The yellowbacks... classics of popular fiction

The yellowjackets or yellowbacks were a great series of bestselling adventure and crime thrillers that had its origins in the mid to late 19th century following on from the 'penny dreadfuls'. They virtually began the mass market revolution of the early 20th century with a clear standard format and imprint/series livery (what would today be called branding). Hodder & Stoughton published the yellowjackets in two main series with series run dates of: 1923-1939 and later 1949-1957.

As the tagline ('where thrillers really began') on the back cover implies, the imprint and series focused on thrillers that were the bestsellers of their time. This current reissue or retro revival if you will, brings back many of these masterpieces, now classics in their own way and extends it further by including key titles from that period that were either great crime or thriller or even general commercial fiction (including sub-genres of noir, horror, gothic, romance, westerns, etc.) influences of their time. There are some perennial favourites and many rarities either lost or not easily available being revived in the current series. Writers and characters ranged from adventure heroes like Bulldog Drummond, Allan Quatermain, Richard Hannay or the Saint through thriller grandmasters Edgar Wallace and E. Phillips Oppenheim, crime and mystery maestros like Patricia Wentworth, GK Chesterton, Agatha Christie and the Detection club, to western and swashbucklers like Zane Grey, Max Brand, Captain Blood and even romance or general fiction classics like Hermina Black, Denise Robins, Marie Corelli or Stella Morton. These were books that had storytelling at their heart and always entertained.

The yellowbacks had both hardback (with varying design elements) and paperback (which built the series look) versions with the latter still carrying the imprint 'yellowjacket'. The current reissues pay tribute to both and use an amalgam of elements from both editions while retaining the complete yellow (or 'mustard-plaster') livery with the author's name in blue beveled type with a 'simulated emboss' effect and a white outer 'outline', and the book title in black. These reissues retain the distinctive size of the original mass market paperback and follow the three main category variations—the thrillers (crime, westerns, mystery, adventure) had blue lettering for the author's name, while Romance and softer general fiction had red; and other categories like humour had green.

For more detail and a full list of titles visit https://www.hachetteindia.com/home/yellowbacks

THE COMPLETE THINKING MACHINE

VOLUME 2

THE COMPLETE THINKING MACHINE

Jacques Heath Futrelle (9 April 1875 – 15 April 1912) was an American journalist and mystery writer who achieved fame for his detective stories featuring 'The Thinking Machine' which were originally published in *The Saturday Evening Post* and the *Boston American*. Futrelle died at age 37 on 15 April 1912, on the RMS Titanic. He refused to board a lifeboat, insisting that his wife board instead. Interestingly Futrelle was used as the lead character in Max Allan Collins' disaster series novel *The Titanic Murders* (1999), which was about two murders aboard the Titanic.

THE COMPLETE THINKING MACHINE

Jacques Futrelle

VOLUME 2

The Complete Thinking Machine
First published by Chapman & Hall, Limited, London in 1907

This Hodder Yellowback edition © Hachette India 2023
(Registered Name: Hachette Book Publishing India Pvt. Ltd.)
An Hachette UK Company www.hachetteindia.com

1

All rights reserved. No part of the publication may be reproduced, stored in a retrieval system (including but not limited to computers, disks, external drives, electronic or digital devices, e-readers, websites), or transmitted in any form or by any means (including but not limited to cyclostyling, photocopying, docutech or other reprographic reproductions, mechanical, recording, electronic, digital versions) without the prior written permission of the publisher, nor be otherwise circulated in any form of binding or cover other than that in which it is published and without a similar condition being imposed on the subsequent purchaser.

The texts in these editions in most cases have been reprinted as is, with minimal editorial changes and by and large no bowdlerizing for political correctness; though in some editions, a few words and phrases considered archaic, or those considered offensive now, along with archaic punctuation may have been modified in places to make the text more accessible to today's readers. The narratives, language, beliefs, social mores and/or cultural depictions, in these volumes are a reflection of their times and must be viewed as such. They may also contain certain cultural, racial and gender prejudices and stereotypes that may be outdated or clearly wrong then and wrong today; but their removal would be tantamount to claiming these prejudices never existed. The Publisher does not endorse or support those depictions or stereotypes; and these books have been made available for a discerning audience that will read it for entertainment value and a chronicle/record of popular fiction of past times.

Cover design by Priya Singh adapted from the original classic yellowjacket by Hodder & Stoughton.

Cover illustration by Ishan Trivedi.

Series note: Some of the books in the series (unless otherwise credited) may have cover or inside illustrations from the original yellowbacks or early editions, and while full restoration has been attempted, some images may be grainy or faded due to the condition of the original material. The end notes or bonus material or blurb details may have been sourced from the public domain or free use publications such as Wikipedia and attribution is hereby made also allowing similar free use reproduction from here. Sources requiring further specific attribution may write in and further detailing and/or corrections shall be made in subsequent printings/editions.

Reprint specifications may be subject to change including but not limited to finishes, paper, colour sections.

ISBN: 978-93-5731-091-8

Hachette Book Publishing India Pvt. Ltd.
4th & 5th Floors, Corporate Centre,
Plot No. 94, Sector 44, Gurugram – 122 003, India

Typeset in Electra LT STD 10/12.5 pt by Manipal Technologies Limited, Manipal

Printed and bound in India by Manipal Technologies Limited, Manipal

CONTENTS

1. Problem of the Ghost Woman	1
2. A Piece of String	15
3. Problem of the Green-Eyed Monster	31
4. Problem of the Hidden Million	50
5. Problem of the Interrupted Wireless	62
6. Mystery of the Golden Dagger	80
7. Problem of the Knotted Cord	113
8. Problem of the Lost Radium	126
9. The Haunted Bell	147
10. Problem of the Missing Necklace	187
11. Problem of the Motor Boat	205
12. Problem of the Opera Box	223
13. Five Millions by Wireless	241
14. Problem of the Organ Grinder	266
15. Problem of the Perfect Alibi	279
16. Problem of the Red Rose	296
17. The Silver Box	316
18. Problem of the Stolen Bank Notes	334

1

PROBLEM OF THE GHOST WOMAN

Ruby Reagan, expert cracksman, was busily, albeit quietly, engaged in the practice of his profession. His rubber soles fell silently upon the deep carpet as he stepped into the utter gloom of the study and closed the door noiselessly behind him. For a long time he stood perfectly still, listening, feeling with that vague single sense for the presence of some one else; then he flashed his electric light. A flat topped library table was directly in front of him, littered over with books, and to his left were the bulky outlines of a roll top desk. There were some chairs, a cabinet or so, and rows of bookcases.

His scrutiny, brief but comprehensive, seemed to satisfy Reagan; for the light went out suddenly, and, turning in his tracks, he slid the bolt of the door into its socket slowly, to avoid even a click. Next he released the grips on one of the windows, for it might be necessary to leave the room that way in the event of some one entering by the single door. Then he settled down to work. First was the desk, and after a long, minute inspection of the lock he dropped on his knees before it and began trying his skeleton keys. The electric flash, with the light fixed, was on the left leaf of the desk, brightly illuminating the lock and lending a deeper glow of ruby red to his hair. On the right leaf of the desk, within instant reach, was his revolver.

It was nearly half an hour before the lock yielded, and then, with a sigh of relief, Reagan carefully pushed up the roll top. Inside he found a metal box. From a score of pigeonholes he dragged forth papers of all descriptions, ruthlessly scattering them about him after a quick examination of each in turn. Then he went through drawer after drawer, carefully scrutinizing each article before he laid it down.

"Guess it's in the box," he mused at length.

Sitting flat upon the floor, with the box between his knees, he lavished his talents upon it. After a few minutes the lock clicked, and the metal lid lifted. Again Reagan smiled, for here were packages and packages of banknotes. But after a moment they too were spilled out on the floor. It was something else he sought.

"Now, that's funny," he told himself finally. "It isn't here." He paused thoughtfully, while his eyes rested lovingly upon the packages of money. "Of course, if I can't get what I want I'll take what I can get," he went on at last. And he proceeded to stuff the money away in his pockets.

Several times he ran his fingers slowly through his red hair. It was plain that he was deeply puzzled. He was on the point of rising to continue his investigations in other directions, when he heard something. It was a voice – a quiet, soothing, pleasant voice – about fourteen inches behind his right ear.

"Don't try to get your revolver, please!" the voice advised. "If you do, I'll shoot!"

Involuntarily Reagan's hand darted out toward the weapon on the leaf of the desk; but it was drawn back as suddenly when he heard a sharp click behind him. Nonplussed for the moment, he sat down again on the floor, half expecting a shot. It didn't come, and he screwed his head around to see why.

What he saw astounded him. It was a diaphanous, floating, lacy, white something—the figure of a girl. Or was it a girl? The head was sheathed in white, the features covered by a misty, hazy, veily thing, and in the dim reflected light the whole figure seemed ridiculously unsubstantial. It was a girl's voice, though.

"Sit perfectly still, please, and don't make any noise!" the voice advised again. Yes, it was a girl's voice.

Reagan noted the small, gold mounted revolver in her right hand, with the barrel, at just that moment, on a direct line with his head and only a foot or so away; and he noted that it remained steadily where it was without one tremor or quiver.

"Yes'm," he said at last.

The white figure walked around him – or did it float? – and picked up his revolver from the desk.

"This is Mr Reagan, isn't it?" she inquired.

"Yes'm," responded Reagan. The admission was surprised out of him.

"Did you find it?"

"No'm."

Was this thing real? Reagan rubbed his eyes doubtfully. He was dreaming, of course. He would wake up in a minute. He opened his eyes again. Yes, there she was. But she wasn't real, – she couldn't be real, – she was a ghost. She was certainly not in the room when he entered, and she could not have come in since, because he had bolted the door on the inside.

"I shall trouble you now, Mr Reagan," the ghost woman went on, "to take all that money from your pocket and put it back in the box."

Reagan stared at the end of the revolver a moment, and the ghost woman wriggled it. That was real enough, anyway. Promptly and without a word he began to disgorge packages of banknotes. Then at last looked up again.

"You put back only eight packages," said the ghost woman calmly. "You took out nine."

"Yes'm," said Reagan.

He fished through his pockets again, in a semi-hypnotic condition, produced more money, and deposited it with the other. He closed the metal lid and snapped the lock.

"That will do very nicely," she said approvingly. "Now I shall trouble you, please, to go on about your business."

Reagan started to rise, awkwardly enough, on hands and knees. The ghost woman stepped back a little; but still she was not far enough away, for when Reagan suddenly came to his feet his outstretched arms struck her violently beneath the wrists and sent the two revolvers flying upward. With another quick movement he swept the electric light from the desk, extinguishing it. There was a sound of scuffling feet in the darkness, as of persons struggling, a little despairing cry, then finally a pistol shot.

Reagan stumbled blindly about the room, seeking the door. He found it at last, still bolted on the inside, and tugged at it frantically. Then came the sound of heavy feet running along the hall outside toward the study, and Reagan stopped. The window! It was the only way now! The shot had aroused the household. He rushed toward the window; but it refused to move.

The clamor was at the door. Desperately Reagan sought for the side grips on the window; but they seemed to have disappeared. The door trembled as some heavy body was hurled against it. The bolt would yield – it was yielding – Reagan heard the woodwork crack. Then deliberately he drove his clenched fist through the glass, took one step on a chair and hurled himself straight through. The door crashed under the onslaught and swung inward.

On the following morning Chester Mills, a wealthy merchant, called on Detective Mallory, chief of the bureau of criminal investigation.

"I own a large country estate forty miles out of town," Mills began abruptly. "Yesterday was the last day of the month. I went to the bank and drew nine hundred dollars, and placed it in a metal box in my desk at home and locked both the box and desk.

"I went to bed at eleven o'clock. About two o'clock this morning I heard a pistol shot in the study. I jumped out of bed and rushed into the hall toward the study, meeting on the way one of my servants, O'Brien. We found the study locked, and started to smash the door in. As we did so we heard a great crash of glass inside.

"Then we did smash the door, and O'Brien turned on the electric lights. One of the two windows was smashed out as if somebody had jumped or been thrown through it; my desk had been ransacked, and my papers scattered all over the floor. The desk was standing open, and I picked up the box. It had a bullet hole in it. The ball went in the top and came out the side. I found it sticking in the desk. It was thirty-two caliber. Here it is."

Mills tossed the misshapen leaden missile on the table, and Detective Mallory examined it.

"Then I found the first real puzzle," Mills went on. "I opened the box and counted the money. Instead of any of it being missing, there was more there than there was when I put the box in the desk. Where there had been only nine hundred dollars, verified by the paying teller and myself, there was now nine hundred and ten dollars – an extra ten-dollar bill."

Detective Mallory chewed his cigar frantically.

"O'Brien found a soft black hat in the room, near the door," continued Mills, "a revolver, thirty-eight caliber, with every chamber loaded, an overcoat, an electric flashlight which had been thrown to the floor and broken, and a very complete kit of burglar's tools. I straightened the women folk all out, had the house searched, and went back to bed. So far as I have been able to find out, nothing was stolen – nothing is missing."

"Well, in that case—" began the detective.

"I haven't started yet," interrupted Mills tersely. "The window was out, as I said; so when we went to bed again we left O'Brien in the study on watch. About half-past three o'clock

I was awakened again by a scream – a woman. Again I jumped out and ran along toward the study. The lights were going, but there was no sign of O'Brien. I presumed then that his attention had been attracted by the scream and he had gone to investigate. But—Well, O'Brien has disappeared. No one has seen or heard of him since – there's not a trace."

Detective Mallory sat for a long time silently smoking, and staring into the eyes of his caller.

At this point the problem came under the observation of that eminent logician, Professor Augustus S. F. X. Van Dusen – The Thinking Machine. As Hutchinson Hatch, reporter, related the known facts, the distinguished man of science permitted his eyes to narrow down to mere slits of watery blue, and the tall, dome-like forehead was deeply furrowed.

"Why was any shot fired?" Hatch demanded of the scientist in perplexity. "And who fired it? Were there two burglars? Did they fight? Was one wounded? There were bloodstains on the ground outside the window; but we can see that whoever jumped out might have cut himself on the glass. And why was the hole shot in the tin box? Not to break the lock, obviously; for it could have been taken along. Where does the odd ten-dollar bill in the box figure? Where is O'Brien? Who was the woman who screamed that second time? Why did she scream? Why wasn't something stolen?"

Having relieved himself of this torrent of questions, Hatch dropped back into his chair expectantly and lighted a cigarette. The Thinking Machine permitted two disapproving eyes to settle on the young man for a moment.

"And still you haven't asked the one vital question," he remarked tartly. "That is, What particular object in that study, or supposed to be in that study, is of such great importance to some one unknown that two bold, daring I might say, attempts were made to get it in the same night?"

"It seems to me it would be impossible to learn that, until—"

"Nothing is impossible, Mr Hatch. It is merely a little sum in arithmetic. Two and two make four; not sometimes but all the time. This problem, at the moment, seems remarkably disjointed, particularly when we consider the disappearance of O'Brien. First, then, is Mr Mills positive nothing was stolen?"

"Absolutely so," replied Hatch. "He has checked off every paper, and accounted for every article."

The furrows in the tall brow deepened perceptibly, and for a long time the crabbed little scientist sat silent. "How much blood was found outside?" he asked suddenly.

"Quite a good deal of it," Hatch responded. "It looks as if some one, whoever jumped or was thrown out, received some nasty cuts. The edges of the glass are stained."

The Thinking Machine nodded. "It is established beyond all question that the woman who screamed that second time was not one of those in the house?" he asked.

"Oh, yes," returned Hatch confidently. "They had all retired after the first fright, and the second didn't even arouse them. They didn't know of O'Brien's disappearance until morning."

"The police have found nothing yet?"

"Not yet. The articles left in the room, of course, – the hat and coat and burglar's tools, – are clues that they are working on. They might establish identity by their aid."

"Well, we'll have to find the man who jumped," remarked the scientist placidly. "When we do that, we can go somewhere with this affair."

"Yes, when we do that," Hatch agreed, with a grin.

"Of course we can do it!" snapped The Thinking Machine. "Here we seek a man with neither hat nor overcoat, who is cut up with glass, possibly badly wounded."

"But he's the sort of man who would scuttle to cover like a scared rabbit," Hatch protested. "Wouldn't matter how badly hurt he was, if he could walk he would hide."

"You seem to think, Mr Hatch, that leaping through a window, taking all the glass with you, and falling twenty feet to a hard pavement, is a trivial affair," declared the scientist crabbedly. "If this man wasn't badly hurt, it's a miracle; therefore—" He stopped abruptly and squinted at the newspaper man. "I'm going to state a case and ask you a question," he went on suddenly. "Before I do it I'll write the answer you will give on this bit of paper. You are an intelligent man; so I'll demonstrate to you how intelligent minds run in the same channel."

He scribbled a few words hurriedly, folded the paper twice, and handed it to the reporter.

"Now you are the burglar," he resumed, "a man perhaps well known to the police. You jumped from that window and hurt yourself seriously. You need medical attention; yet you can't afford to run the slightest risk of capture. You have no hat or coat. You go to physician, not too near the scene of the affair, and you tell a story to account for your condition. What could you say to do away with all suspicion, and make yourself perfectly safe, at least for the moment?"

Hatch smiled whimsically as he turned and twisted the scrap of paper in his fingers, then lighted a cigarette and got down to the matter in hand seriously.

"I think," he said at last slowly, and feeling unaccountably sheepish about it, "that the safest story to tell the physician would be that I had been thrown from an automobile, lost my hat, say, cut myself going head foremost through the glass front when the car ran away, badly bruised by the violence with which I hit the ground; and all that sort of thing."

The Thinking Machine glared at him aggressively for an instant, then arose and left the room. Hatch drew a long breath, then opened the folded paper reluctantly. He found only these words:

"Runaway automobile – cut by diving through glass front— hat lost—bruises and other lacerations by fall to ground."

When the scientist returned, he wore his hat and overcoat.

"Mr Hatch, go at once to Mr Mills, and inquire if he has yet learned of anything being missing from the study – a paper of some sort, in all probability," he instructed. "Then, without mentioning the matter to him, take other steps to learn the nature of any litigation which might be pending in which he is concerned – I imagine something is either now going on or will be going on in a few days. Run by this evening to see me."

"Are you going with me?" inquired the reporter.

"No, no," responded the scientist impatiently. "I'm going to see the man who jumped out of the window."

When Ruby Reagan, expert cracksman, awoke to consciousness he found himself gazing straight into two squinting blue eyes, magnified beyond all proportion by the thick spectacles through which he saw them. The eyes were set far back in a thin, drawn face, and above them was a shock of straw yellow hair.

"Be perfectly quiet," said The Thinking Machine. "You are safe enough, and in a day or so you will be all right."

"Who are you?" demanded Reagan suspiciously.

"I am acting for the gentleman who employed you to get that – that document from Mr Mills's study," replied the scientist glibly. "You are in my home. The doctor fixed you up, and I brought you here as soon as I found you. He doesn't suspect anything. He thinks you were injured in an automobile accident, as you said."

The cracksman closed his eyes to think about it. Weakly, for he had lost much blood, he gradually pieced together a shattered recollection of events of the last few hours,– the jump, his hurts, that staggering run through deserted streets to get away from that place, the final collapse at the very door of a physician, the muttered story he told to account for his wounds. Then he looked again into the inscrutable face of The Thinking Machine. It all seemed regular enough.

"The cops don't know?" he demanded suddenly.

"No," replied The Thinking Machine emphatically. "Who fired the shot?"

"The ghost lady," replied the cracksman promptly. "Guess she didn't mean to, though, cause she seemed as anxious to be quiet as I was."

"And of course you jumped when you heard some one at the door?"

"Betcher neck!" replied Reagan grimly. "The cops ain't never had me yet, an' I don't intend to break no record."

"And the ghost lady," resumed the scientist. "Tell me about her."

And then the story of the strange happenings in the study that night as Reagan recalled them was told. "And I didn't get the paper at that," he concluded.

"You say the ghost lady was all in white?"

"Sure," was the reply. "I don't know really whether she was a ghost or not; but she started the mix-up." He was silent for a moment. "But le'me tell you she must have been a ghost. She couldn't have got in that room any other way. She slid in through the keyhole or something."

"And she called you by name, you say?"

"Yes. That's another thing that makes me think she's a ghost. How did she know my name. And why did she ask me if I got it?"

Hutchinson Hatch called an hour later. There was something of elation, excitement nearly, in his manner. He found The Thinking Machine stretched out in a huge chair in the laboratory, with unruffled brow, and idly twiddling fingers.

"The litigation, Mr Hatch," said the latter without turning.

"Well, there are a dozen cases in which he is interested one way or another," Hatch informed him; "but there is one particularly—"

"Something about property rights, I imagine?" interrupted the scientist.

"Yes," said the reporter. "There's a fortune involved, and a vast deal of real estate. A business partner of Mills, Martin Pendexter by name, died three or four years ago and his grandson, now about twenty-two years old, is suing to recover certain money and property from Mills, alleging that Mills assumed it as his own when Pendexter died. Mills has steadfastly refused to go into the matter, or even discuss it, and finally the boy brought the suit. It has been postponed several times; but it's to come up for hearing soon."

"Mr Mills, then, holds title to this property?" inquired The Thinking Machine.

"I presume if he hadn't felt safe in his position he would not have permitted the matter to go into court," replied Hatch. "I figure that Mills does hold a release from Pendexter of the property, and intends to produce it in court. He has advised the boy several times not to sue; but would never give a reason."

"Oh!" and for a long time the scientist sat silent. "Of course—of course," he mused, half aloud. "Then the ghost woman was one of the—"

"And there's another thing," Hatch rushed on impatiently. "Detective Downey told me a little while ago the police have established the identity of at least one person who was in the study that night, by the kit of tools left behind. His name is Ruby Reagan."

"Ruby Reagan," repeated the scientist thoughtfully. "Oh, yes. He's asleep in the next room there."

The Thinking Machine was talking; Mills, Detective Mallory, and Hutchinson Hatch were listening.

"There is no puzzle about it at all," declared the scientist. "Briefly what happened was this: A burglar was employed by a man who is suing you, Mr Mills, to go into your study and find, if indeed such a thing is in existence, the document upon which you must depend to prove your title to the Pendexter property now in dispute.

"Well, this burglar went to that study and looked for that document—vainly, I may say here. While looking for that he found the money in the box. He was tempted then, contrary to orders, perhaps, and put this money in his pocket. Later he was compelled at the point of a revolver to put the money back in the box, and in his hurry to obey orders he put in a ten-dollar bill of his own. The person who compelled him to replace the money was—was—"

He paused, wrote something on a slip of paper, and passed it to Mills.

"What!" exclaimed Mills incredulously.

"No names, please – yet, anyway," broke in the scientist. "Anyway, it was a woman, I may say a woman of great courage, even audacity. She had gained possession of the burglar's revolver, and with two weapons ordered him to go. The burglar precipitated a struggle, a shot was fired by accident, perhaps, and that is the shot which went through the tin box. The burglar jumped through the window and escaped. The woman, who was in the room, perhaps behind the curtain of the door when the burglar entered, had come there to get that particular document he was seeking. At the time he jumped we can imagine how she managed to get out into the hall when the door flew open, and you and your man O'Brien entered.

"The next we know of that woman she was with the others screaming. A little logic shows us that after that first fright, when the house was perfectly still again, the woman, not knowing O'Brien was on watch, returned to that study again to seek that document. He was sitting in the dark, heard her, and flashed on the electric lights. She was surprised, she screamed, was recognized by O'Brien, and then for some consideration that does not appear – probably a bribe—induced O'Brien to disappear. Again she avoided discovery, and if an investigation had been made she would have been found in bed, I dare say.

"Being totally ignorant now, of the incidents leading up to the pistol shot and the burglar's escape, the first point that the logical mind can seize upon is the finding of more money in the tin box than was known to be there. Therefore, we know that that box had been opened, and we know that the burglar was either an honest man or was compelled to be honest. We know too from the fact that a thirty-eight caliber revolver was found, that there was a second revolver — the one from which the shot was fired. Burglars are not honest. Was this one compelled to be honest? What honest person could be in that room — lone with that burglar, remember? You see instantly a thousand possibilities.

"Without pursuing those possibilities at the moment, it came down to a question of finding the burglar – the dishonest one, I may say. That was not difficult, only tedious work on the telephone, seeking a doctor who had treated a man who was probably — probably, you note — injured in an automobile accident. I found your Ruby Reagan, Mr Mallory, and from him I learned just what happened at first – a woman in white, a ghost woman, obviously some woman in the house. White lacy gowns are not popular for street wear at two o'clock in the morning."

"I wonder if this is absolutely necessary, Mr Van Dusen?" interrupted Mills. His face was white. "I think I understand, and I assure you the matter has taken a personal turn which may mean a great deal to me and my family."

The Thinking Machine waved his hand as if the matter was dismissed.

"For your benefit, Mr Mills," continued the scientist, "I will state that the motive for the girl's act was one which reflected her great courage, and her loyalty to you – perhaps at the same time her regard for another man. Do you follow me? In some way – perhaps the man told her – she learned of the plan to engage Reagan for the work, and she could have learned of that only from the man by a relationship which partook of love for him. Her loyalty to you and a natural desire to save this man's name in your eyes, led her to seek in person to recover the document. It merely happened that they both visited the study the same night."

The Thinking Machine stopped as if that was all.

"But here, go on," Detective Mallory insisted. "I want to know the rest."

"Suppose, Mr Mallory, that you find Reagan for yourself?" suggested The Thinking Machine after a long pause. "I did it. Surely you can."

"Where is he? Where did you see him?"

"I saw him at my house," responded the scientist calmly. "I left him there to come here; but a man who confesses what he confessed to me doesn't stay at a place like that if he can help it. The matter is as I have stated it, Mr Mills. Your reason for refusing to give the young man any explanation of your holding the property is a good one, I dare say, so I'll not question it."

"I'll tell you," flamed Mills suddenly. "He is not really the grandson of Pendexter. I will be compelled to show that if he sues me – that is why I have advised him not to sue."

"I imagined as much," said The Thinking Machine.

Ruby Reagan left the home of The Thinking Machine in a cab late that night. And a few days later the Pendexter suit was withdrawn by the plaintiff.

2

A PIECE OF STRING

It was just midnight. Somewhere near the center of a cloud of tobacco smoke, which hovered over one corner of the long editorial room, Hutchinson Hatch, reporter, was writing. The rapid click-click of his typewriter went on and on, broken only when he laid aside one sheet to put in another. The finished pages were seized upon one at a time by an office boy and rushed off to the city editor. That astute person glanced at them for information and sent them on to the copy desk, whence they were shot down into that noisy, chaotic wilderness, the composing room.

The story was what the phlegmatic head of the copy desk, speaking in the vernacular, would have called a "beaut." It was about the kidnapping that afternoon of Walter Francis, the four-year-old son of a wealthy young broker, Stanley Francis. An alternative to the abduction had been proposed in the form of a gift to certain persons, identity unknown, of fifty thousand dollars. Francis, not unnaturally, objected to the bestowal of so vast a sum upon anyone. So he told the police, and while they were making up their minds the child was stolen. It happened in the usual way—closed carriage, and all that sort of thing.

Hatch was telling the story graphically, as he could tell a story when there was one to be told. He glanced at the clock, jerked out another sheet of copy, and the office boy scuttled away with it.

"How much more?" called the city editor.

"Just a paragraph," Hatch answered.

His type writer clicked on merrily for a couple of minutes and then stopped. The last sheet of copy was taken away, and he rose and stretched his legs.

"Some guy wants yer at the 'phone," an office boy told him.

"Who is it?" asked Hatch.

"Search me," replied the boy. "Talks like he'd been eatin' pickles."

Hatch went into the booth indicated. The man at the other end was Professor Augustus S. F. X. Van Dusen. The reporter instantly recognized the crabbed, perpetually irritated voice of the noted scientist, The Thinking Machine.

"That you, Mr Hatch?" came over the wire.

"Yes."

"Can you do something for me immediately?" he queried. "It is very important."

"Certainly."

"Now listen closely," directed The Thinking Machine. "Take a car from Park-sq., the one that goes toward Worcester through Brookline. About two miles beyond Brookline is Randall's Crossing. Get off there and go to your right until you come to a small white house. In front of this house, a little to the left and across an open field, is a large tree. It stands just in the edge of a dense wood. It might be better to approach it through the wood, so as not to attract attention. Do you follow me?"

"Yes," Hatch replied. His imagination was leading him a chase.

"Go to this tree now, immediately, tonight," continued The Thinking Machine. "You will find a small hole in it near the level of your eye. Feel in that hole, and see what is there – no matter what it is – then return to Brookline and telephone me. It is of the greatest importance."

The reporter was thoughtful for a moment; it sounded like a page from a Dumas romance.

"What's it all about?" he asked curiously.

"Will you go?" came the counter question.

"Yes, certainly."

"Goodbye."

Hatch heard a click as the receiver was hung up at the other end. He shrugged his shoulders, said "Goodnight" to the city editor, and went out. An hour later he was at Randall's Crossing. The night was dark — so dark that the road was barely visible. The car whirled on, and as its lights were swallowed up Hatch set out to find the white house. He came upon it at last, and, turning, faced across an open field toward the wood. Far away over there outlined vaguely against the distant glow of the city, was a tall tree.

Having fixed its location, the reporter moved along for a hundred yards or more to where the wood ran down to the road. Here he climbed a fence and stumbled on through the dark, doing sundry injuries to his shins. After a disagreeable ten minutes he reached the tree.

With a small electric flash light he found the hole. It was only a little larger than his hand, a place where decay had eaten its way into the tree trunk. For just a moment he hesitated about putting his hand into it – he didn't know what might be there. Then, with a grim smile, he obeyed orders.

He felt nothing save crumblings of decayed wood, and finally dragged out a handful, only to spill it on the ground. That couldn't be what was meant. For the second time he thrust in his hand, and after a deal of grabbing about produced – a piece of string. It was just a plain, ordinary, common piece of string — white string. He stared at it and smiled.

"I wonder what Van Dusen will make of that?" he asked himself.

Again his hand was thrust into the hole. But that was all – the piece of string. Then came another thought, and with that due regard for detail which made him a good reporter he went looking around the big tree for a possible second opening of some sort. He found none.

About three quarters of an hour later he stepped into an all-night drug store in Brookline and 'phoned to The Thinking Machine. There was an instant response to his ring.

"Well, well, what did you find?" came the query.

"Nothing to interest you, I imagine," replied the reporter grimly. "Just a piece of string."

"Good, good!" exclaimed The Thinking Machine. "What does it look like?"

"Well," replied the newspaper man judicially, "it's just a piece of white string-cotton, I imagine — about six inches long."

"Any knots in it?"

"Wait till I see."

He was reaching into his pocket to take it out, when the startled voice of The Thinking Machine came over the line.

"Didn't you leave it there?" it demanded.

"No; I have it in my pocket."

"Dear me!" exclaimed the scientist irritably. "That's bad. Well, has it any knots in it?" he asked with marked resignation.

Hatch felt that he had committed the unpardonable sin. "Yes," he replied after an examination. "It has two knots in it – just plain knots – about two inches apart."

"Single or double knots?"

"Single knots."

"Excellent! Now, Mr Hatch, listen. Untie one of those knots – it doesn't matter which one – and carefully smooth out the string. Then take it and put it back where you found it. 'phone me as soon after that as you can."

"Now, tonight?"

"Now, immediately."

"But-but—" began the astonished reporter.

"It is a matter of the utmost consequence," the irritated voice assured him. "You should not have taken the string. I told you merely to see what was there. But as you have brought it away you must put it back as soon as possible. Believe me, it is of the highest importance. And don't forget to 'phone me."

The sharp, commanding tone stirred the reporter to new action and interest. A car was just going past the door, outward bound. He raced for it and got aboard. Once settled, he untied one of the knots, straightened out the string, and fell to wondering what sort of fool's errand he was on.

"Randall's Crossing!" called the conductor at last.

Hatch left the car and retraced his tortuous way along the road and through the wood to the tall tree, found the hole, and had just thrust in his hand to replace the string when he heard a woman's voice directly behind him, almost in his ear. It was a calm, placid, convincing sort of voice. It said:

"Hands up!"

Hatch was a rational human being with ambitions and hopes for the future; therefore his hands went up without hesitation. "I knew something would happen," he told himself.

He turned to see the woman. In the darkness he could only dimly trace a tall, slender figure. Steadily poised just a couple of dozen inches from his nose was a revolver. He could see that without any difficulty. It glinted a little, even in the gloom, and made itself conspicuous.

"Well," asked the reporter at last, as he stood reaching upward, "it's your move."

"Who are you?" asked the woman. Her voice was steady and rather pleasant.

The reporter considered the question in the light of all he didn't know. He felt it wouldn't be a sensible thing to say just who he was. Somewhere at the end of this thing The Thinking Machine was working on a problem; he was presumably helping in a modest, unobtrusive sort of way; therefore he would be cautious.

"My name is Williams," he said promptly. "Jim Williams," he added circumstantially.

"What are you doing here?"

Another subject for thought. That was a question he couldn't answer; he didn't know what he was doing there; he was wondering himself. He could only hazard a guess, and he did that with trepidation.

"I came from him," he said with deep meaning.

"Who?" demanded the woman suspiciously.

"It would be useless to name him," replied the reporter.

"Yes, yes, of course," the woman mused. "I understand."

There was a little pause. Hatch was still watching the revolver. He had a lively interest in it. It had not moved a hair's breadth since he first looked at it; hanging up there in the night it fairly stared him out of countenance.

"And the string?" asked the woman at last.

Now the reporter felt that he was in the mire. The woman herself relieved this new embarrassment.

"Is it in the tree?" she went on.

"Yes."

"How many knots are in it?"

"One."

"One?" she repeated eagerly. "Put your hand in there and hand me the string. No tricks, now!"

Hatch complied with a certain deprecatory manner which he intended should convey to her the impression that there would be no tricks. As she took the string her fingers brushed against his. They were smooth and delicate. He knew that even in the dark.

"And what did he say?" she went on.

Having gone this far without falling into anything, the reporter was willing to plunge—felt that he had to, as a matter of fact.

"He said yes," he murmured without shifting his eyes from the revolver.

"Yes?" the woman repeated again eagerly. "Are you sure?"

"Yes," said the reporter again. The thought flashed through his mind that he was tangling up somebody's affairs sadly – he didn't know whose. Anyhow, it was a matter of no consequence to him, as long as that revolver stared at him that way.

"Where is it?" asked the woman.

Then the earth slipped out from under him. "I don't know," he replied weakly.

"Didn't he give it to you?"

"Oh, no. He-he wouldn't trust me with it."

"How can I get it, then?"

"Oh, he'll fix it all right," Hatch assured her soothingly. "I think he said something about tomorrow night."

"Where?"

"Here."

"Thank God!" the woman gasped suddenly. Her tone betrayed deep emotion; but it wasn't so deep that she lowered the revolver.

There was a long pause. Hatch was figuring possibilities. How to get possession of the revolver seemed the imminent problem. His hands were still in the air, and there was nothing to indicate that they were not to remain there indefinitely. The woman finally broke the silence.

"Are you armed?"

"Oh, no."

"Truthfully?"

"Truthfully."

"You may lower your hands," she said, as if satisfied; "then go on ahead of me straight across the field to the road. Turn to your left there. Don't look back under any circumstances. I shall be behind you with this revolver pointing at your head. If you attempt to escape or make any outcry I shall shoot. Do you believe me?"

The reporter considered it for a moment. "I'm firmly convinced of it," he said at last.

They stumbled on to the road, and there Hatch turned as directed. Walking along in the shadows with the tread of small feet behind him he first contemplated a dash for liberty; but that would mean giving up the adventure, whatever it was. He had no fear for his personal safety as long as he obeyed orders, and he intended to do that implicitly. And besides, The Thinking Machine had his slender finger in the pie somewhere. Hatch knew that, and knowing it was a source of deep gratification.

Just now he was taking things at face value, hoping that with their arrival at whatever place they were bound for he would be further enlightened. Once he thought he heard the woman sobbing, and started to look back. Then he remembered her warning, and thought better of it. Had he looked back he would have seen her stumbling along, weeping, with the revolver dangling limply at her side.

At last, a mile or more farther on, they began to arrive somewhere. A house sat back some distance from the road.

"Go in there!" commanded his captor.

He turned in at the gate, and five minutes later stood in a comfortably furnished room on the ground floor of a small house. A dim light was burning. The woman turned it up. Then almost defiantly she threw aside her veil and hat and stood before him. Hatch gasped. She was pretty—bewilderingly pretty – and young and graceful and all that a young woman should be. Her cheeks were flushed.

"You know me, I suppose?" she exclaimed.

"Oh yes, certainly," Hatch assured her.

And saying that, he knew he had never seen her before.

"I suppose you thought it perfectly horrid of me to keep you with your hands up like that all the time; but I was dreadfully frightened," the woman went on, and she smiled a little uncertainly. "But there wasn't anything else to do."

"It was the only thing," Hatch agreed.

"Now I'm going to ask you to write and tell him just what happened," she resumed. "And tell him, too, that the other matter must be arranged immediately. I'll see that your letter is delivered. Sit here!"

She picked up the revolver from the table beside her and placed a chair in position. Hatch walked to the table and sat down. Pen and ink lay before him. He knew now he was trapped. He couldn't write a letter to that vague "him" of whom he had talked so glibly, about that still more vague "it" – whatever that might be. He sat dumbly staring at the paper.

"Well?" she demanded suspiciously.

"I – I can't write it," he confessed suddenly.

She stared at him coldly for a moment as if she had suspected just that, and he in turn stared at the revolver with a new and vital interest. He felt the tension, but saw no way to relieve it.

"You are an imposter!" she blurted out at last. "A detective?"

Hatch didn't deny it. She backed away toward a bell call near the door, watching him closely, and rang vigorously several times. After a little pause the door opened, and two men, evidently servants, entered.

"Take this gentleman to the rear room up stairs," she commanded without giving them a glance, "and lock him up. Keep him under close guard. If he attempts to escape, stop him! That's all."

Here was another page from a Dumas romance. The reporter started to explain; but there was a merciless gleam, danger even, in the woman's eyes, and he submitted to orders. So, he was led up stairs a captive, and one of the men took a place on guard inside the room.

The dawn was creeping on when Hatch fell asleep. It was about ten o'clock when he awoke, and the sun was high. His guard, wide eyed and alert, still sat beside the door. For several minutes the reporter lay still, seeking vainly some sort of explanation of what was happening. Then, cheerfully:

"Goodmorning."

The guard merely glared at him.

"May I inquire your name?" the reporter asked.

There was no answer.

"Or the lady's name?"

No answer.

"Or why I am where I am?"

Still no answer.

"What would you do," Hatch went on casually, "if I should try to get out of here?"

The guard handled his revolver carelessly. The reporter was satisfied. "He is not deaf, that's certain," he told himself.

He spent the remainder of the morning yawning and wondering what The Thinking Machine was about; also he had a few casual reflections as to the mental state of his city editor at his failure to appear and follow up the kidnapping story. He finally dismissed all these ideas with a shrug of his shoulders, and sat down to wait for whatever was coming.

It was in the early afternoon that he heard laughter in the next room. First there was a woman's voice, then the shrill cackle of a child. Finally he distinguished some words.

"You ticky!" exclaimed the child, and again there was the laugh.

The reporter understood "you ticky," coupled with the subsequent peal, to be a sort of abbreviated English for "you tickle." After awhile the merriment died away and he heard the child's insistent demand for something else.

"You be hossie."

"No, no," the woman expostulated.

"Yes, you be hossie."

"No, let Morris be hossie."

"No, no. You be hossie."

That was all. Evidently some one was "hossie," because there was a sound of romping; but finally even that died away. Hatch yawned away another hour or so under the constant eye of his guard, and then began to grow restless. He turned on the guard savagely.

"Isn't anything ever going to happen?" he demanded.

The guard didn't say.

"You'll never convict yourself on your own statement," Hatch burst out again in disgust.

He stretched out on a couch, bored by the sameness which had characterized the last few hours of his adventure. His attention was attracted by some movement at the door, and he looked up. His guard heard, too, and with revolver in hand went to the door, carefully unlocking it. After a few hurriedly whispered words he left the room, and Hatch was meditating an instant rush for a window, when the woman entered. She had the revolver now. She was deathly white and gripped the weapon menacingly. She did not lock the door—only closed it – but with her own person and the attention compelling revolver she blocked the way.

"What is it now?" asked Hatch wearily.

"You must not speak or call, or make the slightest sound," she whispered tensely. "If you do, I'll kill you. Do you understand?"

Hatch confessed by a nod that he understood. He also imagined that he understood this sudden change in guard, and the warning. It was because some one was about to enter or had entered the house. His conjecture was partially confirmed instantly by a distant rapping on a door.

"Not a sound, now!" whispered the woman.

From somewhere below he heard the sound of steps as one of the servants answered the knock. After a short wait he heard two voices mumbling. Suddenly one was raised clearly.

"Why, Worcester can't be that far," it protested irritably.

Hatch knew. It was The Thinking Machine. The woman noted a change in his manner and drew back the hammer of the revolver. The reporter saw the idea. He didn't dare call. That would be suicide. Perhaps he could attract attention, though; drop a key, for instance. The sound might reach The Thinking Machine and be interpreted aright. One hand was in a pocket, and slowly he was drawing out a key. He would risk it. Maybe —

Then came a new sound. It was the patter of small feet. The guarded door was pushed open and a tousle-headed child, a boy, ran in.

"Mama, mama!" he called loudly. He ran to the woman and clutched at her skirts.

"Oh, my baby! what have you done?" she asked piteously. "We are lost, lost!"

"Me 'faid," the child went on.

With the door — his avenue of possible escape — open, Hatch did not drop the key. Instead, he gazed at the woman, then down at the child. From below he again heard The Thinking Machine.

"How far is the car track, then?"

The servant answered something. There was a sound of steps, and the front door closed. Hatch knew that The Thinking Machine had come and gone; yet he was strangely calm about it, quite himself, despite the fact that a nervous finger still lay on the trigger of the pistol.

From his refuge behind his mother's skirts the boy peered around at Hatch shyly. The reporter gazed, gazed, all eyes, and then was convinced. The boy was Walter Francis, the kidnapped boy whose pictures were being published in every newspaper of a dozen cities. Here was a story — the story — the superlative story.

"Mrs Francis, if you wouldn't mind letting down that hammer —" he suggested modestly. "I assure you I contemplate no harm, and you-you are very nervous."

"You know me, then?" she asked.

"Only because the child there, Walter, called you mama."

Mrs Francis lowered the revolver hammer so recklessly that Hatch involuntarily dodged. And then came a scene, a scene with tears in it, and all those things which stir men, even reporters. Finally the woman dropped the revolver on the floor and swept the boy up in her arms with a gesture of infinite tenderness. He cuddled there, content. At that moment Hatch could have walked out the door, but instead he sat down. He was just beginning to get interested.

"They sha'n't take you!" sobbed the mother.

"There is no immediate danger," the reporter assured her. "The man who came here for that purpose has gone. Meanwhile, if you will tell me the facts, perhaps—perhaps I may be able to be of some assistance."

Mrs Francis looked at him, startled. "Help me?"

"If you will explain, perhaps I can do something," said Hatch again.

Somewhere back in a remote recess of his brain he was remembering. And as it became clearer he was surprised that he had not remembered sooner. It was a story of marital infidelity, and its principals were Stanley Francis and his wife—this bewilderingly pretty young woman before him. It had been only eight or nine months back.

Technically she had deserted Stanley Francis. There had been some violent scene and she left their home and little son. Soon afterward she went to Europe. It had been rumored that divorce proceedings would follow, or at least a legal separation, but nothing had ever come of the rumors. All this Mrs Francis told to Hatch in little incoherent bursts, punctuated with sobs and tears.

"He struck me, he struck me!" she declared with a flush of anger and shame, "and I went then on impulse. I was desperate. Later, even before I went to Europe, I knew the legal status of the affair; but the thought of my boy lingered, and I resolved to come back and get him – abduct him, if necessary. I did that, and I will keep him if I have to kill the one who opposes me."

Hatch saw the mother instinct here, that tigerish ferocity of love which stops at nothing.

"I conceived the plan of demanding fifty thousand dollars of my husband under threat of abduction," Mrs Francis went on. "My purpose was to make it appear that the plot was that of professional – what would you call it? – kidnappers. But I did not send the letter demanding this until I had perfected all my plans and knew I could get the boy. I wanted my husband to think it was the work of others, at least until we were safe in Europe, because even then I imagined there would be a long legal fight.

"After I stole the boy and he recognized me, I wanted him as my own, absolutely safe from legal action by his father. Then I wrote to Mr Francis, telling him I had Walter, and asking that in pity to me he legally give me the boy by a document of some sort. In that letter I told how he might signify his willingness to do this; but of course I would not give my address. I placed a string, the one you saw, in that tree after having tied two knots in it. It was a silly, romantic means of communication he and I used years ago in my girlhood when we both lived near here. If he agreed that I should have the child, he was to come or send some one last night and unties one of the two knots."

Then, to Hatch, the intricacies passed away. He understood clearly. Instead of going to the police with the second letter from his wife, Francis had gone to The Thinking Machine. The Thinking Machine sent the reporter to untie the knot, which was an answer of "Yes" to Mrs Francis's request for the child. Then she would have written giving her address, and there would have been a clue to the child's whereabouts. It was all perfectly clear now.

"Did you specifically mention a string in your letter?" he asked.

"No. I merely stated that I would expect his answer in that place, and would leave something there by which he could signify 'Yes' or 'No,' as he did years ago. The string was one of the odd little ideas of my girlhood. Two knots meant 'No'; one knot meant 'Yes'; and if the string was found by anyone else it meant nothing."

This, then, was why The Thinking Machine did not tell him at first that he would find a string and instruct him to untie one of the knots in it. The scientist had seen that it might have been one of the other tokens of the old romantic days.

"When I met you there," Mrs Francis resumed. "I believed you were an imposter – I don't know why, I just believed it – yet your answers were in a way correct. For fear you were not what you seemed – that you were a detective – I brought you here to keep you until I got the child's release. You know the rest."

The reporter picked up the revolver and whirled it in his fingers. The action, apparently, did not disturb Mrs Francis.

"Why did you remain here so long after you got the child?" asked Hatch.

"I believed it was safer than in a city," she answered frankly. "The steamer on which I planned to sail for Europe with my boy leaves to-morrow. I had intended going to New York tonight to catch it; but now—"

The reporter glanced down at the child. He had fallen asleep in his mother's arms. His tiny hand clung to her. The picture was a pretty one. Hatch made up his mind.

"Well, you'd better pack up," he said. "I'll go with you to New York and do all I can."

It was on the New York – bound train several hours later that Hatch turned to Mrs Francis with an odd smile.

"Why didn't you load that revolver?" he asked.

"Because I was horribly afraid some one would get hurt with it," she replied laughingly.

She was gay with that gentle happiness of possession which blesses woman for the agonies of motherhood, and glanced from time to time at the berth across the aisle where her baby was asleep. Looking upon it all, Hatch was content. He didn't know his exact position in law; but that didn't matter, after all.

Hutchinson Hatch's exclusive story of the escape to Europe of Mrs Francis and her boy was remarkably complete; but all the facts were not in it. It was a week or so later that he detailed them to The Thinking Machine.

"I knew it," said the scientist at the end. "Francis came to me, and I interested myself in the case, practically knowing every fact from his statement. When you heard me speak in the house where you were a prisoner I was there merely to convince myself that the mother did have the baby. I heard it call her and went away satisfied. I knew you were there, too, because you had failed to 'phone me the second time as I expected, and I knew intuitively what you would do when you got the real facts about Mrs Francis and her baby. I went away so that the field might be clear for you to act. Francis himself is a detestable puppy. I told him so."

And that was all that was ever said about it.

3

PROBLEM OF THE GREEN-EYED MONSTER

With coffee cup daintily poised in one hand, Mrs Lingard van Safford lifted wistful, bewitching eyes towards her husband, who sat across the breakfast table partially immersed in the morning papers.

"Are you going out this morning?" she inquired.

Mr van Safford grunted inarticulately.

"May I inquire," she went on placidly, and a dimple snuggled at a corner of her mouth, "if that particular grunt means that you are or are not?"

Mr van Safford lowered his newspaper and glanced at his wife's pretty face. She smiled charmingly.

"Really, I beg your pardon," he apologized, "I hardly think I will go out. I feel rather listless, and I must write some letters. Why?"

"Oh, nothing particularly," she responded.

She took a last sip of her coffee, brushed two or three tiny crumbs from her lap, laid her napkin aside, and arose. Once she turned and glanced back; Mr van Safford was reading again.

After a while he finished the papers and stood looking out a window, yawning prodigiously at the prospect of letters to be written. His wife entered and picked up a handkerchief which had fallen beside her chair. He merely glanced around.

She was dressed for the street – immaculately, stunningly gowned as only a young and beautiful and wealthy woman can gown herself.

"Where are you going, my dear?" he inquired, languidly.

"Out," she responded archly.

She passed through the door. He heard her step and the rustle of her skirts in the hall, then he heard the front door open and close. For some reason, not quite clear even to himself, it surprised him; she had never done a thing like that before. He walked to the front window and looked out. His wife went straight down the street, and turned the first corner. After a time he wandered away to the library to nurse an emotion he had never felt before. It was curiosity.

Mrs van Safford did not return home for luncheon, so he sat down alone. Afterwards he mouched about the house restlessly for an hour or so, then he went down town. He appeared at home again just in time to dress for dinner.

"Has Mrs van Safford returned?" was his first question of Baxter, who opened the door.

"Yes, sir, half an hour ago," responded Baxter. "She's dressing."

Mr van Safford ran up the steps to his own apartments. At dinner his wife was radiant, rosily radiant. The flush of perfect health was in her cheeks and her eyes sparkled beneath their long lashes. She smiled brilliantly upon her husband. To him it was all as if some great thing had been taken out of his life, leaving it desolate, then as suddenly returned. Unnamed emotions struggled within him prompted by that curiosity of the morning, and a dozen questions hammered insistently for answers, But he repressed them gallantly, and for this he was duly rewarded.

"I had such a delightful time today!" his wife exclaimed, after the soup. "I called for Mrs Blacklock immediately after I left here, and we were together all day shopping. We had luncheon down town."

Oh! That was it! Mr van Safford laughed outright from a vague sense of relief which he could not have called by name, and toasted his wife silently by lifting his glass. Her eyes sparkled at the compliment. He drained the glass, snapped the slender stem in his fingers, laughed again and laid it aside. Mrs van Safford dimpled with sheer delight.

"Oh, Van, you silly boy!" she reproved softly, and she stroked the hand which was prosaically reaching for the salt.

It was only a little while after dinner that Mr van Safford excused himself and started for the club, as usual. His wife followed him demurely to the door and there, under the goggling eyes of Baxter, he caught her in his arms and kissed her impetuously, fiercely even. It was the sudden outbreak of an impulsive nature – the sort of thing that makes a woman know she is loved. She thrilled at his touch and reached two white hands forward pleadingly. Then the door closed, and she stood staring down at the tip of her tiny boot with lowered lids and a little, melancholy droop at the corners of her mouth.

It was after ten o'clock when Mr van Safford awoke on the following morning. He had been at his club late – until after two—and now drowsily permitted himself to be overcome again by the languid listlessness which is the heritage of late hours. At ten minutes past eleven he appeared in the breakfast room.

"Mrs van Safford has been down I suppose?" he inquired of a maid.

"Oh yes, sir," she replied. "She's gone out."

Mr van Safford lifted his brows inquiringly.

"She was down a few minutes after eight o'clock, sir," the maid explained, "and hurried through her breakfast."

"Did she leave any word?"

"No, sir."

"Be back to luncheon?"

"She didn't say, sir."

Mr van Safford finished his breakfast silently and thoughtfully. About noon he, too, went out. One of the first persons he met down town was Mrs Blacklock, and she rushed toward him with outstretched hand.

"I'm so glad to see you," she bubbled, for Mrs Blacklock was of that rare type which can bubble becomingly. "But where, in the name of goodness, is your wife? I haven't seen her for weeks and weeks?"

"Haven't seen her for—" Mr van Safford repeated, slowly.

"No," Mrs Blacklock assured him. "I can't imagine where she is keeping herself."

Mr van Safford gazed at her in dumb bewilderment for a moment, and the lines about his mouth hardened a little despite his efforts to control himself.

"I had an impression," he said deliberately, "that you saw her yesterday – that you went shopping together?"

"Goodness, no. It must be three weeks since I saw her."

Mr van Safford's fingers closed slowly, fiercely, but his face relaxed a little, masking with a slight smile, a turbulent rush of mingled emotions.

"She mentioned your name," he said at last, calmly. "Perhaps she said she was going to call on you. I misunderstood her."

He didn't remember the remainder of the conversation, but it was of no consequence at the moment. He had not misunderstood her, and he knew he had not. At last he found himself at his club, and there idle guesses and conjectures flowed through his brain in an unending stream. Finally he arose, grimly.

"I suppose I'm an ass," he mused. "It doesn't amount to anything, of course, but—"

And he sought to rid himself of distracting thoughts over a game of billiards; instead he only subjected himself to open derision for glaringly inaccurate play. Finally he flung down the cue in disgust, strode away to the 'phone and called up his home.

"Is Mrs van Safford there?" he inquired of Baxter.

"No, sir. She hasn't returned yet."

Mr van Safford banged the telephone viciously as he hung up the receiver. At six o'clock he returned home. His wife was still out. At half past eight he sat down to dinner, alone. He didn't enjoy it; indeed hardly tasted it. Then, just as he finished, she came in with a rush of skirts and a lilt of laughter. He drew a long breath, and set his teeth.

"You poor, deserted dear!" she sympathized, laughingly.

He started to say something, but two soft, clinging arms were about his neck, and a velvety cheek rested against his own, so – so he kissed her instead. And really he wasn't at all to be blamed. She sighed happily, and laid aside her hat and gloves.

"I simply couldn't get here any sooner," she explained poutingly as she glanced into his accusing eyes. "I was out with Nell Blakesley in her big, new touring car, and it broke down and we had to send for a man to repair it, so—"

He didn't hear the rest; he was staring into her eyes, steadily, inquiringly. Truth shone triumphant there; he could only believe her. Yet – yet – that other thing! She hadn't told him the truth! In her face, at last, he read uneasiness as he continued to stare, and for a moment there was silence.

"What's the matter, Van?" she inquired solicitously. "Don't you feel well?"

He pulled himself together with a start and for a time they chatted of inconsequential things as she ate. He watched her until she pushed her dessert plate aside, then casually, quite casually:

"I believe you said you were going to call on Mrs Blacklock to-morrow?"

She looked up quickly.

"Oh no," she replied. "I was with her all day yesterday, shopping. I said I had called on her."

Mr van Safford arose suddenly, stood glaring down at her for an instant, then turning abruptly left the house. Involuntarily she had started up, then she sat down again and wept softly over her coffee. Mr van Safford seemed to have a very definite purpose for when he reached the club he went straight to a telephone booth, and called Miss Blakesley over the wire.

"My wife said something about – something about—" he stammered lamely, "something about calling on you tomorrow. Will you be in?"

"Yes, and I'll be so glad to see her," came the reply. "I'm dreadfully tired of staying cooped up here in the house, and really I was beginning to think all my friends had deserted me."

"Cooped up in the house?" Mr van Safford repeated. "Are you ill?"

"I have been," replied Miss Blakesley. "I'm better now, but I haven't been out of the house for more than a week."

"Indeed!" remarked Mr van Safford, sympathetically. "I'm awfully sorry, I assure you. Then you haven't had a chance to try your-your – 'big new touring car'?"

"Why, I haven't any new touring car," said Miss Blakesley. "I haven't any sort of a car. Where did you get that idea?"

Mr van Safford didn't answer her; rudely enough he hung up the telephone and left the club with a face like marble. When finally he stopped walking he was opposite his own house. For a minute he stood looking at it much as if he had never seen it before, then he turned and went back to the club. There was something of fright, of horror even, in his white face when he entered.

As Mr van Safford did not go to bed that night it was not surprising that his wife should find him in the breakfast room when she came down about eight o'clock. She smiled. He stared at her with a curt: "Good morning!" Then came an ominous silence. She finished her breakfast, arose and left the house without a word. He watched her from a window until she disappeared around the corner, just four doors below, then overcome by fears, suspicions, hideous possibilities, he ran out of the house after her.

She had not been out of his sight more than half a minute when he reached the corner, yet now – now she was gone. He looked on both sides of the street, up and down, but there was no sign of her – not a woman in sight. He knew that she would not have had time to reach the next street below, then he readily saw the two obvious possibilities. One was that she had stepped into a waiting cab and been driven away at full speed; another that she had entered one of the nearby houses. If so, which house? Who did she know in this street? He turned the problem over in his mind several times, and then he was convinced that she had hurried away in waiting cab. That emotion which had begun as curiosity was now a raging, turbulent torrent.

On the following morning Mrs van Safford came down to breakfast at fifteen minutes of eight. She seemed a little tired, and there was a trace of tears about her eyes. Baxter looked at her curiously.

"Has Mr van Safford been down yet?" she asked.

"No, Madam," he replied.

"Did he come in at all last night?"

"Yes, Madam. About half past two, I let him in. He had forgotten his key."

Now as a matter of fact at that particular moment Mr van Safford was standing just around the corner, four doors down, waiting for his wife. Just what he intended to do when she appeared was not quite clear in his mind, but the affair had gone to a point where he felt that he must do something. So he waited impatiently, and smoked innumerable cigars. Two hours passed. He glanced around the corner. No one in sight. He strolled back to the house, and met Baxter in the hall.

"Has Mrs van Safford come down?" he asked of the servant.

"Yes, sir," was the reply. "She went out more than an hour ago."

Martha opened the door.

"Please, sir," she said, "there's a young gentleman having a fit in the reception room."

Professor Augustus S. F. X. Van Dusen – The Thinking Machine – turned away from his laboratory table and squinted at her aggressively. Her eyes were distended with nervous excitement, and her wrinkled hands twisted the apron she wore.

"Having a fit?" snapped the scientist.

"Yes, sir," she gasped.

"Dear me! Dear me! How annoying!" expostulated the man of achievement, petulantly. "Just what sort of a fit is it – epileptic, apoplectic, or merely a fit of laughter?"

"Lord, sir, I don't know," Martha confessed helplessly. "He's just a-walking and a-talking and a-pulling his hair, sir."

"What name?"

"I – I forgot to ask, sir," apologized the aged servant, "it surprised me so to see a gentleman a – wiggling like that. He said, though he'd been to Police Headquarters and Detective Mallory sent him."

The eminent logician dried his hands and started for the reception room. At the door he paused and peered in. With no knowledge of just what style of fit his visitor had chosen to have he felt the necessity of this caution. What he saw was not alarming – merely a good-looking young man pacing back and forth across the room with quick, savage stride. His eyes were blazing, and his face was flushed with anger. It was Mr van Safford.

At sight of the diminutive figure of The Thinking Machine, topped by the enormous yellow head, the young man paused and his anger-distorted features relaxed into something closely approaching surprise.

"Well?" demanded The Thinking Machine, querulously.

"I beg your pardon," said Mr van Safford with a slight start. "I-I had expected to find a – a – rather a different sort of person."

"Yes, I know," said The Thinking Machine grumpily. "A man with a black moustache and big feet. Sit down."

Mr van Safford sat down rather suddenly. It never occurred to anyone to do other than obey when the crabbed little scientist spoke. Then, with an incoherence which was thoroughly convincing, Mr van Safford laid before The Thinking Machine in detail those singular happenings which had so disturbed him. The Thinking Machine leaned back in his chair, with finger tips pressed together, and listened to the end.

"My mental condition — my suffering – was such," explained Mr van Safford in conclusion, "that when I proved to my own satisfaction that she had twice misrepresented the facts to me, wilfully, I – I could have strangled her."

"That would have been a nice thing to do," remarked the scientist crustily. "You believe, then, that there may be another—"

"Don't say it," burst out the young man passionately. He arose. His face was dead white. "Don't say it," he repeated, menacingly.

The Thinking Machine was silent a moment, then glanced up in the blazing eyes and cleared his throat.

"She never did such a thing before?" he asked.

"No, never."

"Does she – did she – ever speculate?"

Mr van Safford sat down again.

"Never," he responded, positively. "She wouldn't know one stock from another."

"Has her own bank account?"

"Yes – nearly four hundred thousand dollars. This was her father's gift at our wedding. It was deposited in her name, and has remained so. My own income is more than enough for our uses."

"You are rich, then?"

"My father left me nearly two million dollars," was the reply. "But this all doesn't matter. What I want—"

"Wait a minute," interrupted The Thinking Machine testily. There was a long pause. "You have never quarrelled seriously?"

"Never one cross word," was the reply.

"Remarkable," commented The Thinking Machine ambiguously. "How long have you been married?"

"Two years – last June."

"Most remarkable," supplemented the scientist. Mr van Safford stared. "How old are you?"

"Thirty."

"How long have you been thirty?"

"Six months – since last May."

There was a long pause. Mr van Safford plainly did not see the trend of the questioning.

"How old is your wife?" demanded the scientist.

"Twenty-two, in January."

"She has never had any mental trouble of any sort?"

"No, no."

"Have you any brothers or sisters?"

"No."

"Has she?"

"No."

The Thinking Machine shot out the questions crustily and Mr van Safford answered briefly. There was another pause, and the young man arose and paced back and forth with nervous energy. From time to time he glanced inquiringly at the pale, wizened face of the scientist. Several thin lines had appeared in the dome – like brow, and he was apparently oblivious of the other's presence.

"It's a most intangible, elusive affair," he commented at last, and the wrinkles deepened. "It is, I may say, a problem without a given quantity. Perfectly extraordinary."

Mr van Safford seemed a little relieved to find some one express his own thoughts so accurately.

"You don't believe, of course," continued the scientist, "that there is anything criminal in—"

"Certainly not!" the young man exploded, violently.

"Yet, the moment we pursue this to a logical conclusion," pursued the other, "we are more than likely to uncover something which is, to put it mildly, not pleasant."

Mr van Safford's face was perfectly white; his hands were clenched desperately. Then the loyalty to the woman he loved flooded his heart.

"It's nothing of that kind," he exclaimed, and yet his own heart misgave him. "My wife is the dearest, noblest, sweetest woman in the world. And yet—"

"Yet you are jealous of her," interrupted The Thinking Machine. "If you are so sure of her, why annoy me with your troubles?"

The young man read, perhaps, a deeper meaning than The Thinking Machine had intended for he started forward impulsively. The Thinking Machine continued to squint at him impersonally, but did not change his position.

"All young men are fools," he went on, blandly, "and I may add that most of the old ones are, too. But now the question is: What purpose can your wife have in acting as she has, and in misrepresenting those acts to you? Of course we must spy upon her to find out, and the answer may be one that will wreck your future happiness. It may be, I say. I don't know. Do you still want the answer?"

"I want to know – I want to know," burst out Mr van Safford, harshly. "I shall go mad unless I know."

The Thinking Machine continued to squint at him with almost a gleam of pity in his eyes – almost but not quite. And the habitually irritated voice was in no way softened when he gave some explicit and definite instructions.

"Go on about your affairs," he commanded. "Let things go as they are. Don't quarrel with your wife; continue to ask your questions because if you don't she'll suspect that you suspect; report to me any change in her conduct. It's a very singular problem. Certainly I have never had another like it."

The Thinking Machine accompanied him to the door and closed it behind him.

"I have never seen a man in love," he mused, "who wasn't in trouble."

And with this broad, philosophical conclusion he went to the 'phone. Half an hour later Hutchinson Hatch, reporter, entered the laboratory where the scientist sat in deep thought.

"Ah, Mr Hatch," he began, without preliminary, "did you ever happen to hear of Mr and Mrs van Safford?"

"Well, rather," responded the reporter with quick interest. "He's a well known club-man, worth millions, high in society and all that; and she's one of the most beautiful women I ever saw. She was a Miss Potter before marriage."

"It's wonderful the memories you newspaper men have," observed the scientist. "You know her personally?"

Hatch shook his head.

"You must find some one who knows her well," commanded The Thinking Machine, "a girl friend, for instance – one who might be in her confidence. Learn from her why Mrs van Safford leaves her house every morning at eight o'clock, then tells her husband she has been with some one that we know she hasn't seen. She has done this every day for four days. Your assiduity in this may prevent a divorce."

Hatch pricked up his ears.

"Also find out just what sort of an illness Miss Nell Blakesley has – or is – suffering. That's all."

An hour later Hutchinson Hatch, reporter, called on Miss Gladys Beekman, a young society woman who was an intimate of Mrs van Safford's before the latter's marriage. Without feeling that he was dallying with the truth Hatch informed her that he called on behalf of Mr van Safford. She began to smile. He laid the case before her emphatically, seriously and with great detail. The more he explained the more pleasantly she smiled. It made him uncomfortable but he struggled on to the end.

"I'm glad she did it," exclaimed Miss Beekman. "But I – I couldn't believe she would."

Then came a sudden gust of laughter which left Hutchinson Hatch, reporter, with the feeling that he was being imposed upon. It continued for a full minute – a hearty, rippling, musical laugh. Hatch grinned sheepishly. Then, without an excuse, Miss Beekman arose and left the room. In the hall there came a fresh burst, and Hatch heard it dying away in the distance.

"Well," he muttered grimly. "I'm glad I was able to amuse her."

Then he called upon a Mrs Francis, a young matron whom he had cause to believe was also favoured with Mrs van Safford's friendship. He laid the case before her, and she laughed! Then Hutchinson Hatch, reporter, began to get mule-headed about it. He visited eight other women who were known to be on friendly terms with Mrs van Safford. Six of them intimated that he was an impertinent, prying, inquisitive person, and – the other two laughed! Hatch paused a moment and rubbed his fevered brow.

"Here's a corking good joke on somebody," he told himself, "and I'm beginning to think it's me."

Whereupon he took his troubles to The Thinking Machine. That distinguished gentleman listened in pained surprise to the simple recital of what Hatch had not been able to learn, and spidery wrinkles on his forehead assumed the relative importance of the canals on Mars.

"It's astonishing!" he declared, raspily.

"Yes, it so struck me," agreed the reporter.

The Thinking Machine was silent for a long time; the watery blue eyes were turned upward and the slender white fingers pressed tip to tip. Finally he made up his mind as to the next step.

"There seems only one thing to do," he said. "And I won't ask you to do that."

"What is it?" demanded the reporter.

"To watch Mrs van Safford and see where she goes."

"I wouldn't have done it before, but I will now." Hatch responded promptly. The bull-dog in him was aroused. "I want to see what the joke is."

It was ten o'clock next evening when Hatch called to make a report. He seemed a little weary and tremendously disgusted.

"I've been right behind her all day," he explained, "from eight o'clock this morning until twenty minutes past nine tonight when she reached home. And if the Lord'll forgive me—"

"What did she do?" interrupted The Thinking Machine, impatiently.

"Well," and Hatch grinned as he drew out a notebook, "she walked eastward from her house to the first corner, turned, walked another block, took a down town car, and went straight to the Public Library. There she read a Henry James book until fifteen minutes of one, and then she went to luncheon in a restaurant. I also had luncheon. Then she went to the North End on a car. After she got there she wandered around aimlessly all afternoon, nearly. At ten minutes of four she gave a quarter to a crippled boy. He bit it to see if it was good, found it was, then bought cigarettes with it. At half past four she left the North End and went into a big department store. If there's anything there she didn't price I can't remember it. She bought a pair of shoe-laces. The store closed at six, so she went to dinner in another restaurant. I also had dinner. We left there at half past seven o'clock and went back to the Public Library. She read until nine o'clock, and then went home. Phew!" he concluded.

The Thinking Machine had listened with growing and obvious disappointment on his face. He seemed so cast down by the recital that Hatch tried to cheer him.

"I couldn't help it you know," he said by way of apology. "That's what she did."

"She didn't speak to anyone?"

"Not a soul but clerks, waiters and library attendants."

"She didn't give a note to anyone or receive a note?"

"No."

"Did she seem to have any purpose at all in anything she did?"

"No. The impression she gave me was that she was killing time."

The Thinking Machine was silent for several minutes. "I think perhaps—" he began.

But what he thought Hatch didn't learn for he was sent away with additional instructions. Next morning found him watching the front of the van Safford house again. Mrs van Safford came out at seven minutes past eight o'clock, and walked rapidly eastward. She turned the first corner and went on, still rapidly, to the corner of an alley. There she paused, cast a quick look behind her, and went in. Hatch was some distance back and ran forward just in time to see her skirts trailing into a door.

"Ah, here's something anyhow," he told himself, with grim satisfaction.

He walked along the alley to the door. It was like the other doors along in that it led into the back hall of a house, and was intended for the use of tradesmen. When he examined the door he scratched his chin thoughtfully; then came utter bewilderment, an amazing sense of hopeless insanity. For there, staring at him from a door-plate, was the name: "van Safford." She had merely come out the front door and gone into the back!

Hatch started to rap and ask some questions, then changed his mind and walked around to the front again, and up the steps.

"Is Mrs van Safford in?" he inquired of Baxter, who opened the door.

"No, sir," was the reply. "She went out a few minutes ago."

Hatch stared at him coldly a minute, then walked away.

"Now this is a particularly savoury kettle of fish," he soliloquized. "She has either gone back into the house without his knowledge, or else he has been bribed, and then—"

And then, he took the story to The Thinking Machine. That imperturbable man of science listened to the end, then arose and said "Oh!" three times. Which was interesting to Hatch in that it showed the end was in sight, but it was not illuminating. He was still floundering.

The Thinking Machine started into an adjoining room, then turned back.

"By the way, Mr Hatch," he asked, "did you happen to find out what was the matter with Miss Blakesley?"

"By George, I forgot it," returned the reporter, ruefully.

"Never mind, I'll find out."

At eleven o'clock Hutchinson Hatch and The Thinking Machine called at the van Safford home. Mr van Safford in person received them; there was a gleam of hope in his face at sight of the diminutive scientist. Hatch was introduced, then:

"You don't know of any other van Safford family in this block?" began the scientist.

"There's not another family in the city," was the reply. "Why?"

"Is your wife in now?"

"No. She went out this morning, as usual."

"Now, Mr van Safford, I'll tell you how you may bring this matter to an end, and understand it all at once. Go upstairs to your wife's apartments – they are probably locked – and call her. She won't answer but she'll hear you. Then tell her you understand it all, and that you're sorry. She'll hear that, as that alone is what she has been waiting to hear for some time. When she comes out bring her down stairs. Believe me I should be delighted to meet so clever a woman."

Mr van Safford was looking at him as if he doubted his sanity.

"Really," he said coldly, "what sort of child's play is this?"

"It's the only way you'll ever coax her out of that room," snapped The Thinking Machine belligerently, "and you'd better do it gracefully."

"Are you serious?" demanded the other.

"Perfectly serious," was the crabbed rejoinder. "She has taught you a lesson that you'll remember for sometime. She has been merely going out the front door every day, and coming in the back, with the full knowledge of the cook and her maid."

Mr van Safford listened in amazement.

"Why did she do it?" he asked.

"Why?" retorted The Thinking Machine. "That's for you to answer. A little less of your time at the club of evenings, and a little less of selfish amusement, so that you can pay attention to a beautiful woman who has, previous to her marriage at least, been accustomed to constant attention, would solve this little problem. You've spent every evening at your club for months, and she was here alone probably a great part of that time. In your own selfishness you had never a thought of her, so she gave you a reason to think of her."

Suddenly Mr van Safford turned and ran out of the room. They heard him as he took the stairs, two at a time.

"By George!" remarked Hatch. "That's a silly ending to a cracking good mystery, isn't it?"

Ten minutes later Mr and Mrs van Safford entered the room. Her pretty face was suffused with colour: he was frankly, outrageously happy. There were mutual introductions.

"It was perfectly dreadful of Mr van Safford to call you gentlemen into this affair," Mrs van Safford apologized, charmingly. "Really I feel very much ashamed of myself for—"

"It's of no consequence, madam," The Thinking Machine assured her. "It's the first opportunity I have ever had of studying a woman's mind. It was not at all logical, but it was very – very instructive. I may add that it was effective, too."

He bowed low, and turning picked up his hat.

"But your fee?" suggested Mr van Safford.

The Thinking Machine squinted at him sourly. "Oh, yes, my fee," he mused. "It will be just five thousand dollars."

"Five thousand dollars?" exclaimed Mr van Safford.

"Five thousand dollars," repeated the scientist.

"Why, man, it's perfectly absurd to talk—"

Mrs van Safford laid one white hand on her husband's arm. He glanced at her and she smiled radiantly.

"Don't you think I'm worth it, Van?" she asked, archly.

He wrote the cheque. The Thinking Machine scribbled his name across the back in a crabbed little hand, and passed it on to Hatch.

"Please hand that to some charitable organization," he directed. "It was an excellent lesson, Mrs van Safford. Goodday."

Professor Augustus S. F. X. Van Dusen, scientist, and Hutchinson Hatch, reporter, walked along side by side for two blocks, without speaking. The reporter broke the silence.

"Why did you want to know what was the matter with Miss Blakesley?" he asked.

"I wanted to know if she really had been ill or was merely attempting to mislead Mr van Safford," was the reply. "She was ill with a touch of grippe. I got that by 'phone. I also learned of Mr van Safford's club habits by 'phone from his club."

"And those women who laughed – what was the joke about?"

"The fact that they laughed made me see that the affair was not a serious one. They were intimate friends with whom the wife had evidently discussed doing just what she did do," explained the scientist. "All things considered in this case the facts could only have been as logic developed them. I imagined the true state of affairs from your report of Mrs van Safford's day of wandering; when I knew she went in the back door of her own house, I saw the solution. Because, Mr Hatch," and the scientist paused and shook a long finger in the reporter's face, "because two and two always make four – not sometimes, but all the time."

4

PROBLEM OF THE HIDDEN MILLION

The gray hand of Death had already left its ashen mark upon the wrinkled, venomous face of the old man, who lay huddled up in bed. Save for the feverishly brilliant eyes—cunning, vindictive, hateful – there seemed to be no spark of life in the aged form. The withered lips were mute, and the thin, yellow, claw-like hands lay helplessly outstretched on the white sheets. All physical power was gone; only the brain remained doggedly alive. Two men and two women stood beside the death bed. Upon each in turn the glittering eyes rested with the merciless, unreasoning hatred of age. Crouched on the floor was a huge St. Bernard dog; and on a perch across the room was a parrot which screeched abominably.

The gloom of the wretched little room was suddenly relieved by a ruddy sunbeam which shot athwart the bed and lighted the scene fantastically. The old man noted it, and his lips curled into a hideous smile.

"That's the last sun I'll ever see," he piped feebly. "I'm dying-dying! Do you hear? And you're all glad of it, every one of you. Yes, you are! You are glad of it because you want my money. You came here to make me believe you were paying a last tribute of respect to your old grandfather. But that isn't it. It's the money you want – the money! But I've got a surprise for you. You'll never get the money. It's hidden safely – you'll never get it. You all hate me, you have hated me for years, and after that sun dies you'll all hate me worse. But not more than I hate you. You'll all hate me worse then, because I'll be gone and you'll never know where the money is hidden. It will lie there safely where I put it, rotting and crumbling away; but you shall never warm your fingers with it! It's hidden-hidden-hidden!"

There was rasping in the shrunken throat, a deeply drawn breath, then the figure stiffened and a distorted soul passed out upon the Eternal Way.

Martha held a card within the blinding light of the reflector, and Professor Augustus S. F. X. Van Dusen, with his hands immersed to the elbows in some chemical mess, squinted at it.

"Dr Walter Ballard," he read. "Show him in."

After a moment Dr Ballard entered. The scientist was still absorbed in his labors, but paused long enough to jerk his head toward a chair. Dr Ballard accepted this as an invitation and sat down, staring curiously at the singular, childlike figure of this eminent man of science, at the mop of tangled, straw yellow hair, the enormous brow, and the peering blue eyes.

"Well?" demanded the scientist abruptly.

"I beg your pardon," began Dr Ballard with a little start. "Your name was mentioned to me sometime ago by a newspaper reporter, Hutchinson Hatch, whom I chanced to meet in his professional capacity. He suggested then that I come and see you, but I thought it useless. Now the affair in which we were both interested at that time seems hopelessly beyond solution, so I come to you for aid.

"We want to find one million dollars in gold and United States bonds, which were hidden by my grandfather, John Walter Ballard, sometime before his death just a month ago. The circumstances are altogether out of the ordinary."

The Thinking Machine abandoned his labors, and dried his hands carefully, after which he took a seat facing Dr Ballard. "Tell me about it," he commanded.

"Well," began Dr Ballard reminiscently, as he settled back in his chair, "the old man – my grandfather – died, as I said, a month ago. He was nearly eighty-six, and the last five or six years of his life he spent as a recluse in a little hut twenty miles from the city, a place some distance from any other house. He had a spot of ground there, half an acre or so, and lived like a pauper, despite the fact that he was worth at least a million dollars. Previous to the time he went there to live, there had been an estrangement with my family, his sole heirs. My family consists of myself, wife, son, and daughter.

"My grandfather lived in the house with me for ten years before he went out to this hut; and why he left us then is not clear to any member of my family, unless," and he shrugged his shoulders, "he was mentally unbalanced. Anyway, he went. He would neither come to see us, nor would he permit us to go to see him. As far as we know, he owned no real property of any sort, except this miserable little place, worth altogether — furnishing and all – not more than a thousand or twelve hundred dollars.

"Well, about a month ago some one stopped at the hut for something and found he was ill. I was notified, and with my wife, son and daughter went to see what we could do. He took occasion on his death bed to heap vituperation upon us, and incidentally to state that something like a million dollars was left behind, but hidden.

"For the sake of my son and daughter, I undertook to recover this money. I consulted attorneys, private detectives, and in fact exhausted every possible method. I ascertained beyond question that the money was not in a bank anywhere; and hardly think he would have left it there, because of course, if he had, even with a will disinheriting us, the law would have turned it over to us. He had no safe deposit vault as far as one month's close search revealed, and the money was not hidden in the house or grounds. He stated on his death bed that it was in bonds and gold, and that we should never find it. He was just vindictive enough not to destroy it, but to leave it somewhere, believing we should never find it. Where did he hide it?"

The Thinking Machine sat silent for several minutes, with his enormous yellow head tilted back, and slender fingers pressed together. "The house and grounds were searched?" he asked.

"The house was searched from cellar to garret," was the reply. "Workmen, under my directions, practically wrecked the building. Floors, ceilings, walls, chimney, stairs, – everything, – little cubby holes in the roof, the foundation of the chimney, the pillars, even the flag stones leading from the gate to the door, – everything was examined. The joists were sounded to see if they were solid, and a dozen of them were cut through; the posts on the veranda were cut to pieces; and every stick of furniture was dissected—mattresses, beds, chairs, tables, bureaus—all of it. Outside in the grounds the search was just as thorough. Not one square inch but what was overturned. We dug it all up to a depth of ten feet. Still nothing."

"Of course," said the scientist at last, "the search of the house and grounds was useless. The old man was shrewd enough to know that they would be searched. Also it would appear that the search of banks and safety deposit vaults was equally useless. He was shrewd enough to foresee that too. We shall, for the present, assume that he did not destroy the money or give it away; so it is hidden. If the brain of man is clever enough to conceal a thing, the brain of man is clever enough to find it. It's a little problem in subtraction, Dr Ballard." He was silent for a moment. "Who was your grandfather's attending physician?"

"I was. I was present at his death. Nothing could be done. It was merely the collapse consequent upon old age. I issued the burial certificate."

"Were any special directions left as to the place or manner of burial?"

"No."

"Have all his papers been examined for a clue as to the possible hiding place?"

"Everything. There were no papers to amount to anything."

"Have you those papers now?"

Dr Ballard silently produced a packet and handed it to the scientist.

"I shall examine these at my leisure," said The Thinking Machine. "It may be a day or so before I communicate with you."

Dr Ballard went his way. For a dozen hours The Thinking Machine sat with the papers spread out before him, and the keen, squinting, blue eyes dissected them, every paragraph, every sentence, every word. At the end he arose and bundled up the papers impatiently.

"Dear me! Dear me!" he exclaimed irritably. "There's no cipher – that's certain. Then what?"

Devastating hands had wrought the wreck of the little hut where the old man died. Standing in the midst of its litter, The Thinking Machine regarded it closely and dispassionately for a long time. The work of destruction had been well done.

"Can you suggest anything?" asked Dr Ballard impatiently.

"One mind may read another mind," said The Thinking Machine, "when there is some external thing upon which there can come concentration as a unit. In other words, when we have a given number the logical brain can construct either backward or forward. There are so many thousands of ways in which your grandfather could have disposed of this money, that the task becomes tremendous in view of the fact that we have no starting point. It is a case for patience, rather than any other quality; therefore, for greater speed, we must proceed psychologically. The question then becomes, not one of where the money is hidden, but one of where that sort of man would hide it.

"Now what sort of man was your grandfather?" the scientist continued. "He was crabbed, eccentric, and possibly not mentally sound. The cunning of a diseased brain is greater than the cunning of a normal one. He boasted to you that the money was in existence, and his last words were intended to arouse your curiosity; to hang over you all the rest of your life and torment you. You can imagine the vindictive, petty brain like that putting a thing safely beyond your reach — but just beyond it — near enough to tantalize, and yet far enough to remain undiscovered. This seems to me to be the mental attitude in this case. Your grandfather knew that you would do just what you have done here; that is, search the house and lot. He knew too that you would search banks and safety deposit vaults, and with a million at stake he knew it would be done thoroughly. Knowing this, naturally he would not put the money in any of those places.

"Then what? He doesn't own any other property, as far as we know, and we shall assume that he did not buy property in the name of some other person; therefore, what have we left? Obviously, if the money is still in existence, it is hidden on somebody's else property. And the minute we say that, we have the whole wide world to search. But again, doesn't the deviltry and maliciousness of the old man narrow that down? Wouldn't he have liked to remember as a dying thought that the money was always just within your reach, and yet safely beyond it? Wouldn't it have been a keener revenge to have you dig over the whole place, while the money was hidden just six feet outside in a spot where you would never dig? It might be sixty, or six hundred, or six thousand. But then we have the law of probability to narrow those limits; so—"

Professor Van Dusen turned suddenly and strolled across the uneven ground to the property line. Walking slowly and scrutinizing the ground as he went, he circled the lot, returning to the starting point. Dr Ballard had followed along behind him.

"Are all your grandfather's belongings still in the house?" asked the scientist.

"Yes, everything just as he left it; that is, except his dog and a parrot. They are temporarily in charge of a widow down the road here."

The scientist looked at Dr Ballard quickly. "What sort of dog is it?" he inquired.

"A St. Bernard, I think," replied Dr Ballard wonderingly.

"Do you happen to have a glove or something that you know your grandfather wore?"

"I have a glove, yes."

From the debris which littered the floor of the house, a well worn glove was recovered.

"Now, the dog, please," commanded the scientist.

A short walk along the country road brought them to a house, and here they stopped. The St. Bernard, a shaggy, handsome, boisterous old chap, with wise eyes, was led out in leash. The Thinking Machine thrust the glove forward, and the dog sniffed at it. After a moment he sank down on his haunches, and with head thrust forward and upward, whined softly. It was the call of the brute soul to its master.

The Thinking Machine patted the heavy-coated head, and with the glove still in his hand made as if to go away. Again came the whine, but the dog sank down on the floor, with his head between his forepaws, regarding him intently. For ten minutes the scientist sought to coax the animal to follow him, but still he lay motionless.

"I don't mind keepin' that dog here; but that parrot is powerful noisy," said the woman after a moment. She had been standing by watching the scientist curiously. "There ain't no peace in the house."

"Noisy-how?" asked Dr Ballard.

"He swears, and sings and whistles, and does 'rithmetic all day long," the woman explained. "It nearly drives me distracted."

"Does arithmetic?" inquired The Thinking Machine.

"Yes," replied the woman, "and he swears just terrible. It's almost like havin' a man about the house. There he goes now."

From another room came a sudden, squawking burst of profanity, followed instantly by a whistle, which caused the dog on the floor to prick up his ears.

"Does the parrot talk well?" asked the scientist.

"Just like a human bein'," replied the woman, "an' just about as sensible as some I've seen. I don't mind his whistling, if only he wouldn't swear so, and do all his figgerin' out loud."

For a minute or more the scientist stood staring down at the dog in deep thought. Gradually there came some subtle change in his expression. Dr Ballard was watching him closely.

"I think perhaps it would be a good idea for me to keep the parrot for a few days," suggested the scientist finally. He turned to the woman. "Just what sort of arithmetic does the bird do?"

"All kinds," she answered promptly. "He does all the multiplication table. But he ain't very good in subtraction."

"I shouldn't be surprised," commented The Thinking Machine. "I'll take the bird for a few days, doctor, if you don't mind."

And so it came to pass that when The Thinking Machine returned to his apartments he was accompanied by as noisy and vociferous a companion as one would care to have.

Martha, the aged servant, viewed him with horror as he entered. "The perfessor do be gettin' old," she muttered. "I suppose there'll be a cat next."

Two days later Dr Ballard was called to the telephone. The Thinking Machine was at the other end of the wire.

"Take two men whom you can trust and go down to your grandfather's place," instructed the scientist curtly. "Take picks, shovels, a compass, and a long tape line. Stand on the front steps facing east. To your right will be an apple tree some distance off that lot on the adjoining property. Go to that apple tree. A boulder is at its foot. Measure from the edge of that stone twenty-six feet due north by the compass, and from that point fourteen feet due west. You will find your money there. Then please have some one come and take this bird away. If you don't, I'll wring its neck. It's the most blasphemous creature I ever heard. Goodbye."

Dr Ballard slipped the catch on the suit case and turned it upside down on the laboratory table. It was packed – literally packed – with United States bonds. The Thinking Machine fingered them idly.

"And there is this too," said Dr Ballard.

He lifted a stout sack from the floor, cut the string, and spilled out its contents beside the bonds. It was gold – thousands and thousands of dollars. Dr Ballard was frankly excited about it; The Thinking Machine accepted it as he accepted all material things.

"How much is there of it?" he asked quietly.

"I don't know," replied Dr Ballard.

"And how did you find it?"

"As you directed – twenty-six feet north from the boulder, and fourteen feet west from that point."

"I knew that, of course," snapped The Thinking Machine; "but how was it hidden?"

"It's rather peculiar," explained Dr Ballard. "Fourteen feet brought the man who had measured it to the edge of an old, dried up well, twelve or fifteen feet deep. Not expecting any such thing, he tumbled into it. In his efforts to get out he stepped upon a stone which protruded from one side. That fell out, and revealed the wooden box, which contained all this."

"In other words," said the scientist, "the money was hidden in such a manner that it would in time have come to be buried twelve or fifteen feet below the surface, because the well, being dry, would ultimately, of course, have been filled in."

Dr Ballard had been listening only hazily. His hands had been plowing in and out of the heap of gold. The Thinking

Machine regarded him with something like contempt about his thin-lipped mouth.

"How – how did you ever do it?" asked Dr Ballard at last.

"I am surprised that you want to know," remarked The Thinking Machine cuttingly. "You know how I reached the conclusion that the money was not hidden either in the house or lot. The plain logic of the thing told me that, even before the search you had made demonstrated it. You saw how logic narrowed down the search, and you saw my experiment with the dog. That was purely an experiment. I wanted to see the instinct of the animal. Would it lead him anywhere? – perhaps to the spot where the money had been hidden? It did not.

"But the parrot? That was another matter. It just happens that once before I had an interesting experience with a bird – a cockatoo which figured in a sleep walking case – and naturally was interested in this bird. Now, what were the circumstances in this case? Here was a bird that talked exceptionally well, yet that bird had been living for five years alone with an old man. It is a fact that, no matter how well a parrot may talk, it will forget in the course of time, unless there is some one around it who talks. This old man was the only person near this bird; therefore, from the fact that the bird talks, we know that the old man talked; from the fact that the bird repeated the multiplication table, we know that the old man repeated it; from the fact that the bird whistles, we know that the old man whistled, perhaps to the dog. And in the course of five years under these circumstances, a bird would have come to that point where it would repeat only the words or sounds that the old man used.

"All this shows too that the old man talked to himself. Most people who live alone a great deal do that. Then came a question as to whether at any time the old man had ever repeated the secret of the hiding place within the hearing of the bird – not once but many times, because it takes a parrot a long time to learn phrases. When we know the vindictiveness which lay behind the old man's actions in hiding the money, when we know how the thing preyed on his mind, coupled with the fact that he talked to himself, and was not wholly sound mentally, we can imagine him doddering about the place alone, repeating the very thing of which he had made so great a secret. Thus, the bird learned it, but learned it disjointedly, not connectedly; so when I brought the parrot here, my idea was to know by personal observation what the bird said that didn't connect – that is, that had no obvious meaning, I hoped to get a clue which would result, just as the clue I did get did result.

"The bird's trick of repeating the multiplication table means nothing except it shows the strange workings of an unbalanced mind. And yet, there is one exception to this. In a disjointed sort of way, the bird knows all the multiplication tables to ten, except one. For instance – listen!"

The Thinking Machine crept stealthily to a door and opened it softly a few inches. From somewhere out there came the screeching of the parrot. For several minutes they listened in silence. There was a flood of profanity, a shrill whistle or two, then the squawking voice ran off into a monotone.

"Six times one are six, six time two are twelve, six times three are eighteen, six times four are twenty-four – and add two."

"That's it," explained the scientist, as he closed the door. "'Six times four are twenty-four – and add two.' That's the one table the bird doesn't know. The thing is incoherent, except as applied to a peculiar method of remembering a number. That number is twenty-six. On one occasion I heard the bird repeat a dozen times, 'Twenty-six feet to the polar star.' That could mean nothing except the direction of the twenty-six feet- due north. One of the first things I noticed the bird saying was something about fourteen feet to the setting sun – or due west. When set down with the twenty-six, I could readily see that I had something to go on.

"But where was the starting point? Again, logic. There was no tree or stone inside the lot, except the apple tree which your workmen cut down, and that was more than twenty-six feet from the boundary of the lot in all directions. There was one tree in the adjoining lot, an apple tree with a boulder at its foot. I knew that by observation. And there was no other tree, I knew also, within several hundred feet; therefore, that tree, or boulder rather, as a starting point – not the tree so much as the boulder, because the tree might be cut down, or would in time decay. The chances are the stone would have been allowed to remain there indefinitely. Naturally your grandfather would measure from a prominent point – the boulder. That is all. I gave you the figures. You know the rest."

For a minute or more, Dr Ballard stared at him blankly. "How was it you knew," he asked, "that the directions should have been first twenty-six feet north, then fourteen feet west, instead of first fourteen west, and then twenty-six feet north?"

"I didn't know," replied The Thinking Machine. "If you had failed to find the money by those directions, I should merely have reversed the order."

Half an hour later Dr Ballard went away, carrying the money and the parrot in its cage. The bird cursed The Thinking Machine roundly, as Dr Ballard went down the steps.

5

PROBLEM OF THE INTERRUPTED WIRELESS

Seven bells sounded. The door of the wireless telegraph office on the main deck of the transatlantic liner Uranus was opened quietly, and a man thrust his head out. One quick glance to his right, along the narrow, carpeted passage, showed it to be deserted; another glance to his left showed a young woman approaching, with steps made uncertain by the rolling and pitching of the ship. In one hand she carried a slip of paper, folded once. The man paused only to see this much, then withdrew his head and closed the door abruptly.

The young woman paused opposite the wireless office, and thoughtfully conned over something on the slip of paper. Finally she leaned against the wall, erased a word with a pencil, wrote in another, then laid a hand on the knob of the door as if to enter. The door was locked. She hesitated for an instant, then rapped. There was a pause, and she rapped the second time.

"What is it?" came a man's voice from inside.

"I wish to send a message," responded the young woman.

"Who is that?" came another query.

PROBLEM OF THE INTERRUPTED WIRELESS 63

"It's Miss Bellingdame," was the impatient response. "I desire to get a wireless to a friend on the Breslin which has just been sighted to the north."

Again there was a pause. "It's impossible to send any message now," came the short, harsh answer at last. "It may not be possible to send it at all."

"Why?" demanded Miss Bellingdame. "It's a matter of the utmost importance. I must send it!"

"Can't be done – it's out of the question," came the positive, quick spoken answer. "There has been an – an accident."

Miss Bellingdame was silent for a moment, as she seemed to ponder a note of deep concern, excitement even, in the voice.

"Well, can't it be sent after the accident has been repaired?" she asked at last.

There was no answer.

"Is that Mr Ingraham talking?" Miss Bellingdame demanded.

Still there was no answer. She remained there for a minute, perhaps, staring at the locked door, then turned and retraced her steps. A few minutes later she was reclining in a deck chair, gazing thoughtfully out over the treacherous, dimpling Atlantic with a troubled expression on her face.

At just about the moment she sat down the telephone buzz in the Captain's cabin sounded, and Captain Deihl impatiently laid aside a remarkably promising pinochle hand to answer it.

"Captain Deihl?" came a short, sharp query over the wire.

"Yes."

"This is Mr Tennell, sir. I'm in the wireless office. Can you come at once, and have someone send Dr Maher?"

"What's the matter?" demanded the Captain gruffly.

"I can't very well tell you over the 'phone, sir," came the response; "but you and Dr Maher are needed immediately."

With a slightly puzzled expression on his bronzed face, Captain Deihl turned to Dr Maher, the ship's surgeon who had been his opponent in the pinochle game and now sat staring idly out of the window.

"Tennell wants both of us down in the wireless office at once," the Captain explained. "He won't say what's the matter."

"Wants me?" inquired Dr Maher. "Somebody hurt?"

"I don't know. Come along."

Captain Deihl led the way along the hurricane deck, down to the main deck, and along the narrow passage to the wireless office. The door was still locked. He rapped sharply, impatiently.

"Who's there?" came from inside.

"Captain Deihl. Open the door!"

The key turned in the lock, and First Officer Tennell's white face – white even beneath the deep tan – appeared.

"What's the matter, Mr Tennell?" demanded the Captain brusquely.

"Please step inside, sir," and the first officer opened the door. "There's what's the matter?"

With a gesture the first officer indicated the corner of the cabin where the wireless operator's desk stood. Sitting before it, as if he had dropped back utterly exhausted, was the operator, Charles Ingraham. His head had fallen forward on his breast, and the arms hung straight down, flabbily. His back was toward them, and against the white of his shirt, just beneath the left arm, a heavy handled knife showed. A thin line of scarlet dyed the shirt just below the knife handle.

Captain Deihl stood stockstill for one instant, then turning suddenly closed and locked the door behind him. Dr Maher took two steps forward, wrested the knife from the wound with a slight effort, flung it on the floor, then dropped on his knees beside the chair.

"What is all this, Mr Tennell?" demanded Captain Deihl at last.

"I don't know, sir," was the reply. "I found him like that."

Dr Maher arose after a moment, with a hopeless shake of his head, and minutely examined the wound. It was a clean cut

PROBLEM OF THE INTERRUPTED WIRELESS 65

incision; the knife had been driven in and allowed to remain. The blade had passed between the ribs and had reached the heart. Dr Maher noted these things, then stooped and picked up the knife. It was a long, heavy, broad bladed, dangerous looking weapon. After satisfying himself, the surgeon passed it to Captain Deihl.

"It was murder," he said tersely. "He could not have stabbed himself in that position. You keep the knife; it may be the only clue."

"Murder!" the Captain repeated involuntarily. "How long has – has he been dead?"

"Perhaps ten minutes – certainly not more than twenty," was the surgeon's reply. "The body is still warm, and the blood flows."

"Murder!" repeated Captain Deihl. "Who could have killed him? What could have been the motive?"

He stood staring at the knife silently for a time, then lifted two keen, inquisitive eyes to those of his first officer. Dr Maher too was staring straight into Tennell's face, and slowly, under the sharp scrutiny, the blood mounted again to the tanned cheeks.

"What are your orders, sir?" inquired the first officer steadily.

"How long were you in this room, Tennell, before you called me?" asked Captain Deihl.

"Two or three minutes," was the reply. "I was in my cabin forward, preparing the dispatches which were to go ashore, according to your order, sir. The wireless was going then; for I could hear it. I noticed after a time that it stopped; so, having completed my dispatches, I brought them here directly. I found Mr Ingraham just as you see him."

"H'm!" mused the Captain. He was still staring thoughtfully into the other's face. "Was the door locked?"

"No, sir. It was closed."

"And this knife, Mr Tennell?" The Captain examined it again and then passed it to his first officer. "Do you know it? Have you seen it before?"

Without any apparent reason the first officer's face whitened again and he dropped down on the bench, with hands gripping each other fiercely. Dr Maher was staring at him; Captain Deihl seemed surprised.

"You know whose knife it is then?" asked the Captain finally.

"Yes," and the first officer's head dropped forward. "It's mine."

There was a long dead silence. The hands of the first officer were working nervously, with heavy fingers threading in and out. Dr Maher turned away suddenly and idly fingered some papers on the operator's desk.

Captain Deihl's heavy face grew set and stern. "Did you kill him, Tennell?" he asked.

"No!" Tennell burst out. "No!"

"But it is your knife?"

"It would be useless for me to deny it, sir," replied the first officer, and he arose. "It was given to me by Mr Forbes, the second officer, only a few weeks ago, and he could identify it instantly. I lost the knife yesterday, and last night – I shall ask you to corroborate this, sir – I posted a notice in the fo'c'sle offering a reward to anyone who should find it and return it to me."

Dr Maher turned suddenly upon them. "And isn't it true, Mr Tennell," he demanded, "that you and Ingraham had some – some serious disagreement a few days ago?"

Again the first officer's face blanched. "That is true, yes," he replied steadily. "It was a matter of ship's discipline. This was Mr Ingraham's second trip with us, and on other ships he had been allowed certain liberties which the discipline of this ship compelled me to curtail. There was a disagreement, yes."

Dr Maher nodded as if satisfied, and turned again to the desk.

Captain Deihl stood staring straight into the eyes of his first officer for a time, and then cleared his throat. "I want to believe you, Tennell," he admitted at last. "I have known you and believed in you for fourteen years. Now tell me why you call me here, show me this, and then admit things which – which you must confess make it look black for you. Now, Harry Tennell, if you ever in your life told me the truth, tell it now – man to man!"

The first officer read the friendliness behind the stern, commanding voice, and there was a grateful softening of the glaring eyes. "Man to man, John Deihl, I'll tell you the truth; but it's hard to believe, and I doubt if you will understand it," he said slowly, deliberately. "I did have a row with this man," and he indicated the crumpled figure in the chair, – "a nasty row in the hearing of half a dozen of the crew. That was several days ago. Today I came here in the course of my duties, and found him like this. I recognized the knife instantly as mine – the one I had lost. I am not a coward, John Deihl, – no man knows that better than you do, – yet for a moment I was overcome by a feeling of terror. Here was the fact of the quarrel, my knife as the weapon of death, myself alone in the cabin with this man while the body was still warm. It all flashed across my mind in instant – I was frightened at the utter helplessness of my position. No one had seen me enter this cabin, I knew, and the thought came that perhaps I might leave it without being seen, keep my mouth shut, and allow some one else to discover this." The first officer paused and sought vainly to read the expressions on the faces of the two men before him.

"I even went so far as to draw the knife out of the wound, with the purpose of flinging it overboard," the first officer continued slowly; "then my senses came back. I knew my duty again. I replaced the knife in the wound, precisely as I found it, and called you. You are a severe man, but you're a just man, John Deihl, and you know I am not the man to stab another in the back; you know, John Deihl, that fourteen years with me as shipmate and fellow officer has never shown you a weak spot in my courage; you know me, John Deihl and I know you." The voice dropped suddenly. "That's all."

Captain Deihl had stood motionless, with stern, set face and keen, cold eyes searching those of the first officer. At last he reached out a hand and gripped the one that met it. "I believe you, Harry," he said quietly.

Dr Maher turned quickly and regarded the two with a slight cynical uplifting of his lip. "I understand then," he said unpleasantly, "that this is to be a matter of friendship rather than of evidence?"

The first officer's face flamed, and he took one step toward the surgeon, with clenched fists.

"Go to your cabin, Mr Tennell!" ordered Captain Deihl curtly. "Remain there till further orders come from me!"

The first officer paused, involuntarily straightened himself, and lifted one hand to his cap. "Yes, sir," he said.

"And you are not to mention this matter to anyone," Captain Deihl directed.

"I understand, sir."

But news travels quickly aboard ship; so that within less than an hour the tragedy had become a matter of general discussion. Miss Bellingdame was reclining comfortably in a deck chair, when a casual acquaintance, Clarke Matthews, dropped into a seat beside her, and informed her of it. She struggled to her feet, stood staring at him dully for an instant with whitening face, swayed, and fell prone to the deck. It was fully half an hour before the stewardess and her assistants saw the eyelids flutter and open weakly; and at the end of another half hour the stewardess sought out the Captain. She found him at his desk in his cabin, with Second Officer Forbes.

"We must get those dispatches off, Mr Forbes," the Captain was saying. "Have the ship canvassed, first and second cabin, steerage and crew, to see if by any chance there is a man, woman, or child who can operate the wireless. Attend to it at once!"

Forbes touched his cap and went out. The Captain turned to the stewardess inquiringly.

"Please, sir, Miss Bellingdame is almost insane from the shock of the murder," the stewardess informed him. "It's hard to make her keep in her state room, let alone the berth. Dr Maher doesn't seem to be able to do her any good. She insists on seeing the body."

"Why?" asked Captain Deihl in surprise. "Was she acquainted with Ingraham?"

"She was engaged to be married to him, sir," replied the stewardess. "Poor child! I don't know what to do for her."

Captain Deihl stared at her blankly for an instant, then arose suddenly and accompanied her to Miss Bellingdame's state room. She was sitting up in her berth, pallid as the sheets about her. One of the stewardess's assistants sat near trying to soothe her.

"Is it true, Captain?" she demanded.

Captain Deihl nodded grimly.

She extended her hands convulsively and clutched his arm, then her head sank forward against it and she sobbed bitterly. "Do you know who – who did it?" she asked at last.

"We don't know, madam," he replied gently. "We are doing all we can; but—"

"Somebody told me your first officer had been arrested," she interrupted suddenly. "He is tall and dark, with a heavy moustache, isn't he?"

"Yes," replied the Captain. "Why?"

For a little while she was silent as she struggled to regain control of her voice, and then: "May I say something to you in private, Captain?"

"Do you know – do you suspect—?" he began.

"I must!" she insisted.

At a gesture from Captain Deihl the stewardess and her assistant left them alone together. Fifteen minutes later he emerged and summoned Second Officer Forbes to his cabin.

"Mr Forbes, proceed at once to Mr Tennell's cabin and formally place him under arrest," he ordered shortly. "You had better put him in irons, and keep an armed guard beside him day and night until we land. Don't take any chances with him."

"Yes, sir."

Two hours later Second Officer Forbes appeared in the cabin again. "We have canvassed the ship, sir," he reported. "There is not a wireless operator aboard, or even a telegraph operator."

"What is our speed?"

"A little better than seventeen knots, sir."

"We should land then about five o'clock tomorrow afternoon," the Captain mused. "Very well, Mr Forbes; we shall have to do without an operator."

Captain Deihl paced slowly, thoughtfully, back and forth across the bridge. Above the stars glittered coldly down upon the silent, sinister sea as it slid past the Uranus in green, oily swells. The encompassing night was unbroken by a single glint of light save that which Nature gave grudgingly. The Captain gazed upon it all with unseeing eyes and grimly set lips.

Two bells sounded – one o'clock. As the echo of the last stroke was borne away on the wind Captain Deihl suddenly became conscious of the sharp, venomous hiss of the wireless. The wireless! He paused incredulously, and glanced aloft. A spark sputtered at the top of the foremast, winked and flashed and spat viciously in the rhythmic dots and dashes of the Continental code. The wireless was working! Some one was sending! The Captain knew that no sound accompanied the receipt of a message, even with the automatic attachment; therefore that sputtering and hissing was some one sending, and if that was true it meant—

PROBLEM OF THE INTERRUPTED WIRELESS 71

He ran down the ladder to the hurricane deck, and disappeared down a companion – way to the deck below.

Professor Augustus S. F. X. Van Dusen listened to Captain Deihl's recital of the circumstances surrounding the murder of Charles Ingraham, with a slight frown of annoyance on his wizened face. As he talked the man of the sea turned from time to time to Dr Maher for confirmation of the facts. Each time such corroboration was given with a short nod of the head.

"Now, there are a few other little things," Captain Deihl continued deliberately, "that are not known to Dr Maher here. For instance, I personally went to the fo'c'sle to see if Tennell had posted a notice there offering a reward for the knife on the night before the murder, and found that statement correct. Here is the notice. You will see the description fits perfectly the knife with which the murder was committed."

The Thinking Machine accepted a sheet of paper which Deihl offered, glanced at it, then handed it back.

"I don't know if Dr Maher even knows just why I ordered Tennell under arrest," continued the Captain. "Miss Bellingdame's story decided me. She was going to the wireless office to send a message, when she saw a man – it was First Officer Tennell – thrust his head out the door and look around, as if he contemplated escape. She thought it rather curious that he should slam the door when he saw her; but it meant nothing particularly. Then, at a time when we now know Ingraham was dead, she carried on a conversation with some one in the wireless office, through the locked door. Tennell had not mentioned this to me, and coming as it did it seemed so conclusive that I ordered his arrest."

"It was conclusive from the first," remarked Dr Maher.

"And then hearing the wireless that night after I had taken pains to assure myself that there was no operator aboard!" Captain Deihl resumed, and his face reflected his bewilderment. "I went straight from the bridge to the wireless office, to find it silent, dark, and the door locked. I called. There was no answer, and I smashed in the door. There was no sign of anyone having been in there – everything was precisely as we left it when the body was removed."

For a long time there was silence. Dr Maher drummed impatiently on the arm of his chair; The Thinking Machine sat motionless, his slender figure all but engulfed in the huge chair.

"As I understand it," remarked The Thinking Machine at last, "Tennell is now in the hands of the police, and the body is—"

"Ashore awaiting burial," the Captain supplied. "Miss Bellingdame has asked permission of the authorities to take charge of it."

Dr Maher arose and went to the window, where he stood looking out. The Thinking Machine lowered his squint eyes and stared steadily at the ship's surgeon.

"The case against the first officer seems perfectly clear thus far," said the scientist after a pause. "Why do you come to me?"

Captain Deihl's bronzed face reddened as if he was embarrassed, and he cleared his throat. "Because I know Harry Tennell," he said bluntly. "Circumstances are compelling me to believe that he is a murderer, and my reason won't let me believe it. Why, man, I've known him for years, and I simply can't make myself believe what I have to believe! The police are deaf to the bare suggestion of his innocence, and I – I came here."

"All of which is rather to the credit of your heart than to your head," interposed Dr Maher cynically.

"Have you any cause to suspect anyone but Tennell, Captain?" inquired The Thinking Machine. He was squinting at the back of Dr Maher's head. "Can you imagine any other motive than the apparent one?"

"No," replied Captain Deihl. "I can imagine nothing; but I would gamble my right arm that Harry Tennell didn't kill him."

Again there was silence. The Captain was gazing vainly into the drawn, inscrutable face of the diminutive scientist, who lay back with finger tips pressed together and eyes turned steadily upward.

"Dr Maher," inquired the scientist at last, "the wound was made by a knife. Was it clean cut?"

"Yes."

"Was the knife driven to the hilt?"

"Yes. It required considerable strength."

"And I believe Captain Deihl says there was a thin trickle of blood from the wound before you pulled the knife out?"

"That's correct," was the short answer.

"Therefore is a point for Tennell, as it shows the knife had been withdrawn and replaced. And so the real problem is to find what message Ingraham was sending when he was murdered," said the scientist quietly. "Neither of you happens to know?"

"The same thought came to me while Captain Deihl was talking to Tennell," said Dr Maher quickly. "It was shortly after seven bells in the afternoon—that is, half-past three o'clock – when the crime was discovered. Now, the last message to be sent, according to the time check on it, was sent shortly after twelve. Yet, if we believe Tennell, the operator was sending a message just before he was struck down, or possibly at that moment. Well, there was nothing to show for that message – no scrap of paper – nothing."

The Thinking Machine glanced at Dr Maher as if surprised. "Therefore the message Ingraham was sending," he put in, "was either stolen or was being composed as he sent it. Is that clear?"

There was a pause. Captain Deihl nodded, and Dr Maher began drumming on the window sill.

"That being true," the scientist went on incisively, "the next step is to learn who aboard the Uranus could read the code – the Continental code too, mind you, not the Morse – as a message was being sent. Is that clear?"

"Yes; go on," said Captain Deihl.

"When we find the person who could read the Continental code, we also find the person who in all probability was operating the wireless at one o'clock the night of the murder. Is that clear?"

"Yes, yes."

"And when we find the person who operated the wireless logic shows us, incontrovertibly, that we have either the murderer of Ingraham, or some one who was in the plot. Remember, the ship had been canvassed in a search for an operator. None came forward; therefore we know that the operator—an operator – was aboard, but for divers reasons preferred to remain unknown. We know that as certainly as that two and two make four, not sometimes but all the time."

Dr Maher turned and dropped back into his chair, with a new interest evident in every line of his face.

"With these facts in hand it is a simple matter, albeit perhaps a tedious one, to find what message was sent from the ship both by the operator and by the unknown at night," The Thinking Machine resumed. He was silent for a moment, then arose and left the room. He was gone for perhaps ten minutes. "Now, Captain Deihl, and you, Dr Maher, have you formed any opinion as to the exact method of the murder? Was the murderer inside the cabin with Ingraham, or was he killed by a knife thrust through an open window? You know the arrangement of the place better than I. What is your opinion?"

Captain Deihl considered the matter carefully as he sought to recall every minute detail of the cabin as he found it. "Since you have brought up the question," he said slowly at last, "it seems to me that he must have been stabbed by some one outside, through the window. His left side was toward the window, and the window was open, as it was warm, and he was in his shirt sleeves. Yes, it was within easy reach, and I'm inclined to believe—What do you think, Maher?"

"I agree with you perfectly," was the prompt response. "The angle of the knife indicates that an arm had been dropped inside the state room, and there was an upward thrust, where if a person had been in the room the natural angle would have been downward, unless that person had been lying on the floor."

"All of which being true, is a point in favour of Tennell," said The Thinking Machine curtly. "You found him inside the cabin with the body, and we must suppose from your own statement, Dr Maher, that he would have had to lie down to inflict the wound. I may say that the strongest point in his favour is the fact that he did not throw away the knife. He knew it to be his; had opportunity to get rid of it, but didn't; therefore—" He shrugged his shoulders and was silent for a moment.

"All things depend upon the point of view, gentlemen," he continued after a time. "There are half a dozen casual facts, several of which I have specified, which incline me to a belief in Tennell's innocence; and only two against him, these being the motive and the knife. Strong, you say? Yes; but the knife is turned in his favour. Now let us assume Tennell's innocence for a moment, and build our hypothesis on facts that we know. It is always possible to reconstruct a happening by the logic of its units. Let us see this rule applied to this case.

"We are reasonably certain that whatever message Ingraham was sending just before, or at the moment of his death, was not a written message. I have your word, Dr Maher, that there was not a trace of any message after the one about noon. Shall we suppose that there was a written message and it was stolen from his desk by the hand that slew? Hardly. Let us take the simple view first. He was sending a message somewhere as he composed it. Now, anyone aboard that ship who knew the Continental code could have read that message, because the wireless has that fault. That being true, we shall admit that somebody did read it, or was reading it as it went.

"Right here we come to what may prove to be the solution. It was necessary for the person who read the message to stop it, and perhaps to silence the man who sent it, even at the cost of a life. Therefore, the importance of the message to the person who read it was life and death. A blow was struck; the message was stopped. But the knife? Tennell says he lost it; anyone might have found it.

"The message is stopped; the man is dead. The next vital necessity which the murderer feels is self protection. How? Can a message be sent which will counteract the one which was stopped by the murder? If this can be done, it is vitally necessary. Some one then – the murderer – takes another tremendous chance, enters the office, and is sending another message, possibly a continuation of the interrupted message, when Captain Deihl becomes aware of it. He goes to investigate, and the probabilities are that the unknown operator escapes by way of the window and regains a state room unobserved.

"That's clear, isn't it? Well, now, what possible motive might lie back of it all? Well, one for instance. Suppose the English police, after the Uranus sailed, had reason to suspect there was some person aboard who as wanted there; they could have reached the Uranus by wireless. But no such report reached the Uranus, you say, Captain? That is, no such report reached you, you mean. The operator might have received such a report; but for reasons of his own kept it to himself. Do you see?

"Let us conjecture a bit. What if a big reward was offered for some person aboard the Uranus, and a statement of the fact reached it by wireless? What if the operator was that peculiar type of man who would hold that information to himself on the chance of discovering and delivering over that person who was wanted to the police of this country, thus holding the reward all to himself? Do you see the possibilities? Now, what if that person who was wanted was an operator as well, and able to read the unwritten message the regular operator was sending, – a message, understand, which meant capture and punishment, – is that a motive for murder?

"This is all partly conjectures, partly fact – merely a discussion of the possibilities. Still, our murderer is unknown. As I have said, the capture of the guilty person may be simple; but it may be tedious. When I hear from—"

There was a sharp, ringing of the telephone bell in the next room. The scientist arose abruptly and went out. After a few minutes he returned.

"You allowed Miss Bellingdame to leave the Uranus on a motor boat, I understand, before you docked?" he inquired placidly.

"Yes," replied Captain Deihl. "She requested it, and Dr Maher suggested that it would perhaps be best as she was very ill and weak from the shock following the tragedy."

"I shall be able to put my conjectures to a test at once then," said The Thinking Machine as he put on his hat. "First, I must ask some questions of Miss Bellingdame, however. Suppose you gentlemen wait for me at police headquarters? I shall be there in an hour or so."

The Thinking Machine and Hutchinson Hatch, reporter, were sitting together in a small reception room adjoining the telegraph office in the Hotel Teutonic. Opposite them was Miss Bellingdame, still pale and weary looking, with traces of grief on her face.

"Our close relationship with Mr Igraham prompted us to call upon you and offer our condolences at this time," The Thinking Machine was saying glibly; "and at the same time to ask if we could be of any service to you?"

"I appreciate the feeling, but hardly think there is anything you can do," Miss Bellingdame responded, "unless, indeed, it is to relieve me of the painful task of taking charge of the body, and—"

"Just what I was going to suggest," interrupted the little scientist. "With your permission I shall send a telegram at once to friends at home and tell them to make preparations. If you will excuse me?" And he arose.

Miss Bellingdame nodded, and he went to the small window of the telegraph office, wrote a despatch, and handed it in. After a moment he resumed his seat.

"It is singular that Charlie should never have mentioned your name in his letters home," continued The Thinking Machine as he dropped back into his chair.

"Well, our acquaintance was rather brief," replied Miss Bellingdame. "I met him abroad, and at his suggestion came directly over with him. Now that everything has happened, I hardly know just what I shall do next."

The telegraph sounder clicked sharply, and distinctly.

"And when were you to have been married?" interrupted the scientist gently.

Miss Bellingdame was listening intently. "Married?" she repeated absently. "Oh, yes, we were to have been married, to be sure."

Hatch strove vainly to read the expression which was creeping into her face. She was leaning forward, gripping the arms of the chair in which she sat with wide, staring, frightened eyes, and every instant her face grew whiter. Suddenly she arose.

"Really you must pardon me," she gasped hurriedly. "I am ill!"

She turned quickly and almost ran out of the room. The Thinking Machine walked out and into the arms of Detective Mallory in the lobby.

"Are your men placed?" demanded the scientist abruptly.

"Yes," was the complacent answer. "Did it work?"

"It worked," replied The Thinking Machine enigmatically. "Come on. Let us go to headquarters."

The Thinking Machine's conjecture was faulty only in one point, and that was his surmise that the message which had been sent at night from the Uranus after the murder had been to counteract the message which Ingraham was sending when he was killed. Instead, Miss Bellingdame, herself an operator, had picked up the wireless station ashore and ordered a motor boat out to meet her and take her off. Every other statement was correct as he had stated it.

"And simple," he told Hatch and Captain Deihl. "Mr Hatch, to whom I telephoned while you, Captain, were with me, was able to find the interrupted message at sea; in fact, it had been relayed in to the station here for information. It stated that Miss Florence Hogarth, wanted for poisoning in England, and for whom there was a reward of one thousand pounds, was aboard the Uranus as Miss Bellingdame, and that instead of having dark hair her hair was straw blond, as the result of a little peroxide. You see, therefore, the logic of the units was correct. It is always so. She went to pieces when she read the sounder at the hotel, which was a prearranged affair in the hands of a Continental operator. The message I sent was a dummy."

Subsequent developments proved that instead of being engaged to the murdered operator, Miss Bellingdame, or Miss Hogarth, had never seen him until she came aboard the Uranus. It never appeared just how Ingraham had discovered her identity.

6

MYSTERY OF THE GOLDEN DAGGER

I

"All animals have the same appetites and the same passions. The reasoning faculty is the one thing which lifts man above what we are pleased to call the lower animals. Logic is the essence of the reasoning faculty. Therefore logic is that power which enables the mind of man to reconstruct from one fact a series of incidents leading to a given result. One result may be as surely traced back to its causes as the specialist may reconstruct a skeleton from a fraction of bone."

Thus clearly, pointedly Professor Augustus S. F. X. Van Dusen had once explained to Hutchinson Hatch, reporter, the analytical power by which he had solved some of the most perplexing mysteries that had ever come to the attention of either the police or the press. It was a text from which sermons might be preached. No one knew this better than Hatch.

Professor Van Dusen is the foremost logician of his time. His name has been honored at home and abroad until now it embraces as honorary initials nearly all those letters which had not been included in it in the first place. The Thinking Machine! This phrase applied once in a newspaper to the scientist had clung tenaciously. It was the name by which he was known to the world at large.

In a dozen ways he had proved his right to it. Hatch remembered vividly the scientist's mysterious disappearance from a prison cell once; then there had been the famous automobile mystery, and more lately the strange chain of circumstances whose history has been written as "The Scarlet Thread." This little text, as given above, was one afternoon, when Hatch had casually called on The Thinking Machine. It transpired that a few hours later he had returned to lay before the logician still another mystery.

On his return to his office Hatch had been dispatched in a rush on a murder story. In following up the threads of this he had learned every fact the police had, had written his story, and then presented himself at the Beacon Hill home of The Thinking Machine. It was then 11 o'clock at night. The Thinking Machine had received him, and the facts, in substance, were laid before him as follows:

A man who had given the name of Charles Wilkes called at the real estate office of Henry Holmes & Co., on Washington Street on October 14, just thirty-two days prior to the beginning of the story, as Hatch recited it. He was a man of possibly thirty years, stalwart, good-looking and clean-cut in appearance. There had been nothing about him to attract particular attention. He had said that he was eastern agent for a big manufacturing concern, and travelled a great deal.

"I want a six or seven room house in Cambridge," he had explained. "Something quiet, where I won't have too many neighbors. My wife is extremely nervous, and I want to get a couple of blocks from the street cars. If you have a house, say in the middle of a big lot somewhere in the outskirts of Cambridge, I think that will do."

"What price?" a clerk had asked.

"Anywhere from $45 to $60," he replied.

It just happened that Henry Holmes & Co. had such a house. An office man went with Mr Wilkes to see it. Mr Wilkes was pleased and paid the first month's rent of $60 to the man who had accompanied him.

"I won't go back to the office with you," he said. "Everything is all right. I'll have my stuff moved out in a couple of days and let your collector come for next month's rent when it is due."

Mr Wilkes was a very pleasant man; the clerk had found him so and was gratified at the transaction, which gave his firm such a desirable tenant. He did not ask for Mr Wilkes' address, nor did he think to ask any questions as to where the household goods were at the moment. In the light of subsequent events this lack of caution temporarily hid, at least for a time, it seemed, the key which would have solved a mystery.

The month passed and in the office of Holmes & Co. the matter had been forgotten until the rent came due. Then a collector, Willard Clements, the regular Cambridge collector for the firm went to the Cambridge house. He found the front door locked. The shutters were still over the windows. There was no indication that anyone at all had either occupied the house or used it. That was an impression to be gathered by a casual outside inspection. Clements had gone around the house; the back door stood wide open.

Clements went inside the house and must have remained there for half an hour. When he came out his face was white, his lips quivered, and the madness of terror was in his eyes. He ran staggeringly around the house and down the walk to the street. A few minutes later he rushed into a police station and there poured out a babbling, incoherent story. The usually placid face of the officer in charge was overspread with surprise as he listened.

Three men were detailed to visit the house and investigate Clements' story. Two of these men went with Clements through the back door, which still stood open, and the third, Detective

Fahey, began an examination of the premises. Entering through the back door, the kitchen lay to his left. There was nothing to show that it had been occupied for many months. A hurried glance satisfied him, and he passed into the main body of the house. This consisted of a parlour, a dining room and a bedroom. Here, too, he found nothing. The dust lay thick over floors, mantels and window sills.

From the hall, stairs led to three sleeping rooms above. Under these stairs a short flight lead to the cellar. The door stood open, and a damp, chilly breath came up. Utter darkness lay below. The detective shrugged his shoulders and turned to go upstairs where the other men were.

He found them in the smallest of the three rooms, bending over a bed. Clements stood at the door, which had been broken in, still with the pallor of death on his face and his hands working nervously.

"Find anything?" asked the detective briskly.

"My God, no," gasped Clements. "I wouldn't go back in that room for a million dollars."

The detective laughed and passed in.

"What is it?" he asked.

"A girl," was the reply.

"What happened to her?"

"Stabbed," was the laconic answer.

The other two men stood aside and the detective looked down at the body. It was that of a girl possibly twenty or twenty-two years old. She had been pretty, but the hand of death had obliterated many traces of it now. Her hair, of a rich, ruddy gold, mercifully veiled somewhat the ravages of death; her hands lay outstretched on the white of the bed.

She was dressed for the street. Her hat still clung to her hair, fastened by a long, black-headed pin. Her clothing, of dark brown, was good but not rich. A muff lay beside her and her coat was open.

It was not necessary for Detective Fahey to ask the immediate cause of death. A stab wound in the breast showed that.

"Where's the knife?" he asked.

"Didn't find any."

"Any other wounds?"

"Can't tell until the medical examiner arrives. She's just as we found her."

"Here, O'Brien," instructed the detective, "run out and 'phone to Dr Loyd and tell him to come up as fast as he can get here. It's probably only suicide."

One of the men went out, and the detective picked up and examined the muff. From it he drew out a small purse. He opened this to find a withered rose – nothing else. There was no money, no card, no key – nothing which might immediately throw light on the girl's identity.

After a while Dr Loyd came. He remained in the room alone for ten minutes or so, while the policemen went carefully over the upper rooms of the house. When the doctor opened the door and stepped out he carried something in his hand.

"It's murder," he told the detective.

"How do you know?"

"There are two wounds in the back, where she could not possibly have inflicted them herself. And I found this beneath the body."

In his open hand lay a dagger—a dagger of gold. The handle was strangely and intricately fashioned and might, from its appearance, have been cut from a solid bar of gold. In the end blazed a single splendid gem – a diamond. It was probably of three or four karats and pure white. The steel blade was bright at the hilt but stained red.

"Great Scott!" exclaimed the detective as he examined it. "With a clue like that, the end is already in sight."

This was the story that Hutchinson Hatch told to The Thinking Machine. The scientist listened carefully, as he lay stretched out in a chair with his enormous yellow head resting easily against a cushion. He asked only three questions.

"How long had the girl been dead?"

"The medical examiner says it is impossible to tell within more than a few days," Hatch replied. "He gave it as his opinion that it was a week or ten days."

"What was in the cellar?"

"I don't know. No one looked."

"Who broke in the door? Clements?"

"Yes."

"I shall go with you tomorrow," said The Thinking Machine. "I want to look at the dagger and also the cellar."

II

It was 10 o'clock next day when Hutchinson Hatch and The Thinking Machine called on Dr Loyd. The medical examiner willingly displayed the golden dagger, and in technical terms explained just what had caused the girl's death. Minus the medical phraseology his opinion was that the wound in the breast had been the first inflicted and that the dagger point had punctured the heart. One of the wounds in the back had also reached the same vital spot; the other wound was superficial.

The Thinking Machine viewed the body and agreed with the medical examiner. He had, meanwhile, carefully examined the dagger, handle and blade, and had a photograph of it made. Then, with Hatch, he proceeded to the Cambridge house.

"It isn't suicide, is it?" asked Hatch on the way.

"No," was the quick response. "The only question thus far in my mind, is whether or not the girl was killed in that house."

"Why was a man such a fool as to leave a dagger of that value where it would be found – or any dagger for that matter?" Hatch asked.

"A dozen reasons," replied the scientist. "A possible one is, that whoever killed her may have been frightened away before he could regain possession of the weapon. Remember it was found underneath her body. Presumably she fell backwards and covered the dagger. A slight noise – any one of a dozen things – might have caused the person who killed her to run away rather than try to get the weapon again. Against that of course is the value of the dagger. I know little about jewels, but knowing as little as I do, I should say the value was in the thousands."

"The very reason why it wouldn't be left," said Hatch.

"Quite true," said the other. "Yet the value of the dagger may have been the very reason it was left."

Hatch turned quickly and stared at The Thinking Machine with a question in his eyes.

"I mean," The Thinking Machine explained, "that the dagger is nearly as good as the name and the address of its owner, because it can be traced immediately. Its owner would never have left it under any circumstances."

Hatch was puzzled. He did not follow, as yet, the intricate reasoning of the scientist. It seemed that the one solid, substantial clue, as he regarded it, was to be eliminated without a hearing. The Thinking Machine went on:

"Suppose it had been someone's purpose to kill this girl and, on the face of it, immediately direct attention to some other person as the criminal? In that event, what would have done it more effectively than to kill her with a stolen dagger belonging to some other man and leave it?"

"Oh," exclaimed Hatch. "I think I see what you mean. The fact that a person owns this knife is not, then, to be taken against him?"

"On the contrary," said The Thinking Machine sharply. "It's almost a vindication, unless the person who killed her is mad."

A few minutes later, they arrived at the house. It was a two-story frame structure, back thirty or forty feet from the street, in the centre of a small plot of ground. The nearest house was three or four hundred feet away. Hatch was somewhat surprised at the care with which The Thinking Machine examined the premises before he entered the house. Scarcely a foot of ground had not been critically gone over.

Then they entered through the back door. Here, in the kitchen, The Thinking Machine showed the same care in his examination. He squinted aggressively at the sink and casually turned the water on. Then he examined the rusty range. Thence he went to the dining room, where there was the same minute examination. The parlour, hall, and the lower bedroom were examined, after which the two men went up stairs.

"In which room was the girl found?" asked The Thinking Machine.

"The back room," Hatch replied.

"Well, let's examine the other two first," and the scientist led the way to the front of the house. His examination seemed to be confined largely to the water arrangements. He examined each faucet in turn and turned the water on. He went through the same program in the bathroom.

This done, there remained only the room of death. It was precisely as the Medical Examiner had left it, except that the girl's body was gone. The sheets whereon she lay and the pillows were closely scrutinized. Then The Thinking Machine straightened up.

"Any running water in here?" he asked.

"I don't see any," Hatch replied.

"All right, now for the cellar."

The reporter could not even conjecture what The Thinking Machine expected to find in the cellar. It was low ceiling, damp and chilly. By the light of the electric bulb, which the scientist produced, they could see only the furnace, which stood rustily at about the centre. The Thinking Machine examined this for ashes, but found none. Then he wandered aimlessly about the place, taking it all in seemingly in one long, comprehensive squint. Finally he turned to Hatch.

"Let's go," he suggested.

Three-quarters of an hour later, the two men were again in the apartments on Beacon Hill. The scientist dropped into his accustomed place in the big chair and sat silent for a long time. Hatch waited impatiently.

"Has a picture of this dagger been printed yet?" asked The Thinking Machine at last.

"In every newspaper in Boston, today."

"Dear me, dear me," exclaimed the scientist. "It would have been perfectly easy to find the owner of the dagger if pictures of it hadn't been printed."

"Do you think it probable that its owner is the criminal?"

"No, unless, as I said, he was insane, but it would have been interesting to know how the knife passed out of his possession. Was it given away? If so, to whom? A thing of that value would never be given to anyone who was not near and dear to the one who gave it. It is not the kind of gift a man would make to a woman, but is rather a kind of gift a King might make to a loyal subject. It is Oriental in appearance and naturally suggests the Orient. But as I said, the person who owned it did not use it to kill the girl."

"Then what did happen to it?" asked Hatch, curiously.

"Probably it was stolen. Here is the problem: A girl whose name we don't know was murdered by a person we don't know. We do know that this dagger was used to kill her. Therefore find the man who owned the dagger originally and learn how it passed out of his hands. That may lead us directly to the man who rented the house. When we find the man who rented the house, we find possibly the man who stole the dagger and the man who may have killed or may know who killed the girl."

"That seems perfectly clear," Hatch remarked smilingly. "That is, the nature of the problem itself is clear, but the solution is as far away as ever."

The Thinking Machine arose abruptly and passed into the adjoining room. After a while Hatch heard the telephone bell. It was half an hour or so before The Thinking Machine returned.

"The person who owns the knife will call to see me this afternoon at 3 o'clock," he announced.

Hatch half rose in his astonishment, then sank down again.

"Whoever it is will be arrested the moment the police learn of it," he said after a pause.

"On what charge?"

"Murder. It's a plain circumstantial case."

"If he is arrested," said the scientist, "there will be some international complications."

"Who is he?" asked Hatch.

"His name will appear in due time. Meanwhile find out for me if there has ever been a report to the police of any robbery, in which a dagger is mentioned in any way."

Wonderingly, Hatch went away to obey instructions. He found no trace of any such robbery for half a dozen years back. There were several entries on the police books, and of these he made a record.

At 1 o'clock that afternoon he was again in Cambridge working with the police and half a dozen reporters in an effort to get some light on the question of the girl's identity. Later he went to the real estate office of Henry Holmes & Co. seeking further light there. It was not forthcoming.

"Did this man, Wilkes, sign anything?" he asked; "A lease, or anything of that sort? A sample of his handwriting might be useful now."

"No," was the reply. "We did not consider a lease necessary."

Meanwhile the police had apparently exhausted every means of finding out who and what Charles Wilkes was. It was clear from the beginning, to them at least, that the name Wilkes was a fictitious one. There was no reason to suppose that if Wilkes rented the house with the deliberate intention of murder that he would give his real name. By the wildest stretch of the imagination they could find no motive for the murder. It was not any of the ordinary things. Yet it was deliberate. They regarded the golden dagger as the key to the entire mystery. There they stopped.

At 3 o'clock Hatch returned to the home of The Thinking Machine. He had hardly been ushered into the little reception room when the doorbell rang and the scientist in person appeared. Accompanying him was a stranger; dark, swarthy and with the coal black beard of the Orient.

Hatch was introduced to him as Ali Hassan. Then The Thinking Machine produced the photograph of the dagger.

"Is this the correct picture?" he asked.

The stranger examined it closely.

"It seems to be," he said at last.

"Is there another dagger like that in existence?"

"No."

"How did it come into your possession?"

"It was a gift to me from the Sultan of Turkey," was the reply.

III

Gravely Mr Hassan sat down while The Thinking Machine resumed his seat in the big chair opposite. Hatch was leaning forward eagerly to catch every word. The story of the man who owned the wonderful golden dagger was one which the great public would naturally want to know.

"Now," began The Thinking Machine, "would you mind telling us a little of the history of the dagger?"

"It is not a story to be told to infidels," was the reply. "I mean, of course, unbelievers. I will answer any question that you see fit to ask if I can do so."

A little expression of perplexity crept into the squinting eyes of The Thinking Machine; then it passed as suddenly as it came.

"You are a Mohammedan?" he asked.

"Yes."

"Is there any religious significance attached to the dagger?"

"Yes, it is sacred. A gift from the Sultan – my imperial master – and blessed by the royal hand is always sacred to a subject. It may not be even seen by the eyes of an unbeliever."

Hatch straightened up a little, and The Thinking Machine readjusted himself in the big chair.

"You were educated at Oxford?" he asked irrelevantly.

"Yes. I left there in 1887."

"You did not embrace the Christian religion?"

"No. I am a Mohammedan, loyal to my master."

"Would you mind saying for what service the Sultan so honored you?"

"I cannot say that. It was a service to the crown at a time when I was secretary of the Turkish Embassy in England."

"Under what circumstances did this dagger leave your possession?" asked The Thinking Machine quietly.

"It has not left my possession," was the equally quiet reply. "It would be sacrilege if it did. Therefore I still have it – closely guarded."

Frankly, Hutchinson Hatch was amazed. His manner showed it clearly. The Thinking Machine was still leaning back in the chair staring upward.

"I understand then," he said after a little pause, "that the dagger, of which this is a photograph, is in your possession now?"

"It has not been out of my possession at any time since it was given to me," was the startling reply.

"Then how do you account for this photograph?"

"I don't account for it."

"But Dr Loyd – the dagger – I had it in my hands," Hatch interposed in bewilderment.

"You are mistaken," replied the Turk quietly. "It is still in my possession."

"Will you produce it?" asked The Thinking Machine calmly.

"I will not," was the firm response. "I have explained that it is not to be seen by the eyes of unbelievers."

"If a charge of murder should be laid against you, would you produce it?" insisted The Thinking Machine.

"I would not."

"To avoid an arrest?"

"There is no danger of an arrest," was the still calm response. "I am connected with the Turkish delegation in Washington and I am responsible there. I am entitled to the protection of my own government. If there is any charge against me it must come that way."

There was a long silence. Hatch was bursting with questions, which were silenced by a slight gesture from The Thinking Machine. Under the peculiar circumstances the scientist realized that what Mr Hassan had said was true. It is one of the idiosyncrasies of international law.

"You know, of course, that a woman has been murdered with that dagger, don't you?" asked the scientist.

"I have heard that a woman has been murdered."

"Do you attribute any magical properties to the weapon?"

"Oh, no."

"Just where is it at present? Would you produce it if your government ordered you to do so?"

"My government will not order me to do so."

Hatch was annoyed. All this was tommyrot. If Mr Hassan had his dagger, then there were more than one of them in existence. Dr Loyd had one; the reporter knew that. Whether it was a clever counterfeit he did not know; but the dagger used to kill the girl was certainly in possession of the medical examiner.

"If that dagger should ever by any chance pass out of your possession, Mr Hassan, what would happen?" asked The Thinking Machine.

"I am sworn to protect it with my life. If it should pass out of my possession I should kill myself. It is customary and so understood in my country."

"Oh," exclaimed the scientist, suddenly. "How long will you be in Boston?"

"For several days, probably," was the reply. "Meanwhile, if I can be of any further service to you, I should do so gladly."

"How long have you been here?"

"About a week."

"Were you ever in Boston before?"

"Once, a couple of years ago, when I first came to this country."

Mr Hassan arose and took up his hat. He had formally told Hatch and The Thinking Machine goodday and was at the door when he turned back.

"I understand," he said, "that this dagger is supposed now to be in the possession of Dr Loyd, the Medical Examiner?"

"Yes," said the scientist.

Mr Hassan went away. Hatch sat nursing his wrath a moment, and then came the explosion. It was inevitable; a righteous protest against an insult to his intelligence and that of the eminent scientist who had become interested in the case.

"Mr Hassan is a liar, else there are two daggers," he burst out.

"Mr Hassan is a gentleman of the Turkish legation, Mr Hatch," said The Thinking Machine reprovingly. "Do you know Mr Loyd very well?"

"Yes."

" 'phone him immediately and ask him to have that dagger secretly removed to a safety deposit vault," instructed the scientist. "Then you had better go out and work with the police to see if they yet have any clue to the girl's identity. Mr Hassan will produce the dagger if he has it."

The remainder of that day and a part of the next Hatch spent running down the small possibilities, trying to settle some of the minor questions, which were naturally aroused in his mind. There was a result – a very definite result – and when he again appeared before The Thinking Machine, he felt that he had accomplished something.

"It occurred to me," he explained, "that there was a possibility that this man Wilkes had communicated with or advertised for this girl that was dead. I searched the want columns of three newspapers. At last I found this."

He extended a small clipping to The Thinking Machine, who took it and studied it a moment. This clipping was an advertisement for an intelligent young woman as companion and gave the street and number of the house in Cambridge where the girl had been found.

"Very good," said The Thinking Machine, and he rubbed his hands briskly together. "It looks, Mr Hatch, as if it might be a long tedious work to establish the name of this girl. It may take weeks. I should meanwhile take that clipping and turn it over to the police, and let them make the search. I see it is dated October 19, which is four days from the time Wilkes rented the house. Yet the girl had been dead for not more than ten days. There is a lapse of time in there to be accounted for. Find out if this advertisement appeared more than once, and also get the original copy of it from the newspaper. It might be in Wilkes's handwriting. In that case it would be a substantial clue."

"Have you heard anything more about Hassan's dagger?" inquired the reporter.

"No, but he will produce it. Did you phone Dr Loyd in reference to it?"

"I 'phoned yesterday, as you suggested, and was then informed that Dr Loyd had left the city. I 'phoned twice this

MYSTERY OF THE GOLDEN DAGGER

morning, but got no answer from the house. I presume he has not returned."

"No answer?" asked The Thinking Machine quickly. "No answer? Dear me, dear me!" He arose and paced back and forth across the room twice, then paused before the reporter. "That's bad, bad, bad!" he said.

"Why?" asked Hatch.

The Thinking Machine turned suddenly and entered the adjoining room. When he came out there was a new expression on his face – an expression which Hatch could not read.

"Dr Loyd was found at 1 o'clock today in his home, bound and gagged," he explained shortly. "The only servant there was insensible from some drug. It was burglars. They ransacked the house from top to bottom."

"What-what does that mean?" asked Hatch, wonderingly.

Just then the door from the hall opened and Martha, the aged servant of The Thinking Machine, appeared.

"Mr Hassan, sir," she said.

The Turk appeared in the door behind her, gravely courteous, suave, and dignified as ever.

"Ah," explained The Thinking Machine. "You have brought the dagger?"

"I talked with the Turkish Minister in Washington by telephone and he explained the necessity of my producing it," said Mr Hassan. "I have it here to convince you."

"I thought it was in Washington?" Hatch blurted out.

"Here it is," was the Turk's response. He produced a richly jeweled box. In it lay the golden dagger. The Thinking Machine lifted it. The blade was bright and without a trace of a stain. With a quick movement The Thinking Machine twisted the handle and part of it came off. A few drops of a pungent liquid ran out on the floor.

IV

Mr Hassan left Boston that night for Washington. He took the dagger with him. The Thinking Machine made no objection, and the very existence of the man was as yet unknown to the police.

"When it is necessary to produce that dagger," he explained to Hatch, "it can be done through regular channels, if Hassan is still alive. It seems very probable now that international law may have to take a hand in the case."

"Do you consider it possible that Hassan in person had any connection with the affair?" Hatch asked.

"Anything is possible," was the short reply. "By the way, Mr Hatch, it might be interesting to know a little more about this real estate collector, Clements, who discovered the girl's body. He might have known about the house being unoccupied. There are still possibilities in every direction, but the real problem hangs on the golden dagger."

"In that event, it seems to come back to Hassan," said the reporter doggedly.

"I would advise you, Mr Hatch, to settle the points I asked about the advertisement. Then see Dr Loyd; ask him if he still has the dagger. If you get the original copy of the advertisement, turn it over to the police. You need not mention Hassan to them as yet."

It was early that evening when Hatch saw Dr Loyd.

"Did the burglars get the dagger?" he asked.

"I have nothing to say," was the reply.

"Have you the dagger now?"

"I have nothing to say."

"Did you turn it over to the District Attorney?"

"I have nothing to say."

The result of this was that Hatch went away firmly convinced that Dr Loyd did not have the dagger; that the burglars, whoever they were, had taken it away; that they were probably in the employ of Hassan and robbed Loyd's house for the specific purpose of regaining possession of the dagger.

Later Hatch made an investigation of the circumstances attending the publication of the advertisement. It had appeared four times on alternate days. The original copy of it was found and given to him. It was the bold handwriting of a man. This he turned over to the police, with all information as to the advertisement.

Then began a long, minute search, which ultimately resulted in the discovery of the whereabouts of half a dozen girls reported missing. But the fact that they were found immediately removed them as possibilities. From the first, the search for Wilkes had been unceasing. It was generally assumed that the name Wilkes was fictitious.

On the morning of the second day Hatch appeared at his office weary, discouraged and disgusted. But weariness fled when the city editor excitedly approached him.

"They have Wilkes," he said. "They got him late last night in Worcester. The real estate clerk has positively identified him. He will be at police headquarters within an hour or so. Get the story."

"Who is he?" asked Hatch.

"I don't know. He doesn't deny his identity, and insists that his name is Wilkes. He was found at a hotel registered as Charles Wingate."

The first editions of the afternoon papers flamed with the announcement of the capture of the supposed murderer. Meanwhile Hatch and the other reporters had heard Wilkes's story at second-hand. The police saw fit to put as much mystery about it as they could. Having heard this story Hatch immediately went with it to see The Thinking Machine.

"They've caught Wilkes," he explained. "His name is Wilkes, so far as anybody knows. He registered as Wingate because he was frightened. He knows the police of the entire country were looking for him."

"What about the house?" asked The Thinking Machine.

"He tells what appears to be a straight story. He says he rented the house for himself and wife intending to remain there for several months. He did not take a lease. On the day he was to move in his wife grew very ill – a more than usually serious attack of the nervous trouble with which she is afflicted. Then on the advice of physicians he took her away to Cuba rather than to start up housekeeping.

"He inserted the advertisement in the newspaper before he knew how serious this illness was. They remained in Cuba together for two or three weeks, and she is still there, he says. On the day after his return this murder affair came up and he considered it advisable, until it was all cleared up, to stay out of sight."

"What is his business?" asked The Thinking Machine.

"He is Eastern agent for a big cutlery concern in Cleveland. His headquarters are in Boston. He has only recently been appointed and is not known in Boston. Almost from the time of his appointment, he had been travelling. It was an oversight, he says, that he did not notify the real estate people of his determination not to occupy the house. He had rented it by the month anyway."

The Thinking Machine was silent. The blue eyes were turned upward and the long, slender fingers pressed tip to tip. Hatch, eagerly watching his face, saw perplexed wrinkles at times, which immediately disappeared. It was the working of the man's brain.

"Does he know the girl?"

"He is confident that he does not. He never saw, so he says, anyone who answered the advertisement."

"Of course he would say that," snapped The Thinking Machine. "Has he seen the body?"

"He is to see it this afternoon."

"Have the police any idea of the identity of the girl?"

"I think not," said Hatch. "There are the usual boasts about being able to clear it up within a few hours, but it means nothing."

Again there was silence as the scientist sat thoughtfully squinting at the ceiling.

"Does she know Hassan?" he asked, finally.

"I don't know," Hatch replied. "Remember that no one knows Hassan but you and I, and I haven't seen this man Wilkes yet."

"Will you be able to see him?"

"I don't know. It depends upon the gracious goodness of the police."

"We will go and see him now," declared The Thinking Machine emphatically.

A few minutes later, they were ushered into the office of the chief of the State Police. There were mutual introductions, Hatch officiating. The chief had at various times heard of his distinguished visitor, but had never before met him. Instead he had regarded him as an amusing myth.

"Would it be possible for me to see Mr Wilkes?" asked The Thinking Machine.

"No, not now," was the reply.

"I thought the purpose of this office was to aid justice," snapped the scientist.

"It is," said the chief, and a flush came to his face.

"Well, I know the man who owns the dagger with which the girl was killed," said the scientist emphatically. "I want to see if this is the man."

The chief arose from his desk in astonishment and stood leaning over it toward his visitors.

"You know – you know—" he began. "Who is it?"

"May I see Wilkes?" insisted the other.

"Well, under the circumstances, I suppose, perhaps—"

"Now," said The Thinking Machine.

The chief pressed a button. After a moment one of his men came in.

"Bring Wilkes in here," directed the police official.

The man went out and after a time returned with Wilkes, who had been undergoing the third degree in another room. The prisoner's face was white and every move indicated his tense nervous condition.

"Mr Wilkes, when did the dagger pass out of your possession?" asked The Thinking Machine, suddenly, as he extended the photograph of the golden dagger.

"I have never seen such a dagger," was the reply, after a long, deliberate study of the picture.

"Did you not receive an order for a blade for it?" asked The Thinking Machine.

"No."

"Mr Wilkes, I know possibly more of this affair than the police do as yet. You can supply those facts that I haven't. Now who-who-is the girl who was murdered with this dagger?"

What little color that had been in the prisoner's face was gone now, and he trembled violently. Suddenly he sank down in the chair, burying his face on his arms.

"I don't know, I don't know, I don't know," he sobbed.

Yet that afternoon, when Wilkes stood beside the body of the murdered girl he looked at her long and earnestly then with a wailing cry he lunged forward, half fainting.

"Alice, Alice!" he gasped.

V

Wilkes, or Wingate, as he had been last known, told a story as to his knowledge of the dead girl, which was on its face straight-forward and to the point. In a little room adjoining that in which the body lay he had been revived with a stimulant, and, once himself again, he talked freely. The thing which impressed the police most was the detail which he gave; The Thinking Machine had nothing to say as to what he thought of this recital. He merely observed it without comment.

Briefly here is the story, denuded of extraneous verbiage:

The girl was Alice Gorham. There was no shadow of doubt about the identification. She was the daughter of a man who had been for a long time connected with the Steel Trust offices in Cleveland. Misfortune had finally come to her father and then in her last year at Vassar she had been compelled to return home. Shortly after that her father had died suddenly, leaving her nothing; her mother had died several years previously. She was an only child.

According to his story, Wilkes had been acquainted with her since her childhood. His father, too, had been in the Steel Trust at one time and had left it to take a partnership in the cutlery concern which he now represented. The girl's age, so far as Wilkes's story went, was about twenty-one years.

Since the death of her father, when she had been thrown upon her own resources, she had been employed as companion to an aged woman in Cleveland. There had been some disagreement between them, and the girl decided to come East. She had been in Boston only a few weeks at the time she was found dead.

"That's all I know about it," said Wilkes in conclusion. "Naturally, the shock was very great when I saw her in there dead. I knew that she had come to Boston. I knew, too, that she had disappeared from where she lived, for both my wife and myself, before we went to Cuba, had called and inquired for her."

"You have no idea where she was from the time she disappeared until the time she was found dead, which was at the most not more than fourteen days ago?" asked The Thinking Machine.

"None," replied Wilkes.

"Do you know of any love affair – any man in the case?" insisted The Thinking Machine.

"No, I never heard of one."

"Of course, you read the newspaper accounts of this affair. Did you, then, from the detailed description of the girl printed, associate her in any way with the girl who was dead?"

"I did, yes, but not directly. The thing which impressed me most in the newspaper accounts was the reiterated statement that the man who rented the house must have been the murderer. This placed it directly to me. Then frankly I got frightened and tried to hide my identity for the moment under another name. It was very foolish, of course, but the circumstances seemed to point so conclusively to me that-that I did what I did."

"When did you last see Miss Gorham?"

"In Cleveland seven months ago."

"That's all," said The Thinking Machine, and he arose as if to go.

"Now what do you know of this?" asked the State police chief.

"I shall call on you tomorrow and explain just what I know and how I learned it," was the reply.

"Who is the man who owned that dagger?" the chief continued.

"You mean the dagger that was stolen from Dr Loyd?" asked The Thinking Machine. There was a touch of irony in his tone.

"Who-how-what do you know about that?"

"Let's go, Mr Hatch," said The Thinking Machine suddenly. "I'll see you tomorrow, chief."

Once outside, The Thinking Machine led the way toward the Scollay Square subway.

"Where to now?" asked Hatch.

"To the house in Cambridge," explained The Thinking Machine. "I want to look it over again. I have an idea I overlooked a few things."

"Do you think Wilkes killed Miss Gorham?" asked Hatch.
"I don't know."
"Do you think now that Hassan did it?"
"I don't know."

Further questioning seemed useless, and both men were silent until they stood inside the Cambridge house. Then again, The Thinking Machine went over the structure from cellar to attic, but more carefully, with more detail than even before. Particularly this was true as to the cellar. Not one square inch of the floor surface escaped his eyes. Once he picked up a small scrap of cloth — black cloth, and examined it. Later, on hands and knees, he studied the soft ground flooring in a remote corner. Hatch stood looking on curiously.

"See this?" The Thinking Machine asked.

Hatch looked by the light of the electric bulb and saw only a few indentations in the soft soil. It was as if something heavy and elaborately carved had been pressed down in the dirt.

"What is it?" he asked.

Without answering The Thinking Machine arose and together they went straight to the room of death upstairs. Here the scientist ruthlessly cut into the smooth wood of the bed. He handed the small chip he removed to the reporter.

"What does that look like?" he asked.

"Mahogany," Hatch replied.

"Good, very good. Now, Mr Hatch, you go to Boston, see this young man, Willard Clements, the real estate collector. Don't be afraid to ask him questions. Ask him pointedly if he happens to be acquainted with a burglar. It will be an interesting experiment. Find out all you can about him and meet me at my apartments at 8 o'clock tonight. I have a little further work to do here."

"Lord, did he do it?" asked Hatch.

"I don't know," was the reply. "It would be interesting to know what he knows."

Had Hatch not known the peculiar methods of The Thinking Machine, he would have been bewildered by these instructions. As it was, he was merely seeking in his own mind a possible connecting thread between Clements and the mystery. Disregarding Clements for the moment, he could only see Wilkes, who knew the girl, or Hassan, who owned the dagger, in the affair.

Once alone, The Thinking Machine did several things which would have sadly puzzled an outsider. From the back door he examined the ground and even stooped and stared at the grass. Slowly he walked along, half stooping, toward the back of the plot of ground. There he shook the picket fence, which barred his way. It was apparently a new fence, yet a whole panel of it fell. Outside was an alley.

From this point he went to the house of the nearest neighbor and asked many questions about strangers who might have been in the other yard. None had been seen. Finally, he asked the way and was directed to the nearest police station.

"Have many burglaries been reported in this neighborhood lately?" he asked, after he had introduced himself.

"Three of four. Why?"

"Have you heard of any furnished house, at present unoccupied, which has been robbed?"

"Yes, the old Essex estate – about four blocks from here."

"What was stolen, exactly?"

"We don't know. The owners of the house are in Europe now, and we have no means of learning just what is missing. We have caught the men who robbed it."

"What are their name, please?"

"One is called 'Reddy' Blake, the other gave the name of Johnson."

"Where were they caught?"

"In the house. They had a wagon and were trying to move out a heavy mahogany sideboard."

"When was this?"

"Oh, a week or so ago. They got three years each."

"No other similar cases?"

"No."

"Thank you," and The Thinking Machine went away. That night Hutchinson Hatch called on the scientist and found him with a telegram in his hands.

"Did you see Clements?" asked The Thinking Machine, "and did you ask him if he knew a burglar?"

"I did," said Hatch, smiling slightly. "He wanted to fight."

The Thinking Machine unfolded the telegram and handed it to the reporter.

"This might interest you," he said.

Hatch took the yellow slip and read the following:

"Ali Hassan committed suicide this morning."

"Why that's a confession," said the reporter.

VI

There was a gathering of a half a dozen persons in the office of the Chief of Police on the morning of the following day. They were the chief, The Thinking Machine, Charles Wilkes, Detective Fahey, Willard Clements and Hutchinson Hatch. The summons to Clements had been in the nature of a great surprise to that young man. First he had been indignant, but gradually this passed, and there came instead a cowering attitude.

Every one, even the chief, was waiting the pleasure of The Thinking Machine. Hatch, still firmly convinced that Hassan, the Turk, was the criminal, was almost as much surprised as Clements by his presence.

Detective Fahey sat silently by, chewing his cigar and with a slightly amused smile on his face; the chief didn't smile.

He had felt the vital power of this diminutive man with the enormous yellow head.

"Now, Mr Clements," The Thinking Machine began, and the young man started slightly, "I don't believe that you killed Miss Gorham. Perhaps the worst charge that can be laid to you is burglary, or, rather, illicit knowledge of burglary. Your friends, 'Reddy' Blake and this man Johnson have already partially confessed. Now, will you tell the rest of it?"

"Confessed what? What are you talking about?" demanded the young man.

"Never mind, then," said The Thinking Machine, impatiently. He turned to the chief. "Fortune has favored us a good deal in this case," he said. "Particularly is this true in the arrest of Mr Wilkes. I may compliment you chief on the ability your men displayed in getting Mr Wilkes."

The chief bowed gravely.

"But he is not the murderer."

The scientist went on:

"By telegraph and cable I have verified his story in full. You may have done so yourself. Here are the answers I received to the wires I sent. I think, perhaps, they will convince you. Meanwhile, you have the real murderer in Charlestown prison now. It is 'Reddy' Blake, or Johnson."

At the second mention of these two names every eye was again turned on Clements. A sudden change had come over his face. He was now frightened; the color was surging back into Wilkes's countenance.

"Proofs, proofs," said the chief, shortly.

"It will be useless," continued The Thinking Machine, "to rehearse Mr Wilkes's story. It is proven. Therefore, what remains? Let's begin with the dagger and see what it leads to.

"I saw this dagger. It is an extraordinary weapon. Its value must be in the thousands. On it I saw, cut into the handle, the crescent of Turkey, together with half a dozen symbols, religious and otherwise, of that empire. It was a simple matter, comparatively, to call up on the 'phone some one who knew of these things, preferably a Turk. There is a Turk in one of the oriental stores on Boylston Street.

"I talked to him and described the dagger in detail. He is an educated man, knows his country and its customs and was able to say that such a dagger could only have been what I had previously supposed it to have been — a gift from a prince or ruler to a loyal subject for duty well done. I asked if he knew of such a weapon being in this country. He said he did not, but that a certain Turkish gentleman, then in Boston, had once signally served his master, and there was a possibility that he had been rewarded by such a gift. What was his name? Ali Hassan.

"Mr Hassan was stopping at the Hotel Teutonic. I wrote a note to him. He called and readily identified a photograph of the golden dagger as his property. Remember that this was a photograph of the dagger with which the girl was slain.

"He amazed me a little by stating that the dagger was then in his possession. At the same time he explained that it was a sacred object and not for the eyes of infidels. For a time this was puzzling. Then I asked what would be the result if, by any chance, the dagger should pass out of his possession. He replied that he would kill himself. That was an illuminating point. He had lied; he did not have the dagger. If any one else had known that he did not have it, it would have been his death. He saved his life thus far by lying. It has been done before. I may say, too, that the idea of a duplicate dagger was not tenable."

"If this man owns the dagger and admits it," interrupted the chief, "I will have him immediately arrested."

"There are two reasons why you can't do that," said The Thinking Machine, quietly. "The first is that Mr Hassan was a secretary of the Turkish legation in Washington; the second, he is dead."

There was a pause while the chief and the remainder of the party absorbed this.

"Dead," exclaimed the chief. "How?"

"Suicide by poison," was the brief response. "Anyway, I had established the ownership of the dagger. I also learned that Hassan had been in Boston only five days at the time the body was found. The girl had been dead for a week or ten days – possibly ten days. Therefore, Hassan did not kill Miss Gorham. That was conclusive.

"Then came the question of how the dagger passed out of his possession. Obviously it was not a gift. Stolen? Probably. When? Mr Hassan showed in a way that he had not been in Boston for two years. But burglars operate all over the country. Therefore, burglars. It is perfectly possible that the dagger was stolen some time in Washington by 'Reddy' Blake and his gang, and for some reason they kept it instead of selling it. No man, not even a 'fence,' would have tried to dispose of a four-carat diamond. In the second place, Mr Hassan would not have dared to report the loss of the dagger to the police. Blake, of course, could not know this. He kept the weapon. The safest place for it was on his person."

The Thinking Machine lay back in his chair, squinting at the ceiling, while his listeners leaned forward eagerly. The chief was fascinated, amazed by the strange story. The scientist resumed:

"It was stated in the hearing of Mr Hassan and also published that the dagger was in the possession of Medical Examiner Loyd. It is easy to see how employees of this man burglarized Loyd's home and recovered the weapon. Its possession meant life to Hassan. Immediately after this burglary he returned to Washington. There he committed suicide, probably by order of his superiors. I had wired the facts, not intending to cause his death, of course, but to have the dagger produced here when necessary. That disposes, I think, of the ownership of the weapon, and places it in the hands of 'Reddy' Blake or his pals."

The Thinking Machine turned suddenly on Clements.

"As collector for Henry Holmes & Co. you know Cambridge well, I should imagine. You have opportunities, which fall to few men—legitimately—to know where rich hauls may be made. You were also in a position to know practically every vacant house in Cambridge. Knowing this you might know, too, the best vacant house for a rendezvous for thieves. In passing, you might have learned that the house rented by Mr Wilkes had not been occupied. It is perfectly possible that you did not even know the house had been rented until the bill for rent was placed in your hands. These are possibilities; now here are facts.

"You went to that house to collect rent. The front door was locked and the shutters up. In the natural course of events you would have satisfied yourself that it was unoccupied. You might have shouted to attract someone's attention, but in the ordinary course of events you would not have gone upstairs to look further, unless you had asked something. You found something in a back room and probably behind a door that was closed. You broke open that door. Why did you go to that room? Why did you break down that door?

"Let's see. Suppose for a moment that you were one of the most valued members of a gang of burglars – valued because you appear the gentleman and can go places and learn things without attracting attention. Suppose this house was a hiding place for stolen goods. Suppose the girl, answering Mr Wilkes's advertisement for a companion, should have gone to that house and found it locked. It is not improbable that she should have gone around the house, believing it to be occupied, to find someone.

"Suppose she had come upon a party of thieves. It would have been a natural consequence for them to fear a spy and attempt to get rid of her.

"What more possible than that they should have locked her up? She was at least four hundred feet from the nearest house, and forty, fifty or sixty feet from the street and behind thick walls. Her screams would not have been heard.

"There we have the girl a prisoner in the hands of the men who had the golden dagger. The murder may have followed at any time. It happened but a few days ago. Meanwhile the burglars had taken from their loot a bed and its furnishings, providing a place for the girl to sleep. You, Mr Clements, knew that the girl had been a prisoner upstairs. That is why you went to that room. I will not say that you knew of the murder at that time. You discovered that. You were frightened at this hideous ending of an affair in which you had been interested. Perhaps you were a little angry, too. It may have been that the burglars had taken away the stolen stuff, sold it and left you out in the division. Is that right?"

Clements stared at him with glassy eyes, then suddenly leaned forward with his head in his hands, and sobbed bitterly. It was practically a confession.

"How did it come that you considered burglars in the first place?" asked the chief.

"I made two examinations of the house. The first was not thorough. I examined the faucets to see if the water was on, and if there was a possible trace of blood on them anywhere. It was not impossible that the murderer of Miss Gorham got blood on his hands and left a thumb or finger print when he washed it off. I found none. He was careful.

"On the second examination I looked particularly for a trace of burglars in the cellar. There I found, freshly pressed down in the soft soil, the imprint of what must have been a carved piano leg and beside it a large imprint indicating that a grand piano had been leaned against the wall. People don't keep pianos in the cellar. Therefore, if one were there, it was hidden. Naturally burglars. The bed was not handsome, but was of mahogany. Nobody moving out would leave a mahogany bed. Still burglars. There is no path leading from the back of the house to the back fence. Yet there is a straight line across the grass to a certain panel in that fence where people have walked frequently. That panel of the fence fell out when I shook it; there is no gate. Burglars, even at night, would not move their loot in at the front; it would be comparatively easy to bring in large objects, such as a piano, through the alley, tearing down a fence panel and then to the house. Therefore burglars.

"Now, burglars do not steal pianos and mahogany beds in a wagon from a house that is occupied. The police informed me that burglars – 'Reddy' Blake, among them – had been robbing an unoccupied furnished house. They could have stolen a piano or anything else. Therefore the chain is complete."

"Admitting that is all true," interrupted the chief, "how did you explain the fact that the man who killed Miss Gorham left the dagger? If he had been a burglar, as you say, wouldn't he have been the last man to leave a thing of that value?"

"All men are fools when they kill people," said The Thinking Machine. "They are frightened, half-witted, and do all kinds of inexplicable things. Suppose there had been a sudden violent noise in the house, made by one of his pals just at the moment the girl fell backward, covering the knife with her body. The murderer might have run, leaving it where it was. I don't state this as a fact, but as a strong probability. He might have intended to return for the knife, but if he had meanwhile been arrested, as Blake and Johnson were, this would have been impossible. I think that is all."

"Why is it that Mr Wilkes did not see the stolen goods when he went to look at the house?" asked the chief.

"Because they were in the cellar. You didn't go into the cellar, did you, Mr Wilkes?"

"No; oh, no," Wilkes replied.

"And remember, the girl wasn't in the house then," The Thinking Machine added. "She went to answer the advertisement which appeared after Mr Wilkes had rented the house."

Then Hutchinson Hatch, who had been an interested listener, had a question.

"Why did you ask Mr Wilkes if he had ever seen the knife or had given an order for a blade for it?"

"The blade in the dagger was of American make," replied the scientist. "The original had been broken. Peculiarly enough the new blade was made by the cutlery company which Mr Wilkes represents. It was not impossible, therefore, that this dagger had been in his possession."

There was a long silence. The chief and Detective Fahey removed their half-chewed cigars and looked inquiringly at each other. Fahey shook his head – he had no questions. At last the chief turned to The Thinking Machine:

"If, as you say, Blake or Johnson killed Miss Gorham, how can we prove it? This is not proof – it is theory."

"Simply enough. Do the men occupy the same cell in Charlestown?"

"I hardly think so. Members of a gang that way are rarely kept in the same cell."

"In that case," said The Thinking Machine, "let the warden go to each man and tell him that the other has turned state's evidence, accusing his pal of the murder."

Johnson confessed.

7

PROBLEM OF THE KNOTTED CORD

With the brilliant glare of the noonday sun shining full into his upturned eyes, a venerable man sat beside an open window. The gray-crowned head was a noble one, but strength and rugged manhood was gone; there was only the weakness of years and disaster, illumined and softened by a smile – the appealing, pathetic smile of helplessness. The window framed a vista of green landscape, broken by a dimpled splotch of blue where the sea ran in and lapped the shore, and, far away, a village sprinkled on the hills. But he looked upon it all with sightless eyes—eyes which turned instinctively toward the light as the blind ever seek a ray through their enshrouding gloom. A grateful tang of salt air drifted in, and he breathed deeply of its fragrance.

For a long time he sat thus, silently, then from a distant room came the trill of a song. His smile grew into an expression of infinite tenderness as he listened, and then the closing of a door broke the melody. He sat expectantly for a minute or so, and gradually his mind wandered back into the dreamy thoughtfulness which the voice had interrupted. After awhile he heard a light step in the hall, and then some other sound which he could not interpret. The steps approached the door of the room where he sat, and paused.

"Is that you, deary?" he asked gently.

There was no response, and he turned his sightless eyes expectantly toward the entrance.

"What is it, Mildred?" he inquired.

Again he heard the peculiar sound to which he had been unable to attach a meaning, but still there was no answer.

"Mildred!" he called sharply. He turned quickly in his chair, with a vague uneasiness in his manner, and gripped the arms as if to rise. "Mildred!" he repeated. "Why don't you answer me?"

Suddenly there came an answer – a heart-racking, terrifying answer – shriek after shriek of agony, terror, helplessness. It was here, in this very room in which he stood, but the impenetrable pall of blindness veiled it all. There was a shuffling as of feet for an instant, a gurgling, despairing cry, then the old man tottered forward toward the door.

"Mildred, Mildred, Mildred!" he called despairingly. "What is it, child!"

There was a sound as of a soft body falling, then came utter silence. With straining heart and groping hands the old man kept on blindly seeking. Again he caught the meaningless sound, which he had heard before. One outstretched hand brushed against something which was instantly removed beyond reach. Intuitively he knew that something – somebody – menaced him, that Mildred his granddaughter was now or had been in peril—perhaps it was worse. There was some quick movement to his right, and the old man stretched out his quivering hands straight before him with a pitiful, helpless gesture.

"I am blind!" he said simply.

For a moment he stood there, with hands still outstretched, waiting. For what? He didn't know. At last from the hall outside came a sliding, whispering sound, and the front door closed noiselessly. Instantly he started in that direction. Despite his blindness, he knew his way here in the little house where he had lived for years alone with his granddaughter.

In the hall another thought came to him. Whoever – whatever – it was, had come and gone. And Mildred? He turned and started back toward the room he had just left. One aged hand slipped along the wall to the door frame, and he turned in. For an instant he listened. He heard nothing.

"Mildred?" he called. "My God, child! where are you? What has happened?"

Still silence. He entered and began groping around pitifully. Mildred must be there, somewhere. And finally, as he groped on, he came upon her. One foot struck some yielding obstacle, and he dropped on his knees beside it. A touch of his fingers on the face told him it was Mildred. She was breathing faintly – a gurgle, which as he listened grew fainter.

His brain was instantly awakened to the full possibilities. She had been stabbed, or struck down, perhaps. There had been no shot, and yet, as his hands moved rapidly over the slender form, he found no wound on head, face, or body. The faint gasping breath grew fainter as he listened – she was dying under his hands, and he was helpless, unable to see even what was the matter.

"Mildred, Mildred, Mildred!" he repeated, and he shook the inert body in a frenzy of fear and anxiety.

And then came the end. There was a last faint gurgle, a spasmodic twitching of the body, and it lay rigid. And there crouching on the floor beside his dead, the aged grandfather was found a few minutes later. His sightless eyes were dry and staring, and his lip moved silently in prayer.

One of the first things to come under the observation of the police when they began their investigation of the strange murder of pretty little Mildred Barrett – she was hardly fourteen years old – was the fact that if her grandfather, Wendell Curtis Barrett, had not been blind, he could have saved her life. The girl had been strangled, garroted, with manila twine – a plain cord which is in every day use for the tying of heavy bundles.

This twine had been drawn so tight about the child's throat that it sank deep into the white soft flesh and slowly strangled her to death. Had her grandfather been able to see, had he not overlooked the possibility of such a thing, he could probably have saved her by cutting the twine. This, at least, was what the medical examiner said.

Outside attention had been attracted to the tragedy by two men who were driving past the little house overlooking the sea. They heard the child's screams and stopped to investigate, entering by that front door through which, not more than a few seconds before, the slayer of the child had passed. But they had seen no one, nor had they heard anything except the child's screams. They immediately notified the police. The strangler's cord was not found until Detective Mallory arrived with a couple of his men and Hutchinson Hatch, a newspaper reporter.

The detective examined the garroter's twine closely. There was one knot in it just where it pressed down upon the windpipe; and another at the back of the neck where powerful fingers had drawn it tight and fastened it with a knot similar to the running of a lasso.

"It's a good job, all right," commented Detective Mallory heartlessly enough as he scrutinized the two knots. "It was prepared for just such a purpose, and well prepared at that."

"It isn't unlike the garroting cord that the thugs of India use," remarked Hatch.

"Is that so?" inquired the detective, as he turned quickly on the newspaper man. They had met before many times, and there was a professional friendship between them which amounted almost to enmity. "That may be useful to know."

The reporter remained at the house and in the neighborhood for several hours while the detectives continued their investigations, and then summarized the entire affair, with every established fact, for the benefit of Professor Augustus S.

F. X. Van Dusen – The Thinking Machine. They were well acquainted, these two, an acquaintance which had begun with the chess game incident which had given to the noted scientist the soubriquet by which he had since become known beyond the narrow pale of science. On a dozen or more occasions The Thinking Machine had interested himself in every day problems at the request of the newspaper man, and had invariably woven a woof from tangled, disconnected threads which the reporter brought to him.

"It's absolutely astounding," the reporter told the scientist now, "not only the method of the murder – right within reach, almost, of a man who was totally blind – but there is nothing to indicate any motive, so – "

"Begin at the beginning, Mr Hatch," interrupted The Thinking Machine crustily. "When you do a sum in arithmetic you put down all the figures, don't you? Well, give me all the figures."

"Well, here is every known fact in the case," explained the reporter. "Mr Barrett is about seventy-two years old; his granddaughter Mildred was a little less than fourteen. She was the only relative he had in the world, and had lived with him in the little house, which he owns, since the death of her father, who was killed in the Spanish-American War. They kept no servant, as the child, with a little assistance from the old man, was able to do practically all the simple housework. Occasionally they called in a woman who lived half a mile away to assist in house cleaning and the heavier work. It seems that Barrett has an income of about a thousand a year, and they were able to live comfortably on this.

"Very few persons ever called at the house, and preceding the tragedy there was no caller, at least that Barrett knows of. The child was somewhere in the rear of the house, and he was sitting in his own room. He heard no voices, no sound, nothing except the child singing, until she came along the hall, evidently to his room. The grim horror of the whole thing from that time on has unnerved the old man so that he is almost in a state of collapse.

"To me the mystery of the thing is intensified by the fact that the murdered girl is a mere child. Her extreme youth would indicate at least that there could have been no love affair, certainly from all I have been able to learn there was not. And her youth, too, would make it seem improbable that she could have had an enemy who would have gone to such an extreme. Besides, she seems to have been a sweet-tempered, sunny little girl, intelligent, bright, and lovable. Nothing whatever was stolen. There is positively no clue in the world, not even a vagrant footprint, or any small thing that might have been left to indicate who was there – that is, of course, except the cord with which she was strangled."

"Would the old man have benefited by the child's death?" inquired The Thinking Machine.

"In no way at all," Hatch replied positively, "nor would anyone else. There is no property tied up, as far as anyone can find out, and the miserable little sum which it cost him to keep the child is not so much as he would have had to pay to employ a servant in her absence."

The Thinking Machine sat for a long time with the squint blue eyes turned upward, and his white slender fingers pressed tip to tip. Minute wrinkles in his enormous brow grew momentarily deeper. "It's a remarkable crime, Mr Hatch," he said at last, "perhaps the most remarkable that I have ever met. As you say, the youth of the child removes all the ordinary motives." He was silent for a moment. "Our greatest criminals are never caught, and rarely ever heard of, Mr Hatch," he went on musingly. "The greatest crimes are never discovered, as a matter of fact. One might readily conceive of a brain so keen, so accurate, that in, say, a murder, there would be nothing to indicate one. I think perhaps in this case we have a difficult one. It would be best for me to see and talk with Mr Barrett in person."

They found the aged blind man, and he repeated for them in the minutest detail every fact as he remembered it. The Thinking Machine listened throughout with keen attention, and at the end asked some questions.

"You say, Mr Barrett, that in addition to your granddaughter's footsteps and voice you heard some other slight sound. Could you describe it?"

"I hardly think so," was the reply. "It was strange – peculiar."

"Was it the sound of a human voice, or of something being moved?" insisted the scientist.

"It could have been made by the human voice, I suppose; but it also could have been made by twanging a rubber band. It sounded guttural, unreal, uncanny."

"And the thing you touched when you started toward your granddaughter, after she screamed?" asked the scientist. "What did that seem to be? Clothing, flesh, wood, some one's hair, or what?"

"I – I – don't know," said Barrett helplessly. "It was a sense of having touched something, rather than actual contact with it. It might have been hair, but I don't know what it was."

The Thinking Machine stared at him curiously for a moment. "How long have you been blind, Mr Barrett?"

"Only about two years."

The Thinking Machine nodded as if he understood, and then for an hour he sat questioning the old man. Never for a moment did the wrinkles leave his brow, and never for a moment was his tense attention relaxed. At the end he arose, and Hatch looked at him inquiringly. He shook his head.

He spent another hour in an examination of the strangler's cord, the knots, the body, and of the premises. Every nook and corner of the little house was searched with the utmost care, and every foot of the little plot of ground surrounding it was carefully gone over. Gradually his radius of observation widened until he had covered the ground a hundred feet every way from the house in every direction. Then he went inside again. One of the detectives, Cunningham, met him in the hall.

"There is no question whatever of the innocence of the two men who say they heard the girl scream and came in?" he asked.

"There doesn't seem to be," replied Cunningham. "We have taken pains to confirm their stories, and to be certain of their identity. They seem to be all right."

"I imagined so," remarked the scientist. "What about the woman who came here occasionally to assist in the housework?"

"We also looked into that. She had been spending the day with a friend in a village a dozen miles away. We have proof of that."

The Thinking Machine turned and walked into the room where Barrett sat. "Would you be prepared to say," he asked, "that the sounds you heard were made by an animal of any sort? That is, I mean an ape, say, or a baboon?"

"I couldn't say," replied Barrett.

"Or that the hair you touched was bristly like the hair of an animal?"

"I couldn't say," replied Barrett. "I don't even know that it was hair. Whatever it was, it was instantly withdrawn beyond my reach and I had a singular intuitive feeling of being in great peril myself."

For the second time The Thinking Machine picked up and examined the strangler's cord. Again he shook his head.

"What do you make of it?" Hatch ventured at last.

The Thinking Machine squinted at him dully. "I don't make anything of it," he replied frankly. "There is no starting point. I have all unknown quantities. When every conceivable motive is eliminated as seems to be the case here, we must naturally turn to that thing which does things without motive – a brute – say, an ape." He held up the knotted cord. "But those knots were never tied by any but human hands; a directing intelligence fashioned the noose, and human hands applied it. That is indisputable, so we haven't even the ape to start with. This is perhaps the first case I have ever been interested in where all possibilities seem to be removed."

Hatch stared at the scientist a little blankly for a moment. He had never before heard just such an admission from him. "Well," asked the reporter helplessly, "where are we going with it?"

The Thinking Machine didn't say. Instead, he planted his No. 8 hat more firmly on his enormous straw yellow head, and returned to his apartments.

It was ten minutes of one o'clock that night, and Hatch had just finished writing the story of the tragedy for his newspaper, when there came a call for him on the telephone. It was The Thinking Machine.

"Do you know of any crime similar to this any time recently?" asked the scientist. "I mean a crime where the circumstances resembled these in any manner?"

The reporter was thoughtful for a moment. "No," he replied.

"Well, I'm very much afraid that there will be another just like it," volunteered The Thinking Machine enigmatically.

"Why, who – what?" asked Hatch in amazement.

"Of course I don't know who," retorted the scientist crabbedly. "If I did I would prevent it. I may say I know what, but it doesn't do us any good. Goodnight."

Three days later came another tragedy. Bartow Gillespie and his brother James were found dead in a room together ten miles from the scene of the Barrett affair. Bartow, the eldest, had been strangled to death precisely as Mildred Barrett had been. James Gillespie lay five feet away, with a bullet in his brain. The murderer's revolver had fallen between them. One shot had been fired—the shot which entered James's head at the base of his brain.

The Thinking Machine and Hatch were on the scene of this second crime within a few hours. Again there was a detailed examination to be made, and the scientist made it conscientiously, from the strangler's cord, identical in every way with the one that had slain Mildred Barrett, to the revolver with its one empty chamber. The Thinking Machine weighed the weapon in his hand thoughtfully, and then turned to Detective Mallory.

"Whose is this?" he asked.

"If I knew that we could not only solve this mystery, but also the Barrett affair," retorted the detective grimly.

Then The Thinking Machine did a singular thing. He bent down to within a few inches of the upturned face of James Gillespie, and squinted steadily for a minute or more into the dead, glassy eyes. This done, he ran his slender white fingers through the dead man's hair several times.

"I know whose revolver it is now," he said as he arose. "It belonged to the other dead man there – Bartow Gillespie."

Detective Mallory regarded him in amazement for an instant, and then a slight smile about his lips showed what he thought of it.

"I suppose, professor," he said, "you are going to tell us that Bartow Gillespie killed his brother, and then strangled himself with this cord?"

"No," replied the scientist almost pleasantly.

"Well, then," Mallory ventured, "it's going to be that Bartow Gillespie shot his brother, and then his brother strangled him to death with the cord?"

"No," said the scientist again. "I was going to tell you that James Gillespie attacked his brother Bartow, and attempted to strangle him – did strangle him; that there was a struggle – these two overturned chairs show that; and that Bartow Gillespie, with the strangler's cord about his throat, killed his brother with the revolver. Remember, please, that when James Gillespie murdered Mildred Barrett, he was dealing with a child, but here he was dealing with a man, and a powerful man, who fought fiercely after the knot was fastened.

"We may assume that the revolver was Bartow Gillespie's, and that it was in his possession at the time he was attacked. Why? Because if it had been in James Gillespie's possession he would probably have finished his work by shooting his brother, when his brother began his struggle. Certainly James Gillespie did not kill himself, because the wound is in the back of his head. I am stating these things not as facts but as probabilities. When we know positively that the weapon was Bartow Gillespie's, then the probabilities become facts."

There was still a light, skeptical expression about Detective Mallory's mouth. "And on the other hand," he said, "we have the probability that the strangler came here and killed Bartow Gillespie, that the sound of the struggle attracted James Gillespie's attention, that he came in to investigate, that he was threatened and started to go out, and that the strangler fired the shot which struck him in the back of the head."

"Disproved flatly by two points," said The Thinking Machine curtly. "First, the fact that the strangler deliberately left his revolver, if we accept your hypothesis and second, by the fact that—" He paused and turning stared curiously down into the face of James Gillespie.

Detective Mallory waited impatiently for a moment; then, "And the second is what?" he asked.

"Do you know the motive for the murder of the Barrett child?" asked the scientist irrelevantly.

"No," said Detective Mallory in some surprise.

"And do you know the motive for this double crime, under your hypothesis?"

"No."

"Well, the motive is written here," and the scientist turned and thrust a long finger into the pallid face of James Gillespie. "It is in the eyes, in the mouth, and still again it's written here." He pulled aside the tumbled hair, and disclosed a bare spot. "Here is a scar, left months, perhaps years, ago by some serious injury."

"Why, I don't see —" began the detective protestingly.

"Of course, you don't see!" snapped The Thinking Machine. "What was found in James Gillespie's pockets?"

"I don't know that there has been an examination," said Mallory. "We always leave those things to the medical examiner, where there is no doubt of a man's identity."

With deft fingers the scientist ransacked the slain man's clothes. From a hip pocket he drew a little bundle and threw it on the table before Mallory. "And there is your final proof," he said. "It isn't even necessary now to prove that the revolver was Bartow Gillespie's – we know it – know it as inevitably as that two and two make four, Mr Mallory, not sometimes but all the time."

The little bundle that he had thrown on the table was a roll of plain manila twine – just a couple of yards. At last the detective was beginning to see.

"But what possible motive?" he asked.

"I told Mr Hatch when I investigated the Barrett affair that when all conceivable human motives were eliminated, as seemed to be the fact in this case, there remained only the thing – the creature, which will act without motive – an ape, for instance," interrupted The Thinking Machine. "I told him afterward that there would probably be a second crime under the same circumstances, and also that we were powerless to prevent it. This is the crime. There is no motive for either.

"The old scar on this man's head, the expression of his face, and his eyes particularly, show conclusively that he was a maniac – just a shade the intellectual superior of an ape, with all the cunning of humanity distorted and diseased into a homicidal mania. An examination of his brain at the autopsy will prove all this even to you, Mr Mallory. How long he has been a maniac I don't know; your investigations will develop that. That is all, I think. Goodday."

The Thinking Machine and Hutchinson Hatch walked down the street together.

"How is it," inquired the reporter, "that James Gillespie didn't kill Barrett at the same time he killed the little girl?"

"I don't know," was the reply. "It is difficult enough, Mr Hatch, to follow the mental workings of a sane man; when we have a maniac, no one can say what he will do next. We don't look into the matter, but I dare say that Gillespie never knew that child he killed, and could have had no motive."

And subsequently this proved to be true.

8

PROBLEM OF THE LOST RADIUM

One ounce of radium! Within his open palm Professor Dexter held practically the world's entire supply of that singular and seemingly inexhaustible force which was, and is, one of the greatest of all scientific riddles. So far as known there were only a few more grains in existence — four in the Curie laboratory in Paris, two in Berlin, two in St. Petersburg, one at Leland Stanford University and one in London. All the remainder was here – here in the Yarvard laboratory, a tiny mass lumped on a small piece of steel.

Gazing at this vast concentrated power Professor Dexter was a little awed and a little appalled at the responsibility which had suddenly devolved upon him, naturally enough with this culmination of a project which he had cherished for months. Briefly this had been to gather into one cohesive whole the many particles of the precious substance scattered over the world for the purpose of elaborate experiments as to its motive power practicability. Now here it was.

Its value, based on scarcity of supply, was incalculable. Millions of dollars would not replace it. Minute portions had come from the four quarters of the globe, in each case by special messenger, and each separate grain had been heavily insured by Lloyd's at a staggering premium. It was only after months

PROBLEM OF THE LOST RADIUM

of labour, backed by the influence of the great university of Yarvard in which he held the chair of physics, that Professor Dexter had been able to accomplish his purpose.

At least one famous name had been loaned to the proposed experiments, that of the distinguished scientist and logician, Professor Augustus S. F. X. Van Dusen – so called The Thinking Machine. The interest of this master mind in the work was a triumph for Professor Dexter, who was young and comparatively unknown. The elder scientist – The Thinking Machine – was a court of last appeal in the sciences and from the moment his connection with Professor Dexter's plans was announced his fellows all over the world had been anxiously awaiting a first word.

Naturally the task of gathering so great a quantity of radium had not been accomplished without extensive, and sometimes sensational, newspaper comment all over the United States and Europe. It was not astonishing, therefore that news of the receipt of the final portion of the radium at Yarvard had been known in the daily press and with it a statement that Professors Van Dusen and Dexter would immediately begin their experiments.

The work was to be done in the immense laboratory at Yarvard a high-ceilinged room with roof partially of glass, and with windows set high in the walls far above the reach of curious eyes. Full preparations had been made; – the two men were to work together, and a guard was to be stationed at the single door. This door led into a smaller room, a sort of reception hall, which in turn connected with the main hallway of the building.

Now Professor Dexter was alone in the laboratory, waiting impatiently for The Thinking Machine and turning over in his mind the preliminary steps in the labour he had undertaken. Every instrument was in place, all else was put aside for these experiments, which were either to revolutionize the motive power of the world or else demonstrate the utter uselessness of radium as a practical force.

Professor Dexter's line of thought was interrupted by the appearance of Mr Bowen, one of the instructors of the University.

"A lady to see you, Professor," he said as he handed him a card. "She said it was a matter of great importance to you."

Professor Dexter glanced at the card as Mr Bowen turned and went out through the small room into the main hallway. The name, Mme. Therese du Chastaigny, was wholly unfamiliar. Puzzled a little and perhaps impatient too, he carefully laid the steel with its burden of radium on the long table, and started out into the reception room. Almost in the door he stumbled against something, recovered his equilibrium with an effort and brought up with an undignified jerk.

The colour mounted to his modest ears as he heard a woman laugh – a pleasant, musical, throaty sort of ripple that under other circumstances would have been agreeable. Now, being directed at his own discomfiture, it was irritating, and the Professor's face tingled a little as a tall woman arose and came towards him.

"Please pardon me," she said contritely, but there was still a flicker of a smile upon her red lips. "It was my carelessness. I should not have placed my suit case in the door." She lifted it easily and replaced it in that identical position. "Or perhaps," she suggested, inquiringly, "someone else coming out might stumble as you did?"

"No," replied the Professor, and he smiled a little through his blushes. "There is no one else in there."

As Mme. du Chastaigny straightened up, with a rustle of skirts, to greet him Professor Dexter was somewhat surprised at her height and at the splendid lines of her figure. She was apparently of thirty years and seemed from a casual glance, to be five feet nine or ten inches tall. In addition to a certain striking indefinable beauty she was of remarkable physical power if one might judge from her poise and manner. Professor Dexter glanced at her and then at the card inquiringly.

"I have a letter of introduction to you from Mme. Curie of France," she explained as she produced it from a tiny chatelaine bag. "Shall we go over here where the light is better?"

She handed the letter to him and together they seated themselves under one of the windows near the door into the outer hallway. Professor Dexter pulled up a light chair facing her and opened the letter. He glanced through it and then looked up with a newly kindled interest in his eyes.

"I should not have disturbed you," Mme. du Chastaigny explained pleasantly, "had I not known it was a matter of the greatest possible interest to you."

"Yes?" Professor Dexter nodded.

"It's radium," she continued. "It just happens that I have in my possession practically an ounce of radium of which the world of science has never heard."

"An ounce of radium!" repeated Professor Dexter, incredulously. "Why, Madame, you astonish, amaze me. An ounce of radium?"

He leaned further forward in his chair and waited expectantly while Mme. du Chastaigny coughed violently. The paroxysm passed after a moment.

"That is my punishment for laughing," she explained, smilingly. "I trust you will pardon me. I have a bad throat – and it was quick retribution."

"Yes, yes," said the other courteously, "but this other – it's most interesting. Please tell me about it."

Mme. du Chastaigny made herself comfortable in the chair, cleared her throat, and began.

"It's rather an unusual story," she said apologetically, "but the radium came into my possession in quite a natural manner. I am English, so I speak the language, but my husband was

French as my name indicates, and, he, like you, was a scientist. He was little known to the world at large, however, as he was not connected with any institution. His experiments were undertaken for amusement and gradually led to a complete absorption of his interest. We were not wealthy as Americans count it, but we were comfortably well off.

"That much for my affairs. The letter I gave you from Mme. Curie will tell you the rest as to who I am. Now when the discovery of radium was made by M. and Mme. Curie my husband began some investigations along the same line and they proved to be remarkably successful. His efforts were first directed towards producing radium, with what object, I was not aware at that time. In the course of months he made grain after grain by some process unlike that of the Curies', and incidentally he spent practically all our little fortune. Finally he had nearly an ounce."

"Most interesting!" commented Professor Dexter. "Please go on."

"It happened that during the production of the last quarter of an ounce, my husband contracted an illness which later proved fatal," Mme. du Chastaigny resumed after a slight pause, and her voice dropped. "I did not know the purpose of his experiments; I only knew what they had been and their comparative cost. On his death bed he revealed this purpose to me. Strangely enough it was identical with yours as the newspapers have announced it – that is, the practicability of radium as a motive power. He was at work on plans looking to the utilization of its power when he died but these plans were not perfected and unfortunately were in such shape as to be unintelligible to another."

She paused and sat silent for a moment. Professor Dexter watching her face, traced a shadow of grief and sorrow there and his own big heart prompted a ready sympathy.

"And what," he asked, "was your purpose in coming to me now?"

"I know of the efforts you have made and the difficulties you have encountered in gathering enough radium for the experiments you have in mind," Mme. du Chastaigny continued, "and it occurred to me that what I have, which is of no possible use to me, might be sold to you or to the university. As I said, there is nearly an ounce of it. It is where I can put my hands on it, and you of course are to make the tests to prove it is what it should be."

"Sell it?" gasped Professor Dexter. "Why, Madame, it's impossible. The funds of the college are not so plentiful that the vast fortune necessary to purchase such a quantity would be forthcoming."

A certain hopeful light in the face of the young woman passed and there was a quick gesture of her hands which indicated disappointment.

"You speak of a vast fortune," she said at last. "I could not hope, of course, to realize anything like the actual value of the substance – a million perhaps? Only a few hundred thousands? Something to convert into available funds for me the fortune which has been sunk."

There was almost an appeal in her limpid voice and Professor Dexter considered the matter deeply for several minutes as he stared out the window.

"Or perhaps," the woman hurried on after a moment, "it might be that you need more radium for the experiments you have in hand now, and there might be some sum paid me for the use of what I have? A sort of royalty? I am willing to do anything within reason."

Again there was a long pause. Ahead of him, with this hitherto unheard of quantity of radium available, Professor Dexter saw rosy possibilities in his chosen work. The thought gripped him more firmly as he considered it. He could see little chance of a purchase – but the use of the substance during his experiments! That might be arranged.

"Madame," he said at last, "I want to thank you deeply for coming to me. While I can promise nothing definite I can promise that I will take up the matter with certain persons who may be able to do something for you. It's perfectly astounding. Yes, I may say that I will do something, but I shall perhaps, require several days to bring it about. Will you grant me that time?"

Mme. du Chastaigny smiled.

"I must of course," she said, and again she went off into a paroxysm of coughing, a distressing, hacking outburst which seemed to shake her whole body. "Of course," she added, when the spasm passed, "I can only hope that you can do something either in purchasing or using it."

"Could you fix a definite price for the quantity you have – that is a sale price – and another price merely for its use?" asked Professor Dexter.

"I can't do that offhand of course, but here is my address on this card – Hotel Teutonic. I expect to remain there for a few days and you may reach me any time. Please, now please," and again there was a pleading note in her voice, and she laid one hand on his arm, "don't hesitate to make any offer to me. I shall be only too glad to accept it if I can."

She arose and Professor Dexter stood beside her.

"For your information," she went on, "I will explain that I only arrived in this country yesterday by steamer from Liverpool and my need is such that within another six months I shall be absolutely dependent upon what I may realize from the radium."

She crossed the room, picked up the suit case and again she smiled, evidently at the recollection of Professor Dexter's awkward stumble. Then with her burden she turned to go.

"Permit me, Madame," suggested Professor Dexter, quickly as he reached for the bag.

"Oh no, it is quite light," she responded easily.

There were a few commonplaces and then she went out. Gazing through the window after her Professor Dexter noted, with certain admiration in his eyes the graceful strong lines of her figure as she entered a carriage and was driven away. He stood deeply thoughtful for a minute considering the possibilities arising from her casual announcement of the existence of this unknown radium.

"If I only had that too," he muttered as he turned and re-entered his work room.

An instant later, a cry – a wild amazed shriek – came from the laboratory and Professor Dexter, with pallid face, rushed out through the reception room and flung open the door into the main hallway. Half a dozen students gathered about him and from across the hall Mr Bowen, the instructor, appeared with startled eyes.

"The radium is gone — stolen!" gasped Professor Dexter.

The members of the little group stared at one another blankly while Professor Dexter raved impotently and ran his fingers through his hair. There were questions and conjectures; a babble was raging about him when a new figure loomed up in the picture. It was that of a small man with an enormous yellow head and an eternal petulant droop to the corners of his mouth. He had just turned a corner in the hall.

"Ah, Professor Van Dusen," exclaimed Professor Dexter, and he seized the long, slender hand of The Thinking Machine in a frenzied grip.

"Dear me! Dear me!" complained The Thinking Machine as he sought to extract his fingers from the vice. "Don't do that. What's the matter?"

"The radium is gone — stolen!" Professor Dexter explained.

The Thinking Machine drew back a little and squinted aggressively into the distended eyes of his fellow scientist.

"Why that's perfectly silly," he said at last. "Come in, please, and tell me what happened."

With perspiration dripping from his brow and hands atremble, Professor Dexter followed him into the reception room, whereupon The Thinking Machine turned, closed the door into the hallway and snapped the lock. Outside Mr Bowen and the students heard the click and turned away to send the astonishing news hurtling through the great university. Inside Professor Dexter sank down on a chair with staring eyes and nervously twitching lips.

"Dear me, Dexter, are you crazy?" demanded The Thinking Machine irritably. "Compose yourself. What happened? What were the circumstances of the disappearance?"

"Come – come in here – the laboratory and see," suggested Professor Dexter.

"Oh, never mind that now," said the other impatiently. "Tell me what happened?"

Professor Dexter paced the length of the small room twice then sat down again, controlling himself with a perceptible effort. Then, ramblingly but completely, he told the story of Mme. du Chastaigny's call, covering every circumstance from the time he placed the radium on the table in the laboratory until he saw her drive away in the carriage. The Thinking Machine leaned back in his chair with squint eyes upturned and slender white fingers pressed tip to tip.

"How long was she here?" he asked at the end.

"Ten minutes, I should say," was the reply.

"Where did she sit?"

"Right where you are, facing the laboratory door."

The Thinking Machine glanced back at the window behind him.

"And you?" he asked.

"I sat here facing her."

"You know that she did not enter the laboratory?"

"I know it, yes," replied Professor Dexter promptly. "No one save me has entered that laboratory today. I have taken particular pains to see that no one did. When Mr Bowen spoke to me I had the radium in my hand. He merely opened the door, handed me her card and went right out. Of course it's impossible that—"

"Nothing is impossible, Mr Dexter," blazed The Thinking Machine suddenly. "Did you at any time leave Mme. du Chastaigny in this room alone?"

"No, no," declared Dexter emphatically. "I was looking at her every moment she was here; I did not put the radium out of my hand until Mr Bowen was out of this room and in the hallway there. I then came into this room and met her."

For several minutes The Thinking Machine sat perfectly silent, squinting upward while Professor Dexter gazed into the inscrutable face anxiously.

"I hope," ventured the Professor at last, "that you do not believe it was any fault of mine?"

The Thinking Machine did not say.

"What sort of a voice has Mme. du Chastaigny?" he asked instead.

The Professor blinked a little in bewilderment.

"An ordinary voice – the low voice of a woman of education and refinement," he replied.

"Did she raise it at any time while talking?"

"No."

"Perhaps she sneezed or coughed while talking to you?"

Unadulterated astonishment was written on Professor Dexter's face.

"She coughed, yes, violently," he replied.

"Ah!" exclaimed The Thinking Machine and there was a flash of comprehension in the narrow blue eyes. "Twice, I suppose?"

Professor Dexter was staring at the scientist blankly.

"Yes, twice," he responded.

"Anything else?"

"Well, she laughed I think."

"What was the occasion of her laughter?"

"I stumbled over a suit case she had set down by the laboratory door there."

The Thinking Machine absorbed that without evidence of emotion, then reached for the letter of introduction which Mme. du Chastaigny had given to Professor Dexter and which he still carried crumpled up in his hand. It was a short note, just a few lines in French, explaining that Mme. du Chastaigny desired to see Professor Dexter on a matter of importance.

"Do you happen to know Mme. Curie's handwriting?" asked The Thinking Machine after a cursory examination. "Of course you had some correspondence with her about this work?"

"I know her writing, yes," was the reply. "I think that is genuine, if that's what you mean."

"We'll see after a while," commented The Thinking Machine.

He arose and led the way into the laboratory. There Professor Dexter indicated to him the exact spot on the work table where the radium had been placed. Standing beside it he made some mental calculation as he squinted about the room, at the highly placed windows, the glass roof above, the single door. Then wrinkles grew in his tall brow.

"I presume all the wall windows are kept fastened?"

"Yes, always."

"And those in the glass roof?"

"Yes."

"Then bring me a tall step – ladder please!"

It was produced after a few minutes. Professor Dexter looked on curiously and with a glimmer of understanding as The Thinking Machine examined each catch on every window, and tapped the panes over with a pen-knife. When he had examined the last and found all locked he came down the ladder.

"Dear me!" he exclaimed petulantly. "It's perfectly extraordinary – most extraordinary. If the radium was not stolen through the reception room, then-then—" He glanced around the room again.

Professor Dexter shook his head. He had recovered his self-possession somewhat, but his bewilderment left him helpless.

"Are you sure, Professor Dexter," asked The Thinking Machine at last coldly, "are you sure you placed the radium where you have indicated?"

There was almost an accusation in the tone and Professor Dexter flushed hotly.

"I am positive, yes," he replied.

"And you are absolutely certain that neither Mr Bowen nor Mme. du Chastaigny entered this room?"

"I am absolutely positive."

The Thinking Machine wandered up and down the long table apparently without any interest, handling the familiar instruments and glittering appliances as a master.

"Did Mme. du Chastaigny happen to mention any children?" he at last asked, irrelevantly.

Professor Dexter blinked again.

"No," he replied.

"Adopted or otherwise?"

"No."

"Just what sort of a suit case was that she carried?"

"Oh, I don't know," replied Professor Dexter. "I didn't particularly notice. It seemed to be about the usual kind of a suit case – sole leather I imagine."

"She arrived in this country yesterday you said?"

"Yes."

"It's perfectly extraordinary," The Thinking Machine grunted. Then he scribbled a line or two on a scrap of paper and handed it to Professor Dexter.

"Please have this sent by cable at once."

Professor Dexter glanced at it. It was:

"Mme. Curie, Paris:

"Did you give Mme. du Chastaigny letter of introduction for Professor Dexter? Answer quick.

"Augustus S. F. X. Van Dusen."

As Professor Dexter glanced at the dispatch his eyes opened a little.

"You don't believe that Mme. du Chastaigny could have—" he began.

"I daresay I know what Mme. Curie's answer will be," interrupted the other abruptly.

"What?"

"It will be no," was the positive reply. "And then—" He paused.

"Then—?"

"Your veracity may be brought into question."

With flaming face and tightly clenched teeth but without a word, Professor Dexter saw The Thinking Machine unlock the door and pass out. Then he dropped into a chair and buried his face in his hands. There Mr Bowen found him a few minutes later.

"Ah, Mr Bowen," he said, as he glanced up, "please have this cable sent immediately."

Once in his apartments The Thinking Machine telephoned to Hutchinson Hatch, reporter, at the office of his newspaper. That long, lean, hungry looking young man was fairly bubbling with suppressed emotion when he rushed into the booth to answer and the exhilaration of pure enthusiasm made his voice vibrant when he spoke. The Thinking Machine readily understood.

"It's about the radium theft at Yarvard that I wanted to speak to you," he said.

"Yes," Hatch replied, "just heard of it this minute – a bulletin from Police Headquarters. I was about to go out on it."

"Please do something for me first," requested The Thinking Machine. "Go at once to the Hotel Teutonic and ascertain indisputably for me whether or not Mme. du Chastaigny, who is stopping there, is accompanied by a child."

"Certainly, of course," said Hatch, "but the story—"

"This is the story," interrupted The Thinking Machine, tartly. "If you can learn nothing of any child at the hotel go to the steamer on which she arrived yesterday from Liverpool and inquire there. I must have definite, absolute, indisputable evidence."

"I'm off," Hatch responded.

He hung up the receiver and rushed out. He happened to be professionally acquainted with the chief clerk of the Teutonic, a monosyllabic, rotund gentleman who was an occasional source of private information and who spent his life adding up a column of figures.

"Hello, Charlie," Hatch greeted him. "Mme. du Chastaigny stopping here?"

"Yep," said Charlie.

"Husband with her?"

"Nope."

"By herself when she came?"

"Yep."

"Hasn't a child with her?"

"Nope."

"What does she look like?"

"A corker!" said Charlie.

This last loquacious outburst seemed to appease the reporter's burning thirst for information and he rushed away to the dock where the steamship, Granada from Liverpool, still lay. Aboard he sought out the purser and questioned him along the same lines with the same result. There was no trace of a child. Then Hatch made his way to the home of The Thinking Machine.

"Well?" demanded the scientist.

The reporter shook his head.

"She hasn't seen or spoken to a child since she left Liverpool so far as I can ascertain," he declared.

It was not quite surprise, it was rather perturbation in the manner of The Thinking Machine now. It showed in a quick gesture of one hand, in the wrinkles on his brow, in the narrowing down of his eyes. He dropped back into a chair and remained there silent, thoughtful for a long time.

"It couldn't have been, it couldn't have been, it couldn't have been," the scientist broke out finally.

Having no personal knowledge on the subject, whatever it was, Hatch discreetly remained silent. After a while The Thinking Machine aroused himself with a jerk and related to the reporter the story of the lost radium so far as it was known.

"The letter of introduction from Mme. Curie opened the way for Mme. du Chastaigny," he explained. "Frankly I believe that letter to be a forgery. I cabled asking Mme. Curie. A 'No' from her will mean that my conjecture is correct; a 'Yes' will mean – but that is hardly worth considering. The question now is: What method was employed to cause the disappearance of the radium from that room?"

The door opened and Martha appeared. She handed a cablegram to The Thinking Machine and he ripped it open with hurried fingers. He glanced at the sheet once, then arose suddenly after which he sat down again, just as suddenly.

"What is it?" ventured Hatch.

"It's 'Yes,' " was the reply.

In the seclusion of his own small laboratory The Thinking Machine was making some sort of chemical experiment about eight o'clock that night. He was just hoisting a graduated glass, containing a purplish, hazy fluid, to get the lamp light through it, when an idea flashed into his mind. He permitted the glass to fall and smash on the floor.

"Perfectly stupid of me," he grumbled and turning he walked into an adjoining room without so much as a glance at the wrecked glass. A minute later he had Hutchinson Hatch on the telephone.

"Come right up," he instructed.

There was that in his voice which caused Hatch to jump. He seized his hat and rushed out of his office. When he reached The Thinking Machine's apartments that gentleman was just emerging from the room where the telephone was.

"I have it," the scientist told the reporter, forestalling a question. "It's ridiculously simple. I can't imagine how I missed it except through stupidity."

Hatch smiled behind his hand. Certainly stupidity was not to be charged against The Thinking Machine.

"Come in a cab?" asked the scientist.

"Yes, it's waiting."

"Come on then."

They went out together. The scientist gave some instruction to the cabby and they clattered off.

"You're going to meet a very remarkable person," The Thinking Machine explained. "He may cause trouble and he may not – any way look out for him. He's tricky."

That was all. The cab drew up in front of a large building, evidently a boarding house of the middle class. The Thinking Machine jumped out, Hatch following, and together they ascended the steps. A maid answered the bell.

"Is Mr. – Mr. – oh, what's his name?" and The Thinking Machine snapped his fingers as if trying to remember. "Mr—, the small gentleman who arrived from Liverpool yesterday—"

"Oh," and the maid smiled broadly, "you mean Mr Berkerstrom?"

"Yes, that's the name," exclaimed the scientist. "Is he in, please?"

"I think so, sir," said the maid, still smiling. "Shall I take your card?"

"No, it isn't necessary," replied The Thinking Machine. "We are from the theatre. He is expecting us."

"Second floor, rear," said the maid.

They ascended the stairs and paused in front of a door. The Thinking Machine tried it softly. It was unlocked and he pushed it open. A bright light blazed from a gas jet but no person was in sight. As they stood silent, they heard a newspaper rattle and both looked in the direction whence came the sound.

Still no one appeared. The Thinking Machine raised a finger and tiptoed to a large upholstered chair which faced the other way. One slender hand disappeared on the other side to be lifted immediately. Wriggling in his grasp was a man – a toyman – a midget miniature in smoking jacket and slippers who swore fluently in German. Hatch burst out laughing, an uncontrollable fit which left him breathless.

"Mr Berkerstrom, Mr Hatch," said The Thinking Machine gravely. "This is the gentleman, Mr Hatch, who stole the radium. Before you begin to talk, Mr Berkerstrom, I will say that Mme. du Chastaigny has been arrested and has confessed."

"Ach, Gott!" raged the little German. "Let me down, der chair in, ef you blease."

The Thinking Machine lowered the tiny wriggling figure into the chair while Hatch closed and locked the door. When the reporter came back and looked, laughter was gone. The drawn wrinkled face of the midget, the babyish body, the toy clothing, added to the pitiful helplessness of the little figure. His age might have been fifteen or fifty, his weight was certainly not more than twenty-five pounds, his height barely thirty inches.

"It iss as we did him in der theatre, und—" Mr Berkerstrom started to explain limpingly.

"Oh, that was it?" inquired The Thinking Machine curiously as if some question in his own mind had been settled. "What is Mme. du Chastaigny's correct name?"

"She iss der famous Mlle. Fanchon, und I am der marvellous midget, Count von Fritz," proclaimed Mr Berkerstrom proudly in play-bill fashion.

Then a glimmer of what had actually happened flashed through Hatch's mind; he was staggered by the sublime audacity which made it possible. The Thinking Machine arose and opened a closet door at which he had been staring. From a dark recess he dragged out a suit case and from this in turn a small steel box.

"Ah, here is the radium," he remarked as he opened the box. "Think of it, Mr Hatch. An actual value of millions in that small box."

Hatch was thinking of it, thinking all sorts of things, as he mentally framed an opening paragraph for this whooping big yarn. He was still thinking of it as he and The Thinking Machine accompanied willingly enough by the midget, entered the cab and were driven back to the scientist's house.

An hour later Mme. du Chastaigny called by request. She imagined her visit had something to do with the purchase of an ounce of radium; Detective Mallory, watching her out a corner of his official eye, imagined she imagined that. The next caller was Professor Dexter. Dumb anger gnawed at his heart, but he had heeded a telephone request. The Thinking Machine and Hatch completed the party.

"Now, Mme. du Chastaigny, please," The Thinking Machine began quietly, "will you please inform me if you have another ounce of radium in addition to that you stole from the Yarvard laboratory?"

Mme. du Chastaigny leaped to her feet. The Thinking Machine was staring upward with squint eyes and finger tips pressed together. He didn't alter his position in the slightest at her sudden move – but Detective Mallory did.

"Stole?" exclaimed Mme. du Chastaigny. "Stole?"

"That's the word I used," said The Thinking Machine almost pleasantly. Into the woman's eyes there leapt a blaze of tigerish ferocity. Her face flushed, then the colour fled and she sat down again, perfectly pallid.

"Count von Fritz has recounted his part in the affair to me," went on The Thinking Machine. He leaned forward and took a package from the table. "Here is the radium. Now have you any radium in addition to this?"

"The radium!" gasped the Professor incredulously.

"If there is no denial Count von Fritz might as well come in, Mr Hatch," remarked The Thinking Machine.

Hatch opened the door. The midget bounded into the room in true theatric style.

"Is it enough, Mile. Fanchon?" inquired the scientist. There was an ironic touch in his voice.

Mme. du Chastaigny nodded, dumbly.

"It would interest you, of course, to know how it came out," went on The Thinking Machine. "I daresay your inspiration for the theft came from a newspaper article, therefore you probably know that I was directly interested in the experiments planned. I visited the laboratory immediately after you left with the radium. Professor Dexter told me your story. It was clever, clever, but there was too much radium, therefore unbelievable. If not true, then why had you been there? The answer is obvious.

"Neither you or anyone else save Mr Dexter entered that laboratory. Yet the radium was gone. How? My first impression was that your part in the theft had been to detain Mr Dexter while someone entered the laboratory or else fished out the radium through a window in the glass roof by some ingenious contrivance. I questioned Mr Dexter as to your precise acts, and ventured the opinion that you had either sneezed or coughed. You had coughed twice – obviously a signal – thus that view was strengthened.

"Next, I examined window and roof fastenings -- all were locked. I tapped over the glass to see if they had been tampered with. They had not. Apparently the radium had not gone through the reception room; certainly it had not gone any other way – yet it was gone. It was a nice problem until I recalled that Mr Dexter had mentioned a suit case. Why did a woman, on business, go out carrying a suit case? Or why, granting that she had a good reason for it, should she take the trouble to drag it into the reception room instead of leaving it in the carriage?

"Now, I didn't believe you had any radium; I knew you had signalled to the real thief by coughing. Therefore I was prepared to believe that the suit case was the solution of the theft. How? Obviously, something concealed in it. What? A monkey? I dismissed that because the thief must have had the reasoning instinct. If not a monkey then what? A child? That seemed more probable, yet it was improbable. I proceeded, however, on the hypothesis that a child carefully instructed had been the actual thief."

Open eyes were opened wider. Mme. du Chastaigny, being chiefly concerned, followed the plain, cold reasoning as if fascinated. Count von Fritz straightened his necktie and smiled.

"I sent a cable to Mme. Curie asking if the letter of introduction was genuine, and sent Mr Hatch to get a trace of a child. He informed me that there was no child just about the time I heard from Mme. Curie that the letter was genuine. The problem immediately went back to the starting point. Time after time I reasoned it out, always the same way – finally the solution came. If not a monkey or a child then what? A midget. Of course it was stupid of me not to have seen that possibility at first.

"Then there remained only the task of finding him. He probably came on the same boat with the woman, and I saw a plan to find him. It was through the driver of the carriage which Mme. du Chastaigny used. I got his number by 'phone at the Hotel Teutonic. Where had Mme. du Chastaigny left a suit case? He gave me an address. I went there.

"I won't attempt to explain how this woman obtained the letter from Mme. Curie. I will only say that a woman who undertakes to sell an ounce of radium to a man from whom she intends to steal it is clever enough to do anything. I may add that she and the midget are theatrical people, and that the idea of a person in a suit case came from some part of their stage performance. Of course the suit case is so built that the midget could open and close it from inside."

"Und it always gets der laugh," interposed the midget, complacently.

After awhile the prisoners were led away. Count von Fritz escaped three times the first day by the simple method of wriggling between the bars of his cell.

9

THE HAUNTED BELL

I

It was a thing, trivial enough, yet so strangely mystifying in its happening that the mind hesitated to accept it as an actual occurrence despite the indisputable evidence of the sense of hearing. As the seconds ticked on, Franklin Phillips was not at all certain that it had happened, and gradually the doubt began to assume the proportions of a conviction. Then, because his keenly-attuned brain did not readily explain it, the matter was dismissed as an impossibility. Certainly it had not happened. Mr Phillips smiled a little. Of course, it was – it must be – a trick of his nerves.

But, even as the impossibility of the thing grew upon him, the musical clang still echoed vaguely in his memory, and his eyes were still fixed inquiringly on the Japanese gong whence it had come. The gong was of the usual type-six bronze discs, or inverted bowls, of graduated sizes, suspended one above the other, with the largest at the top, and quaintly colored with the deep, florid tones of Japan's ancient decorative art. It hung motionless at the end of a silken cord which dropped down sheerly from the ceiling over a corner of his desk. It was certainly harmless enough in appearance, yet – yet—

As he looked the bell sounded again. It was a clear, rich, vibrant note – a boom which belched forth suddenly as if of its own volition, quavered full-toned, then diminished until it was only a lingering sense of sound. Mr Phillips started to his feet with an exclamation.

Now, in the money-marts of the world, Franklin Phillips was regarded as a living refutation of all theories as to the physical disasters consequent upon a long pursuit of the strenuous life – a human antithesis of nerves. He breathed fourteen times to the minute and his heart-beat was always within a fraction of seventy-one. This was true whether there were millions at stake in a capricious market or whether he ordered a cigar. In this calm lay the strength which had enabled him to reach his fiftieth year in perfect mental and physical condition.

Back of this utter normality was a placid, inquiring mind; so now, deliberately, he took a pencil and tapped the bells of the gong one after another, beginning at the bottom. The shrill note of the first told him instantly that was not the one which had sounded; nor was the second, nor the third. At the fourth he hesitated and struck a second time. Then he tapped the fifth. That was it. The gong trembled and swayed slightly from the blow, light as it was, and twice again he struck it. Then he was convinced.

For several minutes he stood staring, staring blankly. What had caused the bell to ring? His manner was calm, cold, quiet, inquisitive – indomitable common-sense inspired the query.

"I guess it was nerves," he said after a moment. "But I was looking at it, and—"

Nerves as a possibility were suddenly brushed ruthlessly aside, and he systematically sought some tangible explanation of the affair. Had a flying insect struck the bell? No. He was positive, because he had been looking directly at it when it sounded the second time. He would have seen an insect. Had something dropped from the ceiling? No. He would have seen that, too.

With alert, searching eyes he surveyed the small room. It was his own personal den – a sort of office in his home. He was alone now; the door closed; everything appeared as usual.

Perhaps a window! The one facing east was open to the lightly stirring air of the first warm evening of spring. The wind had disturbed the gong! He jumped at the thought as an inspiration. It faded when he saw the window-curtains hanging down limply; the movement of the air was too light to disturb even these. Perhaps something had been tossed through the window! The absurdity of that conjecture was proven instantly. There was a screen in the window of so fine a mesh that hardly more than a grain of sand could pass through it. And this screen was intact.

With bewilderment in his face Mr Phillips sat down again. Then recurred to him one indisputable fact which precluded the possibility of all those things he had considered. There had been absolutely no movement – that is, perceptible movement – of the gong when the bell sounded. Yet the tone was loud, as if a violent blow had been struck. He remembered that, when he tapped the bell sharply with his pencil, it swayed and trembled visibly, but the pencil was so light that the tone sounded far away and faint. To convince himself he touched the bell again, ever so lightly. It swayed.

"Well, of all the extraordinary things I ever heard of!" he remarked.

After a while he lighted a cigar, and for the first time in his life his hand shook. The sight brought a faint expression of amused surprise to his lips; then he snapped his fingers impatiently and settled back in his chair. It was a struggle to bring his mind around to material things; it insisted on wandering, and wove fantastic, grotesque conjectures in the drifting tobacco smoke. But at last common-sense triumphed under the sedative influence of an excellent cigar, and the incident of the bell floated off into nothingness. Business affairs – urgent, real, tangible business affairs – focused his attention.

Then, suddenly, clamorously, with the insistent acclaim of a fire-alarm, the bell sounded – once! twice! thrice! Mr Phillips leaped to his feet. The tones chilled him and stirred his phlegmatic heart to quicker action. He took a long, deep breath, and, with one glance around the little room, strode out into the hall. He paused there a moment, glanced at his watch – it was four minutes to nine – then went on to his wife's apartments.

Mrs Phillips was reclining in a chair and listening with an amused smile to her son's recital of some commonplace college happening which chanced to be of interest to him. She was forty or forty-two, perhaps, and charming. Women never learn to be charming until they're forty; until then they are only pretty and amiable – sometimes. The son, Harvey Phillips, arose as his father entered. He was a stalwart young man of twenty, a prototype, as it were, of that hard-headed, masterful financier – Franklin Phillips.

"Why, Frank, I thought you were so absorbed in business that—" Mrs Phillips began.

Mr Phillips paused and looked blankly, unseeingly, as one suddenly aroused from sleep, at his wife and son – the two dearest of all earthly things to him. The son noted nothing unusual in his manner; the wife, with intuitive eyes, read some vague uneasiness.

"What is it?" she asked solicitously. "Has something gone wrong?"

Mr Phillips laughed nervously and sat down near her.

"Nothing, nothing," he assured her. "I feel unaccountably nervous somehow, and I thought I should like to talk to you rather than-than—"

"Keep on going over and over those stupid figures?" she interrupted. "Thank you."

She leaned forward with a gesture of infinite grace and took his hand. He clenched it spasmodically to stop its absurd

THE HAUNTED BELL

trembling and, with an effort all the greater because it was repressed so sternly, regained control of his panic-stricken nerves. Harvey Phillips excused himself and left the room.

"Harvey has just been explaining the mysteries of baseball to me," said Mrs Phillips. "He's going to play on the Harvard team." Her husband stared at her without the slightest heed or comprehension of what she was saying.

"Can you tell me," he asked suddenly, "where you got that Japanese gong in my room?"

"Oh, that? I saw it in the window of a queer old curio shop I pass sometimes on my charity rounds. I looked at it two or three months ago and bought it. The place is in Cranston Street. It's kept by an old German—Wagner, I think his name is. Why?"

"It looks as if it might be very old, a hundred years perhaps," remarked Mr Phillips.

"That's what I thought," responded his wife, "and the coloring is exquisite. I had never seen one exactly like it, so—"

"It doesn't happen to have any history, I suppose?" he interrupted.

"Not that I know of."

"Or any peculiar quality, or—or attribute out of the ordinary?"

Mrs Phillips shook her head.

"I'm sure I don't know what you mean," she replied. "The only peculiar quality I noticed was the singular purity of the bells and the coloring."

Mr Phillips coughed over his cigar.

"Yes, I noticed the bells myself," he explained lamely. "It just struck me that the thing was—was out of the ordinary, and I was a little curious about it." He was silent a moment. "It looks as if it might have been valuable once."

"I hardly think so," Mrs Phillips responded. "I believe thirty dollars is what I paid for it—all that was asked."

That was all that was said about the matter at the time. But on the following morning an early visitor at Wagner's shop was Franklin Phillips. It was a typical place of its kind, half curio and half junk-store, with a coat of dust over all. There had been a crude attempt to enhance the appearance of the place by an artistic arrangement of several musty antique pieces, but, otherwise, it was a chaos of all things. An aged German met Mr Phillips as he entered.

"Is this Mr Wagner?" inquired the financier.

Extreme caution, amounting almost to suspicion, seemed to be a part of the old German's business régime, for he looked at his visitor from head to foot with keen eyes, then evaded the question.

"What do you want?" he asked.

"I want to know if this is Mr Wagner," said Mr Phillips tersely. "Is it, or is it not?"

The old man met his frank stare for a moment; then his cunning, faded eyes wavered and dropped.

"I am Johann Wagner," he said humbly. "What do you want?"

"Some time ago – two or three months – you sold a Japanese gong—" Mr Phillips began.

"I never sold it!" interrupted Wagner vehemently. "I never had a Japanese gong in the place! I never sold it!"

"Of course you sold it," insisted Mr Phillips. "A Japanese gong – do you understand? Six bells on a silken cord."

"I never had such a thing in my life – never had such a thing in my shop!" declared the German excitedly. "I never sold it, so help me! I never saw it!"

Curiosity and incredulity were in Mr Phillips' eyes as he faced the old man.

"Do you happen to have any clerk?" he asked. "Or did you have three months ago?"

"No, I never had a clerk," explained the German with a violence which Mr Phillips did not understand. "There has never been anybody here but me. I never had a Japanese gong here – I never sold one! I never saw one here!"

Mr Phillips studied the aged, wrinkled face before him calmly for several seconds. He was trying vainly to account for an excitement, a vehemence which was as inexplicable as it was unnecessary.

"It's absurd to deny that you sold the bell," he said finally. "My wife bought it of you, here in this place."

"I never sold it!" stormed the German. "I never had it! No women ever came here. I don't want women here. I don't know anything about a Japanese gong. I never had one here."

Deeply puzzled and thoroughly impatient, Mr Phillips decided to forego this attempt at a casual inquiry into the history of the gong. After a little while he went away. The old German watched him cautiously, with cunning, avaricious eyes, until he stepped on a car.

As the cool, pleasant days of early spring passed on the bell held its tongue. Only once, and that was immediately after his visit to the old German's shop, did Mr Phillips refer to it again. Then he inquired casually of his wife if she had bought it of the old man in person, and she answered in the affirmative, describing him. Then the question came to him: Why had Wagner absolutely denied all knowledge of the bell, of its having been in his possession and of having sold it?

But, after a time, this question was lost in vital business affairs which engrossed his attention. The gong still hung over his desk and he occasionally glanced at it. At such times his curiosity was keen, poignant even, but he made no further effort to solve the mystery which seemed to enshroud it.

So, until one evening a wealthy young Japanese gentleman, Oku Matsumi, by name, son of a distinguished nobleman in his country's diplomatic service, came to dinner at the Phillips' home as the guest of Harvey Phillips. They were classmates in Harvard, and a friendship had grown up between them which was curious, perhaps, but explainable on the ground of a mutual interest in art.

After dinner Mr Matsumi expressed his admiration for several pictures which hung in the luxurious dining-room, and so it followed naturally that Mr Phillips exhibited some other rare works of art. One of these pictures, a Da Vinci, hung in the little room where the gong was. With no thought of that, at the moment, Mr Phillips led the way in and the Japanese followed.

Then a peculiar thing happened. At sight of the gong Mr Matsumi seemed amazed, startled, and, taking one step toward it, he bent as if in obeisance. At the same time his right hand was thrust outward and upward as if describing some symbol in the air.

...Utter silence! A suppliant throng, bowed in awed humility with hands outstretched, palms downward, and yellow faces turned in mute prayer toward the light which fluttered up feebly from the sacred fire upon the stony, leering countenance of Buddha. The gigantic golden image rose cross-legged from its pedestal and receded upward and backward into the gloom of the temple. The multitude shaded off from bold outlines within the glow of the fire to a shadowy, impalpable mass in the remotest corners; hushed of breath, immovably staring into the drooping eyes of their graven-god.

Behind the image was a protecting veil of cloth of gold. Presently there came a murmer, and the suppliants, with one accord, prostrated themselves until their heads touched the bare, cold stones of the temple floor. The murmur grew into the weirdly beautiful chant of the priests of Buddha. The flickering light for an instant gave an appearance of life to the heavy-lidded, drooping eyes, then it steadied again and they seemed fixed on the urn wherein the fire burned.

After a moment the curtain of gold was thrust aside in three places simultaneously, and three silken-robed priests appeared.

Each bore in his hand a golden sceptre. Together they approached the sacred fire and together they thrust the sceptres into it. Instantly a blaze spouted up, illuminating the vast, high-roofed palace of worship, and a cloud of incense arose. The sweetly sickening odor spread out, fanlike, over the throng.

The three priests turned away from the urn, and each, with slow, solemn tread, made his way to an altar of incense with the flaming torch held aloft. They met again at the feet of Buddha and prostrated themselves, at the same time extending the right hand and forming some symbol in the air. The chant from behind the golden veil softened to a murmur, and the murmur grew into silence. Then:

"Gautama!"

The name came from the three together – the tone was a prayer. It reverberated for an instant in the recesses of the great temple; then the multitude, with one motion, raised themselves, repeated the single word and groveled again on their faces.

"Siddhartha, Beloved!"

Again the three priests spoke and again the supplicants moved as one, repeating the words. The burning incense grew heavy, the sacred fire flickered, and shadows flitted elusively over the golden, graven face of the Buddha.

"Sayka-muni, Son of Heaven!"

The moving of the multitude as it swayed and answered was in perfect accord. It was as if one heart, one soul, one thought had inspired the action.

"O Buddha! Wise One! Enlightened One!" came the voices of the priests again. "Oh, Son of Kapilavastu! Chosen One! Holy One who found Nirvana! Your unworthy people are at your feet. Omnipotent One! We seek your gracious counsel!"

The voices in chorus had risen to a chant. When they ceased there was the chill of suspense; a little shiver ran through the temple; there was a hushed movement of terrified anxiety. Of all the throng only the priests dared raise their eyes to the cold, graven face of the image. For an instant the chilling silence; then boldly, vibrantly, a bell sounded – once!

"Buddah has spoken!"

It was a murmurous whisper, almost a sigh, plaintive, awestricken. The note of the bell trembled on the incense-laden air, then was dissipated, welded into silence again. Priests and people were cowering on the bare stones; the lights flared up suddenly, then flickered, and the semi-gloom seemed to grow sensibly deeper. Behind the veil of gold the chant of the priests began again. But it was a more solemn note – a despairing wail. For a short time it went on, then died away.

Again the sacred fire blazed up as if caught by a gust of wind, but the glow did not light the Buddha's face now – it was concentrated on a bronze gong which dropped down sheerly on a silken cord at Buddha's right hand. There were six discs, the largest at the top, silhouetted against the darkness of the golden veil beyond. From one of these bells the sound had come, but now they hung mute and motionless. Only the three priests raised reverential eyes to it, and one, the eldest rose.

"O Voice of Buddha!" he apostrophized in a moving, swinging chant – and the face of the graven – god seemed swallowed up in the shadows – "we, your unworthy disciples, await! Each year at the eleventh festival we supplicate! But thrice only hast thou spoken in the half-century, and thrice within the eleventh day of your speaking our Emperor has passed into the arms of Death and Nirvana. Shall it again be so, Omnipotent One?"

The chant died away and the multitude raised itself to its knees with supplicating hands thrust out into the darkness toward the dim-lit gong. It was an attitude of beseeching, of prayer, of entreaty.

And again, as it hung motionless, the bell sounded. The tone rolled out melodiously, clearly – Once! Twice! Thrice! Those who gazed at the miracle lowered their eyes lest they be stricken blind. And the bell struck on – Four! Five! Six! A plaintive, wailing cry was raised; the priests behind the veil of gold were chanting again. Seven! Eight! Nine! The people took up the rolling chant as they groveled, and it swelled until the ancient walls of the temple trembled. Ten! Eleven!

Utter silence! A supplicant throng, bowed in awed humility, with hands outstretched, palms downward, and yellow faces turned in mute prayer toward the light which fluttered up feebly from the sacred fire upon the stony, leering countenance of Buddha!...

Mr Matsumi straightened up suddenly to find his host staring at him in perturbed amazement.

"Why did you do that?" Mr Phillips blurted uneasily.

"Pardon me, but you wouldn't understand if I told you," replied the Japanese with calm, inscrutable face. "May I examine it, please?" And he indicated the silent and motionless gong.

"Certainly," replied the financier wonderingly.

Mr Matsumi, with a certain eagerness which was not lost upon the American, approached the gong and touched the bells lightly, one after another, evidently to get the tone. Then he stooped and examined them carefully – top and bottom. Inside the largest bell – that at the top – he found something which interested him. After a close scrutiny he again straightened up, and in his slant eyes was an expression which Mr Phillips would have liked to interpret.

"I presume you have seen it before?" he ventured.

"No, never," was the reply.

"But you recognized it!"

Mr Matsumi merely shrugged his shoulders.

"And what made you do that?" By "that" Mr Phillips referred to Mr Matsumi's strange act when he first saw the bell.

Again the Japanese shrugged his shoulders. An exquisite, innate courtesy which belonged to him was apparently forgotten now in contemplation of the gong. The financier gnawed at his mustache. He was beginning to feel nervous – the nervousness he had felt previously, and his imagination ran riot.

"You have not had the gong long?" remarked Mr Matsumi after a pause.

"Three or four months."

"Have you ever noticed anything peculiar about it?"

Mr Phillips stared at him frankly.

"Well, rather!" he said at last, in a tone which was perfectly convincing.

"It rings, you mean – the fifth bell?"

Mr Phillips nodded. There was a tense eagerness in the manner of the Japanese.

"You have never heard the bell ring eleven times?"

Mr Phillips shook his head. Mr Matsumi drew a long breath – whether it was relief the other couldn't say. There was silence. Mr Matsumi closed and unclosed his small hands several times.

"Pardon me for mentioning the matter under such circumstances," he said at last, in a tone which suggested that he feared giving offence, "but would you be willing to part with the gong?"

Mr Phillips regarded him keenly. He was seeking in the other's manner some inkling to a solution of a mystery which each moment seemed more hopelessly beyond him.

"I shouldn't care to part with it," he replied casually. "It was given to me by my wife."

"Then no offer I might make would be considered?"

"No, certainly not," replied Mr Phillips tartly. There was a pause. "This gong has interested me immensely. I should like to know its history. Perhaps you can enlighten me?"

THE HAUNTED BELL

With the imperturbability of his race, Mr Matsumi declined to give any information. But, with a graceful return of his former exquisite courtesy, he sought more definite knowledge for himself.

"I will not ask you to part with the gong," he said, "but perhaps you can inform me where your wife bought it?" He paused for a moment. "Perhaps it would be possible to get another like it?"

"I happen to know there isn't another," replied Mr Phillips. "It came from a little curio shop in Cranston Street, kept by a German named Johann Wagner."

And that was all. This incident passed as the other had, the net result being only further to stimulate Mr Phillips' curiosity. It seemed a futile curiosity, yet it was ever present, despite the fact that the gong still hung silent.

On the next evening, a balmy, ideal night of spring, Mr Phillips had occasion to go into the small room. This was just before dinner was announced. It was rather close there, so he opened the east window to a grateful breeze, and placed the screen in position, after which he stooped to pull out a drawer of his desk. Then came again the quick, clangorous boom of the bell – One! Two! Three! Four! Five! Six! Seven!

At the first stroke he straightened up; at the second he leaned forward toward the gong with his eyes riveted to the fifth disc. As it continued to ring he grimly held on to jangling nerves and looked for the cause. Beneath the bells, on top, all around them he sought. There was nothing! nothing! The sounds simply burst out, one after another, as if from a heavy blow, yet the bell did not move. For the seventh time it struck, and then with white, ghastly face and chilled, stiff limbs Mr Phillips rushed out of the room. A dew of perspiration grew in the palms of his quavering hands.

It was a night of little rest and strange dreams for him. At breakfast on the following morning Mrs Phillips poured his coffee and then glanced through the mail which had been placed beside her.

"Do you particularly care for that gong in your room?" she inquired.

Mr Phillips started a little. That particular object had enchained his attention for the last dozen hours, awake and asleep.

"Why?" he asked.

"You know I told you I bought it of a curio dealer," Mrs Phillips explained. "His name is Johann Wagner, and he offers me five hundred dollars if I will sell it back to him. I presume he has found it is more valuable than he imagined, and the five hundred dollars would make a comfortable addition to my charity fund."

Mr Phillips was deeply thoughtful. Johann Wagner! What was this new twist? Why had Wagner denied all knowledge of the gong to him? Having denied, why should he now make an attempt to buy it back? In seeking answers to these questions he was silent.

"Well, dear?" inquired his wife after a pause. "You didn't answer me."

"No, don't sell the gong," he exclaimed abruptly. "Don't sell it at any price. I – I want it. I'll give you a cheque for your charity."

There was something of uneasiness in her devoted eyes. Some strange, subtle, indefinable air which she could not fathom was in his manner. With a little sigh which breathed her unrest she finished her breakfast.

On the following morning still another letter came from Johann Wagner. It was an appeal – an impassioned appeal – hurriedly scrawled and almost incoherent in form. He must have the gong! He would give five thousand dollars for it. Mrs Phillips was frankly bewildered at the letter, and turned it over to her husband. He read it through twice with grimly-set teeth.

"No," he exclaimed violently; "it sha'n't be sold for any price!" Then his voice dropped as he recollected himself. "No, my dear," he continued, "it shall not be sold. It was a present from you to me. I want it, but" – and he smiled whimsically – "if he keeps raising the price it will add a great deal to your charity fund, won't it?"

Twice again within thirty-six hours Mr Phillips heard the bell ring—once on one occasion and four on the other. And now visibly, tangibly, a great change was upon him. The healthy glow went from his face. There was a constant twitching of his hands; a continual, impatient snapping of his fingers. His eyes lost their steady gaze. They roved aimlessly, and one's impression always was that he was listening. The strength of the master spirit was being slowly destroyed, eaten up by a hideous gnawing thing of which he seemed hopelessly obsessed. But he took no one into his confidence; it was his own private affair to work out to the end.

This condition was upon him at a time when the activity of the speculative centres of the world was abnormal, and when every faculty was needed in the great financial schemes of which he was the centre. He, in person, held the strings which guided millions. The importance of his business affairs was so insistently and relentlessly thrust upon him that he was compelled to meet them. But the effort was a desperate one, and that night late, when a city slept around him, the bell sounded twice.

When he reached his downtown office next day an enormous amount of detail work lay before him, and he attacked it with a feverish exaltation which followed upon days and nights of restlessness. He had been at his desk only a few minutes when his private telephone clattered. With an exclamation he arose; comprehending, he sat down again.

Half-a-dozen times within the hour the bell rang, and each time he was startled. Finally he arose in a passion, tore the desk-telephone from its connecting wires and flung it into the waste-basket. Deliberately he walked around to the side of his desk and, with a well-directed kick, smashed the battery-box. His secretary regarded him in amazement.

"Mr Camp," directed the financier sharply, "please instruct the office operator not to ring another telephone-bell in this office – ever."

The secretary went out and he sat down to work again. Late that afternoon he called on his family physician, Doctor Perdue, a robust individual of whom it was said that his laugh cured more patients than his medicine. Be that as it may, he was a successful man, high in his profession. Doctor Perdue looked up with frank interest as he entered.

"Hello, Phillips!" was his greeting. "What can I do for you?"

"Nerves," was the laconic answer.

"I thought it would come to that," remarked the physician, and he shook his head sagely. "Too much work, too much worry and too many cigars; and besides, you're not so young as you once were."

"It isn't work or cigars," Phillips replied impatiently. "It's worry – worry because of some peculiar circumstances which – which—"

He paused with a certain childish feeling of shame, of cowardice. Doctor Perdue regarded him keenly and felt of his pulse.

"What peculiar circumstances?" he demanded.

"Well, I – I can hardly explain it myself," replied Mr Phillips, between tightly-clenched teeth. "It's intangible, unreal, ghostly – what you will. Perhaps I can best make you understand it by saying that I'm always – I always seem to be waiting for something."

Doctor Perdue laughed heartily; Mr Phillips glared at him.

"Most of us are always waiting for something," said the physician. "If we got it there wouldn't be any particular object in life. Just what sort of thing is it you're always waiting for?"

Mr Phillips arose suddenly and paced the length of the room twice. His under jaw was thrust out a little, his teeth crushed together, but in his eyes lay a haunting, furtive fear.

"I'm always waiting for a – for a bell," he blurted fiercely, and his face became scarlet. "I know it's absurd, but I awake in the night trembling, and lie for hours waiting, waiting, yet dreading the sound as no man ever dreaded anything in this world. At my desk I find myself straining every nerve, waiting, listening. When I talk to any one I'm always waiting, waiting, waiting! Now, right this minute, I'm waiting, waiting for it. The thing is driving me mad, man, mad! Don't you understand?"

Doctor Perdue arose with grave face and led the financier back to his seat.

"You are behaving like a child, Phillips!" he said sharply. "Sit down and tell me about it."

"Now, look here, Perdue," and Mr Phillips brought his fist down on the desk with a crash, "you must believe it – you've got to believe it! If you don't, I shall know I am mad."

"Tell me about it," urged the physician quietly.

Then haltingly, hesitatingly, the financier related the incidents as they had happened. Incipient madness, fear, terror, blazed in his eyes, and at times his pale lips quivered as a child's might. The physician listened attentively and nodded several times.

"The bell must be – must be haunted!" Mr Phillips burst out in conclusion. "There's no reasonable way to account for it. My common-sense tells me that it doesn't sound at all, and yet I know it does."

Doctor Perdue was silent for several minutes.

"You know, of course, that your wife did buy the bell of the old German?" he asked after a while.

"Why, certainly, I know it. It's proved absolutely by the letters he writes trying to get it back."

"And your fear doesn't come from anything the Japanese said?"

"It isn't the denial of the German; it isn't the childish things Mr Matsumi said and did; it's the actual sound of the bell that's driving me insane – it's the hopeless, everlasting, eternal groping for a reason. It's an inanimate thing and it acts as if – it acts as if it were alive!"

The physician had been sitting with his fingers on Mr Phillips' wrist. Now he arose and mixed a quieting potion which the other swallowed at a gulp. Soon after his patient went home somewhat more self-possessed, and with rigid instructions as to the regularity of his life and habits.

"You need about six months in Europe more than anything else," Doctor Perdue declared. "Take three weeks, shape up your business and go. Meanwhile, if you won't sell the gong or throw it away, keep out of its reach."

Next morning a man – a stranger was found dead in the small room where the gong hung. A bullet through the heart showed the manner of death. The door leading from the room into the hall was locked on the outside; an open window facing east indicated how he had entered and suggested a possible avenue of escape for his slayer.

Attracted by the excitement which followed the discovery of the body, Mr and Mrs Phillips went to investigate, and thus saw the dead man. The wife entered the room first, and for an instant stood speechless, staring into the white, upturned face. Then came an exclamation.

"Why, it's the man from whom I bought the gong!" She turned to find her husband peering over her shoulder. His face was ashen to the lips, his eyes wide and staring.

"Johann Wagner!" he exclaimed.

Then, as if frenzied, he flung her aside and rushed to where the gong hung silent and motionless. He seemed bent on destruction as he reached for it with gripping fingers. Suddenly he staggered as if from a heavy blow in the face, and covered both eyes with his hands.

"Look!" he screamed.

There was a smudge of fresh, red blood on the fifth bell. Mrs Phillips glanced from the bell to him inquiringly.

He stood for a moment with hands pressed to his eyes, then laughed mirthlessly, demoniacally.

II

Here a small brazier spouting a blue flame, there a retort partially filled with some purplish, foul-smelling liquid, yonder a sinuous copper coil winding off into the shadows, and moving about like an alchemist of old, the slender, childlike figure of Professor Augustus S. F. X. Van Dusen, Ph.D., LL.D., F.R.S., M.D., etc., etc. A ray of light shot down blindingly from a reflector above and brilliantly illuminated the laboratory table. The worker leaned forward to peer at some minute particle under the microscope, and for an instant his head and face were thrown out against the darkness of the room like some grotesque, disembodied thing.

It was a singular head and face – a head out of all proportion to body, domelike, enormous, with a wilderness of straw-yellow hair. The face was small, wizened, petulant even; the watery blue eyes, narrow almost to the disappearing point, squinted everlastingly through thick spectacles; the mouth drooped at the corners. The small, white hands which twisted and turned the object-glass into focus were possessed of extraordinarily long, slender fingers.

This man of the large head and small body was the undisputed leader in contemporaneous science. His was the sanest, coldest, clearest brain in scientific achievement. His word was the final one. Once upon a time a newspaperman, Hutchinson Hatch, had dubbed him The Thinking Machine, and so it came about that the world at large had heard of and knew him by that title. The reporter, a tall, slender young man, sat now watching him curiously and listening. The scientist spoke in a tone of perpetual annoyance; but a long acquaintance had taught the reporter that it was what he said and not the manner of its saying that was to be heeded.

"Imagination, Mr Hatch, is the single connecting link between man and the infinite," The Thinking Machine was saying. "It is the one quality which distinguishes us from what we are pleased to call the brute creation, for we have the same passions, the same appetites, and the same desires. It is the most valuable adjunct to the scientific mind, because it is the basis of all scientific progress. It is the thing which temporarily bridges gaps and makes it possible to solve all material problems – not some, but all of them. We can achieve nothing until we imagine it. Just so far as the human brain can imagine it can comprehend. It fails only to comprehend the eternal purpose, the Omnipotent Will, because it cannot imagine it. For imagination has a limit, Mr Hatch, and beyond that we are not to go — beyond that is Divinity."

This wasn't at all what Hatch had come to hear, but he listened with a sort of fascination.

"The first intelligent being," the irritated voice went on, "had to imagine that when two were added to two there would be a result. He found it was four, he proved it was four, and instantly it became immutable – a point in logic, a thing by which we may solve problems. Thus two and two make four, not sometimes, but all the time."

"I had always supposed that imagination was limitless," Hatch ventured for a moment, "that it knows no bounds."

The Thinking Machine squinted at him coldly.

"On the contrary," he declared, "it has a boundary beyond which the mind of man merely reels, staggers, collapses. I'll take you there." He spoke as if it were just around the corner. "By aid of a microscope of far less power than the one there, the atomic or molecular theory was formulated. You know that –

it is that all matter is composed of atoms. Now, imagination suggested and logic immutably demonstrates that the atoms themselves are composed of other atoms, and that those atoms in turn are composed of still others, ad infinitum. They are merely invisible, and imagination — I am not now stating a belief, but citing an example of what imagination can do — imagination can make us see the possibility of each of those atoms, down to infinity, being inhabited, being in itself a world relatively as distant from its fellows as we are from the moon. We can even imagine what those inhabitants would look like."

He paused a minute; Hatch blinked several times.

"But the boundary lies the other way — through the telescope," continued the scientist. "The most powerful glass ever devised has brought no suggestion of the end of the universe. It only brings more millions of worlds, invisible to the naked eye into sight. The stronger the glass, the more hopeless the task of even conjecturing the end, and here, too, the imagination can apply the atomic theory, and logic will support it. In other words, atoms make matter, matter makes the world, which is an inconceivably tiny speck in our solar system, an atom; therefore, all the millions and millions of worlds are mere atoms, infinitesimal parts of some far greater scheme. What greater scheme? There is the end of imagination! There the mind stops!"

The immensity of the conception made Hatch gasp a little. He sat silent for a long time, awed, oppressed. Never before in his life had he felt of so little consequence.

"Now, Mr Hatch, as to this little problem that is annoying you," continued The Thinking Machine, and the matter-of-fact tone was a great relief. "What I have said has had, of course, no bearing on it, except in so far as it demonstrates that imagination is necessary to solve a problem, that all material problems may be solved, and that, in meeting them, logic is the lever. It is a fixed quantity; its simplest rules have enabled me to solve petty affairs for you in the past, so—"

The reporter came to himself with a start. Then he laid before this master brain the circumstances which cast so strange a mystery about the death by violence of Johann Wagner, junk-dealer, in the home of Franklin Phillips, millionaire. But his information was only from the time the police came into the affair. Mr Phillips, Doctor Perdue and Mr Matsumi alone knew of the ringing of the bell.

"The blood-spot on one of the bells," Hatch told the scientist in conclusion, "may be the mark of a hand, but its significance doesn't appear. Just now the police are working on two queer points which they developed. First, Detective Mallory recognized the dead man as 'Old Dutch' Wagner, long suspected of conducting a 'fence' – that is, receiving and disposing of stolen goods; and second, one of the servants in the Phillips' household, Giles Francis, has disappeared. He hasn't been seen since eleven o'clock on the night before the body was found, and then he was in bed sound asleep. Every article of his clothing, except a pair of shoes, trousers, and pajamas, was left behind."

The Thinking Machine turned away from the laboratory table and sank into a chair. For a long time he sat with his enormous yellow head thrown back and his slender, white fingers pressed tip to tip.

"If Wagner was shot through the heart," he said at last, "we know that death was instantaneous; therefore he could not have made the blood-mark on the bell." It seemed to be a statement of fact. "But why should there be such a mark on the bell?"

"Detective Mallory thinks that—" began the reporter.

"Oh, never mind what he thinks!" interrupted the other testily. "What time was the body found?"

"About half-past nine yesterday morning."

"Anything stolen?"

"Nothing. The body was simply there, the window open and the door locked, and there was the blood-mark on the bell."

THE HAUNTED BELL 169

There was a pause. Cobwebby lines appeared on the broad forehead of the scientist and the squint eyes narrowed down to mere slits. Hatch was watching him curiously.

"What does Mr Phillips say about it?" asked The Thinking Machine. He was still staring upward and his thin lips were drawn into a straight line.

"He is ill, just how ill we don't know," responded the newspaper man. "Doctor Perdue has, so far, not permitted the police to question him."

The scientist lowered his eyes quickly.

"What's the matter with him?" he demanded.

"I don't know. Doctor Perdue has declined to make any statement."

Half an hour later The Thinking Machine and Hatch called at the Phillips' house. They met Doctor Perdue coming out. His face was grave and preoccupied; his professional air of jocundity was wholly absent. He shook hands with The Thinking Machine, whom he had met years before beside an operating-table, and reéntered the house with him. Together the three went to the little room-the scene of the tragedy.

The Japanese gong still swung over the desk. The crabbed little scientist went straight to it, and for five minutes devoted his undivided attention to a study of the splotch on the fifth bell. From the expression of his face Hatch could gather nothing. What the scientist saw might or might not have been illuminating. Was the splotch the mark of a hand? If it were, Hatch argued, it offered no clew, as the intricate lines of the flesh were smeared together, obliterated.

Next The Thinking Machine critically glanced about him, and finally threw open the window facing east. For a long time he stood silently squinting out; and, save for the minute lines in his forehead, there was no indication whatever of his mental workings. The little room was on the second floor and jutted out at right angles across a narrow alley which ran beneath them to the kitchen in the back. The dead-wall of the next building was only four feet from the Phillips' wall, and was without windows, so it was easily seen how a man, unobserved, might climb up from below despite an arc-light above the wide front door of an apartment-house across the street, visible in the vista of the alley.

"Do you happen to know, Perdue," asked The Thinking Machine at last, "if this west window was ever opened?"

"Never," replied the physician. "Detective Mallory questioned the servants about it. It seems that the kitchen is beneath, somewhat to the back, and the odors of cooking came up."

"How many outside doors has this house?"

"Only two," was the reply: "the one you entered, and one opening into the alley below us."

"Both were found locked yesterday morning?"

"Yes. Both doors have spring-locks, therefore each locks itself when closed."

"Oh!" exclaimed the scientist suddenly.

He turned away from the window, and, for a second time, examined the still and silent gong. Somewhere in his mind seemed to be an inkling that the gong might be more closely associated than appeared with the mystery of death, and yet, watching him curiously, Doctor Perdue knew he could have no knowledge of the sinister part it had played in the affair. With a penknife The Thinking Machine made a slight mark on the under side of each bell in turn; then squinted at them, one after another. On the inside of the top bell – the largest – he found something – a mark, a symbol perhaps – but it seemed meaningless to Hatch and Doctor Perdue, who were peering over his shoulder.

It was merely a circle with three upward rays and three dots inside it.

"The manufacturer's mark, perhaps," Hatch suggested.

"Of course, it's impossible that the bell could have had anything to do—" Doctor Perdue began.

"Nothing is impossible, Perdue," snapped the scientist crabbedly. "Do not say that. It annoys me exceedingly." He continued to stare at the symbol. "Just where was the body found?" he asked after a little.

"Here," replied Doctor Perdue, and he indicated a spot near the window.

The Thinking Machine measured the distance with his eye.

"The only real problem here," he remarked musingly, after a moment, as if supplementing a previous statement, "is what made him lock the door and run?"

"What made-who?" Hatch asked eagerly.

The Thinking Machine merely squinted at him, through him, beyond him with glassy eyes. His thoughts seemed far away and the cobwebby lines in his forehead grew deeper. Doctor Perdue was apparently at the moment too self-absorbed to heed.

"Now, Perdue," demanded The Thinking Machine suddenly, "what is really the matter with Mr Phillips?"

"Well, it's rather—" he started haltingly, then went on as if his mind were made up: "You know, Van Dusen, there's something back of all this that hasn't been told, for reasons which I consider good ones. It might interest you, because you are keen on these things, but I doubt if it would help you. And besides, I should have to insist that you alone should hear it."

He glanced meaningly at Hatch, whom he knew to be present only in his capacity as reporter.

"There's something else – about the bell," said The Thinking Machine quickly. It was not a question, but a statement.

"Yes, about the bell," acquiesced the physician, as if a little surprised that the other should know. "But as I said it—"

"I undertook to get at the facts here to aid Mr Hatch," explained The Thinking Machine; "but I can assure you he will print nothing without my permission."

Doctor Perdue looked at the newspaperman inquiringly; Hatch nodded.

"I guess perhaps it would be better for you to hear it from Phillips himself," went on the physician. "Come along. I think he would be willing to tell you."

Thus the scientist and the reporter met Franklin Phillips. He was in bed. The once masterful financier seemed but a shadow of what he had been. His strong face was now white and haggard, and lined almost beyond recognition. The lips were pale, the hands nervously clutched at the sheet, and in his eyes was horror—hideous horror. They glittered at times, and only at intervals reflected the strength, the power which once lay there. His present condition was as pitiable as it was inexplicable to Hatch, who remembered him as the rugged storm-centre of half a dozen spectacular financial battles.

Mr Phillips talked willingly—seemed, indeed, relieved to be able to relate in detail those circumstances which, in a way, accounted for his utter collapse. As he went on volubly, yet coherently enough, his roving eyes settled on the petulant, inscrutable face of The Thinking Machine as if seeking, above all things, belief. He found it, for the scientist nodded time after time, and gradually the lines in the dome-like forehead were dissipated.

"Now I know why he ran," declared the scientist positively, enigmatically. The remark was hopelessly without meaning to the others. "As I understand it, Mr Phillips," he asked, "the east window was always open when the bell sounded?"

"Yes, I believe it was, always," replied Mr Phillips after a moment's thought.

"And you always heard it when the window was open?"

"Oh, no," replied the financier. "There were many times when the window was open that I didn't hear anything."

A fleeting bewilderment crossed the scientist's face, then was gone.

"Of course, of course," he said after a moment. "Stupid of me. I should have known that. Now, the first time you ever noticed it the bell rang twice – that is, twice with an interval of, say, a few seconds between?"

"Yes."

"And you had had the gong, then, two or three months?"

"About three months – yes."

"The weather remained cool during that time? Late winter and early spring?"

"I presume so. I don't recall. I know the first time I heard the bell was an early, warm day of spring, because my window had not previously been opened."

The Thinking Machine was dreamily squinting upward. As he stared into the quiet, narrow eyes a certain measure of confidence seemed to return to Mr Phillips. He raised himself on an elbow.

"You say that once you heard the bell ring late at night — twice. What were the circumstances?"

"That was the night preceding a day of some important operations I had planned," explained Mr Phillips, "and I was in the little room for a long time after midnight going over some figures."

"Do you remember the date?"

"Perfectly. It was Tuesday, the eleventh of this month," – and, for an instant, memory called to Mr Phillips' face an expression which financial foes know well. "I remember, because next day I forced the market up to a record price on some railway stocks I control."

The Thinking Machine nodded.

"This servant of yours who is missing, Francis, was rather a timid sort of man, I imagine."

"Well, I could hardly say," replied Mr Phillips doubtfully.

"Well, he was," declared The Thinking Machine flatly. "He was a good servant, I dare say?"

"Yes, excellent."

"Would it have been within his duties to close a window which might have been left open at night?"

"Certainly."

"Rather a big man?"

"Yes, six feet or so – two hundred and ten pounds, perhaps."

"And Mr Matsumi was, of course, small?"

"Yes, small even for a Japanese."

The Thinking Machine arose and placed his fingers on Mr Phillips' wrist. He stood thus for half a minute.

"Did you ever notice any odor after the bell rang?" he inquired at last.

"Odor?" Mr Phillips seemed puzzled. "Why, I don't see what an odor would have to do—"

"I didn't expect you to," interrupted The Thinking Machine crustily. "I merely want to know if you noticed one."

"No," retorted Mr Phillips shortly.

"And could you explain your precise feelings?" continued the scientist. "Did the effect of the bell's ringing seem to be entirely mental, or was it physical? In other words, was there any physical exaltation or depression when you heard it?"

"It would be rather difficult to say – even to myself," responded Mr Phillips. "It always seemed to be a shock, but I suppose it was really a mental condition which reacted on my nerves."

The Thinking Machine walked over to the window and stood with his back to the others. For a minute or more he remained there, and three eager pairs of eyes were fixed inquiringly on the back of his yellow head. Beneath the irritated voice, behind the inscrutable face, in the disjointed questioning, they all knew intuitively there was some definite purpose, but to none came a glimmer of light as to its nature.

"I think, perhaps, the matter is all clear now," he remarked musingly at last. "There are two vital questions yet to be answered. If the first of these is answered in the affirmative,

I know that a mind – I may say a Japanese mind – of singular ingenious quality conceived the condition which brought about this affair; if in the negative, the entire matter becomes ridiculously simple."

Mr Phillips was leaning forward, listening greedily. There was hope and fear, doubt and confidence, eagerness and a certain tense restraint in his manner. Doctor Perdue was silent; Hatch merely waited.

"What made the bell ring?" demanded Mr Phillips.

"I must find the answer to the two remaining questions first," returned The Thinking Machine.

"You mentioned a Japanese," said Mr Phillips. "Do you suspect Mr Matsumi of any connection with the – the mystery?"

"I never suspect persons of things, Mr Phillips," said The Thinking Machine curtly. "I never suspect – I always know. When I know in this case I shall inform you. Mr Hatch and I are going out for a few minutes. When we return the matter can be disposed of in ten minutes."

He led the way out and along the hall to the little room where the gong hung. Hatch closed the door as he entered. Then for the third time the scientist examined the bells. He struck the fifth violently time after time, and after each stroke he thrust an inquisitive nose almost against it and sniffed. Hatch stared at him in wonderment. When the scientist had finished he shook his head as if answering a question in the negative. With Hatch following he passed out into the street.

"What's the matter with Phillips?" the reporter ventured, as they reached the sidewalk.

"Scared, frightened," was the tart rejoinder. "He's merely morbidly anxious to account for the bell's ringing. If I had been absolutely certain before I came out I should have told him. I am certain now. You know, Mr Hatch, when a thing is beyond immediate understanding it instantly suggests the supernatural to some minds. Mr Phillips wouldn't confess it, but he sees back of the ringing of that bell some uncanny power – a threat, perhaps – and the thing has preyed upon him until he's nearly insane. When I can arrange to make him understand perfectly why the bell rings he will be all right again."

"I can readily see how the ringing of the bell strikes one as uncanny," Hatch declared grimly. "Have you an idea what causes it?"

"I know what causes it," returned the other irritably. "And if you don't know you're stupid."

The reporter shook his head hopelessly.

They crossed the street to the big apartment – house opposite, and entered. The Thinking Machine inquired for and was shown into the office of the manager. He had only one question.

"Was there a ball, or reception, or anything of that sort held in this building on Tuesday night, the eleventh of this month?" he inquired.

"No," was the response. "There has never been anything of that sort here."

"Thanks," said The Thinking Machine. "Goodday."

Turning abruptly he left the manager to figure that out as best he could, and, with Hatch following, ascended the stairs to the next floor. Here was a wide, airy hallway extending the full length of the building. The Thinking Machine glanced neither to right nor left; he went straight to the rear, where a plate-glass window enframed a panorama of the city. From where they stood the city's roofs slanted down toward the heart of the business district, half a mile away.

As Hatch looked on The Thinking Machine took out his watch and set it two and a half minutes forward, after which he turned and walked to the other end of the hall. Here, too, was a plate-glass window. For just a fraction of an instant he stood staring straight out at the Phillips' home across the way; then, without a word, retraced his steps down the stairs and into the street.

Hatch's head was overflowing with questions, but he choked them back and merely trailed along. They reëntered the Phillips' house in silence. Doctor Perdue and Harvey Phillips met them in the hallway. An expression of infinite relief came into the physician's face at the sight of The Thinking Machine.

"I'm glad you're back so soon," he said quickly. "Here's a new development and a singular one." He referred evidently to a long envelope he held. "Step into the library here."

They entered, and Doctor Perdue carefully closed the door behind them.

"Just a few minutes ago Harvey received a sealed envelope by mail," he explained. "It inclosed this one, also sealed. He was going to show it to his father, but I didn't think it wise because of – because —"

The Thinking Machine took the envelope in one slender hand and examined it. It was a perfectly plain white one, and bore only a single line written in a small, copper-plate hand with occasional unexpected angles:

"To be opened when the fifth bell rings eleven times."

Something as nearly approaching complacent satisfaction as Hatch had ever seen overspread the petulant countenance of The Thinking Machine, and a long, aspirated "Ah!" escaped the thin lips. There was a hushed silence. Harvey Phillips, to whom nothing of the mystery was known beyond the actual death of Wagner, sought to read what it all meant in Doctor Perdue's face. In turn Doctor Perdue's eyes were fastened on The Thinking Machine.

"Of course, you don't know whom this is from, Mr Phillips?" inquired the scientist of the young man.

"I have no idea," was the reply. "It seemed to amaze Doctor Perdue here, but, frankly, I can't imagine why."

"You don't know the handwriting?"

"No."

"Well, I do," declared The Thinking Machine emphatically. "It's Mr Matsumi's." He glared at the physician. "And in it lies the key to this affair of the bell. The mere fact that it came at all proves everything as I saw it."

"But it can't be from Matsumi," protested the young man. "The postmark on the outside was Cleveland."

"That means merely that he is running away to escape arrest on a charge of murder."

"Then Matsumi killed Wagner?" Hatch asked quickly.

"I didn't say it was a confession," responded the scientist curtly. "It is merely a history of the bell. I dare say—"

Suddenly the door was thrown open and Mrs Phillips entered. Her face was ashen.

"Doctor, he is worse-sinking rapidly!" she gasped. "Please come!"

Doctor Perdue glanced from her pallid face to the impassive Thinking Machine.

"Van Dusen," he said solemnly, "if you can do anything to explain this thing, do it now. I know it will save a man's reason – it might save his life."

"Is he conscious?" inquired the scientist of Mrs Phillips.

"No, he seems to have utterly collapsed," she explained. "I was talking to him when suddenly he sat up in bed as if listening, then shrieked something I didn't understand and fell back unconscious."

Doctor Perdue was dragged out of the room by the wife and son. The Thinking Machine glanced at his watch. It was three and a half minutes past four o'clock. He nodded, then turned to Hatch.

"Please go into the little room and close the window," he instructed. "Mr Phillips has heard the bell again, and I imagine Doctor Perdue needs me. Meanwhile, put this envelope in your pocket." And he handed to Hatch the mysterious sealed packet.

It was twenty minutes past nine o'clock that evening. In the little room where the gong hung were Franklin Phillips, pale and weak, but eager; Doctor Perdue, The Thinking Machine, Harvey Phillips and Hatch. For four hours Doctor Perdue and the scientist had labored over the unconscious financier, and finally a tinge of color returned to the pale lips; then came consciousness.

"It was my suggestion, Mr Phillips, that we are here," explained The Thinking Machine quietly. "I want to show you just why and how the bell rings, and incidentally clear up the other points of the mystery. Now, if I should tell you that the bell will sound a given number of times at a given instant, and it should sound, you would know that I was aware of the cause?"

"Certainly," assented Mr Phillips eagerly.

"And then if I demonstrated tangibly how it sounded you would be satisfied?"

"Yes, of course – yes."

"Very good." And the scientist turned to the reporter: "Mr Hatch, 'phone the Weather Bureau and ask if there was a storm about midnight preceding the finding of Wagner's body; also if there was thunder. And get the direction and velocity of the wind. I know, of course, that there was thunder, and that the wind was either from the east, or there was no wind. I know it, not from personal observation, but by the pure logic of events."

The reporter nodded.

"Also I will have to ask you to borrow for me somewhere a violin and a champagne-glass."

There happened to be a violin in the house. Harvey Phillips went for it, and Hatch went to the 'phone. Five minutes later he reappeared; Harvey Phillips had preceded him.

"Light wind from the east, four miles an hour," Hatch reported tersely. "The storm threatened just before midnight. There was vivid lightning and heavy thunder."

To prosaic Doctor Perdue these preliminaries smacked a little of charlatanry. Mr Phillips was interested, but impatient.

The Thinking Machine, watch in hand, lay back in his chair, squinting steadily upward.

"Now, Mr Phillips," he announced, "in just thirty-three and three-quarter minutes the bell will ring. It will sound ten times. I am taking pains to reproduce the exact conditions under which the bell has always sounded since you have known it, because if I show you there can be no doubt."

Mr Phillips was leaning forward, gripping the arms of his chair.

"Meanwhile, I will reconstruct the events, not as they might have happened, but as they must have happened," continued The Thinking Machine. "They will not be in sequence, but as they were revealed to me by each added fact, for logic, Mr Phillips, is only a sum in arithmetic, and the answer based on every known fact must be correct as inevitably as that two and two make four—not sometimes, but all the time.

"Well, a man was found dead here—shot. His mere presence indicated burglary. The open window showed how he probably entered. Considering only these superficial facts, we see instantly that more than one person might have entered that window. Yet it is hardly likely that two thieves entered, and one killed the other before they got their booty, for nothing was stolen, and it is still less likely that one man came here to commit suicide. What then?

"The blood mark on the bell. It was made by a human hand. Yet a man shot instantly dead could not have made it. Therefore we know there was another person. The door locked on the outside absolutely confirmed this. Ordinarily, I dare say, the door is never locked? No? Then who locked it? Certainly not a second thief, for he would not have risked escaping through the house after a shot which, for all he knew, had aroused every one. Ergo, some one in the house locked the door. Who?

"One of your servants, Giles Francis, is missing. Did he hear some one in the room? No, for he would have alarmed the household. What happened to him? Where is he? There is, of course, a chance that he ran out to find an officer and was disposed of in some way by an outside confederate of the man inside. But remember, please, the last we know of him he was asleep in bed. The vital point, therefore, is, what aroused him? From that we can easily develop his subsequent actions."

The Thinking Machine paused and glanced casually at his watch, then toward the east window, which was open with the screen in.

"We know," he resumed, "that if Francis had been aroused by burglars, or by a sound which he attributed to burglars, he would have awakened other servants. We must suppose he was awakened by some noise. What is most probable? Thunder! That would account for his every act. So let's say for the moment that it was thunder, that he remembered this window was open, partially dressed himself and came here to close it. This was, we will also presume, just before midnight. He met Wagner here, and in some way got Wagner's revolver. Then the fatal shot was fired.

"From this point, as the facts developed, Francis' acts became more difficult of comprehension. I could readily see how, when Wagner fell, Francis might have placed his hand over the heart to see if he were dead, and thus stained his hands; but why did Francis then smear blood on the fifth bell of the gong, leave this room, locking the door behind him, and run into the street? In other words, why did he lock the door and run?

"I had already attached considerable importance to the gong, primarily because of the blood, and had examined the bells closely. I even scratched them to assure myself that they were bronze and not a precious metal which would attract thieves. Then, Mr Phillips, I heard your story, and instantly I knew why Francis locked the door and ran. It was because he was frightened—horribly, unspeakably frightened. Naturally there was a nerve-racking shock when he found he had killed a man. Then as he stood, horror-stricken perhaps, the bell rang. It affected him as it did you, Mr Phillips, but under circumstances which were inconceivably more terrifying to a timid man. The bell rang six, seven, eight – perhaps a dozen times. To Francis, looking down upon a man he had killed, it was maddening, inexplicable. He placed his hand on it to stop the sound, then, crazed with terror, ran out of the room, locking the door behind him, and out of the house. The outer door closed with a spring-lock. He will return in time, because, of course, he was justified in killing Wagner."

Again The Thinking Machine glanced at his watch. Eighteen minutes of the specified thirty-three had elapsed.

"Now, as to the bell itself," he went on, "its history is of no consequence. It's Japanese and we know it's extremely old. We must assume from Mr Matsumi's conduct that it is an object of – of, say, veneration. We can imagine it hanging in a temple; perhaps it rang there, and awed multitudes listened. Perhaps they regarded it as prophetic. After its disappearance from Japan – we don't know how – Mr Matsumi was naturally amazed to see it here, and was anxious to buy it. You refused to listen to him, Mr Phillips. Then he went to Wagner and offered, we'll say, several thousand dollars for it. That accounts for Wagner's letters and his presence here. He came to steal the thing which he couldn't buy. His denial of all knowledge of the bell is explained readily by Detective Mallory's statement that he had long been suspected of handling stolen goods. He denied because he feared a trap.

"I may add that I attributed an ingenuity of construction to the bell which it did not possess. When I asked if you ever noted any odor when it sounded, Mr Phillips, I had an idea that perhaps your present condition had been brought about by a subtle poison in which the gong had once been immersed, particles of which, when the bell sounded, might have been cast off and drawn into the lungs. I can assure you, however, that there was no poison. That is all, I think."

"But the sealed letter—" began Doctor Perdue.

"Oh, I opened that," was the casual rejoinder; but Doctor Perdue, as he looked, read a warning in the scientist's face. "It related to another matter entirely."

Doctor Perdue gazed at him a moment and understood. Unconsciously Hatch felt of the pocket where he had placed the letter. It was still there. He, too, understood. The Thinking Machine arose, glanced out of the window, then turned to the reporter.

"Now, Mr Hatch," he requested, "please go across the street to the apartment-house, and open the rear window in the hall where we were. See that it remains open for twenty minutes; then return here. Keep out of the hall while the window is open, and if possible, keep others out."

Without a word or question, Hatch went out. The Thinking Machine dropped back into his chair, glanced at his watch, then scribbled something on a card which he handed to Doctor Perdue.

"By the way," he remarked irrelevantly, "there's an excellent compound for nervous indigestion I ran across the other day."

Doctor Perdue read the card. On it was:

"Letter dangerous. Probably predicts death. Has religious significance. Would advise Phillips not be informed."

"I'll try it some time," remarked Doctor Perdue.

There was a silence of two or three minutes. The Thinking Machine was idly twirling his watch in his slender fingers; Mr Phillips sat staring at the bell, but there was no longer fright in his manner; it seemed rather curiosity.

"In just three minutes," said The Thinking Machine at last. A pause. "Now, two!" Again a pause. "Now, one! Be perfectly calm and listen!" Another pause, then suddenly: "Now!"

"Boom!" rang the bell, as if echoing the word. Despite himself, Mr Phillips started a little, and the scientist's fingers closed on his pulse. "Boom!" again came the note. The bell hung motionless; the musical clangor seemed to roll out methodically, rhythmically. Three! Four! Five! Six! Seven! Eight! Nine! Ten!

When the last note sounded, The Thinking Machine was staring into Mr Phillips' face, seeking understanding. He found only bewilderment, and with quick impatience picked up the violin and bow.

"Here!" he exclaimed curtly. "Watch the champagne glass."

He tapped the fragile glass, and it sang shrilly. Then, on the violin, he sought the accompanying chord. Four times he drew the bow across the strings, and the glass was silent. Then the violin caught the pitch and the glass, three or four feet away, sang with it. Louder and louder the violin note grew, then suddenly, with a crash, the thin receptacle collapsed, shattered, tumbled to pieces before their eyes. Mr Phillips stared in the utmost astonishment.

"A little demonstration in natural philosophy," explained The Thinking Machine. "In other words, vibration. Vibration sounded the glass, just as vibration sounded the bell on the gong there. You saw me sound the glass; the note which sounds the bell is a clock on a direct line half a mile away due east."

Mr Phillips stared first at the shattered glass, then at the scientist. After a moment he understood, and an inexpressible feeling of relief swept over him.

"But the bell didn't always sound when the window was open," objected Doctor Perdue, after a moment.

"The bell can only sound when this window and both hall windows on the second floor across the way are open – on warm nights, for instance," replied The Thinking Machine. "Then, too, the wind must be from the east, or else there must be none. A gust of air, a person passing through the hall, any one of a dozen things would interrupt the sensitive sound-waves and prevent all strokes of the clock reaching the bell here, while some of them might. Of course, any bell on the gong may be sounded with a violin, or, if they are true notes, with a piano, and I knew this at first. But Mr Phillips had once heard the bell long after midnight—say two o'clock in the morning. Pianos and violins are not going so late, except perhaps at a ball. There was no ball across the street that night; therefore we came to the obvious remainder—a clock. It is visible from the rear window of the second-floor hall over there. It's all logic, logic!"

There was a pause. Doctor Perdue, looking into the face of his patient, was reassured by what he saw there, and something of his own professional jocundity asserted itself.

"Instead of being a thing to make you nervous, Phillips," he said at last with a smile, "it seems to me that the bell is an excellent and reliable timepiece."

Mr Phillips glanced at him quickly and the drawn, white face was relieved by a slight smile. After a while Hatch returned and for some time the little party sat in the room talking over the affair. Their conversation was interrupted at last by the clangor of the bell, and every person present rose and stared at it anew with the exception of The Thinking Machine. His squint eyes were still turned upward – he didn't even alter his position. There were eleven strokes of the bell, then silence.

"Eleven o'clock," remarked The Thinking Machine placidly. "You left the windows open over there, Mr Hatch."

Hatch nodded.

Mr Phillips was in bed sleeping when Doctor Perdue and The Thinking Machine, accompanied by Hatch, went away.

"Suppose we drop in at my place and look at that letter?" suggested the doctor.

The Thinking Machine, in Doctor Perdue's office, took the sealed packet from the reporter and opened it. Doctor Perdue was peering over his shoulder. The scientist squinted down the page with inscrutable face, then crumpled up the letter, struck a match and ignited it.

"But-but—" protested Doctor Perdue quickly, and Hatch saw that some strange pallor suddenly overspread his face, "it said that – that eleven strokes meant-meant—"

"You're a fool, Perdue!" snapped The Thinking Machine, and he glared straight into the physician's eyes. "Didn't I show why and how the bell rang? Do you expect me to account for every barbaric superstition of a half-civilized race regarding the bell."

The paper burned, and The Thinking Machine crumpled up the ashes and dropped them in a waste-basket.

Two days later Franklin Phillips was himself again; on the fourth day he appeared at his office. On the sixth the market began to feel the master's clutch; on the eighth Francis was taken into custody and related a story identical with that told by The Thinking Machine to account for his disappearance; on the eleventh Franklin Phillips was found dead in bed. On his forehead was a pallid, white spot, faintly visible. It was a circle with three dots inside and three rays extending out from it.

10

PROBLEM OF THE MISSING NECKLACE

Mr Bradlee Cunnyngham Leighton was clever. His most ardent enemies admitted that. Scotland Yard, for instance, not only admitted it but insisted on it. It wasn't any half hearted insistence, either, for in the words of Herbert Conway, one of the Yard's chief operators, he was smooth—"so smooth that he made ice feel like sandpaper." Whether or not Mr Leighton was aware of this delicate compliment does not appear. It was perfectly possible that he was, although he had never mentioned it. He was a well bred gentleman and was aware of many things that he never mentioned.

In his person Mr Leighton had the distinguished honour of closely resembling the immaculate villain of melodrama. In his mental attainments, however, Scotland Yard gave him credit for being a genius—far beyond the cigarette smoking mummer of crime who is always transparent and is inevitably caught. Mr Leighton had never been caught. Perhaps that was why Scotland Yard insisted on his cleverness and was prepared to argue the point.

Mr Leighton went everywhere. At those functions where the highest in the social world met, there was Mr Leighton. He was on every matron's selected list of guests, a charming addition to any gathering. Scotland Yard knew this. Of course it may have been only the merest chance that he was always present at those functions where valuable jewels had been "lost" or "mislaid." Yet Scotland Yard did not regard it as chance. That it did not was another compliment to Mr Leighton.

From deep down in its innermost conscience Scotland Yard looked up to Mr Leighton as the master mind, if not the actual vital instrument, in a long series of baffling jewel robberies. There was a finesse and delicacy—not to mention regularity—about these robberies that annoyed Scotland Yard. Yet believing all this Scotland Yard had never been so indiscreet as to mention the matter to Mr Leighton. As a matter of fact Scotland Yard had never seen its way clear to mentioning it to anyone.

Conway had some ideas of his own about Mr Leighton whom he exalted to a position that would have surprised if not flattered him. Conway perhaps, more nearly expressed the opinion of Scotland Yard in a few brief remarks than I could at greater length.

"He's a crook and the cleverest in the world," he said of Mr Leighton, almost enthusiastically. "He got the Hemingway jewels, the Cheltenham bracelet and the Quez shiners all right. I know he got them. But that doesn't do any good – merely knowing it. I can't put a finger on him because he's too blooming smooth. I think I've got him and then – I haven't."

This was before the Varron necklace affair. When that remarkable episode came to be known to Scotland Yard Conway's admiration for Mr Leighton increased immeasurably. He knew that Leighton was the responsible one—he knew it in his own head and heart—but that was all. He gnawed his scrubby moustache fiercely and set to work to prove it, feeling beforehand that it was a vain task.

The absolute simplicity of the thing – and in this it was like the others—was its most puzzling feature. Lady Varron had tendered a reception to the United States Ambassador at her

London house. She had gathered about her a most distinguished company. There were representatives of England, France and Russia; there were some of the most beautiful women of the continent; there were two American Duchesses; there were a chosen few of the American colony – and Mr Leighton. It maybe well to repeat that he went everywhere.

Lady Varron on this occasion wore the famous Varron necklace. Its intrinsic value was said to be £40,000; associations made it priceless. She was dancing with the American Ambassador when she slipped on the smooth floor and fell, dragging him down with her. It was an undignified, unromantic thing, but it happened. Mr Leighton chanced to be one of those nearest and rushed to her assistance. In an instant Lady Varron and the Ambassador were the centre of a little group. It was Mr Leighton who lifted Lady Varron to her feet.

"It's nothing," she assured him, smiling uncertainly. "I was a little awkward, that's all."

Mr Leighton turned to assist the Ambassador but found him standing again and puffing inordinately, then turned back to Lady Varron.

"You dropped your necklace," he remarked blandly.

"My necklace?"

Lady Varron's white hand flew to her bare throat, and she paled a little as Mr Leighton and others of the group stood back to look for the jewel. It was not to be seen. Lady Varron controlled herself admirably.

"It must have fallen somewhere," she said finally.

"Are you sure you had it on?" asked another guest solicitously.

"Oh, yes," she replied positively, "but I may have dropped it somewhere else."

"I noticed it just before you – we – fell," said the Ambassador. "It must be here."

But it wasn't. In that respect – that is visible non-existence – it resembled the Cheltenham bracelet. Mr Leighton had, on that occasion, strolled out on the lawn at night with the Honourable Miss Cheltenham and she had dropped the bracelet. That was all. It was never found.

In this Varron affair it would be useless to go into details of what immediately followed the loss of the necklace. It is sufficient to say that it was not found; that men and women stared at each other in bewildered embarrassment and mutual suspicion, and that finally Mr Leighton, who still stood beside Lady Varron, intimated courteously, tactfully, that a personal search of her guests would not be amiss. He did not say it in so many words but the others understood.

Mr Leighton was seconded heartily by the American Ambassador, a Democratic individual with honest ideas which were foremost when a question of personal integrity was involved. But the search was not made and the reception proceeded. Lady Varron bore her loss marvellously well.

"She's a brick," was the audible compliment of one of the American Duchesses whose father owned $20,000,000 worth of soap somewhere in vague America. "I'd have had a fit if I'd lost a necklace like that."

It was not until next day that Scotland Yard was notified of Lady Varron's loss.

"Leighton there?" was Conway's question.

"Yes."

"Then he got it," Conway asserted positively. "I'll get him this time or know why."

Yet at the end of a month he neither had him, nor did he know why. He had intercepted messengers, he had opened letters, telegrams, cable dispatches; he had questioned servants; he had taken advantage of the absence of both Mr Leighton and his valet to search his exquisite apartments. He had done all these things and more – all that a severely conscientious man of his profession could do, and had gnawed his scrubby moustache down to a disreputable ragged line. But of the necklace there was no clue, no trace, nothing.

Then Conway heard that Mr Leighton was going to the United States for a few months.

"To take the necklace and dispose of it," he declared out of the vexation of his own heart. "If he ever gets aboard ship with it I've got him – either I've got him or the United States customs officials will have him."

Conway could not bring himself to believe that Mr Leighton, with all his cleverness, would dare try to dispose of the pearls in England and he flattered himself that Leighton could not have sent them elsewhere – too close a watch had been kept.

It transpired naturally that when the Boston bound liner Romanic sailed from Liverpool four days later not only was Mr Leighton aboard but Conway was there. He knew Leighton, but was secure in the thought that Leighton did not know him.

On the second day out he was disabused on this point. He was beginning to think that it might not be a bad idea to know Leighton casually so when he noticed that immaculate gentleman alone, leaning on the rail, smoking, he sauntered up and joined him in contemplation of the infinite ocean.

"Beautiful weather," Conway remarked after a long time.

"Yes," replied Leighton as he glanced around and smiled. "I should think you Scotland Yard men would enjoy a junket like this?"

Conway didn't do any such foolish thing as start or show astonishment, whatever he might have felt. Instead he smiled pleasantly.

"I've been working pretty hard on that Varron affair," he said frankly. "And now I'm taking a little vacation."

"Oh, that thing at Lady Varron's?" inquired Leighton lazily. "Indeed? I happened to be the one to notice that the necklace was gone."

"Yes, I know it," responded Conway, grimly.

The conversation drifted to other things. Conway found Leighton an agreeable companion, and a democratic one. They smoked together, walked together and played shuffle-board together. That evening Leighton took a hand at "bridge" in the smoking room. For hours Conway stared at the phosphorescent points in the sinister green waters, and smoked.

"If he did it," he remarked at last, "he's the cleverest scoundrel on earth, and if he did not I'm the biggest fool."

Six bells—eleven o'clock struck. The deck was deserted. Conway stumbled along through the dark toward the smoking room. Inside he saw Leighton still at play. As he paused at the open door he heard Leighton's voice.

"I'll play until two o'clock, not later," it said.

Conway made up his mind instantly. He turned, retraced his steps along the deck to Leighton's room where he stopped. He knew Leighton had not burdened himself with a valet and thought he knew why, so without hesitation he drew out several keys and fumbled at the lock. It yielded at last and he stepped inside the state room, closing the door. His purpose was instantly apparent. It was to search.

Now Conway had his own ideas of just how a search should be conducted. First he took Leighton's wearing apparel and patted and pinched it inch by inch; he squeezed up neckties, unrolled handkerchiefs, examined shirts and crumpled up silken hosiery. Then he took the shoes – half a dozen pairs. He had been suspicious of shoes since he once found a dozen diamonds concealed in false heels. But these heels weren't false.

Next, still without haste or apparent disappointment, he turned his attention to the handbag, the suitcase and the steamer trunk all of which he had emptied. Such things had been known to have false bottoms and secret compartments. These had none. He satisfied himself absolutely on this point by every method known to his art.

In due time his examination came down to the room itself. He unmade the bed and closely felt of and scrutinized the mattress, sheets, blankets, pillows, and coverlid. He took the three drawers from the dressing cabinet and looked behind them. He turned over several English newspapers and shook them one by one. He peered into the water pitcher and fumbled around the plumbing in the tiny bath room adjoining. He examined the carpet to see if anything had been hidden beneath it. Finally he climbed on a chair and from this elevated position looked for a crack or crevice where a necklace or unset pearls could be hidden.

"There are still three possibilities," he told himself at the end as he carefully restored the room to its previous condition. "He might have left them in a package in the ship's safe but that's improbable – too risky; he might have left them in a trunk in the hold, which is still more improbable; or he might have them on his person. That is more than likely."

So Conway went out, extinguishing the light and locking the door behind him. He stepped into his own state room a moment and took a mouthful of whiskey which he spat out again. But it must have had some deep, potent effect for a few minutes later when he appeared in the smoking room he was in a lamentable state of intoxication and exhaled whiskey noticeably. His was a maudlin, thick-tongued condition. Leighton glanced up at him with well bred reproach.

It may have been only accident that Conway stumbled over Leighton's feet and noted that he wore flat-soled, loose slippers without heels, and also accident that he embraced him with exaggerated affection as he struggled to recover his equilibrium.

Be those things as they may Leighton excused himself good-naturedly from the bridge party and urged Conway to bed. Conway would only agree on condition that Leighton would assist him. Leighton consented cheerfully and they left the smoking room together, Conway clinging to him as the vine to the oak.

Half way down the deck Conway stumbled and fell despite the friendly supporting arm, and in his effort to save himself his hands slid all the way down Leighton's shapely legs. Then he was deposited in his state room and Leighton returned to his cards smiling.

"And he hasn't got them on him," declared Conway enigmatically to the bare walls. He was not intoxicated now.

It was an easy matter next day for him to learn that Leighton had left nothing in the ship's safe and that his four trunks in the hold were inaccessible, being buried under hundreds of others. Whereupon Conway sat down to wait and learn what new and original ideas of searching Uncle Sam's Customs officers had invented.

At last came a morning when the wireless telegraph operator aboard picked up a signal from shore and announced that the Romanic was less than a hundred miles from Boston light. Later Conway found Leighton leaning on the rail, smoking and gazing shoreward.

It was three hours or so after that that several passengers noticed a motor boat coming toward them. Leighton watched it with idle interest. Finally it circled widely and it became apparent that it was coming along-side the now slow moving liner. When it was only a hundred feet off and the liner was barely creeping along, Leighton grew suddenly interested.

"By Jove," he exclaimed, then shouted: "Hello, Harry!"

"Hello, Leighton," came an answering shout. "Heard you were aboard and came out to meet you."

There was a rapid fire of uninteresting pleasantries as the motor boat slid in under the Romanic's lee and bobbed up and down in her wash. The man aboard stood up with a package of newspapers in his hand.

"Here are some American papers for you," he called.

He flung the bundle and Leighton caught it, left the rail and passed into his state room. He returned after a moment with a bundle of European papers – those Conway had previously seen.

"Catch," he called. "There's something in these that will interest you."

The man in the small boat caught the package and dropped it carelessly on a seat.

Then, suddenly, Conway awoke.

"There goes the necklace," he told himself with a start. A quick grasping movement of his hands attracted Leighton's attention and he smiled inscrutably, daringly into the blazing eyes of the Scotland Yard man. The motor boat with a parting shot of "I'll meet you on the wharf" sped away.

Thoughts began to flow rapidly through Conway's fertile brain. Five minutes later he burst in on the wireless operator and sent a long dispatch to officials ashore. Then from the bow rail he watched the motor boat speeding away in the direction of Boston. It drew off about two miles and remained relatively in that position for nearly all the forty miles into Boston Harbour. It spoke no other craft, passed near none in fact while in Conway's sight, which was until it disappeared in Boston Harbour.

An hour later the Romanic was warped in and tied up. Conway was the first man off. He went straight to a man who seemed to be waiting for him.

"Did you search the motor boat?" he demanded.

"Yes," was the reply. "We nearly tore it to pieces, even took it out of the water. We also searched the man on her, Harry Cheshire. You must have been mistaken."

"Are you sure she spoke no one or got rid of the jewels to another vessel?"

"She didn't go near another vessel," was the reply. "I met her at the Harbour mouth and came in with her."

For an instant Conway's face showed disappointment, then came animation again. He was just beginning to get really interested in the affair.

"Do you know the Customs officer in charge?" he asked.

"Yes."

"Introduce me."

There was an introduction and the three men spoke aside for several minutes. The result of it was that when Leighton sauntered down the gang plank he was invited into a private office. He went smilingly and submitted to a search of his person without anger or the slightest trace of uneasiness. As he came out Conway was standing at the door.

"Are you satisfied?" Leighton asked.

"No," blazed Conway, savagely.

"What? Not after searching me twice and my state room once?"

Conway didn't answer. He didn't dare to at the moment, but he stood by when Leighton's four trunks were taken from the hold, and he saw that they were searched with the same minute care that he had given to the state room. At the fruitless end of it he sat down on one of the trunks and stared at Leighton in a sort of admiration.

Leighton stared back for a moment, smiled, nodded pleasantly and strolled up the dock chatting carelessly with Harry Cheshire. Conway made no attempt to follow them. It wasn't worthwhile — nothing was worthwhile any more.

"But he did get them and he's got them now," he told himself savagely, "or he has disposed of them in some way that I can't find."

The Thinking Machine did not seem to regard the problem as at all difficult when it came to his attention a couple of days later. Hutchinson Hatch, reporter, brought it to him. Hatch had some good friends in the Customs Office where Conway had told his story. He learned from them that that office had refused to have anything to do with the case insisting that the Scotland Yard man must be mistaken.

Crushed in spirit, mangled in reputation and taunted by Leighton's final words Conway took a desolate view of life. Momentarily he lost even that bull-dog tenacity which had never before faltered – lost it all except in so far as he still believed that Leighton was the man. It was about this time Hatch met him. Would he talk? He was burning to talk; caution was a senseless thing anyway. Then Hatch took him gently by the hand and led him to The Thinking Machine.

Conway unburdened himself at length and with vitriolic emphasis. For an hour he went on while the scientist leaned back in his chair with his great yellow head pillowed on a cushion and squinted aggressively at the ceiling. At the end of the hour The Thinking Machine knew as much of the Varron problem as Conway knew and knew as much of Leighton as any man knew, except Leighton.

"How many stones were in the necklace," the scientist asked.

"One hundred and seventy-two," replied Conway.

"Was the man in the motor boat – Harry Cheshire you call him – an Englishman?"

"Yes, in speech, manner and appearance."

For a long time The Thinking Machine twiddled his fingers while Conway and the reporter sat staring at him impatiently. Hatch knew, from the past, that something tangible, something that led somewhere, would come from that wonderful analytical brain; Conway not knowing, was only hopefully curious. But like most men of his profession he wanted action; sitting down and thinking didn't seem to get anywhere.

"You see, Mr Conway," said the scientist at last, "you haven't proven anything. Your investigations, as a matter of fact, indicate that Leighton did not take the pearls, therefore did not bring them with him. There is only one thing that indicates that he might have. That is the throwing of the newspapers into the motor boat. That one act seems to have been a senseless one, unless—"

"Unless the pearls were concealed in the bundle," interrupted the Scotland Yard man.

"Or unless he was amusing himself at your expense and is perfectly innocent," added The Thinking Machine. "It is perfectly possible that if he were an innocent man and discovered that you were on his track that he has merely made a fool of you. If we take any other view of it we must base it on an assumption which has no established fact to support it. We will have to dispose of every other person who might have stolen the necklace and pin it down to Leighton. Further, we will have to assume out of hand that he brought the jewels to this country."

The Scotland Yard man was getting interested.

"That is not good logic, yet when we assume all this for our present purposes the problem is a simple one. And by assuming it we prove that your search of the state room was not thorough. Did you, for instance, happen to look on the under side of the slats in the berth? Do you know that the necklace, or its unset pearls, did not hang down in the drain pipe from the water bowl?"

Conway snapped his fingers in annoyance. These were two things he had not done.

"There are other possibilities of course," resumed The Thinking Machine, "therefore the search for the necklace was useless. Now we must take for granted that, if they came to this country at all, they came in one of those places and you overlooked them. Obviously Mr Leighton would not have left them in the trunks in the hold. Therefore we assume further that he hid them in his state room and threw them into the motor boat.

"In that event they were in the motor boat when it left the Romanic and we must believe they were not in it when it docked. Yet the motor boat neither spoke nor approached any other vessel. The jewels were not thrown into the water. The man Cheshire could not have swallowed one hundred and seventy-two pearls – or any great part of them – therefore, what have we?"

"Nothing," responded Conway promptly. "That's what's the matter. I've had to give it all up."

"Instead of nothing we have the answer," replied The Thinking Machine tartly. "Let's see. Perhaps I can give you the name and address of the man who has the jewels now, assuming of course that Leighton brought them."

He arose suddenly and passed into the adjoining room. Conway turned and stared at Hatch inquiringly with a queer expression on his face.

"Is he anything of a joker?" he asked.

"No, but he's a good deal of a wonder," replied Hatch.

"Do you mean to say that I have been working on this thing for months and months without learning anything about it and all he's got to do is to go in there and get the name and address of the man who has the necklace?" demanded Conway in bewilderment.

"If he went into that room and said he'd bring back the Pacific Ocean in a tea cup I'd believe him," said the reporter. "I know him."

They were interrupted by the tinkling of the telephone bell in the next room, then for a long time the subdued hum of the scientist's irritable voice as he talked over the 'phone. It was twenty-five or thirty minutes before he appeared in the door again. He paused there and scribbled something on a card which he handed to Hatch. The reporter read this: "Henry C. H. Manderling, Scituate, Mass."

"There is the name and address of the man who probably has the jewels now," said The Thinking Machine quite as a matter of fact. "Mr Hatch, you accompany Mr Conway, let him see the surroundings and act as his judgment dictates. You must search this man's house. I don't think you'll have much trouble finding them because they cannot foresee their danger. The pearls will be unset and you will find them possibly in small oil-silk bags, no larger than your little finger. When you find them take steps to apprehend both this man and Leighton. Call Detective Mallory when you get them and bring them here."

"But-but—" stammered Conway.

"Come on," commanded Hatch.

And Conway went.

The sleepy little old town of Scituate sprawls along two or three miles of Massachusetts coast, facing the sea boldly in a series of cliffs which rise up and sink away with the utmost suddenness. The town was settled two or three hundred years ago and nothing has ever happened there since. It was here, atop one of the cliffs, that Henry C. H. Manderling had lived alone for two or three months. He had gone there in the Spring with other city folks who dreamed their Summers away, and occupied a queer little shack through which the salt breezes wandered at will. A tiny barn was attached to the house.

Hutchinson Hatch and the Scotland Yard man found the house without difficulty and entered it without hesitation. There was no one at hand to stop them, or to interfere with the search they made. The simple lock on the door was no obstacle. In less than half an hour the skilful hands of the Scotland Yard man had turned out a score or more small oil-silk bags, no larger than his little finger. He ripped one open and six pearls dropped into his hand.

"They're the Varron pearls all right," he exclaimed triumphantly after an examination. He dropped them all into his pocket.

"Sh-h-h-h!" warned Hatch suddenly.

He had heard a step at the door, then two voices as some one inserted a key in the lock. After a moment the door opened and crouching back in the shadow they heard two men enter.

It was just at that psychological moment that Conway stepped out and faced them.

"I want you, Leighton," he said calmly.

Hatch could not see beyond the Scotland Yard man but he heard a shot and a bullet whistled uncomfortably close to his head. Conway leaped forward; Hatch saw his arm swing and one of the men fell. Then came another shot. Conway staggered a little, took another step forward and again swung his great right arm. There was a scurrying of feet, the clatter of a revolver on the floor and the front door slammed.

"Tie up that chap there," commanded Conway.

He opened the door and Hatch heard him run along the veranda and leap off. He turned his attention to the senseless man on the floor. It was Harry Cheshire. Hatch bound him hand and foot where he lay and ran out.

Conway was racing down the cliff to where a motor boat lay. Hatch saw a man climb into the boat and an instant later it shot out into the water. Conway ran on to where it had been; it was now fifty yards out.

"Not this time, Mr Conway," came Leighton's voice as the boat sped on. The Scotland Yard man stared after it a minute or more then returned to Hatch. The reporter saw that he was pale, very pale.

"Did you bind him?" Conway asked.

"Yes," Hatch responded. "Are you wounded?"

"Sure," replied the Scotland Yard man. "He got me in the left arm. I never knew him to carry a revolver before. It's lucky those two shots were all he had."

The Thinking Machine put the finishing touches on the binding of Conway's wound – it was trivial – then turned to his other visitors. These were Harry Cheshire, or Manderling, and Detective Mallory to whom he had been delivered a prisoner on the arrival of Hatch and Conway in Boston. A general alarm had been sent out for Leighton.

Conway apparently didn't care anything about the wound but he had a frank curiosity as to just what The Thinking Machine had done and how those things which had happened had been brought to pass.

"It was all ridiculously simple," began the scientist at last in explanation. "It came down to this: How could one hundred and seventy-two pearls be transferred from a boat forty miles at sea to a safe place ashore? The motor boat did not speak or approach any other vessel; obviously one could not throw them ashore and I have never heard of such a thing as a trained fish which might have brought them in. Now what are the only other ways they could have reached shore with comparative safety?"

He looked from one to another inquiringly. Each in turn shook his head. Manderling, or Cheshire, was silent.

"There are only two possible answers," said the scientist at last. "One, a submarine boat, which is improbable, and the other birds – homing pigeons."

"By Jove!" exclaimed Conway as he stared at Manderling. "And I did notice dozens of pigeons about the place at Scituate."

"The jewels were on the ship as you suspected," resumed the scientist, "unset and probably suspended in a long oil-silk bag in the drain pipe I mentioned. They were thrown into the motor boat, wrapped in the newspapers. Two miles away from the Romanic they were fastened to homing pigeons and one by one the pigeons were released. You, Mr Conway, could see the boat clearly at that distance but you could not possibly see a bird rise from it. The birds went to their home, Mr Manderling's place at Scituate. Homing pigeons are generally kept in automatically closing compartments and each pigeon was locked in as it arrived. Mr Manderling here and Mr Leighton removed the pearls at their leisure.

"Of course with homing pigeons as a clue we could get somewhere," The Thinking Machine went on after a moment. "There are numerous homing pigeon associations and fanciers and it was possible that one of these would know an Englishman who had, say, twenty-five or fifty birds, and presumably lived somewhere near Boston. One did know. He gave me the name of Henry C. H. Manderling. Harry is a corruption of Henry; and Henry C? Henry Cheshire, or Harry Cheshire – the name Mr Manderling gave when he was searched at the wharf."

"Can you explain how Leighton was able to get the necklace in the first place?" asked Conway curiously.

"Just as he got the other things," replied The Thinking Machine, "by boldness and cleverness. Suppose, when Lady Varron fell, Leighton had had a stout elastic fastened high up at the shoulder, say, inside his coat sleeve and the end of this elastic had a clamp of some sort, and was drawn down until the elastic was taut, and fastened to his cuff? Remember that this man was always waiting for an opportunity, and was always prepared to take advantage of it. Of course he did not plan the thing as it happened.

"Say that the necklace dropped off as he leaned over to help Lady Varron. In the momentary excitement he could, under their very noses, have fastened the clamp to the necklace. Instantly the jewels would have disappeared up his sleeve and he could have submitted to any sort of perfunctory search of his pockets as he suggested."

"That's a trick professional gamblers have to get rid of cards," remarked Detective Mallory.

"Oh, it isn't new then?" asked The Thinking Machine. "Immediately he left the ball-room, he hid this necklace as he had hidden other jewels, and before you knew of the theft, wrote and mailed full directions to Mr Manderling here what to do. You did not intercept any letters, of course, until after you knew of this theft. Leighton had perhaps had other dealings with Mr Manderling in other parts of the world, when he was not so closely watched as in this particular instance. I daresay, however, he had them all planned carefully for fear the very thing that did happen in this case would happen."

Half an hour later Conway shook hands with The Thinking Machine, thanked him heartily and the little party dispersed.

"I had given it up," Conway confessed as he was going out.

"You see," remarked The Thinking Machine, "gentlemen of your profession use too little common sense. Remember that two and two always make four – not some times but all the time."

Leighton has not yet been caught. Manderling made a model prisoner.

11

PROBLEM OF THE MOTOR BOAT

Captain Hank Barber, master mariner, gripped the bow-rail of the Liddy Ann and peered off through the semi-fog of the early morning at a dark streak slashing along through the gray-green waters. It was a motor boat of long, graceful lines; and a single figure, that of a man, sat upright at her helm staring uncompromisingly ahead. She nosed through a roller, staggered a little, righted herself and sped on as a sheet of spray swept over her. The helmsman sat motionless, heedless of the stinging splash of wind-driven water in his face.

"She sure is a – goin' some," remarked Captain Hank, reflectively. "By Ginger! If she keeps it up into Boston Harbour she won't stop this side o' the Public Gardens."

Captain Hank watched the boat curiously until she was swallowed up, lost in the mist, then turned to his own affairs. He was a couple of miles out of Boston Harbour, going in; it was six o'clock of a gray morning. A few minutes after the disappearance of the motor boat Captain Hank's attention was attracted by the hoarse shriek of a whistle two hundred yards away. He dimly traced through the mist the gigantic lines of a great vessel – it seemed to be a ship of war.

It was only a few minutes after Captain Hank lost sight of the motor boat that she was again sighted, this time as she flashed into Boston Harbour at full speed. She fled past, almost under the prow of a pilot boat, going out, and was hailed. At the mess table later the pilot's man on watch made a remark about her.

"Goin'! Well, wasn't she though! Never saw one thing pass so close to another in my life without scrubbin' the paint offen it. She was so close up I could spit in her, and when I spoke the feller didn't even look up – just kept a – goin'. I told him a few things that was good for his soul."

Inside Boston Harbour the motor boat performed a miracle. Pursuing a course which was singularly erratic and at a speed more than dangerous she reeled on through the surge of the sea regardless alike of fog, the proximity of other vessels and the heavy wash from larger craft. Here she narrowly missed a tug; there she skimmed by a slow-moving tramp and a warning shout was raised; a fisherman swore at her as only a fisherman can. And finally when she passed into a clear space, seemingly headed for a dock at top speed, she was the most unanimously damned craft that ever came into Boston Harbour.

"Guess that's a through boat," remarked an aged salt, facetiously as he gazed at her from a dock. "If that durned fool don't take some o' the speed offen her she'll go through all right – wharf an' all."

Still the man in the boat made no motion; the whiz of her motor, plainly heard in a sudden silence, was undiminished. Suddenly the tumult of warning was renewed. Only a chance would prevent a smash. Then Big John Dawson appeared on the string piece of the dock. Big John had a voice that was noted from Newfoundland to Norfolk for its depth and width, and possessed objurgatory powers which were at once the awe and admiration of the fishing fleet.

"You ijit!" he bellowed at the impassive helmsman. "Shut off that power an' throw yer hellum."

There was no response; the boat came on directly toward the dock where Big John and his fellows were gathered. The fishermen and loungers saw that a crash was coming and scattered from the string piece.

"The durned fool," said Big John, resignedly.

Then came the crash, the rending of timbers, and silence save for the grinding whir of the motor. Big John ran to the end of the wharf and peered down. The speed of the motor had driven the boat half way upon a float which careened perilously. The man had been thrown forward and lay huddled up face downward and motionless on the float. The dirty water lapped at him greedily.

Big John was the first man on the float. He crept cautiously to the huddled figure and turned it face upward. He gazed for an instant into wide staring eyes then turned to the curious ones peering down from the dock.

"No wonder he didn't stop," he said in an awed tone. "The durned fool is dead."

Willing hands gave aid and after a minute the lifeless figure lay on the dock. It was that of a man in uniform – the uniform of a foreign navy. He was apparently forty-five years old, large and powerful of frame with the sun-browned face of a seaman. The jet black of moustache and goatee was startling against the dead colour of the face. The hair was tinged with gray; and on the back of the left hand was a single letter "D"– tattooed in blue.

"He's French," said Big John authoritatively, "an' that's the uniform of a Cap'n in the French Navy." He looked puzzled a moment as he stared at the figure. "An' they ain't been a French man-o'-war in Boston Harbour for six months."

After awhile the police came and with them Detective Mallory, the big man of the Bureau of Criminal Investigation; and finally Dr Clough, Medical Examiner. While the detective questioned the fishermen and those who had witnessed the crash Dr Clough examined the body.

"An autopsy will be necessary," he announced as he arose.

"How long has he been dead?" asked the detective.

"Eight or ten hours, I should say. The cause of death doesn't appear. There is no shot or knife wound so far as I can see."

Detective Mallory closely examined the dead man's clothing. There was no name or tailor mark; the linen was new; the name of the maker of the shoes had been ripped out with a knife. There was nothing in the pockets, not a piece of paper or even a vagrant coin.

Then Detective Mallory turned his attention to the boat. Both hull and motor were of French manufacture. Long, deep scratches on each side showed how the name had been removed. Inside the boat the detective saw something white and picked it up. It was a handkerchief – a woman's handkerchief, with the initials "E. M. B." in a corner.

"Ah, a woman's in it!" he soliloquised.

Then the body was removed and carefully secluded from the prying eyes of the press. Thus no picture of the dead man appeared. Hutchinson Hatch, reporter, and others asked many questions. Detective Mallory hinted vaguely at international questions – the dead man was a French officer, he said, and there might be something back of it.

"I can't tell you all of it," he said wisely, "but my theory is complete. It is murder. The victim was captain of a French man-of-war. His body was placed in a motor boat, possibly a part of the fittings of the war ship and the boat set adrift. I can say no more."

"Your theory is complete then," Hatch remarked casually, "except the name of the man, the manner of death, the motive, the name of his ship, the presence of the handkerchief and the precise reason why the body should be disposed of in this fashion instead of being cast into the sea?"

The detective snorted. Hatch went away to make some inquiries on his own account. Within half a dozen hours he had satisfied himself by telegraph that no French war craft had been within five hundred miles of Boston for six months. Thus the mystery grew deeper; a thousand questions to which there seemed no answer arose.

At this point, the day following the events related, the problem of the motor boat came to the attention of Professor Augustus S. F. X. Van Dusen, The Thinking Machine. The scientist listened closely but petulantly to the story Hatch told.

"Has there been an autopsy yet?" he asked at last.

"It is set for eleven o'clock today," replied the reporter. "It is now after ten."

"I shall attend it," said the scientist.

Medical Examiner Clough welcomed the eminent Professor Van Dusen's proffer of assistance in his capacity of M.D., while Hatch and other reporters impatiently cooled their toes on the curb. In two hours the autopsy had been completed. The Thinking Machine amused himself by studying the insignia on the dead man's uniform, leaving it to Dr Clough to make a startling statement to the press. The man had not been murdered; he had died of heart failure. There was no poison in the stomach, nor was there a knife or pistol wound.

Then the inquisitive press poured in a flood of questions. Who had scratched off the name of the boat? Dr Clough didn't know. Why had it been scratched off? Still he didn't know. How did it happen that the name of the maker of the shoes had been ripped out? He shrugged his shoulders. What did the handkerchief have to do with it? Really he couldn't conjecture. Was there any inkling of the dead man's identity? Not so far as he knew. Any scar on the body which might lead to identification? No.

Hatch made a few mental comments on officials in general and skilfully steered The Thinking Machine away from the other reporters.

"Did that man die of heart failure?" he asked, flatly.

"He did not," was the curt reply. "It was poison."

"But the Medical Examiner specifically stated that there was no poison in the stomach," persisted the reporter.

The scientist did not reply. Hatch struggled with and suppressed a desire to ask more questions. On reaching home the scientist's first act was to consult an encyclopædia. After several minutes he turned to the reporter with an inscrutable face.

"Of course the idea of a natural death in this case is absurd," he said, shortly. "Every fact is against it. Now, Mr Hatch, please get for me all the local and New York newspapers of the day the body was found – not the day after. Send or bring them to me, then come again at five this afternoon."

"But-but—" Hatch blurted.

"I can say nothing until I know all the facts," interrupted The Thinking Machine.

Hatch personally delivered the specified newspapers into the hands of The Thinking Machine – this man who never read newspapers – and went away. It was an afternoon of agony; an agony of impatience. Promptly at five o'clock he was ushered into Professor Van Dusen's laboratory. He sat half smothered in newspapers, and popped up out of the heap aggressively.

"It was murder, Mr Hatch," he exclaimed, suddenly. "Murder by an extraordinary method."

"Who-who is the man? How was he killed?" asked Hatch.

"His name is—" the scientist began, then paused. "I presume your office has the book 'Who's Who In America?' Please 'phone and ask them to give you the record of Langham Dudley."

"Is he the dead man?" Hatch demanded quickly.

"I don't know," was the reply.

Hatch went to the telephone. Ten minutes later he returned to find The Thinking Machine dressed to go out.

"Langham Dudley is a ship owner, fifty-one years old," the reporter read from notes he had taken. "He was once a sailor before the mast and later became a ship owner in a small way. He was successful in his small undertakings and for fifteen years has been a millionaire. He has a certain social position, partly through his wife whom he married a year and a half ago. She was Edith Marston Belding, a daughter of the famous Belding family. He has an estate on the North Shore."

"Very good," commented the scientist. "Now we will find out something about how this man was killed."

At North Station they took train for a small place on the North Shore, thirty-five miles from Boston. There The Thinking Machine made some inquiries and finally they entered a lumbersome carry-all. After a drive of half an hour through the dark they saw the lights of what seemed to be a pretentious country place. Somewhere off to the right Hatch heard the roar of the restless ocean.

"Wait for us," commanded The Thinking Machine as the carry-all stopped.

The Thinking Machine ascended the steps, followed by Hatch, and rang. After a minute or so the door was opened and a light flooded out. Standing before them was a Japanese – a man of indeterminate age with the graven face of his race.

"Is Mr Dudley in?" asked The Thinking Machine.

"He has not that pleasure," replied the Japanese, and Hatch smiled at the queerly turned phrase.

"Mrs Dudley?" asked the scientist.

"Mrs Dudley is attiring herself in clothing," replied the Japanese. "If you will be pleased to enter."

The Thinking Machine handed him a card and was shown into a reception room. The Japanese placed chairs for them with courteous precision and disappeared. After a short pause there was a rustle of silken skirts on the stairs, and a woman – Mrs Dudley—entered. She was not pretty; she was stunning rather, tall, of superb figure and crowned with a glory of black hair.

"Mr Van Dusen?" she asked as she glanced at the card.

The Thinking Machine bowed low, albeit awkwardly. Mrs Dudley sank down on a couch and the two men resumed their seats. There was a little pause; Mrs Dudley broke the silence at last.

"Well, Mr Van Dusen, if you—" she began.

"You have not seen a newspaper for several days?" asked The Thinking Machine, abruptly.

"No," she replied, wonderingly, almost smiling. "Why?"

"Can you tell me just where your husband is?"

The Thinking Machine squinted at her in that aggressive way which was habitual. A quick flush crept into her face; and grew deeper at the sharp scrutiny. Inquiry lay in her eyes.

"I don't know," she replied at last. "In Boston, I presume."

"You haven't seen him since the night of the ball?"

"No. I think it was half past one o'clock that night."

"Is his motor boat here?"

"Really, I don't know. I presume it is. May I ask the purpose of this questioning?"

The Thinking Machine squinted hard at her for half a minute. Hatch was uncomfortable, half resentful even, at the agitation of the woman and the sharp, cold tone of his companion.

"On the night of the ball," the scientist went on, passing the question, "Mr Dudley cut his left arm just above the wrist. It was only a slight wound. A piece of court plaster was put on it. Do you know if he put it on himself? If not, who did?"

"I put it on," replied Mrs Dudley, unhesitatingly, wonderingly.

"And whose court plaster was it?"

"Mine—some I had in my dressing room. Why?"

The scientist arose and paced across the floor, glancing once out the hall door. Mrs Dudley looked at Hatch inquiringly and was about to speak when The Thinking Machine stopped beside her and placed his slim fingers on her wrist. She did not resent the action; was only curious if one might judge from her eyes.

"Are you prepared for a shock?" the scientist asked.

"What is it?" she demanded in sudden terror. "This suspense—"

"Your husband is dead—murdered—poisoned!" said the scientist with sudden brutality. His fingers still lay on her pulse. "The court plaster which you put on his arm and which came from your room was covered with a virulent poison which was instantly transfused into his blood."

Mrs Dudley did not start or scream. Instead she stared up at The Thinking Machine a moment, her face became pallid, a little shiver passed over her. Then she fell back on the couch in a dead faint.

"Good!" remarked The Thinking Machine complacently. And then as Hatch started up suddenly: "Shut that door," he commanded.

The reporter did so. When he turned back his companion was leaning over the unconscious woman. After a moment he left her and went to a window where he stood looking out. As Hatch watched he saw the colour coming back into Mrs Dudley's face. At last she opened her eyes.

"Don't get hysterical," The Thinking Machine directed calmly. "I know you had nothing whatever to do with your husband's death. I want only a little assistance to find out who killed him."

"Oh, my God!" exclaimed Mrs Dudley. "Dead! Dead!"

Suddenly tears leapt from her eyes and for several minutes the two men respected her grief. When at last she raised her face her eyes were red, but there was a rigid expression about the mouth.

"If I can be of any service—" she began.

"Is this the boat house I see from this window?" asked The Thinking Machine. "That long, low building with the light over the door?"

"Yes," replied Mrs Dudley.

"You say you don't know if the motor boat is there now?"

"No, I don't."

"Will you ask your Japanese servant, and if he doesn't know, let him go see, please?"

Mrs Dudley arose and touched an electric button. After a moment the Japanese appeared at the door.

"Osaka, do you know if Mr Dudley's motor boat is in the boat house?" she asked.

"No, honourable lady."

"Will you go yourself and see?"

Osaka bowed low and left the room, closing the door gently behind him. The Thinking Machine again crossed to the window and sat down staring out into the night. Mrs Dudley asked questions, scores of them, and he answered them in order until she knew the details of the finding of her husband's body – that is, the details the public knew. She was interrupted by the reappearance of Osaka.

"I do not find the motor boat in the house, honourable lady."

"That is all," said the scientist.

Again Osaka bowed and retired.

"Now, Mrs Dudley," resumed The Thinking Machine almost gently, "we know your husband wore a French naval costume at the masked ball. May I ask what you wore?"

"It was a Queen Elizabeth costume," replied Mrs Dudley, "very heavy with a long train."

"And if you could give me a photograph of Mr Dudley?"

Mrs Dudley left the room an instant and returned with a cabinet photograph. Hatch and the scientist looked at it together; it was unmistakably the man in the motor boat.

"You can do nothing yourself," said The Thinking Machine at last, and he moved as if to go. "Within a few hours we will have the guilty person. You may rest assured that your name will be in no way brought into the matter unpleasantly."

Hatch glanced at his companion; he thought he detected a sinister note in the soothing voice, but the face expressed nothing. Mrs Dudley ushered them into the hall; Osaka stood at the front door. They passed out and the door closed behind them.

Hatch started down the steps but The Thinking Machine stopped at the door and tramped up and down. The reporter turned back in astonishment. In the dim reflected light he saw the scientist's finger raised, enjoining silence, then saw him lean forward suddenly with his ear pressed to the door. After a little he rapped gently. The door was opened by Osaka who obeyed a beckoning motion of the scientist's hand and came out. Silently he was led off the veranda into the yard; he appeared in no way surprised.

"Your master, Mr Dudley, has been murdered," declared The Thinking Machine quietly, to Osaka. "We know that Mrs Dudley killed him," he went on as Hatch stared, "but I have told her she is not suspected. We are not officers and cannot arrest her. Can you go with us to Boston, without the knowledge of anyone here and tell what you know of the quarrel between husband and wife to the police?"

Osaka looked placidly into the eager face.

"I had the honour to believe that the circumstances would not be recognized," he said finally. "Since you know, I will go."

"We will drive down a little way and wait for you."

The Japanese disappeared into the house again. Hatch was too astounded to speak, but followed The Thinking Machine into the carryall. It drove away a hundred yards and stopped. After a few minutes an impalpable shadow came toward them through the night. The scientist peered out as it came up.

"Osaka?" he asked softly.

"Yes."

An hour later the three men were on a train, Boston bound. Once comfortably settled the scientist turned to the Japanese.

"Now if you will please tell me just what happened the night of the ball" he asked, "and the incidents leading up to the disagreement between Mr and Mrs Dudley?"

"He drank elaborately," Osaka explained reluctantly, in his quaint English, "and when drinking he was brutal to the honourable lady. Twice with my own eyes I saw him strike her – once in Japan where I entered his service while they were on a wedding journey, and once here. On the night of the ball he was immeasurably intoxicated, and when he danced he fell down to the floor. The honourable lady was chagrined and angry – she had been angry before. There was some quarrel which I am not comprehensive of. They had been widely divergent for several months. It was, of course, not prominent in the presence of others."

"And the cut on his arm where the court plaster was applied?" asked the scientist. "Just how did he get that?"

"It was when he fell down," continued the Japanese. "He reached to embrace a carved chair and the carved wood cut his arm. I assisted him to his feet and the honourable lady sent me to her room to get court plaster. I acquired it from her dressing table and she placed it on the cut."

"That makes the evidence against her absolutely conclusive," remarked The Thinking Machine, as if finally. There was a little pause, and then: "Do you happen to know just how Mrs Dudley placed the body in the boat?"

"I have not that honour," said Osaka. "Indeed I am not comprehensive of anything that happened after the court plaster was put on except that Mr Dudley was affected some way and went out of the house. Mrs Dudley, too, was not in the ball room for ten minutes or so afterwards."

Hutchinson Hatch stared frankly into the face of The Thinking Machine; there was nothing to be read there. Still deeply thoughtful Hatch heard the brakeman bawl "Boston" and mechanically followed the scientist and Osaka out of the station into a cab. They were driven immediately to Police Headquarters. Detective Mallory was just about to go home when they entered his office.

"It may enlighten you, Mr Mallory," announced the scientist coldly, "to know that the man in the motor boat was not a French naval officer who died of natural causes—he was Langham Dudley, a millionaire ship owner. He was murdered. It just happens that I know the person who did it."

The detective arose in astonishment and stared at the slight figure before him inquiringly; he knew the man too well to dispute any assertion he might make.

"Who is the murderer?" he asked.

The Thinking Machine closed the door and the spring lock clicked.

"That man there," he remarked calmly, turning on Osaka.

For one brief instant there was a pause and silence; then the detective advanced upon the Japanese with hand outstretched. The agile Osaka leapt suddenly, as a snake strikes; there was a quick, fierce struggle and Detective Mallory sprawled on the floor. There had been just a twist of the wrist – a trick of jiu jitsu – and Osaka had flung himself at the locked door. As he fumbled there Hatch, deliberately and without compunction, raised a chair and brought it down on his head. Osaka sank down without a sound.

It was an hour before they brought him around again. Meanwhile the detective had patted and petted half a dozen suddenly acquired bruises, and had then searched Osaka. He found nothing to interest him save a small bottle. He uncorked it and started to smell it when The Thinking Machine snatched it away.

"You fool, that'll kill you!" he exclaimed.

Osaka sat, lashed hand and foot to a chair, in Detective Mallory's office – so placed by the detective for safe keeping.

His face was no longer expressionless; there were fear and treachery and cunning there. So he listened, perforce, to the statement of the case by The Thinking Machine who leaned back in his chair, squinting steadily upward and with his long, slender fingers pressed together.

"Two and two make four, not some times but all the time," he began at last as if disputing some previous assertion. "As the figure two, wholly disconnected from any other, gives small indication of a result, so is an isolated fact of little consequence. Yet that fact added to another, and the resulting fact added to a third, and so on, will give a final result. That result, if every fact is considered, must be correct. Thus any problem may be solved by logic; logic is inevitable.

"In this case the facts, considered singly, might have been compatible with either a natural death, suicide, or murder – considered together they proved murder. The climax of this proof was the removal of the maker's name from the dead man's shoes, and a fact strongly contributory was the attempt to destroy the identity of the boat. A subtle mind lay back of it all."

"I so regarded it," said Detective Mallory. "I was confident of murder until the Medical Examiner—"

"We prove a murder," The Thinking Machine went on serenely. "The method? I was with Dr Clough at the autopsy. There was no shot, or knife wound, no poison in the stomach. Knowing there was murder I sought further. Then I found the method in a slight, jagged wound on the left arm. It had been covered with court plaster. The heart showed constriction without apparent cause, and while Dr Clough examined it I took off this court plaster. Its odour, an unusual one, told me that poison had been transfused into the blood through the wound. So two and two had made four.

"Then – what poison? A knowledge of botany aided me. I recognized faintly the trace of an odour of an herb which is not only indigenous to, but grows exclusively in Japan. Thus a Japanese poison. Analysis later in my laboratory proved it was a Japanese poison, virulent, and necessarily slow to act unless it is placed directly in an artery. The poison on the court plaster and that you took from Osaka are identical."

The scientist uncorked the bottle and permitted a single drop of a green liquid to fall on his handkerchief. He allowed a minute or more for evaporation then handed it to Detective Mallory who sniffed at it from a respectful distance. Then The Thinking Machine produced the bit of court plaster he had taken from the dead man's arm, and again the detective sniffed.

"The same," the scientist resumed as he touched a lighted match to the handkerchief and watched it crumble to ashes, "and so powerful that in its pure state mere inhalation is fatal. I permitted Dr Clough to make public his opinion – heart failure – after the autopsy for obvious reasons. It would reassure the murderer for instance if he saw it printed, and besides Dudley did die from heart failure; the poison caused it.

"Next came identification. Mr Hatch learned that no French war ship had been within hundreds of miles of Boston for months. The one seen by Captain Barber might have been one of our own. This man was supposed to be a French naval officer, and had been dead less than eight hours. Obviously he did not come from a ship of his own country. Then from where?

"I know nothing of uniforms, yet I examined the insignia on the arms and shoulders closely after which I consulted my encyclopædia. I learned that while the uniform was more French than anything else it was really the uniform of no country, because it was not correct. The insignia were mixed.

"Then what? There were several possibilities, among them a fancy dress ball was probable. Absolute accuracy would not be essential there. Where had there been a fancy dress ball? I trusted to the newspapers to tell me that. They did. A short dispatch from a place on the North Shore stated that on the night before the man was found dead there had been a fancy dress ball at the Langham Dudley estate.

"Now it is as necessary to remember every fact in solving a problem as it is to consider every figure in arithmetic. Dudley! Here was the "D" tattooed on the dead man's hand. 'Who's Who' showed that Langham Dudley married Edith Marston Belding. Here was the 'E. M. B.' on the handkerchief in the boat. Langham Dudley was a ship owner, had been a sailor, was a millionaire. Possibly this was his own boat built in France."

Detective Mallory was staring into the eyes of The Thinking Machine in frank admiration; Osaka to whom the narrative had thus far been impersonal, gazed, gazed as if fascinated. Hutchinson Hatch, reporter, was drinking in every word greedily.

"We went to the Dudley place," the scientist resumed after a moment. "This Japanese opened the door. Japanese poison! Two and two were still making four. But I was first interested in Mrs Dudley. She showed no agitation and told me frankly that she placed the court plaster on her husband's arm, and that it came from her room. There was instantly a doubt as to her connection with the murder; her immediate frankness aroused it.

"Finally, with my hand on her pulse – which was normal – I told her as brutally as I could that her husband had been murdered. Her pulse jumped frightfully and as I told her the cause of death it wavered, weakened and she fainted. Now if she had known her husband were dead – even if she had killed him – a mere statement of his death would not have caused that pulse. Further I doubt if she could have disposed of her husband's body in the motor boat. He was a large man and the manner of her dress even, was against this. Therefore she was innocent.

"And then? The Japanese, Osaka, here. I could see the door of the boat house from the room where we were. Mrs Dudley asked Osaka if Mr Dudley's boat was in the house. He said he didn't know. Then she sent him to see. He returned and said the boat was not there, yet he had not gone to the boat house at all. Ergo, he knew the boat was not there. He may have learned it from another servant, still it was a point against him."

Again the scientist paused and squinted at the Japanese. For a moment Osaka withstood the gaze, then his beady eyes shifted and he moved uncomfortably.

"I tricked Osaka into coming here by a ludicrously simple expedient," The Thinking Machine went on steadily. "On the train I asked if he knew just how Mrs Dudley got the body of her husband into the boat. Remember at this point he was not supposed to know that the body had been in a boat at all. He said he didn't know and by that very answer admitted that he knew the body had been placed in the boat. He knew because he put it there himself. He didn't merely throw it in the water because he had sense enough to know if the tide didn't take it out it would rise, and possibly be found.

"After the slight injury Mr Dudley evidently wandered out toward the boat house. The poison was working, and perhaps he fell. Then this man removed all identifying marks, even to the name in the shoes, put the body in the boat and turned on full power. He had a right to assume that the boat would be lost, or that the dead man would be thrown out. Wind and tide and a loose rudder brought it into Boston Harbour. I do not attempt to account for the presence of Mrs Dudley's handkerchief in the boat. It might have gotten there in one of a hundred ways."

"How did you know husband and wife had quarrelled?" asked Hatch.

"Surmise to account for her not knowing where he was," replied The Thinking Machine. "If they had had a violent disagreement it was possible that he would have gone away without telling her, and she would not have been particularly worried, at least up to the time we saw her. As it was she presumed he was in Boston; perhaps Osaka here gave her that impression?"

The Thinking Machine turned and stared at the Japanese curiously.

"Is that correct?" he asked.

Osaka did not answer.

"And the motive?" asked Detective Mallory, at last.

"Will you tell us just why you killed Mr Dudley?" asked The Thinking Machine of the Japanese.

"I will not," exclaimed Osaka, suddenly. It was the first time he had spoken.

"It probably had to do with a girl in Japan," explained The Thinking Machine, easily. "The murder had been a long cherished project, such a one as revenge through love would have inspired."

It was a day or so later that Hutchinson Hatch called to inform The Thinking Machine that Osaka had confessed and had given the motive for the murder. It was not a nice story.

"One of the most astonishing things to me," Hatch added, "is the complete case of circumstantial evidence against Mrs Dudley, beginning with the quarrel and leading to the application of the poison with her own hands. I believe she would have been convicted on the actual circumstantial evidence had you not shown conclusively that Osaka did it."

"Circumstantial fiddlesticks!" snapped The Thinking Machine. "I wouldn't convict a yellow dog of stealing jam on circumstantial evidence alone, even if he had jam all over his nose." He squinted truculently at Hatch for a moment. "In the first place well behaved dogs don't eat jam," he added more mildly.

12

PROBLEM OF THE OPERA BOX

Gradually the lights dimmed and the great audience became an impalpable, shadowy mass broken here and there by the vagrant glint of a jewel or the gleam of white shoulders. There was a preliminary blare of horns, then the crashing anvil chorus of "Il Trovatore" began. Sparks spattered and flashed as the sledges rose and fell in exquisite rhythm while the clangorous music roared through the big theatre.

Eleanor Oliver arose, and moving from the front of the box into the gloom at the rear, leaned her head wearily against the latticed partition. Her mother, beside whom she had been sitting, glanced up inquiringly as did her father and their guest Sylvester Knight.

"What's the matter, my dear?" asked Mrs Oliver.

"Those sparks and that noise give me a headache," she explained. "Father, sit in front there if you wish. I'll stay here in the dark until I feel better."

Mr Oliver took the seat near his wife and Knight immediately lost interest in the stage, turning his chair to face Eleanor. She seemed a little pale and mingled eagerness and anxiety in his face showed his concern. They chatted together for a minute or so and under cover of darkness his hand caught hers and held it a fluttering prisoner.

As they talked the drone of their voices interfered with Mrs Oliver's enjoyment of the music and she glanced back warningly. Neither noticed it for Knight was gazing deeply into the girl's eyes with adoration in his own. She made some remark to him and he protested quickly.

"Please don't," Mrs Oliver heard him say pleadingly as his voice was raised. "It won't be long."

"I'm afraid I'll have to," the girl replied.

"You mustn't," Knight commanded earnestly. "If you insist on it I shall have to do something desperate."

Mrs Oliver turned and looked back at them reprovingly.

"You children chatter too much," she said good-naturedly. "You make more noise than the anvils."

She turned again to the stage and Knight was silent for a moment. Finally the girl said something else that the mother didn't catch.

"Certainly," he replied.

He arose quietly and left the box. The swish and fall of the curtain behind him were smothered in the heavy volume of music. The girl sat white and inert. Knight found her in just that position when he returned with a glass of water. He had been out only a minute or so, and the encore to the chorus was just ending.

He offered the glass to Eleanor but she made no move to take it and he touched her lightly on the arm. Still she did not move and he leaned over and looked at her closely. Then he turned quickly to Mrs Oliver.

"Eleanor has fainted, I think," he whispered uneasily.

"Fainted?" exclaimed Mrs Oliver as she arose. "Fainted?"

She pushed her chair back and in a moment was beside her daughter chafing her hands. Mr Oliver turned and glanced at them with languid interest.

"What's the matter now?" he inquired.

"We'll have to go," replied Mrs Oliver. "Eleanor has fainted."

"Again?" he asked impatiently.

Knight hovered about anxiously, helplessly as the father and mother worked with the girl. Finally in some way he never understood Eleanor was lifted out, still unconscious and white as death, and removed in a waiting carriage to her home. Two physicians were summoned and disappeared into her boudoir while Knight paced back and forth restlessly between the smoking room and the hall. Mrs Oliver was with her daughter; Mr Oliver sat quietly smoking.

"I wouldn't worry," he advised the young man after a few minutes. "She has a trick of fainting like that. You will know more about her after awhile – when she is Mrs Knight."

From somewhere upstairs came a scream and Knight started nervously. It was a shrill, penetrating cry that tore straight through him. Mr Oliver took it phlegmatically, even smiled at his nervousness.

"That's my wife fainting," he explained. "She always does it that way. You know," he added confidentially, "my wife and two daughters are so exhausted with this everlasting social game that they go off like that at any minute. I've talked to them about it but they won't listen."

Heedless of the idle, even heartless, comments of the father Knight stopped in the hall and stood at the foot of the stairs looking up. After a minute a man came down; it was Dr Brander, one of the two physicians who had been called. On his face was an expression of troubled perplexity.

"How is she?" demanded Knight abruptly.

"Where is Mr Oliver?" asked Dr Brander.

"In the smoking room," replied the young man. "What's the matter?"

Without answering the physician went on to the father. Mr Oliver looked up.

"Bring her around all right?" he asked.

"She's dead," replied the physician.

"Dead?" gasped Knight.

Mr Oliver rose suddenly and gripped the physician fiercely by a shoulder. For an instant he gazed and then his face grew deathly pale. With a distinct effort he recovered himself.

"Her heart?' he asked at last.

"No. She was stabbed."

Dr Brander looked from one to the other of the two white faces with troubled lines about his eyes.

"Why it can't be," burst out Knight suddenly. "Where is she? I'll go to her."

Dr Brander laid a detaining hand on his shoulder.

"You can do no good," he said quietly.

For a time Mr Oliver was dumb and the physician curiously watched the struggle in his face. The hand that clung to his shoulder was trembling horribly. At last the father found voice.

"What happened?" he asked.

"She was stabbed," said Dr Brander again. "When we examined her we found the knife – a long, keen, short-handled stiletto. It was driven in with great force directly under her left arm and penetrated the heart. She must have been dead when she was lifted from the box at the opera. The stiletto remained in the wound and prevented any flow of blood while its position and the short handle caused it to be overlooked when she was lifted into the carriage. We did not find the knife for several minutes after we arrived. It was covered by her arm."

"Did you tell my wife?" asked Mr Oliver quickly.

"She was present," the physician went on. "She screamed and fainted. Dr Seaver is attending her. Her condition is – is not very good. Where is your 'phone? I must notify the police."

Mr Oliver started to ask something else, paused and dropped back in his chair only to rise instantly and rush up the stairs. Knight into whose face there had come a deadly calm stood stone-like while Dr Brander used the telephone. At last the physician finished.

"The calling of the police means that Eleanor did not kill herself?" asked the young man.

"It was murder," was the positive reply. "She could not have stabbed herself. The knife went straight in, entering here," and he indicated a spot about four inches below his left arm. "You see," he explained, "it took a very long blade to penetrate the heart."

There was dull despair in Knight's eyes. He dropped down at a table with his head on his arms and sat motionless for a long time. He looked up once and asked a question.

"Where is the knife?"

"I have it," replied Dr Brander. "I shall turn it over to the authorities."

"Now," began The Thinking Machine in his small, irritated voice as Hutchinson Hatch, reporter, stopped talking and leaned back to listen, "all problems are merely sums in addition, when reduced to their primary parts. Therefore this one is simply a matter of putting facts together in order to prove that two and two do not sometimes but always make four."

Professor Augustus S. F. X. Van Dusen, scientist and logician, paused to adjust his head comfortably on the cushion in the big chair, then resumed:

"Your statement of the case, Mr Hatch, gives me these absolute facts: Eleanor Oliver is dead; she died of a stab wound; a stiletto made this wound; it was in such a position that she could hardly have inflicted it herself; and Sylvester Knight, her fiancé, is under arrest. That's all we know isn't it?"

"You forget that she was stabbed while in a box at the opera," the reporter put in, "in the hearing of three or four thousand persons."

"I forget nothing," snapped the scientist. "It does not appear at all that she was stabbed while in that box. It appears merely that she was ill and might have fainted. She might have been stabbed while in the carriage, or even after she was in her room."

Hatch's eyes opened wide at the bare mention of these possibilities.

"The presumption is of course," The Thinking Machine went on a little less aggressively, "that she was stabbed while in the box, but we can't put that down as an absolute fact to work on until we know it. Remember the stiletto was not found until she was in her room."

This gave the reporter something new to think about and he was silent as he considered it. He saw that either of the possibilities suggested by the scientist was tenable, but on the other hand – on the other hand, and there his mind refused to work.

"You have told me that Knight was arrested at the suggestion of Mr Oliver last night shortly after the police learned of the affair," The Thinking Machine went on, musingly. "Now just what have you or the police learned as to him? How do they connect him with the affair?"

"First the police acted on the general ground of exclusive opportunity," the reporter explained. "Then Knight was arrested. The stiletto used was not an ordinary one. It had a blade of about seven inches and was very slender, but instead of a guard on it there was only a gold band. The handle is a straight, highly polished piece of wood. Around it, below the gold band where the guard should have been, there were threads as if it had been screwed into something."

"Yes, yes, I see," the other interrupted impatiently. "It was intended to be carried hidden in a walking cane, perhaps, and was screwed down with the blade in the stick. Go on."

"Detective Mallory surmised that when he saw the stiletto," the reporter continued, "so after Knight was locked up he searched his rooms for the other part – the lower end – of the cane."

"And he found it, without the stiletto?"

"Yes, that's the chain against Knight. First, exclusive opportunity, then the stiletto and the finding of the lower end of the cane in his possession."

"Exclusive fiddlesticks!" exclaimed the scientist irritably. "I presume Knight denies that he killed Miss Oliver?"

"Naturally."

"And where is the stiletto that belongs to his cane? Does he attempt to account for it?"

"He doesn't seem to know where it is – in fact he doesn't deny that the stiletto might be his. He merely says he doesn't know."

The Thinking Machine was silent for several minutes.

"Looks bad for him," he remarked at last.

"Thank you," remarked Hatch dryly. It was one of those rare occasions when the scientist saw a problem exactly as he saw it.

"Miss Oliver and Mr Knight were to be married – when?"

"Three weeks from next Wednesday."

"I suppose Detective Mallory has the stiletto and cane?"

"Yes."

The Thinking Machine arose and found his hat.

"Let's run over to police headquarters," he suggested.

They found Detective Mallory snugly ensconced behind a fat cigar with beatific satisfaction on his face.

"Ah, gentlemen," he remarked graciously – the graciousness of conscious superiority. "We've nailed it to our friend Knight all right."

"How?" inquired The Thinking Machine.

The detective gloated a little – twisted his tongue around the dainty morsel – before he answered.

"I suppose Hatch has told you the grounds of the arrest?" he asked. "Exclusive opportunity and all that? Then you know, too, how I searched Knight's rooms and found the other part of the stiletto cane. Of course that was enough to convict, but early this evening the last link in the chain against him was supplied when Mrs Oliver made a statement to me."

The detective paused in enjoyment of the curiosity he had aroused.

"Well?" asked The Thinking Machine, at last.

"Mrs Oliver heard – understand me – heard Knight threaten her daughter only a few minutes before she was found dead."

"Threaten her?" exclaimed Hatch, as he glanced at The Thinking Machine. "By George!"

Detective Mallory tugged at his moustache complacently.

"Mrs Oliver heard Knight first say something like, 'Please don't. It won't be very long.' Her daughter answered something she couldn't catch after which she heard Knight say positively, 'You mustn't. If you do I shall do something desperate' or something like that. Now as she remembers it the tone was threatening – it must have been raised in anger to be heard above the anvils. Thus the case is complete."

The Thinking Machine and Hatch silently considered this new point.

"Remember this was only three or four minutes before she was found stabbed," the detective went on with conviction. "It all connects up straight from exclusive opportunity to the ownership of the stiletto; from that to the threat and there you are."

"No motive of course?" asked The Thinking Machine.

"Well, the question of motive isn't exactly clear but our further investigations will bring it out all right," the detective admitted. "I should imagine the motive to be jealousy. Of course the story of Knight not knowing where his stiletto is has no weight."

Detective Mallory was so charmed with himself that he offered cigars to his visitors – an unusual burst of generosity – and Hatch was so deeply thoughtful that he accepted. The Thinking Machine never smoked.

"May I see the stiletto and cane?" he asked instead.

The detective was delighted to oblige. He watched the scientist with keen satisfaction as that astute gentleman squinted at the slender blade, still stained with blood, and then as he examined the lower part of the cane. Finally the scientist thrust the long blade into the hollow stick and screwed the handle in. It fitted perfectly. Detective Mallory smiled.

"I don't suppose you'll try to put a crimp in me this time?" he asked jovially.

"Very clever, Mr Mallory, very clever," replied The Thinking Machine, and with Hatch trailing he left headquarters.

"Mallory will swell like a balloon after that," Hatch commented grimly.

"Well, he might save himself that trouble," replied the scientist crustily. "He has the wrong man."

The reporter glanced quickly into the inscrutable face of his companion.

"Didn't Knight do it?" he asked.

"Certainly not," was the impatient answer.

"Who did?"

"I don't know."

Together they went on to the theatre from which Miss Oliver had been removed the night before. There a few words with the manager gained permission to look at the Oliver box – a box which the Olivers held only on alternate nights during the opera season. It was on the first balcony level, to the left as they entered the house.

The first three rows of seats in the balcony ran around to and stopped at the box, one of four on that level and the furthest from the stage. The Thinking Machine pottered around aimlessly for ten minutes while Hatch looked on. He entered the box two or three times, examined the curtains, the partitions, the floor and the chairs after which he led the way into the lobby.

There he excused himself to Hatch and stopped in the manager's office. He remained only a few minutes, afterwards climbing into a cab in which he and Hatch were driven back to police headquarters.

After some wire pulling and a good deal of red tape The Thinking Machine and his companion were permitted to see Knight. They found him standing at the barred cell door, staring out with weary eyes and pallid face.

The Thinking Machine was introduced to the prisoner by Hatch who had previously tried vainly to induce the young man to talk.

"I have nothing to say," Knight declared belligerently. "See my attorney."

"I would like to ask three or four questions to which you can have no possible objection," said The Thinking Machine. "If you do object of course don't answer."

"Well?" demanded the prisoner.

"Have you ever travelled in Europe?"

"I was there for nearly a year. I only returned to this country three months ago."

"Have you ever been interested in any other woman? Or has any other woman ever been interested in you?"

The prisoner stared at his questioner coldly.

"No," he responded, emphatically.

"Your answer to that question may mean your freedom within a few hours," said The Thinking Machine quite calmly. "Tell me the truth."

"That is the truth—on my honour."

The answer came frankly, and there came a quick gleam of hope in the prisoner's face.

"Just where in Italy did you buy that stiletto cane?" was the next question.

"In Rome."

"Rather expensive?"

"Five hundred lira – that is about one hundred dollars."

"I suppose they are very common in Italy?"

"Yes, rather."

Knight pressed eagerly against the bars of his cell and gazed deeply but uncomprehendingly into the quiet squinting blue eyes.

"There has never been any sort of a quarrel—serious or otherwise between you and Miss Oliver?"

"Never," was the quick response.

"Now, only one more question," said The Thinking Machine. "I shall not ask it to hurt you." There was a little pause and Hatch waited expectantly. "Does it happen that you know whether or not Miss Oliver ever had any other love affair?"

"Certainly not," exclaimed the young man, hotly. "She was just a girl—only twenty, out of Vassar just a few months ago and-and—"

"You needn't say any more," interrupted The Thinking Machine. "It isn't necessary. Make your plans to leave here tonight, not later than midnight. It is now four o'clock. Tomorrow the newspapers will exonerate you."

The prisoner seemed almost overcome by his emotions. He started to speak, but only extended an open hand through the bars. The Thinking Machine laid his slender fingers in it with a slight look of annoyance, said "Goodday" mechanically and he and Hatch went out.

The reporter was in a sort of a trance, not an unusual condition in him when in the company of his scientific friend. They climbed into the cab again and were driven away. Hatch was thinking too deeply to note the destination when the scientist gave it to the cabby.

"Do you actually anticipate that you will be able to get Knight out of this thing so easily?" he asked incredulously.

"Certainly," was the response. "The problem is solved except for one or two minor points. Now I am proving it."

"But-but—"

"I will make it all clear to you in due time," interrupted the other.

They were both silent until the cab stopped. Hatch glanced out and recognized the Oliver home. He followed The Thinking Machine up the steps and into the reception hall. There the scientist handed a card to the servant.

"Tell Mr Oliver, please, that I will only take a moment," he explained.

The servant bowed and left them. A short wait and Mr Oliver entered.

"I am sorry to disturb you at such a time, Mr Oliver," said the scientist, "but if you can give me just a little information I think perhaps we may get a full light on this unfortunate affair."

Mr Oliver bowed.

"First, let me ask you to confirm what I may say is my knowledge that your daughter, Eleanor, knew this man. I will ask, too, that you do not mention his name now."

He scribbled hastily on a piece of paper and handed it to Mr Oliver. An expression of deep surprise came into the latter's face and he shook his head.

"I can answer that question positively," he said. "She does not know him. She had never been abroad and he has never been in this country until now."

The Thinking Machine arose with something nearly akin to agitation in his face, and his slender fingers worked nervously.

"What?" he demand abruptly. "What?" Then, after a pause: "I beg your pardon, sir. It startled me a little. But are you sure?"

"Perfectly sure," replied Mr Oliver firmly. "They could not have met in anyway."

For a long time The Thinking Machine stood squinting aggressively at his host with bewilderment plainly apparent in his manner. Hatch looked on with absorbed interest. Something had gone wrong; a cog had slipped; the wheels of logic had been thrown out of gear.

"I have made a mistake, Mr Oliver," said The Thinking Machine at last. "I am sorry to have disturbed you."

Mr Oliver bowed courteously and they were ushered out.

"What is it?" asked Hatch anxiously as they once more took their seats in the cab.

The Thinking Machine shook his head in frank annoyance.

"What happened?" Hatch insisted.

"I've made a mistake," was the petulant response. "I'm going home and start all over again. It may be that I shall send for you later."

Hatch accepted that as a dismissal and went his way wonderingly. That evening The Thinking Machine called him to the 'phone.

"Mr Hatch?"

"Yes."

"Did Miss Oliver have any sisters?"

"Yes, one. Her name is Florence. There's something about her in the afternoon papers in connection with the murder story."

"How old is she?"

"I don't know—twenty-two or three."

"Ah!" came a long, aspirated sigh of relief over the wire. "Run by and bring Detective Mallory up to my place."

"All right. But what was the matter?"

"I was a fool, that's all. Goodbye."

Detective Mallory was still delighted with himself when Hatch entered his office.

"What particular line is your friend Van Dusen working?" he asked a little curiously.

The reporter shrugged his shoulders.

"He asked me to come by and bring you up," he replied. "He has evidently reached some conclusion."

"If it's anything that doesn't count Knight in it's all wind," he said loftily. For once in his life he was confident that he could deliver a blow which would obliterate any theory but his own. In this mood, therefore, he went with Hatch. They found The Thinking Machine pacing back and forth across his small laboratory with his slender hands clasped behind his back. Hatch noted that the perplexed wrinkles had gone.

"In adding up a column of figures," began the scientist abruptly as he sat down, "the oversight of even so trivial a unit as one will make a glaring error in the result. You, Mr Mallory, have overlooked a figure one, therefore your conclusion is wrong. In my first consideration of this affair I also overlooked a figure one and my conclusion toppled over just at the moment when it seemed to be corroborated. So I had to start over; I found the one."

"But this thing against Knight is conclusive," said the detective explosively.

"Except for the figure one," added the scientist.

Detective Mallory snorted politely.

"Now here is the logic of the thing," resumed The Thinking Machine. "It will show how I overlooked the figure one – that is a vital fact – and how I found it."

He dropped back into the reflective attitude which was so familiar to his hearers, squint eyes turned upward and with his fingers pressed tip to tip. For several minutes he was silent while Detective Mallory vented his impatience by chewing his moustache.

"In the beginning," began The Thinking Machine at last, "we have a girl, pretty, young and wealthy in a box at the opera with her parents and her fiancé. It would seem, at first glance, to be as safe a place as her home would be, yet she is murdered mysteriously. A stiletto is thrust into her heart. We will assume that her death occurred in the box; that the knife thrust came while she was in a dead faint. This temporary unconsciousness would account for the fact that she did not scream, as the heart would have been pierced by a sudden thrust before consciousness of pain was awakened.

"Now the three persons who were with her. There seemed no reason to suspect either the father or mother, so we come to Sylvester Knight, her intended husband. There is always to be found a motive, either real or imaginary, for a man to kill his sweetheart. In this case Knight had the opportunity, but not the exclusive opportunity. Therefore, an unlimited field of speculation was opened up."

Detective Mallory raised his hand impressively and started to say something, then thought better of it.

"After Mr Knight's arrest," The Thinking Machine continued, "your investigation, Mr Mallory, drew a net about him. That's what you wanted to say, I believe. There was the stiletto, the other end of the cane and the alleged threats. I admit all these things. On this statement of the case it looked black for Mr Knight."

"That's what," remarked the detective.

"Now a stiletto naturally suggests Italy. The blade with which Miss Oliver was killed bore an Italian manufacturer's mark. I presume you noticed it?"

"Oh, that!" exclaimed the detective.

"Means nothing conclusively," added The Thinking Machine. "I agree with you. Still it was a suggestion. Then I saw the thing that did mean something. This was the fact that the handle of the stiletto was not of the same wood as the part of the cane you found in Mr Knight's room. This difference is so slight that you would hardly notice it even now, but it was there and showed a possible clue leading away from Mr Knight."

Detective Mallory could not readily place his tongue on words to fittingly express his disgust, so he remained silent.

"When I considered what manner of man Mr Knight is and the singular nature of the crime," resumed the scientist, "I had no hesitancy in assuring Mr Hatch that you had the wrong man. After we first saw you we examined the opera box. It was on the left of the theatre and separated from the next box by a latticed partition. It was against this partition that Miss Oliver was leaning.

"Remember, I saw the box after I examined the stiletto and while I was seeking a method by which another person might have stabbed her without entering the box. I found it. By using a stiletto without a guard it would have been perfectly possible for a person in the next box to have killed her by thrusting the blade through the lattice partition. That is exactly what happened."

Detective Mallory arose with a mouth full of words. They tumbled out in incoherent surprise and protest, then he sat down again. The Thinking Machine was still staring upward.

"I then took steps to learn who was in the adjoining box at the time of her death," he continued quietly. "The manager of the theatre told me it was occupied by Mr and Mrs Franklin Dupree, and their guest an Italian nobleman. Italian nobleman! Italian stiletto! You see the connection?

"Then we saw Mr Knight. He assured me, and I believed him, that he had never had any other love affair, therefore no woman would have had a motive in killing Miss Oliver because of him. He was positive, too, that Miss Oliver had never had any other love affair, yet I saw the possibility of some connecting link between her and the nobleman. It was perfectly possible, indeed probable, that he would not know of it. At the moment I was convinced that there had been such an affair.

"Mr Knight also told me that he bought his stiletto cane in Rome; and he paid a price that would seem to guarantee that it would be a perfect one, with the same wood in the handle and lower part, and that he and Miss Oliver had never had any sort of a quarrel."

There was a little pause and The Thinking Machine shifted his position slightly.

"Here I had a motive—jealousy of one man who was thrown over for another; the method of death, through the lattice; a clue to the murderer in the stiletto, and the name of the man. It seemed conclusive but I had overlooked a figure one. I saw that when Mr Oliver assured me that Miss Eleanor Oliver did not know the nobleman whose name I wrote for him; that she could not have known him. The entire structure tumbled. I was nonplussed and a little rude, I fear, in my surprise. Then I had to reconsider the matter from the beginning. The most important of all the connecting links was missing, yet the logic was right. It is always right.

"There are times when imagination has to bridge gaps caused by the absence of demonstrable facts. I considered the matter carefully, then saw where I had dropped the figure one. I 'phoned to Mr Hatch to know if Miss Oliver had a sister. She had. The newspapers to which Mr Hatch referred me told me the rest of it. It was Eleanor Oliver's sister who had the affair with the nobleman. That cleared it. There is the name of the murderer."

He laid down a card on which was scribbled this name and address: "Count Leo Tortino, Hotel Teutonic." Hatch and the detective read it simultaneously, then looked at The Thinking Machine inquiringly.

"But I don't see it yet," expostulated the detective. "This man Knight—"

"Briefly it is this," declared the other impatiently. "The newspapers carried a story of Florence Oliver's love affair with Count Tortino at the time she was travelling in Europe with her mother. According to what I read she jilted him and returned to this country where her engagement to another man was rumoured. That was several months ago. Now it doesn't follow that because the Count knew Florence Oliver that he knew or even knew of Eleanor Oliver.

"Suppose he came here maddened by disappointment and seeking revenge, suppose further he reached the theatre, as he did, while the anvil chorus was on, the party started into the wrong box and the usher mentioned casually that the Olivers were in there. We presume he knew Mrs Oliver by sight, and saw her. He might reasonably have surmised, perhaps he was told, that the other woman was Miss Oliver – and Miss Oliver meant to him the woman who had jilted him. The lattice work offered a way, the din of the music covered the act – and that's all. It doesn't really appear – it isn't necessary to know – how he carried the stiletto about him, or why."

The detective was gnawing his moustache. He was silent for several minutes trying to see the tragedy in this new light.

"But the threats Knight made?" he inquired finally.

"Has he explained them?"

"Oh, he said something about the girl being ill and wanting to go home, and he urged her not to. He told her, he says, that she mustn't go, because he would have to do something desperate. Silly explanation I call it."

"But I dare say it's perfectly correct," commented The Thinking Machine. "Men of your profession, Mr Mallory, never believe the simple things. If you would take the word of an accused man at face value occasionally you would have less trouble." There was a pause, then: "I promised Mr Knight that he would be free by midnight. It is now ten. Suppose you run down to the Teutonic and see Count Tortino. He will hardly deny anything."

Detective Mallory and Hatch found the Count in his room. He was lying face down across a bed with a bullet hole in his temple. A note of explanation confessed the singular error which had led to the murder of Eleanor Oliver.

It was three minutes of midnight when Sylvester Knight walked out of his cell a heartbroken man, but free.

13

FIVE MILLIONS BY WIRELESS

Within the great room, dim, shadowy, mysterious as the laboratory of some alchemist of old, and foul with the pungent odours of strange chemical messes, there blazed a single light, a powerful electrical contrivance fitted with reflector, and so shaded that its concentrated rays beat down fiercely upon a table littered with scientific apparatus; and bending over the table was a man, an odd, almost pathetic little figure, slight to childishness, small of stature, attenuated. His hair was a straw-coloured thatch thrown back impatiently from a domelike brow, increasing in effect the abnormal size of his head. His eyes were narrow slits of pale blue, squinting petulantly through thick spectacles; his wizened, clean-shaven face was white with the pallor of the student; his mouth was a straight, bloodless line. His hands, busy now at some microscopic labour, were slender and almost transparent under the blinding glare from above; his fingers long, sensitive, delicate.

The door opened, and an elderly woman appeared with a tray.

"Some coffee and rolls, sir," she explained. "Really you ought to have something, sir."

"Put them down." The little man didn't lift his eyes from his work; he spoke curtly.

"And if you should ask me, sir," the woman continued, "I'd say you ought to stop whatever you're a-doing of, and take some rest, sir."

"Tut, tut, Martha!" the little man objected. "I've only just begun."

"You've been a-standing right there, sir," Martha denied, in righteous indignation, "ever since Sunday afternoon at four o'clock."

"What time is it now?"

"It's ten o'clock Tuesday morning, sir."

"Dear me, dear me!"

"You haven't slept a wink, sir," Martha complained, "and you haven't eat enough—"

"Martha, you annoy me," the little man interrupted peevishly. "Run along and attend to your duties."

"But, sir, you can't keep a-going like—"

"Very well, then," and there was a childish tone of resignation in the master's voice. "It's Tuesday, you say? Tell me when it's noon Wednesday."

Martha went out with a helpless shrug of her shoulders, leaving him alone.

Hours passed. The coffee, untasted, grew cold. Motionless, the little man continued at his labors with tense eagerness in his narrow eyes, oblivious alike of the things about him, and of exhausted nature. The will beneath the straw-colored thatch knew not weariness.

And this was "The Thinking Machine" – Professor Augustus S.F.X. Van Dusen, Ph.D., F.R.S., M.D., LL.D., et cetera, et cetera—logician, analyst, worker of miracles in the exact sciences, intellectual wizard of his time; this the master mind, exalted by the cumulative genius of generations gone before, which had isolated itself on a pinnacle of achievement through sheer force of applied reason. Once he had been the controversial center of his profession, riding down pet theories and tentative surmises and cherished opinions, and setting up instead precise facts, a few rescued from the chaos he had himself created, more of his own uncovering. Now he was the court of last appeal in the sciences.

The Thinking Machine! No one of the honorary degrees thrust upon him willy-nilly by the universities of the world described him half so accurately as did this title—a chance paradox applied by a newspaper man. Seemingly tireless, calm, unemotional—unless one counted as an emotion the constant note of irritation in his voice—terse of speech, crabbed of manner, and possessed of an uncanny faculty of separating all things into their primal units, he lived in a circumscribed sphere which he had stripped of all illusion. The mental precision which distinguished his laboratory work characterized all else he did. If any man ever reduced human frailties, human virtues, and human motives to mathematics that man was The Thinking Machine.

It has been my pleasure to set down at another time and place some results of The Thinking Machine's investigations along lines disassociated with abstruse problems of his profession, these being chiefly instances in which he had turned the light of cold logic upon perplexing criminal mysteries with well-nigh mathematical precision.

Also, it has been my pleasure to relate at length some of those curious adventures which led to The Thinking Machine's incongruous friendship for Hutchinson Hatch.

Hatch was a newspaper reporter, a young man of vitality and enthusiasm and keen wordliness; he was a breath of the outside to this odd little man, who never read papers, who rarely came into contact with things as they are, who had not even the small vices which bring individuals together. It had been Hatch who first applied the title of The Thinking Machine to the eminent scientist, and the phrase had stuck.

Perhaps not the least interesting of the adventures of these two together was that which culminated in the bestowal upon The

Thinking Machine of the Order of the Iron Eagle, second class, by Emperor Gustavus, of Germania-Austria. It so happened in that case that the fate of an empire and the future of its royal house lay for a time in The Thinking Machine's slender hands. Failure on his part certainly would have changed the history of Europe, and probably the map. This problem was purely intellectual, and came to his attention at a time when physical vitality was at its lowest, after forty-eight hours' unceasing work in his laboratory.

The door opened, and Martha entered.

"Martha," the eminent scientist stormed, "if you've brought me more coffee I shall discharge you!"

"It isn't coffee, sir," she replied. "It's a—"

"And don't tell me it's already twelve o'clock Wednesday."

"It's a card, sir. Two gentlemen who—"

"Can't see them."

Not for an instant had the squinting eyes been raised from the work which engrossed The Thinking Machine. Martha laid the card on the table; he glanced at it impatiently. Herr Von Hartzfeldt!

"He says, sir, it's a matter of the utmost importance," Martha explained.

"Ask him who he is and what he wants."

The unexpectedness of the answer Martha brought back straightened The Thinking Machine where he stood.

"He says, sir," she reported, "that he's the ambassador to the United States from Germania-Austria."

"Show him in at once."

Two gentlemen entered, one Baron Von Hartzfeldt, polished, courtly, distinguished in appearance, a famous figure in the diplomatic world; the other of a more rugged type, shorter, heavier, with bristly hair and beard, and deeply bronzed face. For an instant they stared into the wizened countenance of the little scientist with something like astonishment.

"We have come to you, Mr Van Dusen, in an extremity the gravity of which cannot be exaggerated," Baron Von Hartzfeldt began suavely. "We know, as all the world knows, your splendid achievements in science. We know, too, that you have occasionally consented to investigate more material problems—that is, mysteries of crimes, and—"

"Please come to the point," The Thinking Machine interrupted tartly. "If you hadn't known who I was, and hadn't needed me, you wouldn't have come. Now, what is it? This gentleman—"

"Pardon me," the ambassador begged, in polite confusion at the curt directness of his host. "Admiral Hausen-Aubier, of the royal navy, commanding the Mediterranean Fleet, now visiting your city on his flagship, the Friedrich der Grosse, which lies in the outer harbor."

The admiral bowed ceremoniously, and, accepting a slight movement of The Thinking Machine's hand as an invitation to seats, the two gentlemen sat down. Not until that moment had the scientist realized his own weariness. The big chair offered grateful relaxation to tired limbs, and, with his enormous head tilted back, narrowed eyes turned upward, and slender fingers precisely tip to tip, he waited.

"One of my officers has disappeared from the flagship—rather, has utterly vanished," said Admiral Hausen-Aubier. He spoke excellent English, but there was a guttural undercurrent of excitement in his tone. "He went to his stateroom at midnight; next morning at seven o'clock he was gone. The guard at his door had been drugged with chloroform, and can tell nothing."

"Guard at the door?" questioned The Thinking Machine. "Why?"

Admiral Hausen-Aubier seemed oddly disturbed by the question. He shot a hasty glance at Baron Von Hartzfeldt.

"Ship discipline," explained the diplomat vaguely.

"Was he under arrest?"

"Oh, no!" This from the admiral.

"Do you sleep with a guard at your door?"

"No."

"Any of the other officers?"

"No."

"Go on, please."

"There isn't much to tell." There was bewilderment, deep concern, grief even, in the bronzed face. "The officer's bed had been occupied, but there was no sign of a struggle. It was as if he had arisen, dressed, and gone out. There was no note, no shred or fragment of a clew—nothing. No one saw him from the moment he entered his stateroom and closed his door—not even the guard. There were half a dozen sentries, watchmen, on deck; neither saw nor heard anything out of the ordinary. He isn't aboard ship; we have searched from keel to signal yard; and he didn't go overside in a ship's boat; they are all accounted for. He is not a particularly strong swimmer, and could not have reached shore in that way."

"You say the guard had been chloroformed," The Thinking Machine went back. "Just what happened to him? How do you know he was chloroformed?"

"By the odor," replied the admiral, answering the last question first. "In order to enter the officer's suite it was necessary—"

"Suite, did you say?"

"Yes; that is, he occupied more than one stateroom—"

"I understand. Go on."

"It was necessary to pass through an antechamber. The guard slept there. He says it must have been after one o'clock when he went to sleep. Next morning he was found unconscious, and the officer was gone." He paused. "There can be no question whatever of the guard's integrity. He has been attached to the—the officer for many years."

With eyes all but closed, The Thinking Machine sat motionless for minute after minute, the while thin, spidery lines of though ruffled the domelike brow. At last:

FIVE MILLIONS BY WIRELESS

"The matter hasn't been reported to the police?"

"No." Admiral Hausen – Aubier looked startled.

"Why not?"

"Because," Baron Von Hartzfeldt answered, "when it was brought to my attention in Washington by wire, we decided against that. The affair is extremely delicate. It is inadvisable that the police even should so much as suspect—"

The Thinking Machine nodded.

"How about the secret service?"

"That bureau has been at work on the case from the first," the diplomatist replied; "also half a dozen secret agents attached to the embassy. You must understand, Mr Van Dusen, that it is absolutely essential that no word of the disappearance – not even a hint of it – be allowed to become public. The result would be a – a disaster. I can't say more."

"Perhaps," suggested The Thinking Machine irrelevantly, "perhaps the officer deserted?"

"I would vouch for his loyalty with my life," declared the admiral, with deep feeling.

"Or perhaps it was suicide?"

Again there was a swift interchange of glances between the admiral and the ambassador. Obviously that was a possibility that had occurred to each of them, and yet one that neither dared admit.

"Impossible!" the diplomat shook his head.

"Nothing is impossible," snapped The Thinking Machine curtly. "Don't say that. It annoys me exceedingly." Fell a short silence. Finally: "Just when did your officer disappear?"

"Last Tuesday—almost a week ago," Admiral Hausen-Aubier told him.

"And nothing – nothing – has been heard of him? Or from him? Or from any one else concerning him?"

"Nothing – not a word," Admiral Hausen – Aubier said. "If we could only hear! If we could only know whether he is living or dead!"

"What's his name?"

"Lieutenant Leopold Von Zinckl."

For the first time, The Thinking Machine lowered his eyes and swept the countenances of the two men before him – both grave, troubled, lined with worry. Under his curious scrutiny, the diplomatist retained his self-possession by sheer force of will; but a vital, consuming nervousness seemed to seize upon the man of the sea.

"I mean," and again the scientist was squinting into the gloom above, "I mean his real name."

Admiral Hausen-Aubier's broad face flushed suddenly as if from a blow, and he started to his feet. Some subtle warning form the ambassador caused him to drop back into his seat.

"That is his real name," he said distinctly; "Lieutenant Leopold Von Zinckl."

"May I ask," The Thinking Machine was speaking very slowly, "if his majesty the emperor has been informed of Lieutenant Von Zinckl's disappearance?"

Perhaps The Thinking Machine anticipated the effect of the question; perhaps he did not. Anyway, he didn't look around when Admiral Hausen-Aubier came to his feet with a mighty Teutonic exclamation, and strode the length of the big room, his face dead white beneath the coat of bronze. Baron Von Hartzfeldt remained seated, apparently fascinated by some strange, newly discovered quality in the scientist.

"We have not informed the emperor of the affair as yet," he said, at last, steadily. "We thought it inadvisable to go so far until every effort had been made to—"

The Thinking Machine interrupted him with an impatient gesture of one slender hand.

"As a matter of fact, the situation is like this, isn't it?" he queried abruptly. "Prince Otto Ludwig, heir apparent to the throne of Germania-Austria, has been abducted from the royal suite of the battleship Friedrich der Grosse, in the harbor of a friendly nation?"

FIVE MILLIONS BY WIRELESS 249

There was an instant's amazed silence. Suddenly Admiral Hausen-Aubier covered his face with his hands, and stood, his great shoulders shaking. Straining nerves had broken at last. Baron Von Hartzfeldt, ripe in diplomatic experience, seemed merely astonished, if one might judge by the face of him.

"How do you know that?" he inquired quietly, after a moment. "Outside of the secret service and my own agents, there are not six persons in the world who are aware—"

"How do I know it?" interrupted The Thinking Machine. "You have just told me. Logic, logic, logic!"

"I have told you?" There was blank bewilderment on the diplomatist's face.

"You and Admiral Hausen-Aubier together," The Thinking Machine declared petulantly.

"But how, man, how?" demanded Baron Von Hartzfeldt. "Of course, you knew from the newspapers that his highness, Crown Prince Otto Ludwig, was visiting America; but—"

"I never read newspapers," snapped The Thinking Machine. "I didn't know he was here any more than I knew the battleship Friedrich der Grosse was in the harbor. It's logic, logic – the adding together of the separate units – a simple demonstration of the fact that two and two make four, not sometimes, but all the time."

Admiral Hausen-Aubier, having mastered the emotion which had shaken him, resumed his seat, staring curiously into the wizened face before him.

"Still I don't understand," Baron Von Hartzfeldt insisted. "Logic, you say. How?"

"I'll see if I can make it clear." And there was that in the manner of the eminent man of science which was no compliment to their perspicacity. "You tell me an officer has disappeared, that his guard was chloroformed. The officer was not under arrest, and no other officer aboard ship had a guard. I assume, therefore, for the moment that the officer was a man of consequence, else he was mentally irresponsible. An instant later you tell me how to enter the officer's suite—not stateroom, but suite. Ergo, a man of so much consequence that he occupies a suite; a man of so much consequence that you didn't dare report his disappearance to the police; a man of so much consequence that public knowledge of the affair would precipitate disaster. Do you follow the thread?"

Fascinated, the two listeners nodded.

"Very well," The Thinking Machine resumed, in that odd little tone of irritation. "There are only a few persons in the world of so much consequence as all that – that is, of so much consequence aboard a ship of war. Those are members of the royal household. I am of German descent; hence I am well acquainted with the histories of the German countries. I know that Emperor Gustavus has only one son, Otto Ludwig, the crown prince. I know that no reigning king has ever visited America; therefore logic, inexorable, indisputable logic, tells me that Prince Otto Ludwig is the officer who occupied the royal suite aboard your ship."

He paused, and readjusted himself in the great chair. When he spoke again, it was in the tone of one who is thoughtfully checking off and verifying the units of a problem he has solved. His two visitors were staring at him breathlessly.

"Of course, no royal person save a son of the house of Germania-Austria would be occupying the royal suite on a Germania-Austrian battleship," he said slowly. "Proper adjustment of the actual facts leading straight to the crown prince removed instantly as a possibility a vague suggestion that the officer with the guard at his door, while not a prisoner, was mentally irresponsible. I've made myself clear, I hope?"

"It's marvelous!" ejaculated the diplomatist. "If any man can lead us to the end of this mystery, you are that man!"

"Thanks," returned The Thinking Machine dryly.

"You said," Admiral Hausen-Aubier questioned tensely, "that his highness had been abducted?"

"Certainly."

"Why abducted instead of – of – murdered—" He shuddered a little. "Instead of suicide?"

"That man who is clever enough and bold enough to board your ship and chloroform a guard is not fool enough to murder a man and then drag him out over the guard and throw him into the sea," was the reply, "or to drag him out and then murder him. In either event, such an act would have been useless; and as a rule murderers don't do useless things. As for suicide, it would not have been necessary for the prince to chloroform his guard, or even to leave his stateroom. Remains, therefore, only abduction."

"But who abducted him?" the admiral insisted. "Why? How was he taken away from the ship?"

The Thinking Machine shrugged his narrow shoulders.

"I don't know," he said. "Either one of a dozen ways—aeroplane, rowboat, submarine—" He stopped.

"But–but no one heard anything," the admiral pointed out.

"That doesn't signify."

There seemed nothing to cling to, no tangible fact upon which to base even understanding. Aeroplane—submarine—'twas fantasy, preposterous, unheard of. Hopelessly enough, Admiral Hausen-Aubier turned back to the one vital question:

"At any rate, the prince is alive?"

"I don't know. He was abducted a week ago. You've heard nothing since. He may have been murdered after he was taken away. He may have been. I doubt it."

Admiral Hausen-Aubier arose tragically, with haggard face, a light of desperation in his eyes, his powerful, sun-dyed hands pressed to his temples.

"If he is dead, do you know what it means?" he demanded vehemently. "It means the fall of the royal house of Germania-Austria with the passing of our emperor, who is now nearly eighty; it means the end of our country as a monarchy; it means war, revolution, a-a republic!"

"That wouldn't be so bad," commented The Thinking Machine oddly. "There'll be nothing but republics in a few years; witness France, Portugal, China—"

"You can't realize the acute political situation in my country," Admiral Hausen-Aubier rushed on, heedless of the other's remark. "Already there are dissensions; the emperor holds his kingdom together with a rod of iron, and his people only submit because they expect so much of Prince Otto Ludwig when he ascends the throne. He is popular with his subjects – the crown prince, I mean – and they would welcome him as emperor – welcome him, but no one else. It is absolutely necessary that he be found! The future of my country – our country," and he turned to Baron Von Hartzfeldt, "depends upon finding him."

Seemingly some new thought was born in The Thinking Machine's mind. His eyes opened slightly, and he turned upon Baron Von Hartzfeldt inquiringly. Apparently the ambassador understood, for he nodded.

"He is revealing diplomatic secrets," he said, with a slight movement of his shoulders; "but what he says is true."

"In that case—" The Thinking Machine began; and then he lapsed into silence. For minute after minute he sat, heedless of the nervous pacing of Admiral Hausen-Aubier, heedless of the constant interrogation of the ambassador's eyes.

"In that case—" the ambassador prompted.

"Is Crown Prince Otto Ludwig here incognito, or is it generally known that he is in this country?" the scientist questioned suddenly.

"He is here officially," was the response; "that is, publicly. The government of the United States has received him and entertained him, and you know all that that means."

"Then how do you – have you – accounted for his disappearance?"

"Lies!" Admiral Hausen-Aubier broke in bitterly. "He is supposed to be dangerously ill, confined to his stateroom aboard the Friedrich der Grosse; and no one except the ship's surgeon is permitted to see him. We have lied even to our emperor! He believes the prince is ill; if he understood that his son, the heir apparent, was missing, dead, perhaps – ach, Gott! Every moment I am expecting sailing orders – orders to return home. I can't go back to my king and tell him that the son he intrusted to my care, the hope and salvation of my country, is – is – I can't even say dead – I could only say that I don't know."

There was something magnificent in the bronzed old sailorman – something at once rugged and tender and fierce in his loyalty. The Thinking Machine studied the grief-stricken face curiously. Unashamed, Admiral Hausen-Aubier permitted the tears to gather in his eyes and roll down his furrowed cheeks.

"I don't care for myself," he explained huskily. "I do care for my country, for my prince. In any event, there remains for me only dishonor and death."

"Suicide?" questioned the scientist coldly.

"What else is there?"

"That," The Thinking Machine murmured acridly, "would improve the situation a lot! If I had committed suicide every time I had a problem to solve I should have been very dead by this time." His manner changed. "We know the prince was abducted; he is probably not dead, but we have no word of him or from him; therefore, there remains only—"

"Only what?" The question came from his two visitors simultaneously.

"Only a question of the most effective way of establishing communication with him."

"If we knew how to communicate with him, we'd go get him instead!" declared Admiral Hausen-Aubier grimly. "There are eight hundred men on the battleship who—"

The Thinking Machine arose, stood staring blankly at the two, much as if he had never seen them before; then walked over to his worktable, and shut off the great electric light.

"It's easy enough to communicate with Prince Otto Ludwig," he said, as he returned to them. "There are half a dozen ways."

"Then why, if it is so easy," demanded the diplomatist, "why hasn't he communicated with his ship?"

"There's always a chance that he doesn't want to, you know," was the enigmatic response. "How many persons know of his disappearance?"

"Only five outside of the secret service and the embassy agents," Admiral Hausen-Aubier answered. "They are Baron Von Hartzfeldt here, the guard, the ship's commander, the ship's surgeon, and myself."

"Too many!" The Thinking Machine shook his head slowly. "However, let's go aboard the Friedrich der Grosse. I don't recall that I've ever been on a modern battleship."

Night had fallen as the three men, each eminent in his own profession, boarded a small power boat off Atlantic Avenue, and were hurried away through slashing waters to the giant battleship in the outer harbor. There for an hour or more the little scientist pottered about the magnificent suite which had been occupied by Prince Otto Ludwig. He asked one or two casual questions of the guard; that was all, after which he retired to the admiral's cabin to write a short note.

"If," he remarked, as he addressed an envelope to Hutchinson Hatch, "if the prince is alive we shall hear from him. If he is dead we will not." His eye chanced upon a glaring headline in a newspaper on the desk:

PRINCE OTTO LUDWIG DANGEROUSLY ILL.

Heir to Throne of Germania-Austria

Confined to Suite Aboard the Battle-

Ship "Friedrich der Grosse."

No One Permitted to See Him.

The Thinking Machine glanced at Admiral Hausen-Aubier.

"Lies!" declared the rugged old sailor. "Every day for a week it has been the same. We are compelled to issue bulletins. Ach, Gott! He must be found!"

"Please have this note sent ashore and delivered immediately," the scientist requested. "Meanwhile, I haven't been in bed for three nights. If you'll give me a berth, I'll get some sleep. Wake me if necessary."

"You expect something to happen, then?"

"Certainly. I expect a wireless, but not for several hours-probably not until tomorrow afternoon."

"A wireless?" There was a flicker of hope in the admiral's eyes. "May-may I ask from whom?"

"From Crown Prince Otto Ludwig," said The Thinking Machine placidly. "I'm going to sleep. Goodnight."

Three hours later Admiral Hausen-Aubier in person aroused The Thinking Machine from the lethargy of oblivion which followed upon utter physical and mental exhaustion, and thrust a wireless message under his nose. It said simply:

O.K. Hatch.

The Thinking Machine blinked at it, grunted, then turned over as if to go back to sleep. Struck with some new idea, however, he opened his eyes for an instant.

"Issue a special bulletin to the press," he directed drowsily, "to the effect that Prince Otto Ludwig's condition has taken a sudden turn for the better. He is expected to be up and around again in a few days."

The sentence ended in a light snore.

All that night Admiral Hausen-Aubier, haggard, vigilant, sat beside the wireless operator in his cabinet on the upper deck, waiting, waiting, he knew not for what. Darkness passed, the stars died, and pallid dawn found him there.

At nine o'clock he ordered coffee; at noon more coffee.

At four in the afternoon the thing he had been waiting for came – only three words:

Followed suggestion. Communicate.

"Very indistinct, sir," the operator reported. "An amateur sending."

The Thinking Machine, wide awake now, and below deck discussing high explosives with a gunner's mate, was summoned. Into the wireless cabinet with him came Baron Von Hartzfeldt. For an instant the three men studied in silence this portentous message from the void.

"Keep in touch with him," The Thinking Machine instructed the operator. "What's his range?"

"Hundred miles, sir."

"Strong or weak?"

"Weak, sir."

"Reduce the range."

"I did, sir, and lost him."

"Increase it."

With the receiver clamped to his ears, the operator thrust his range key forward, and listened.

"I lose him, sir," he reported.

"Very well. Set at one hundred." The scientist turned to Baron Von Hartzfeldt and Admiral Hausen-Aubier. "He is alive, and less than a hundred miles away," he explained hurriedly. Then to the operator: "Send as I dictate:

"Is-O-L-there?"

The instrument hissed as the message spanned the abyss of space; in the glass drum above, great crackling electric sparks leaped and roared fitfully, lighting the tense faces of the men in the cabinet. Came dead silence – painful silence – then the operator read the answer aloud:

"Yes."

"Mein Gott ich lobe!" One great exclamation of thanks, and Admiral Hausen-Aubier buried his face in his hands.

To Baron Von Hartzfeldt the whole thing was wizardry pure and simple. The Thinking Machine had summoned the lost out of the void. While a hundred trained men, keen-eyes, indefatigable, wary as ferrets, were searching for the crown prince, along comes this withered, white-faced little man of science, with his monstrous head and his feeble hands, and works a miracle under his very eyes! He listened, fascinated, as The Thinking Machine continued:

"Must-prove-identity-Hausen-Aubier-here-ask-O-L-give-word-or phrase-identify-him."

Suddenly The Thinking Machine whirled about to face the admiral. The answer should prove once for all whether the prince was alive or dead. Minutes passed. Finally—

"It's coming, sir, in German," the operator explained:

"Neujarstag-eine-cigarre."

"New Year's Day-a cigar!" Admiral Hausen-Aubier translated, in obvious bewilderment. Swiftly his face cleared. "I understand. He refers to an incident that he and I alone know. When a lad of twelve he tried to smoke a cigar, and it made him deathly ill. I saved him from—"

"Send," interrupted The Thinking Machine:

"Satisfied-give-terms."

And the operator read:

"Five-million-dollars!"

"Five million dollars!" exclaimed the admiral and the diplomatist, in a breath. "Does he mean ransom?" Baron Von Hartzfeldt asked, aghast. "Five million dollars!"

"Five million dollars, yes," the scientist replied irritably. "We're not dealing with children. We're dealing with shrewd, daring, intelligent men who have played a big game for a big stake; and if you love your country and your king you'd better thank God it's only money they want. Suppose they had demanded a constitution, or even the abdication of your emperor? That might have meant revolution, war—anything." He stared at them an instant, then swung around to the operator. "Send," he commanded:

"We – accept – terms—"

"Why, man, you are mad!" interposed the diplomatist sharply. "It's preposterous!"

But The Thinking Machine said again evenly:

"We-accept-terms-specify-by-mail-place-time-manner-of-settlement."

The crashing of the mighty current in the glass drum ceased as the message was finished, and with strained attention the three men waited. Again a tense pause. At last the operator read:

"Also-assurance-no-prosecution."

And The Thinking Machine dictated:

"Accept."

"Wait a minute!" commanded Admiral Hausen-Aubier hotly. "Do you mean we are promising immunity to the men who abducted—"

"Certainly," replied the scientist. "They're not fools. If we don't promise it, all they have to do is break off communication and wait until such time as you will promise it." He shrugged his shoulders. "Or else stick a knife into your prince, and end the affair. Besides, prosecution means publicity."

With clenched hands, the admiral turned away; no answer seemed possible. Heedless of the things about him, Baron Von Hartzfeldt sat dumbly meditating upon the staggering ransom. It would take days to raise so vast a sum, if he could do it at all; and his private resources, together with those of Admiral Hausen-Aubier, would be drained to the last dollar. Even then it might be necessary to call upon the royal treasury. That would be a confession; out of it would come only dishonor and—death.

The Thinking Machine dictated:

"Accept-we-pledge-Hausen-Aubier's-word-of honor."

And the answer came:

"Satisfied - mailing - details - tonight - will - communicate - tomorrow-noon."

The attenuated thread which had linked them with the unknown was broken. Somewhere off through space they had talked with a man whom human ingenuity had failed to find – 'twas another of the many miracles of modern science.

FIVE MILLIONS BY WIRELESS 259

The morrow brought a typewritten letter incapable of misconstruction. It was the usual thing – an open field, some thirty miles out of the city, a lone tree in the center of the field, a suit case containing the money to be left there. The letter concluded with a paragraph after this fashion:

Your prince's life depends upon rigid adherence to these instructions. If there is any attempt to watch, or to identify us, or molest us, a pistol shot will end the affair; if the bag is there, and the money is in the bag, he will be aboard ship within five hours. Remember, we hold your pledge!

"Crude," commented The Thinking Machine. "I was led to expect better things of them."

"But the money, man, the money?" exclaimed Baron Von Hartzfeldt. "It will be absolutely impossible to get it unless – unless we call upon the royal treasury."

His face was haggard, his eyes inflamed by lack of sleep, and deep furrows lined his usually placid brow. He leaned forward, and stared tensely into the pallid, wizened face of the scientist, who sat with head tilted back, his gaze turned steadily upward, his slender fingers precisely tip to tip.

"Five million dollars in gold," The Thinking Machine observed ambiguously, "would weigh tons. It would take five hundred ten-thousand-dollar notes to make five million dollars, and I doubt if there are that many in existence. It would take five thousand thousand-dollar notes. Absurd! There will have to be two, perhaps three, of the bags."

"But don't you understand," Baron Von Hartzfeldt burst out violently, "that it's impossible to raise that sum? That there will be none of the bags? That some other scheme—"

"Oh, yes, there will be three of the bags," The Thinking Machine asserted mildly. "But, of course, there will be no money in them!"

Admiral Hasuen-Aubier and the diplomatist digested the statement in silence.

"But you have pledged my word of honor—" the old sailorman objected.

"Not to prosecute," the scientist pointed out.

"Absurd!" The ambassador came to his feet. "You have said we are not dealing with children. Why put the empty bags there? If they find they are empty, the prince's life will pay forfeit; if we attempt to surround them and capture them, the result will be the same; and, besides, we will have broken our pledge."

"I've never seen any one so fussy about their pledges as you gentlemen are," observed The Thinking Machine acridly. "Don't worry. I shall not break a pledge; I shall not attempt to surround them and capture them; I shall not, nor shall any one representing me, or any of us, for that matter, be within miles of that particular field after the bags are placed. They shall reach the field unmolested and unwatched."

"You are talking in riddles," declared the diplomatist impatiently. "What do you mean?"

"I mean merely that the men who go to get the bags of money will wait right there until I come, even if it should happen to take two weeks," was the enigmatic response. "Also, I'll say they'll be glad to see me when I get there, and glad to restore Prince Otto Ludwig to his ship without one penny being paid. There will be no prosecution."

"But-but I don't understand," stammered the ambassador.

"I don't expect you to," said The Thinking Machine ungraciously. "Nor do I expect you to understand this."

Impatiently he spread a newspaper before the two men, and indicated an advertisement in black-faced type. It was on the first page, directly beneath a bulletin announcing a sudden change for the better in Prince Otto Ludwig's condition. The admiral read it aloud blankly:

"Wireless is only means communication can not be traced. Use it. Safe for all. Communicate with ship immediately. Would advise you erect private station."

That was all of it. It was addressed to no one, and signed by no one; if it had any meaning at all, it was merely as a curious method of advertising wireless telegraphy. Inquiringly at last the baron and the admiral raised their eyes to those of The Thinking Machine.

"The abductors of Prince Otto Ludwig had not communicated with the ship," he explained tersely, "because they could devise no way they considered absolutely safe. They knew the secret service would be at work. They didn't dare to telegraph in the usual way, nor send a messenger, nor even a letter. Our secret service is an able organization; they understood it was not to be trifled with. All these things considered, I didn't believe the abductors could hit upon a plan of communication which they considered safe. I inserted that advertisement in all the newspapers. It was a suggestion. They understood, and followed it. You will remember their first communication."

Baron Von Hartzfeldt came to his feet suddenly, then sat down again. The miracle hadn't been a miracle, after all. It was merely common sense.

"Jeder verrückte könnte davon denken!" exclaimed the admiral bluntly.

"Quite right," assented The Thinking Machine. "Any fool could have thought of that—but no other fool did!"

Promptly at noon the wireless operator plucked this from the void:

"Is-letter-satisfactory?"

And the scientist dictated an answer:

"Yes-except-we-require-another-day-to-raise-money."

"Granted—"

"Impossible-put-all-money-one-bag-will-use-three."

"Satisfactory-remember-our-warning."

"You-have-our-pledge."

As the last word of the message went hurtling off into space, The Thinking Machine scrambled down the sea ladder and was rowed ashore. From his own home, half an hour later, he called Hutchinson Hatch on the telephone.

"I want," he said, "three large suit cases, one pair of extra-heavy rubber gloves, ten miles of electric wire well insulated, three Edison transformers, one fast automobile, permission to tap the Abington trolley wire, and two dozen ham sandwiches."

Hatch laughed. He was accustomed to the eccentricities of this little man of science.

"You shall have them," he promised.

"Bring everything to my house at midnight."

"Right!"

Looking back upon it later, Hatch decided he had never worked so hard in his life as he did that night; in addition to which he had the satisfaction of not knowing just what he was doing. There were telephone poles to be climbed, and shallow trenches to be dug and immediately filled in so no trace of their existence remained, and miles of electric wire to be hauled through thickly weeded fields. Dawn was breaking when everything seemed to be done.

"This," remarked The Thinking Machine, "is where the ham sandwiches are useful."

They breakfasted upon them, after which The Thinking Machine went away, leaving Hatch to watch the small dial of some sort of an indicator attached to a wire. At noon the scientist returned, and, without a word, took the reporter's place at the dial. At thirty-three minutes past four the hand of the indicator suddenly shot around to one side, and the scientist arose.

"We have caught a fish," he said. "Come on!"

They were in the automobile, speeding along the highway, before Hatch spoke.

"What sort of fish?" he asked curiously.

"I don't know," was the reply. "A person, or persons, have picked up one or more of those suit cases to the bottom of which our electric wire is connected. He is unable to let go –

he, or they, as the case may be. He will be unconscious when we reach him."

"Dead, you mean," said Hatch grimly. "The current from that trolley wire—"

"Unconscious," The Thinking Machine corrected. "The current is reduced. There is a transformer in each of the suit cases. The wiring extends up through the handles where the insulation is stripped off."

Three, four, nearly five, miles they went like the wind; then the motor car stopped with a jerk, and Hatch, taking advantage of his longer legs, galloped off through the open field toward the lone tree in the center. The thing he saw caused him to stop suddenly and raise his hands in horror. Upon the ground in front of him was the convulsed figure of a young man, foreign-looking, distinguished even. His distorted face, livid now, was turned upward, and his hands were gripped to the suit case by the powerful electric current.

"Who is it?" queried the scientist.

"Crown Prince Otto Ludwig, of Germania-Austria!"

"What?" The question came violently, a single burst of amazement. And again: "What?" There was an expression on The Thinking Machine's face the like of which Hatch had never seen there before. "It's a possibility I had never considered. So he wanted the five million—" Suddenly his whole manner changed. "Let's get him to the motor."

With rubber-gloved hands, he cut the wire which held the crown prince prisoner, and the unconscious man fell back limply, as if dead. Five minutes later they had lifted him into the tonneau, and The Thinking Machine bent over him anxiously, with his hand on his wrist.

"Where to?" asked Hatch.

"Anywhere, and fast!" was the reply. "I must think."

Oblivious of the swaying and clatter of the huge car, The Thinking Machine sat silent for minute after minute as it sped on over the smooth road. Finally he seemed satisfied. He leaned forward, and touched Hatch on the shoulder.

"It's all right," he said. "We'll go aboard ship now."

Late that night the crown prince, himself again, but with badly burned hands, explained. He had been stupefied by chloroform, kidnaped, and lowered over the battleship rail in utter darkness. His impression was that he had been taken away in a small boat which had muffled oars. When he recovered, he found himself a prisoner in a deserted country house, with two men on guard. He didn't know the name of either.

Calmly enough, the three of them discussed the affair in all its aspects. They could devise no safe means of communicating with the ship until he suggested the wireless. He even aided in the erection of a station between two tall trees on a remote hill somewhere. One of his guards, meanwhile, had to master the code. He had become fairly proficient when they saw the advertisement in the newspapers.

"But how is it you went to get the money?" the scientist questioned curiously.

"The men feared treachery," was the explanation. "They were willing to take my word of honor that I would get it and return with it, after which I was to be free. A prince of the royal house of Germania-Austria may not break his word of honor."

Tiny corrugations in the domelike brow of the scientist caused Hatch to stare at him expectantly; even as he looked they passed.

"Mr Hatch," he said abruptly, "I have heard you refer to certain newspaper stories as 'peaches' and 'corkers' and what not. How would you class this?"

"This," said the reporter enthusiastically, "this is a bird!"

"It has only one defect," remarked The Thinking Machine. "It cannot be printed."

One eminent scientist who had achieved the seemingly impossible, and one disgusted newspaper reporter were rowed ashore at midnight.

"What do you think of it all, anyhow?" demanded Hatch suddenly.

"I have no opinion to express," declared The Thinking Machine crabbedly. "The prince has come to his own again; that is sufficient."

Some weeks later Professor Augustus S. F. X. Van Dusen was decorated with the Order of the Iron Eagle by Emperor Gustavus, of Germania-Austria. Reflectively he twisted the elaborate jeweled bauble in his slender fingers; then returned to his worktable under the great electric light. For a minute or more tiny corrugations appeared in his forehead; finally they passed as that strange mind of his became absorbed in the thing he was doing.

14

PROBLEM OF THE ORGAN GRINDER

Hutchinson Hatch, reporter, was standing in a corner with both hands in his coat pockets. Just three inches to the left of his second waistcoat button was the point of a stiletto, and he glanced at it from time to time in frank uneasiness, then his eyes returned to the flushed, tense face of the girl who held it. She was Italian. Her eyes were splendidly black, and there was a gleam in them that was anything but reassuring. Her scarlet lips were parted slightly, disclosing small, regular, white teeth clenched tightly together. A brilliant multicolored headdress partially confined her hair and rippled down about her shoulders. Her skirt was barely to her ankles.

"I feel like the third act of an Italian comic opera," Hatch thought grimly. Then aloud, "What is all this?"

"You must be silent, signor!" warned the young woman in excellent English.

"I am going to be," Hatch explained; "but still I should like to—"

"You must be silent, signor!" the girl repeated. "No, don't take your hands from your pockets!"

"But look here!"

The stiletto point was pressed in until he felt it against his flesh. He winced involuntarily, but wisely held his tongue.

It was a time to stand perfectly still and wait. He had come to the tenement in the course of his professional duties, and had rapped on this door to inquire in which apartment a certain family lived. The door had been opened by the young woman—and now this! He didn't understand it; he didn't even make a pretense of conjecturing what it meant. He just kept on standing still.

From outside came the varied noises of a busy city. Inside the gloom grew about him, and gradually the rigid, motionless figure of the girl became a shadowy silhouette. Then an electric arc light outside, which happened to be on a level with a window, spluttered and flashed into brilliance almost blinding him. Through the murk of the room only their motionless figures were visible.

After awhile the reporter heard vaguely a stealthy shuffle of feet as if some one was passing along the hall. Then the door leading from the hall into the next room opened and closed softly. The girl prodded him with the stiletto point to remind him to be silent. It was a needless warning, because now Hatch dimly foresaw some grave and imminent danger to himself in the presence of this third person, whoever it might be. Unconsciously he was concentrating all his forces, mental and physical, for – for something he didn't know what.

The shuffling feet were now in the next room. He heard them moving about as if coming toward the connecting door. Then a hand was laid on the knob, the lock rattled a little, and the door was softly closed. Hatch took a deep breath of relief – whoever this third person might be, he evidently had no business in the room with them just at that moment.

With straining ears and tense nerves the reporter listened, and after awhile came a muffled chatter as of some one talking rapidly and incoherently. Then he heard a man's voice, pleasant neither in tone nor in the expletives used, and several times he heard the chatter—quick, excited, incoherent. At last the man broke out into a string of profanity, objurgations. The chatter rose angrily, and burst finally into a strangling, guttural scream of anguish.

With a chilly creepiness along his spine and nerves strained to the breaking point, Hatch started forward involuntarily. The stiletto point at his breast stopped him. He glared at the rigid figure of the girl and choked back, with an effort, an outburst of emotion. His utter helplessness overwhelmed him.

"Some one is being killed in there!" he protested desperately between gritting teeth.

"Sh-h!" warned the girl.

From the next room came the shuffling of feet again, then a soft thump thrice repeated, and a faint gurgling cry. Hatch shivered a little; the girl was rigid as marble.

"I guess that fixed you!" Hatch heard a man say.

There was silence for a minute or so. The feet moved stealthily again, and the door leading from the other room into the hall opened and closed. The footsteps moved rapidly along, then apparently precaution was forgotten, for they clattered down the steps and were gone.

Suddenly the girl straightened up. "You will remain here, signor," she said, "until I am out of the house? You will raise no alarm for at least five minutes? Believe me, if you do, it will be worse for you; for sometime, somewhere, you will have occasion to regret it! You promise?"

Hatch would not make himself believe that he had the slightest choice in the matter. "I promise, of course," he said.

She bowed a little, half mockingly, flung open the door, and ran out. Hatch heard the swishing of her skirts as she sped down the stairs, then he brought himself together with a huge sigh and a nervous jerking of his limbs.

He strode across the room twice to regain possession of jumping nerves, then paused and lighted a cigarette. What was in the next room? He didn't know. He wanted to know, and yet there was an intangible fear which clung to him and held him back when he started for the door. At last he mastered this absurd weakness, and flung the door open wide, and walked in. At first he saw nothing, and he had expected to see every evidence of a brutal crime. Then in a far corner he noticed what seemed to be a bundle of rags which had been thrown there carelessly. He strode over boldly and poked it with his foot, stooping to examine it.

What he saw brought an exclamation from him; but it was rather of astonishment than of horror. The thing he had found was the body of a monkey. The rags were the tawdry clothing in which organ grinders attire their apish companions. There was a little cap, a coat, and trousers.

"Well! What in the deuce—" exclaimed the reporter. He dropped on his knees beside the tiny body. There were three stab wounds in it – one in the throat and two in the breast. The body was still warm.

"But why," protested Hatch, "should anyone, man or woman, murder a monkey?"

Professor Augustus S. F. X. Van Dusen – The Thinking Machine – didn't hazard a conjecture. "Are you sure it was a monkey that was murdered?" he asked instead. "I mean are you sure that only a monkey was murdered?"

"I am sure," he responded emphatically, "that the monkey was killed while I listened, and certainly there was nothing else that I could find or that I heard to indicate anything beyond that."

"Did you search the place?" queried the scientist.

"Yes."

"Find anything?"

"No, nothing."

"Did you happen to notice, Mr Hatch, if the monkey's clothing had pockets?"

"There were no pockets. I looked for them."

The Thinking Machine lay back in his chair, steadily squinting upward for several minutes, without speaking. Then: "I can comprehend readily why the monkey should have been killed as it was. Any one of half a dozen hypotheses would explain that. But if the monkey didn't have a pocket somewhere in its clothing, then I don't see so readily why — Oh, of course – must have been bigger than I thought," he mused.

"What?" inquired Hatch.

"Are you sure, Mr Hatch, that there had been nothing sewn to the clothing of the monkey?" asked The Thinking Machine, without heeding the question – "that nothing had been ripped loose from the clothing?"

"I can't say as to that," the reporter replied.

"Where is the monkey now?"

"Still there in the room, I suppose. I came straight from there to you here. Of course, my being held up that way wasn't of any actual consequence – it was merely incidental, I thought, to the other."

The Thinking Machine nodded. "Yes," he agreed. "I presume that was merely because you happened to arrive at an inopportune moment, and that method was employed to keep you out of the way until whatever was to be done was done."

The Thinking Machine and the reporter went out together. It was a few minutes past nine o'clock when they reached the tenement. It was dirty and illy lighted, and boldly faced a street which was a center of the Italian colony. Hatch led the way in and up the stairs to the room where he had left the monkey. The little body still lay huddled up, inert, as he had left it.

By the light of an electric bulb The Thinking Machine examined it closely. Twice Hatch saw him shake his head. When The Thinking Machine arose from the floor his face was inscrutable. He led Hatch around that room and the next and through a third which connected, and then they went out.

"It is an extraordinary case, Mr Hatch," he explained as they went on. "There are now three explanations of the affair, either one of which would fit in with every fact that we know. But instead of helping us, these three possibilities make it necessary for us to know more. Two of them must be removed – the remainder will be correct as surely as two and two make four, not sometimes but all the time."

Hatch waited patiently.

"The real problem here," the scientist continued after a moment, "is the identity of the person who owned the monkey. When we get that, we get a starting point."

"That would not seem difficult," Hatch suggested. "It is extremely improbable that anyone knows of the affair except the persons who were responsible for it, perhaps the owner of the monkey and ourselves. An advertisement in the newspapers would bring the owner quickly enough."

"There is always the possibility, Mr Hatch, that the owner is the man who killed the monkey," replied the scientist. "In that event the advertisement would do no good; and there is a question if it would be advisable to let those persons who are responsible for the animal's death know that the matter is being investigated. This is presuming, of course, that some one besides the owner killed it. It will be just as well to let the young woman who held you prisoner believe that the affair is at an end. Any other course just now might indirectly endanger the life of some one who has not yet appeared in the case.

"I am going home now, Mr Hatch," concluded the scientist, "and it is possible that within two or three hours I may devise a plan by which we can find the monkey's owner. If so, I shall communicate with you."

"You can reach me at police headquarters until about midnight," replied the reporter. "I am going up there on another affair."

It was about a quarter past eleven o'clock that night when Hatch scurried away to a telephone and eagerly cried to The Thinking Machine, "I know the man who owned the monkey!"

Ten minutes later he was in the scientist's little reception room. "The man who owned the monkey," he said, "is named Giacomo Bardetto. He is an organ grinder. He was found unconscious in an area way at the other end of the city tonight at ten o'clock. He had been struck down from behind, his organ smashed, his pockets rifled, and no one knows how long he had been unconscious when found. He is now in a hospital, still unconscious. The police know nothing whatever about the monkey incident; but I surmise that the dead monkey was Bardetto's. You might have noticed that a short chain was attached to the monkey's clothing? The other end of that chain is fastened to the hand organ."

"How was Bardetto identified?" asked The Thinking Machine.

"By his organ grinder's license, which was fastened to the inside of a flap on the instrument."

"His home?"

"Here is the address," and the reporter produced a card on which he had jotted down the street and number.

The Thinking Machine studied the card for a moment, then glanced at his watch. It was five minutes of midnight.

"Detective Mallory sent a man there to notify his family of Bardetto's condition," Hatch went on to explain. "But it seems that he has no family or relatives. Mallory, of course, has nothing to lead him to think that the case is anything more than ordinary assault and robbery."

"Let's go see what the case really is, Mr Hatch," said the scientist. "I know in a general way what it is, of course; but it possesses many singular features."

Half an hour later they stood in the room where Bardetto lived. This too was in a tenement and poorly furnished. It seemed to be a combination of bed room, living room, dining room, and kitchen. The Thinking Machine began a minute search of the room. Bureau drawers were pulled out, the bed denuded, articles of furniture moved, and even the oil stove turned upside down. Hatch stood looking on without the slightest idea of the object of the search.

"What are you looking for?" he asked at last.

"I don't know," The Thinking Machine confessed frankly. "The ultimate purpose is to find out why the monkey was killed. I have an idea that there is something here that will answer the question."

And the search continued. Every conceivable point seemed to have been gone over; and Hatch was marveling at the thoroughness of it, when The Thinking Machine dropped on his knees on the floor and wriggled along, minutely inspecting the baseboard at every joint. One of these sounded unlike the others when he rapped it, and he began work at it. Finally the board responded to the prying of a knife and fell out. The Thinking Machine took one look.

"Dear me! Dear me!" he exclaimed in a tone which nearly indicated astonishment.

He plunged both hands into the narrow aperture and tumbled out on the floor package after package of money-crackling, rustling bills – unfolded and with the sheen of newness still on them. There was money and money! Hatch stared with bulging eyes.

"Now I know why the monkey was killed," remarked The Thinking Machine conclusively. "This is what I was looking for, but I didn't know it."

"Great Scott! Whose is it? How much is there? Where did it come from?"

Hatch flung the questions at the diminutive scientist still crouching on the floor. The Thinking Machine glanced at him in petulant reproof at an excitement which the reporter's voice betrayed.

"Whose is it?" he repeated. "Bardetto's. How much is there? I should say from fifty to seventy-five thousand dollars. It's all in two and five dollar bills. Where did it come from? I should say that it came from the—"

The door behind them squeaked a little as it swung on its hinges. Hatch turned quickly. It was the girl. For an instant they stood motionless, staring at each other in mutual astonishment. The Thinking Machine didn't even glance around.

"Put that woman under arrest, Mr Hatch," he commanded irritably, "and close the door! She has no revolver, but look out for a knife."

Hatch pushed the door to with his foot. "Now, signorina," he remarked grimly, "I shall have to ask you to remain silent."

The girl was evidently not one of the screaming kind, but her right hand disappeared into the folds of her dress as she faced him boldly. It was a sinister movement. Hatch smiled a little, and his own right hand went back to his hip. Perhaps he smiled because he had never been guilty of carrying a revolver in all his life.

"Don't do that, signorina!" he advised pleasantly. "Don't make any mistake with that knife! I have never drawn a revolver on a woman, and I don't want to now; but believe me, you must take out the knife and drop it. You must, I say!" and his right hand moved forward the fraction of a foot threateningly.

Staring straight into his eyes without a tremor in her own, the girl produced the stiletto, and it clattered on the floor. Hatch kicked it beyond her reach. The Thinking Machine finally arose from his place on the floor.

"Mr Hatch," he commanded sharply, "take the young woman over in the far corner there and let her sit down. Just so surely as she makes any noise, however slight, it will cost one of us, perhaps even both of us, our lives. Remember that and act accordingly. Don't hesitate an instant because she happens to be a woman. I shall be able alone to take care of whoever else may happen to enter."

The tone was one which was utterly strange to the reporter, coming as it did from this crabbed, irritable little scientist whom he had known so long. It was chilling by reason of its very gravity, and for the first time in his life Hatch felt that his companion considered a situation imminently dangerous. All of which convinced him that if he had ever obeyed orders now was the time. The girl's face was white, but there was a slight, mocking smile wavering about her lips.

The Thinking Machine turned the gas half down, then went over and sat near the door. Silently they waited, five, ten, fifteen minutes; then they heard a quick, muffled tread moving along the hall toward the door.

"If she moves or makes the slightest sound, shoot!" directed The Thinking Machine in a low voice.

He arose and faced the door. Some one fumbled at the lock, and the door swung inward. The figure of a man appeared.

"Hands up!" commanded The Thinking Machine abruptly, and he thrust a glittering something beneath the intruder's nose. The man's hand went up. The Thinking Machine leaned forward suddenly and deftly abstracted a revolver from the stranger's right hand pocket. He gave a sigh of infinite relief as he straightened up, holding the captured revolver in hand.

"It's all right, Mr Hatch," he said to the reporter, who had scarce dared remove his eyes from his prisoner. Then to the man and woman, "It may interest you to know that neither of us had a weapon of either sort until I got this revolver. I stopped you," he told the man, "with a clinical thermometer, and Mr Hatch captured you," he told the woman, "at the point, we may say, of his pipe case."

They were all at police headquarters – The Thinking Machine, Hatch, and the two prisoners. Piled up on Detective Mallory's desk were the packages of bills which the scientist had discovered. They were counterfeit, all of two and five dollar denominations, and excellent in texture, engraving, and printing. But the numbers were at fault; all the twos were the same, and all the fives were the same.

For the enlightenment of Detective Mallory, The Thinking Machine and Hatch repeated in detail those incidents leading up to the capture of the man and the woman.

"There is really little to explain," said the scientist at the end; "although the problem, while it lasted, was one of the most complex and intricate I have ever met. We may dismiss Mr Hatch's first adventure as of no consequence. It just happened that he went to the house on a different matter, and fortunately was dragged into this affair. Now, I have no doubt that the prisoners here will give us the location of the counterfeiter's plant?"

He glanced at the man and woman. They looked at each other, but remained silent.

"I have never met a counterfeiter yet who would give up the hiding place of his plates," remarked Detective Mallory.

"But these are not counterfeiters, Mr Mallory," said The Thinking Machine; "they are merely thieves. Bardetto, the man who was found unconscious, who owned the monkey, is one of the counterfeiters. Let me explain briefly how every fact considered clears up the problem. First, the inevitable logic of the affair shows us that these two prisoners learned in some manner unknown that Bardetto was either a principal or an agent for some big counterfeiting scheme; for we can't believe that they thought this was real money. But instead of reporting the matter to the police they resolved to benefit by it themselves. How? By stealing the bills from Bardetto, this to be followed, perhaps, by immediate flight to Italy. They are both

Italians, and you may know that a clever American counterfeit abroad is almost as good as the genuine; and for that matter these bills would pass in circulation readily here.

"Granting, then, that they did know of Bardetto's part in the scheme, we can readily imagine that they learned that Bardetto had a quantity of the money in his possession; so the robbery was planned. The man here did the work, and was to meet the woman in the vacant rooms of the tenement where Mr Hatch saw her.

"Well, Bardetto was attacked and his pockets rifled. Evidently our prisoner did not find what he sought, and yet he knew that the money had passed into Bardetto's possession, and perhaps too that he had had no opportunity of getting rid of it. Was it in the organ? He smashed it to see. It wasn't. Then, the monkey: was the money concealed about the animal's clothing? That was the next question in the robber's mind.

"Half a dozen reasons, such as some one approaching, would have prevented this man making a search there; so he broke the monkey's chain and took the little brute along with him. In the vacant apartments the man did not meet the woman – we know why – perhaps presumed that she did not come, and so went on with his search. It is extremely probable that the monkey struggled and fought in the hands of a stranger, so the man stabbed it. He had no use for it, anyway. Now, as a matter of fact," and the scientist turned to the man whom he had personally taken prisoner, "you took a pouch or pocket from beneath the monkey's clothing, didn't you?"

The prisoner stared at him an instant, then nodded.

"So he got that counterfeit money which he knew had been in Bardetto's possession," continued The Thinking Machine. "It was not a great deal – not so much as he had anticipated, we'll say – then he and the woman planned to search Bardetto's room for more, knowing he was in the hospital. Perhaps the woman went ahead to reconnoiter. I didn't see her enter, but knew it was a woman because her skirts swished, and told Mr Hatch to lose no time in arresting her.

"The minute I found the money I knew the solution of the affair – the solution that must be correct. Up to that time I had imagined a dozen other things – jewels, letters, papers of some sort. That is why I told Mr Hatch I didn't know what I was searching for." There was a pause. "I think, perhaps, that explanation covers it all."

"I still don't see why Hatch should have been held up," remarked Detective Mallory.

"It might have been merely excess of caution," was the reply, "or the woman might have admitted him first under a misapprehension as to his identity, and was afraid to let him go. It was almost dark in the hall."

"But why should Bardetto entrust the money to the monkey?" Hatch inquired curiously. "It seems to me that it would have been safer for him to carry it himself."

"On the contrary," was the reply. "A man in his position is always expecting arrest. If the money had been found on him, it would have convicted him; if it had been found in his organ, and that should have fallen into other hands and been identified, it would have convicted him. But if the money was on the monkey, which couldn't talk, and he felt himself in danger, it would have been easy to free it, and perhaps it could easily have succeeded in making its escape."

The two prisoners willingly informed Detective Mallory of the whereabouts of the counterfeiter's plant – were apparently even anxious to inform him – and he in person led the raid on it. Plates for the bills were seized, and five expert workers placed under arrest.

From the time Hutchinson Hatch was held up in the vacant room until seven prisoners were in their cells at police headquarters less than twelve hours had elapsed.

15

PROBLEM OF THE PERFECT ALIBI

Skulking along through the dense gloom, impalpably a part of the murky mist which pressed down between the tall board fences on each side, moved the figure of a man. Occasionally he shot a glance behind him, but the general direction of his gaze was to his left, where a fence cut off the small back – yards of an imposing row of brown-stone residences. At last he stopped and tried a gate. It opened noiselessly and he disappeared inside. A pause. A man came out of the gate, closed it carefully and walked on through the alley toward an arc-light which spread a generous glare at the intersection of a street.

Patrolman Gillis was standing idly on a corner, within the light-radius of a street lamp debating some purely personal questions when he heard the steady clack, clack, clack of footsteps a block or more away. He glanced up and dimly he saw a man approaching. As he came nearer the policeman noticed that the man's right hand was pressed to his face.

"Good evening, officer," said the stranger nervously. "Can you tell me where I can find a dentist?"

"Toothache?" inquired the policeman.

"Yes, and it's nearly killing me," was the reply. "If I don't get it pulled I'll – I'll go crazy."

The policeman grinned sympathetically.

"Had it myself – I know what it is," he said. "You passed one dentist down in the other block, but there's another just across the street here," and he indicated a row of brownstone residences. "Dr Paul Sitgreaves. He'll charge you good and plenty."

"Thank you," said the other.

He crossed the street and the policeman gazed after him until he mounted the steps and pulled the bell. After a few minutes the door opened, the stranger entered the house and Patrolman Gillis walked on.

"Dr Sitgreaves here?" inquired the stranger of a servant who answered the bell.

"Yes."

"Please ask him if he can draw a tooth for me. I'm in a perfect agony, and—"

"The doctor rarely gets up to attend to such cases," interrupted the servant.

"Here," said the stranger and he pressed a bill in the servant's hand. "Wake him for me, won't you? Tell him it's urgent."

The servant looked at the bill, then opened the door and led the patient into the reception room.

Five minutes later, Dr Sitgreaves, gaping ostentatiously, entered and nodded to his caller.

"I hated to trouble you, doctor," explained the stranger, "but I haven't slept a wink all night."

He glanced around the room until his eye fell upon a clock. Dr Sitgreaves glanced in that direction. The hands of the clock pointed to 1:53.

"Phew!" said Dr Sitgreaves. "Nearly two o'clock. I must have slept hard. I didn't think I'd been asleep more than an hour." He paused to gape again and stretch himself. "Which tooth is it?" he asked.

"A molar, here," said the stranger, and he opened his mouth.

PROBLEM OF THE PERFECT ALIBI

Dr Sitgreaves gazed officially into his innermost depths and fingered the hideous instruments of torture.

"That tooth's too good to lose," he said after an examination. "There's only a small cavity in it."

"I don't know what's the matter with it," replied the other impatiently, "except that it hurts. My nerves are fairly jumping."

Dr Sitgreaves was professionally serious as he noted the drawn face, the nervous twitching of hands and the unusual pallor of his client.

"They are," he said finally. "There's no doubt of that. But it isn't the tooth. It's neuralgia."

"Well, pull it anyway," pleaded the stranger. "It always comes in that tooth, and I've got to get rid of it some time."

"It wouldn't be wise," remonstrated the dentist. "A filling will save it. Here," and he turned and stirred an effervescent powder in a glass. "Take this and see if it doesn't straighten you out."

The stranger took the glass and gulped down the foaming liquid.

"Now sit right there for five minutes or so," instructed the dentist. "If it doesn't quiet you and you insist on having the tooth pulled, of course—"

He sat down and glanced again at the clock after which he looked at his watch and replaced it in a pocket of his pajamas. His visitor was sitting, too, controlling himself only with an obvious effort.

"This is real neuralgia weather," observed the dentist at last, idly. "Misty and damp."

"I suppose so," was the reply. "This began to hurt about twelve o'clock, just as I went to bed, and finally it got so bad that I couldn't stand it. Then I got up and dressed and came out for a walk. I kept on, thinking that it would get better but it didn't and a policeman sent me here."

There was a pause of several minutes.

"Feel any better?" inquired the dentist, at last.

"No," was the reply. "I think you'd better take it out."

"Just as you say!"

The offending tooth was drawn, the stranger paid him with a sigh of relief, and after a minute or so started out. At the door he turned back.

"What time is it now, please?" he asked.

"Seventeen minutes past two," replied the dentist.

"Thanks," said the stranger. "I'll just have time to catch a car back home."

"Goodnight," said the dentist.

"Goodnight."

Skulking along through the dense gloom, impalpably a part of the murky mist which pressed down between tall board fences on each side, moved the figure of a man. Occasionally he shot a glance behind him, but the general direction of his gaze was to his left, where a fence cut off the small back – yards of an imposing row of brown-stone residences. At last he stopped and tried a gate. It opened noiselessly and he disappeared inside. A pause. A man came out of the gate, closed it carefully and walked on through the alley toward an arc-light which spread a generous glare at the intersection of a street.

Next morning at eight o'clock, Paul Randolph De Forrest, a young man of some social prominence, was found murdered in the sitting room of his suite in the big Avon apartment house. He had been dead for several hours. He sat beside his desk, and death left him sprawled upon it face downward. The weapon was one of several curious daggers which had been used ornamentally on the walls of his apartments. The blade missed the heart only a quarter of an inch or so; death must have come within a couple of minutes.

Detective Mallory went to the apartments, accompanied by the Medical Examiner. Together they lifted the dead man.

PROBLEM OF THE PERFECT ALIBI

Beneath his body, on the desk, lay a sheet of paper on which were scrawled a few words; a pencil was clutched tightly in his right hand. The detective glanced then stared at the paper; it startled him. In the scrawly, trembling, incoherent handwriting of the dying man were these disjointed sentences and words:

"Murdered **** Franklin Chase **** quarrel **** stabbed me **** am dying **** God help me **** clock striking 2 **** goodbye."

The detective's jaws snapped as he read. Here was crime, motive and time. After a sharp scrutiny of the apartments, he went down the single flight of stairs to the office floor to make some inquiries. An elevator man, Moran, was the first person questioned. He had been on duty the night before. Did he know Mr Franklin Chase? Yes. Had Mr Franklin Chase called to see Mr De Forrest on the night before? Yes.

"What time was he here?"

"About half past eleven, I should say. He and Mr De Forrest came in together from the theatre."

"When did Mr Chase go away?"

"I don't know, sir. I didn't see him."

"It might have been somewhere near two o'clock?"

"I don't know, sir," replied Moran again, "I'll – I'll tell you all I know about it. I was on duty all night. Just before two o'clock a telegram was 'phoned for a Mr Thomas on the third floor. I took it and wrote on it the time that I received it. It was then just six minutes before two o'clock. I walked up from this floor to the third-two flights – to give the message to Mr Thomas. As I passed Mr De Forrest's door, I heard loud voices, two people evidently quarrelling. I paid no attention then but went on. I was at Mr Thomas's door possibly five or six minutes. When I came down I heard nothing further and thought no more of it."

"You fix the time of passing Mr De Forrest's door first at, say, five minutes of two?" asked the detective.

"Within a minute of that time, yes, sir."

"And again about two or a minute or so after?"

"Yes."

"Ah," exclaimed the detective. "That fits in exactly with the other and establishes beyond question the moment of the murder." He was thinking of the words "clock striking 2" written by the dying man. "Did you recognize the voices?"

"No, sir, I could not. They were not very clear."

That was the substance of Moran's story. Detective Mallory then called at the telegraph office and indisputable records there showed that they had telephoned a message for Mr Thomas at precisely six minutes of two. Detective Mallory was satisfied.

Within an hour Franklin Chase was under arrest. Detective Mallory found him sound asleep in his room in a boarding house less than a block away from the Avon. He seemed somewhat astonished when informed of his arrest for murder, but was quite calm.

"It's some sort of a mistake," he protested.

"I don't make mistakes," said the detective. He had a short memory.

Further police investigation piled up the evidence against the prisoner. For instance, minute blood stains were found on his hands, and a drop or so on the clothing he had worn the night before; and it was established by three fellow lodgers – young men who had come in late and stopped at his room – that he was not in his boarding house at two o'clock the night before.

That afternoon Chase was arraigned for a preliminary hearing. Detective Mallory stated the case and his statement was corroborated by necessary witnesses. First he established the authenticity of the dying man's writing. Then he proved that Chase had been with De Forrest at half past eleven o'clock; that there had been a quarrel – or argument – in De Forrest's room just before two o'clock; and finally, with a dramatic flourish, he swore to the blood stains on the prisoner's hands and clothing.

The august Court stared at the prisoner and took up his pen to sign the necessary commitment.

"May I say something before we go any further?" asked Mr Chase.

The Court mumbled some warning about anything the prisoner might say being used against him.

"I understand," said the accused, and he nodded, "but I will show that there has been a mistake – a serious mistake. I admit that the writing was Mr De Forrest's; that I was with him at half-past eleven o'clock and that the stains on my hands and clothing were blood stains."

The Court stared.

"I've known Mr De Forrest for several years," the prisoner went on quietly. "I met him at the theatre last night and walked home with him. We reached the Avon about half past eleven o'clock and I went to his room but I remained only ten or fifteen minutes. Then I went home. It was about five minutes of twelve when I reached my room. I went to bed and remained in bed until one o'clock, when for a reason which will appear, I arose, dressed and went out, say about ten minutes past one. I returned to my room a few minutes past three."

Detective Mallory smiled sardonically.

"When I was arrested this morning I sent notes to three persons," the prisoner went on steadily. "Two of these happen to be city officials, one the City Engineer. Will he please come forward?"

There was a little stir in the room and the Court scratched one ear gravely. City Engineer Malcolm appeared inquiringly.

"This is Mr Malcolm?" asked the prisoner. "Yes? Here is a map of the city issued by your office. I would like to ask please the approximate distance between this point—" and he indicated on the map the location of the Avon – "and this." He touched another point far removed.

The City Engineer studied the map carefully.

"At least two and a half miles," he explained.

"You would make that statement on oath?"

"Yes, I've surveyed it myself."

"Thank you," said the prisoner, courteously, and he turned to face the crowd in the rear. "Is Policeman No. 1122 in Court? – I don't know his name?"

Again there was a stir, and Policeman Gillis came forward.

"Do you remember me?" inquired the prisoner.

"Sure," was the reply.

"Where did you see me last night?"

"At this corner," and Gillis put his finger down on the map at the second point the prisoner had indicated.

The Court leaned forward eagerly to peer at the map; Detective Mallory tugged violently at his moustache. Into the prisoner's manner there came tense anxiety.

"Do you know what time you saw me there?" he asked.

Policeman Gillis was thoughtful a moment.

"No," he replied at last. "I heard a clock strike just after I saw you but I didn't notice."

The prisoner's face went deathly white for an instant, then he recovered himself with an effort.

"You didn't count the strokes?" he asked.

"No, I wasn't paying any attention to it."

The colour rushed back into Chase's face and he was silent a moment. Then:

"It was two o'clock you heard strike?" It was hardly a question, rather a statement.

"I don't know," said Gillis. "It might have been. Probably was."

"What did I say to you?"

"You asked me where you could find a dentist, and I directed you to Dr Sitgreaves across the street."

"You saw me enter Dr Sitgreaves' house?"

"Yes."

The accused glanced up at the Court and that eminent jurist proceeded to look solemn.

"Dr Sitgreaves, please?" called the prisoner.

The dentist appeared, exchanging nods with the prisoner.

"You remember me, doctor?"

"Yes."

"May I ask you to tell the Court where you live? Show us on this map please."

Dr Sitgreaves put his finger down at the spot which had been pointed out by the prisoner and by Policeman Gillis, two and a half miles from the Avon.

"I live three doors from this corner," explained the dentist.

"You pulled a tooth for me last night?" went on the prisoner.

"Yes."

"Here?" and the prisoner opened his mouth.

The dentist gazed down him.

"Yes," he replied.

"You may remember, doctor," went on the prisoner, quietly, "that you had occasion to notice the clock just after I called at your house. Do you remember what time it was?"

"A few minutes before two—seven or eight minutes, I think."

Detective Mallory and the Court exchanged bewildered glances.

"You looked at your watch, too. Was that exactly with the clock?"

"Yes, within a minute."

"And what time did I leave your office?" the prisoner asked.

"Seventeen minutes past two – I happen to remember," was the reply.

The prisoner glanced dreamily around the room twice, his eyes met Detective Mallory's. He stared straight into that official for an instant then turned back to the dentist.

"When you drew the tooth there was blood of course. It is possible that I got the stains on my fingers and clothing?"

"Yes, certainly."

The prisoner turned to the Court and surprised a puzzled expression on that official countenance.

"Is anything else necessary?" he inquired courteously. "It has been established that the moment of the crime was two o'clock; I have shown by three witnesses – two of them city officials – that I was two and a half miles away in less than half an hour; I couldn't have gone on a car in less than fifteen minutes – hardly that."

There was a long silence as the Court considered the matter. Finally he delivered himself, briefly.

"It resolves itself into a question of the accuracy of the clocks," he said. "The accuracy of the clock at the Avon is attested by the known accuracy of the clock in the telegraph office, while it seems established that Dr Sitgreaves' clock was also accurate, because it was with his watch. Of course there is no question of veracity of witnesses – it is merely a question of the clock in Dr Sitgreaves' office. If that is shown to be absolutely correct we must accept the alibi."

The prisoner turned to the elevator man from the Avon.

"What sort of a clock was that you mentioned?"

"An electric clock, regulated from Washington Observatory," was the reply.

"And the clock at the telegraph office, Mr Mallory?"

"An electric clock, regulated from Washington Observatory."

"And yours, Dr Sitgreaves?"

"An electric clock, regulated from Washington Observatory."

The prisoner remained in his cell until seven o'clock that evening while experts tested the three clocks. They were accurate to the second; and it was explained that there could have been no variation of either without this variation showing in the delicate testing apparatus. Therefore it came to pass that Franklin Chase was released on his own recognizance, while Detective Mallory wandered off into the sacred precincts of his private office to hold his head in his hands and think.

Hutchinson Hatch, reporter, had followed the intricacies of the mystery from the discovery of De Forrest's body, through the preliminary hearing, up to and including the expert examination of the clocks, which immediately preceded the release of Franklin Chase. When this point was reached his mental condition was not unlike that of Detective Mallory – he was groping hopelessly, blindly in the mazes of the problem.

It was then that he called to see Professor Augustus S. F. X. Van Dusen – The Thinking Machine. That distinguished gentleman listened to a recital of the known facts with petulant, drooping mouth and the everlasting squint in his blue eyes. As the reporter talked on, corrugations appeared in the logician's expansive brow, and these gave way in turn to a network of wrinkles. At the end The Thinking Machine sat twiddling his long fingers and staring upward.

"This is one of the most remarkable cases that has come to my attention," he said at last, "because it possesses the unusual quality of being perfect in each way – that is the evidence against Mr Chase is perfect and the alibi he offers is perfect. But we know instantly that if Mr Chase killed Mr De Forrest there was something the matter with the clocks despite expert opinion.

"We know that as certainly as we know that two and two make four, not some times but all the time, because our reason tells us that Mr Chase was not in two places at once at two o'clock. Therefore we must assume either one of two things – that something was the matter with the clocks – and if there was we must assume that Mr Chase was responsible for it – or that Mr Chase had nothing whatever to do with Mr De Forrest's death, at least personally."

The last word aroused Hatch to a new and sudden interest. It suggested a line of thought which had not yet occurred to him.

"Now," continued the scientist, "if we can find one flaw in Mr Chase's story we will have achieved the privilege of temporarily setting aside his defence and starting over. If, on the contrary, he told the full and exact truth and our investigation proves that he did, it instantly clears him. Now just what have you done, please?"

"I talked to Dr Sitgreaves," replied Hatch. "He did not know Chase – never saw him until he pulled the tooth, and then didn't know his name. But he told me really more than appeared in court, for instance, that his watch had been regulated only a few days ago, that it had been accurate since, and that he knew it was accurate next day because he kept an important engagement. That being accurate the clock must be accurate, because they were together almost to the second.

"I also talked to every other person whose name appears in the case. I questioned them as to all sorts of possibilities, and the result was that I was compelled to accept the alibi – not that I'm unwilling to of course, but it seems peculiar that De Forrest should have written the name as he was dying."

"You talked to the young men who went into Mr Chase's room at two o'clock?" inquired The Thinking Machine casually.

"Yes."

"Did you ask either of them the condition of Mr Chase's bed when they went in?"

"Yes," replied the reporter. "I see what you mean. They agreed that it was tumbled as if someone had been in it."

The Thinking Machine raised his eyebrows slightly.

"Suppose, Mr Hatch, that you had a violent toothache," he asked after a moment, still casually, "and were looking for relief, would you stop to notice the number of a policeman who told you where there was a dentist's office?"

Hatch considered it calmly, as he stared into the inscrutable face of the scientist.

"Oh, I see," he said at last. "No, I hardly think so, and yet I might."

Later Hatch and The Thinking Machine, by permission of Detective Mallory, made an exhaustive search of De Forrest's apartments in the Avon, seeking some clue. When the Thinking Machine went down the single flight of stairs to the office he seemed deeply perplexed.

"Where is your clock?" he inquired of the elevator man.

"In the inside office, opposite the telephone booth," was the reply.

The scientist went in and taking a stool, clambered up and squinted fiercely into the very face of the timepiece. He said "Ah!" once, non-commitally, then clambered down.

"It would not be possible for anyone here to see a person pass through the hall," he mused. "Now," and he picked up a telephone book, "just a word with Dr Sitgreaves."

He asked the dentist only two questions and their nature caused Hatch to smile. The first was:

"You have a pocket in the shirt of your pajamas?"

"Yes," came the wondering reply.

"And when you are called at night you pick up your watch and put it in that pocket?"

"Yes."

"Thanks. Goodbye."

Then The Thinking Machine turned to Hatch.

"We are safe in believing," he said, "that Mr De Forrest was not killed by a thief, because his valuables were undisturbed, therefore we must believe that the person who killed him was an acquaintance. It would be unfair to act hastily, so I shall ask you to devote three or four days to getting this man's history in detail; see his friends and enemies, find out all about him, his life, his circumstances, his love affairs – all those things."

Hatch nodded; he was accustomed to receiving large orders from The Thinking Machine.

"If you uncover nothing in that line to suggest another line of investigation I will give you the name of the person who killed him and an arrest will follow. The murderer will not run away. The solution of the affair is quite clear, unless—" he emphasized the word – "unless some unknown fact gives it another turn."

Hatch was forced to be content with that and for the specified four days laboured arduously and vainly. Then he returned to The Thinking Machine and summed up results briefly in one word: "Nothing."

The Thinking Machine went out and was gone two hours. When he returned he went straight to the 'phone and called Detective Mallory. The detective appeared after a few minutes.

"Have one of your men go at once and arrest Mr Chase," The Thinking Machine instructed. "You might explain to him that there is new evidence – an eye witness if you like. But don't mention my name or this place to him. Anyway bring him here and I'll show you the flaw in the perfect alibi he set up!"

Detective Mallory started to ask questions.

"It comes down simply to this," interrupted The Thinking Machine impatiently. "Somebody killed Mr De Forrest and that being true it must be that that somebody can be found. Please, when Mr Chase comes here do not interrupt me, and introduce me to him as an important new witness."

An hour later Franklin Chase entered with Detective Mallory. He was somewhat pale and nervous and in his eyes lay a shadow of apprehension. Over it all was the gloss of ostentatious nonchalance and self control. There were introductions. Chase started visibly at actual reference to the "important new witness."

"An eye witness," added The Thinking Machine.

Positive fright came into Chase's manner and he quailed under the steady scrutiny of the narrow blue eyes. The

Thinking Machine dropped back into his chair and pressed his long, white fingers tip to tip.

"If you'll just follow me a moment, Mr Chase," he suggested at last. "You know Dr Sitgreaves, of course? Yes. Well, it just happens that I have a room a block or so away from his house around the corner. These are Mr Hatch's apartments." He stated it so convincingly that there was no possibility of doubt. "Now my room faces straight up an alley which runs directly back of Dr Sitgreaves's house. There is an electric light at the corner."

Chase started to say something, gulped, then was silent.

"I was in my room the night of Mr De Forrest's murder," went on the scientist, "and was up moving about because I, too, had a toothache. It just happened that I glanced out my front window." His tone had been courteous in the extreme; now it hardened perceptibly. "I saw you, Mr Chase, come along the street, stop at the alley, glance around and then go into the alley. I saw your face clearly under the electric light, and that was at twenty minutes to three o'clock. Detective Mallory has just learned of this fact and I have signified my willingness to go on the witness stand and swear to it."

The accused man was deathly white now; his face was working strangely, but still he was silent. It was only by a supreme effort that he restrained himself.

"I saw you open a gate and go into the backyard of Dr Sitgreaves's house," resumed The Thinking Machine. "Five minutes or so later you came out and walked on to the cross street, where you disappeared. Naturally I wondered what it meant. It was still in my mind about half past three o'clock, possibly later, when I saw you enter the alley again, disappear in the same yard, then come out and go away."

"I – I was not – not there," said Chase weakly. "You were – were mistaken."

"When we know," continued The Thinking Machine steadily, "that you entered that house before you entered by the front door, we know that you tampered with Dr Sitgreaves's watch and clock, and when we know that you tampered with those we know that you murdered Mr De Forrest as his dying note stated. Do you see it?"

Chase arose suddenly and paced feverishly back and forth across the room; Detective Mallory discreetly moved his chair in front of the door. Chase saw and understood.

"I know how you tampered with the clock so as not to interfere with its action or cause any variation at the testing apparatus. You were too superbly clever to stop it, or interfere with the circuit. Therefore I see that you simply took out the pin which held on the hands and moved them backward one hour. It was then actually a quarter of three – you made it a quarter of two. You showed your daring by invading the dentist's sleeping room. You found his watch on a table beside his bed, set that with the clock, then went out, spoke to Policeman Gillis whose number you noted and rang the front door bell. After you left by the front door you allowed time for the household to get quiet again, then re-entered from the rear and reset the watch and clock. Thus your alibi was perfect. You took desperate chances and you knew it, but it was necessary."

The Thinking Machine stopped and squinted up into the pallid face. Chase made a hopeless gesture with his hands and sat down, burying his face.

"It was clever, Mr Chase," said the scientist finally. "It is the only murder case I know where the criminal made no mistake. You probably killed Mr De Forrest in a fit of anger, left there while the elevator boy was upstairs, then saw the necessity of protecting yourself and devised this alibi at the cost of one tooth. Your only real danger was when you made Patrolman Gillis your witness, taking the desperate chance that he did not know or would not remember just when you spoke to him."

Again there was silence. Finally Chase looked up with haggard face.

"How did you know all this?" he asked.

"Because under the exact circumstances, nothing else could have happened," replied the scientist. "The simplest rules of logic proved conclusively that this did happen." He straightened up in the chair. "By the way," he asked, "what was the motive of the murder?"

"Don't you know?" asked Chase, quickly.

"No."

"Then you never will," declared Chase, grimly.

When Chase had gone with the detective, Hatch lingered with The Thinking Machine.

"It's perfectly astonishing," he said. "How did you get at it anyway?"

"I visited the neighbourhood, saw how it could have been done, learned through your investigation that no one else appeared in the case, then, knowing that this must have happened, tricked Mr Chase into believing I was an eye witness to the incident in the alley. That was the only way to make him confess. Of course there was no one else in it."

One of the singular points in the Chase murder trial was that while the prisoner was convicted of murder on his own statement no inkling of a motive ever appeared.

16

PROBLEM OF THE RED ROSE

Through the open windows of a pleasantly sunny little sitting room a lazy breath of early summer drifted in, and gently stirred the wayward hair of a girl who leaned forward over a small writing desk with her head resting upon one white fore arm, and her face hidden. Her attitude was one of utter collapse, complete abandonment perhaps to grief or perhaps to actual physical suffering; yet there was no movement of the slender, graceful body, nothing to indicate even a passive interest in her surroundings – just this silent, motionless figure, alone.

One arm, the left, swung down listlessly at her side, and in that hand she held a single red rose, a splendid, full blown crimson blossom. The thorny stem touched the floor, and the leaves swayed rhythmically, playthings of the caressing breeze. On the green stem, just below the girl's tightly clenched hand, was a single stain – a drop of blood – as if the thorn had pierced the delicate flesh. On the desk, from which dainty writing trinkets had been pushed back, was a florist's box, open. It was from this box evidently that the red rose had been taken. The wax paper which had been wrapped round the flower was torn.

A Dresden clock on the mantel whirred faintly and chimed the hour of five; but the girl gave not the slightest indication of having heard. And then after a moment a door opened and a maid appeared. She paused as her eyes fell upon the figure of the young woman, made as if to speak, then instead silently withdrew, leaving the door slightly open. She did not seem surprised that no notice was taken of her. A dozen times she had found her young mistress like this, and it was always after the box had come from the florist's with the single red rose. She sighed a little as she went out.

The hands of the clock crept on round the dial slowly, to five minutes past the hour, then to ten, and finally to fifteen. Then there came a scampering of soft feet along the hall, and a white, shaggy little dog thrust his head in at the door inquisitively. Helterskelter he came tumbling in and planted two soiled fore feet in the girl's lap as he awaited the caress which was always ready for him. Now it didn't come. He backed away and regarded her thoughtfully. It must be some new sort of game she was playing. He crouched on the floor and barked playfully; but she didn't look round.

Evidently this was not what was expected of him. He scampered back and forth across the room twice, then returned to the motionless figure and placed his feet in her lap again. She wouldn't look. He barked, whined softly, then off like the wind round the room again. He stopped on her left side this time – the side where the arm swung down, and the hand clutched the rose. His moist tongue caressed the closed hand, and sniffed at it insistently. Suddenly he seemed dazed, and reeled uncertainly as if from an unexpected blow. He whined again as if choking; there was a rattle in his shaggy throat; and then began a violent whirling, twisting, which continued till he fell. After awhile he lay still with all four feet turned upward and glazed, staring eyes. And yet the girl hadn't moved.

The hands of the clock crept on. At five minutes of six o'clock the maid appeared at the door again, paused for a moment, then ventured in. "Will you dress for dinner, ma'am?" she inquired.

The girl didn't answer.

"It's nearly six o'clock, ma'am," said the maid.

Still there was no answer.

The maid approached her young mistress and touched her lightly on the shoulder. 'You'll be late, unless—" she began.

And then something about the unresisting, impassive figure frightened her. She shook the girl sharply and called her name many times. Finally with an effort she raised the shapely head. What she saw in the upturned face wrung scream after scream from her lips, now suddenly ashen, and turning she staggered toward the door with unutterable horror in her widely distended eyes. She clutched at the door frame to steady herself, screamed again, and fell forward, fainting. There they found them: Miss Edna Burdock dead with hideously distorted face, – a face upon which was written some awful agony, – and the rose still clasped so fiercely in her hand that the thorns had pierced the palm; her little dog Tatters dead beside her; and the maid, Goodwin, unconscious. For half an hour two servants worked over the maid; but when at last she opened her eyes she only screamed and babbled incoherently. There were no marks on Miss Burdock's body save the prick of thorns in her left hand – nothing that would indicate the manner of death; nor was there the slightest thing to explain the death of the dog.

"The police are not at all certain that Miss Burdock's death was due to anything more mysterious than heart failure," Hutchinson Hatch, reporter, was explaining. "In that event, of course—"

"In that event, of course," interrupted Professor Augustus S. F. X. Van Dusen – The Thinking Machine – crabbedly, "their theory must be that the pet dog died at the same time of the same disease?"

"That seems to be about the way they look at it, although there are several curious features," the reporter went on; "for instance, the expression on her face." He shuddered a little.

"I saw her. It was awful. The dog too. There was not a mark or scratch on the dog—not even the prick of a thorn like that in the girl's palm, therefore heart failure seems to be the only thing that will cover the case, unless—"

"Fidldesticks!" exclaimed the irritable little scientist. "Persons who die of heart failure don't show suffering in their faces, and little dogs don't have heart failure. What did the autopsy show?"

"Nothing illuminating," responded the reporter. "There was no trace of poison in Miss Burdock's system; a blood test showed her blood to be about normal, and yet she was dead. There was a peculiar constriction of the heart, and the same thing was true of the dog. The medical examiner's report brought out these facts; but there was no poison – they were just dead."

"When did this happen, Mr Hatch?"

"Yesterday afternoon, Monday."

"You tell me the maid found the body. Has she said anything about noticing any odor when she entered the room?"

"Not a word; but there are curious things—"

"In a minute, Mr Hatch," interrupted The Thinking Machine impatiently. "Were the windows open?"

"Yes," replied the reporter. "She was sitting at her desk, between two open windows."

The man of science dropped back in his chair, and for a long time sat silent with the perpetually squinting eyes turned upward, and slender white fingers pressed tip to tip. Hatch lighted a cigarette, smoked it, and threw the butt away before he spoke.

"There are peaches in the market, I think, Mr Hatch," said the scientist at last. "When you go out, buy one, cut the meat off, crush the kernel, take it to the maid, and ask her to smell it. Ask her if she noticed yesterday any odor similar to that when she entered the room and was near the girl's body."

Hatch absorbed the instructions wonderingly, then ventured a remark. "I presume you are thinking of poison. Isn't there a chance that despite the normal condition of her blood some sort of poison was introduced into her system — I mean that the thorns of the rose might have been poisoned, for instance."

"You say there was no scratch or thorn prick on the dog?" asked The Thinking Machine in answer.

"No mark of any sort."

"And the dog is dead. That answers your question, Mr Hatch." He relapsed into silence.

"Poison on the thorns could not have killed both of them, because only the woman's hand showed the marks?" Hatch asked.

"Precisely," was the reply. "Unless we allow for coincidence, and that has never been reduced to a scientific law, we must say that both the woman and the dog died of the same cause. When we know that, we prove that the thorn prick had nothing to do with the woman's death. Two and two make four, Mr Hatch, not sometimes but all the time. And so what have we left?"

"I don't see that we have anything left," remarked Hatch frankly. "If there is no outward cause, how can we—"

"The mere fact that there is no apparent cause, or outward cause, as you term it, makes the manner of death of both the woman and the dog perfectly plain," declared The Thinking Machine belligerently. "There is no mystery about that at all – it's obvious. Our problem is not what killed her, but who killed her."

"Yes, that seems quite clear," the reporter admitted.

Minute after minute passed while the scientist sat staring upward. Finally he lowered his eyes to the face of the newspaper man. "Where did this red rose come from?" he demanded.

"I was going to tell you about that," responded Hatch. "It came from Lamperti's, a florist. The police are investigating it now. It seems, according to a statement of the manager of the shop, that on June 16 he received a special delivery letter from Washington with only a typewritten, unsigned slip of paper inclosed. This directed that one dozen red roses be sent to Miss Burdock, one at a time on specified days, Mondays, Wednesdays, and Saturdays. They accepted the order, – there was no way to return the money anyway, – and so—"

He paused to gaze curiously into the eyes of The Thinking Machine. They were drawn down to mere slits of watery blue and some subtle change had altered the straight line of the lips.

"Well, well!" grumbled the scientist. "Go on!"

"As a rule the long box with the one rose was delivered at the house by one of the wagons of the company," the reporter continued; "but some days when the wagon was not going in that direction the box was sent by a messenger boy. This last rose went to her by messenger."

"And have all the roses been sent?"

"So the manager says."

"And where is the red rose – the one she had in her hand when found?"

"Detective Mallory has it in charge, I suppose," explained the reporter. "He has an idea that Miss Burdock was killed by poison on the thorns; so he stripped them off and sent them to a chemist to see if any trace of poison could be found. I presume he kept the flower and the box it came in."

"That's just like Mallory," commented the scientist testily. "Whenever the police want to keep a cat's teeth from falling out they cut off its tail. Now tell me something about Miss Burdock herself. Who was she? What was she? What were her circumstances?" He settled back in his chair for a categorical answer.

"She was the only daughter of Plympton Burdock; a man who is not wealthy, but who is well to do," answered Hatch. "She lived at home with her father, her mother, and a younger brother, a chap about eighteen or nineteen years old. She was something of a social favorite, although not yet quite twenty-one, and went about a great deal; so—"

"So naturally a great many men, some of whom admired her," The Thinking Machine finished for him. "Now who are the men? Tell me about her love affairs?"

"It hasn't appeared yet that there was a love affair, in the sense you mean. At least, if there was no one knew of it."

"Doesn't the maid Goodwin know?" insisted the scientist.

"She says she doesn't."

"But somebody sent the rose. The mere fact that she received the one rose a dozen times indicates that some one was interested in her. Therefore, who was it? Who?"

"That's what the police are trying to find out now."

The Thinking Machine arose suddenly, picked up his hat and planted it aggressively on his enormous yellow head. "I'm going to the florist's," he said. "You get the peach and see the maid Goodwin. Meet me at police headquarters in an hour."

It required ten minutes for The Thinking Machine to reach the florist's shop, and in five minutes more the manager was at liberty.

"All I want to know," the scientist explained, "is the day you sent the first rose of that dozen to Miss Burdock, and I should like to see your records of delivery. That is, when a package is delivered either by your wagon or by messenger you get a receipt for it? Yes. I should like to see those, please."

The manager obligingly consulted his records. "The letter with the inclosure was received on June 16," he explained as he ran his finger down the book. "It came in the morning mail. June 16 was Monday; therefore the first rose of the dozen was sent that afternoon, Monday."

"Are you absolutely certain of that?" demanded The Thinking Machine. "A — a person's life may depend on that record."

The manager stared at him in frank astonishment, then arose. "I can make sure," he said. He went to a cabinet and took out another book – a delivery receipt book, and fluttered the leaves through his fingers. At last he laid it before The Thinking Machine and indicated an entry with his finger. "There it is," he said. "Monday, June 16, at five-thirty in the afternoon. The book was signed by Edna Burdock in person. See."

The Thinking Machine squinted down at the entry for a minute or more in silence. "From that date forward one rose was sent every Monday, Wednesday, and Saturday without a break until the dozen were delivered?" he asked at last.

"Yes; that was the direction. Run through the book on the dates it should have been sent and see, if you like."

The scientist heeded the suggestion, and for ten minutes or so was engrossed in the record. "These slips?" he inquired, as he looked up. "I find three of them."

"Those were the occasions when we didn't happen to have a wagon going in that direction," the manager explained; "so the box was sent by special messenger. Each messenger took a receipt and returned it here. In that way those receipts became a part of our record."

The Thinking Machine scrutinized the slips carefully, made a note of the dates on them, then closed the record book. That seemed to be all. Fifteen minutes later Plympton Burdock, father of the dead girl, received a card from a servant, glanced at it, nodded, and The Thinking Machine was ushered in.

"I should not have disturbed you, believe me, if the necessity for it had not been pressing in the interest of justice," the scientist apologized. "Just one or two questions, please."

Burdock regarded the little man curiously, and motioned to a seat.

"First," began The Thinking Machine, "was your daughter engaged to be married at the time of her-her death?"

"No," replied Burdock.

"She did receive attention, however?"

"Certainly. All girls of her age do. Really, Mr-Mr," and he glanced at the card, – "Mr Van Dusen, this matter is entirely beyond discussion. We believe, my wife and I, that death was due to natural causes, and have so informed the police. I hope it may go no further."

The Thinking Machine looked at him sharply with some strange new expression in his squint eyes. "The investigation won't stop now, Mr Burdock," he said coldly. "I don't know your object in-in seeking to stop it."

"I don't want to stop it," declared Burdock quickly. "We are convinced that no good can come of an investigation, because there is no ground for suspicion, and certainly it is not pleasant to have one's family affairs constantly pawed over when it is a foregone conclusion that nothing will result except unpleasant notoriety which merely adds to the burden that we now have to bear."

The Thinking Machine understood and nodded. It was almost an apology. "Well, just one more question, please," he said. "What is the name of the man whose attentions to your daughter you in person forbade?"

"How do you know of that?" blazed Burdock quickly.

"What is his name?" repeated The Thinking Machine.

"I will not discuss the matter further with you," was the reply.

"In the interests of justice I demand his name!" The Thinking Machine insisted.

Burdock stared at the slight figure before him with growing horror in his face. "You don't mean to say you suspect—" He stopped. "My God! if I thought that I'd—How was she killed, if she was killed?" he concluded.

"His name, please," urged The Thinking Machine. "If you don't give it to me, you will place me under the necessity of asking the police to compel you to give it. I'd prefer not to."

Burdock seemed not to heed the speech. His face had gone perfectly white, and he stood staring past the scientist, out the window. His hands were clenched tightly and the fingers were working. "If he did! If he did!" he repeated fiercely. Suddenly he recovered himself and glared down at his visitor. "I beg your pardon," he said simply. His name is-is Paul K. Darrow."

"Of this city," said The Thinking Machine. It was not a question; it was a statement of fact.

"Of this city," repeated Burdock,—"at least formerly of this city. He left here, I am informed, four or five weeks ago."

The Thinking Machine went his way, leaving Burdock sitting with his face in his hands. A few minutes later he appeared in Detective Mallory's office at police headquarters. The officer was sitting with his feet on his desk, smoking furiously, with a dozen deep wrinkles in his brow. He hailed the scientist almost cordially, something unusual for him.

"What do you make of it?" he demanded as he arose.

"Let me see your directory for a moment, please," replied The Thinking Machine. He bent over the book, ran down a page or so of the D's, then finally looked up.

"We don't seem to be able to establish a crime, even," Detective Mallory confessed. "I had the thorns examined, and the chemist reports that there is not a trace of poison about them."

"Silly in the first place," remarked The Thinking Machine ungraciously enough. "Is the rose here?"

The detective produced it from a drawer of his desk, whereupon The Thinking Machine did several things with it which he didn't understand. First he waved it about in the air at arm's length, then took two steps forward and sniffed. Then he waved it about much closer to him and sniffed. Detective Mallory looked on in mingled curiosity and disgust. Finally the scientist held it close to his nose and sniffed, then examined the petals closely, after which he laid it on the desk again.

"And the box the rose was delivered in?" queried the scientist.

Silently the detective produced that. The Thinking Machine sniffed at it cautiously, then turned it over to examine the handwriting on the address.

"Know who wrote this?" he inquired.

"Some one at the florist's," was the reply.

"Can you lend me a man for half an hour or so?" asked the scientist next.

"Oh, I suppose so," grumbled Detective Mallory. "But what's it all about, anyway?"

"Perhaps I may be able to tell you at the end of the half hour," The Thinking Machine assured him. "Meanwhile lend me the man you said I could have."

Detective Downey was called in, and the diminutive scientist led him into the hall, where he gave him some definite directions. Downey went out the front door at full speed. The Thinking Machine returned to Detective Mallory's private room, to find the officer sulking, like a boy.

"Where'd you send him?" he growled.

"Wait till he comes back and I'll tell you," was the reply. "It isn't necessary to get excited about something that we know nothing of. I'm saving you some excitement."

He dropped back into a chair and sat there idly twiddling his thumbs while Detective Mallory glared at him. After a few minutes the door was thrown open violently and Hutchinson Hatch entered. He was frankly excited.

"Well?" demanded The Thinking Machine without looking round.

"When she smelled that crushed kernel she fainted!" said Hatch explosively.

"Fainted?" repeated the scientist. "Fainted?" The tone was hardly one of surprise, and yet—

"Yes, she took one whiff, and screamed and went right over," the reporter rushed on.

"Dear me! Dear me!" commented The Thinking Machine. He sat still looking up. "Wait a few minutes," he advised. "Let's see what Downey gets."

At the end of fifteen minutes Downey returned. His chief glared at him curiously as he entered and handed a piece of paper to The Thinking Machine. That imperturbable man of science examined the paper closely, then handed it to Detective Mallory.

"Is that the handwriting on the flower box?" he asked.

Mallory, Downey, and Hatch compared it together. The verdict was unanimous: "Yes."

"Then the man who wrote it is the man you want," declared The Thinking Machine flatly. "His name is Paul K. Darrow. Detective Downey knows his address."

Two days passed. Professor Van Dusen stood beside his laboratory table poking idly at the dismembered legs of a frog with a short copper wire. Each time the point touched the flesh there was a spasmodic twitching of the limbs, a simulation of living contraction and extension. There beside the table Hutchinson Hatch found him.

"Watch this a moment, Mr Hatch," requested the scientist. "It bears, in a way, on our problem in hand."

Then began a rhythmic swinging of his slender hand, not unlike the beat of the musician's baton, the wire touching the frog's legs at each downward swing. Hatch had seen a similar demonstration before.

"Watch the strokes," said the scientist, "and watch the legs after the twentieth."

"Fourteen, fifteen, sixteen," Hatch counted. Each time the wire touched, and each time came the spasmodic motion. "Seventeen, eighteen, nineteen, twenty."

The Thinking Machine, instead of touching the twenty-first time, held the wire aloft. At the instant it would have touched the flesh, according to the beat, there came the same quick, spasmodic twitch, and then the legs were still.

"You see the effect is precisely as if I had touched them the twenty-first time," explained The Thinking Machine, "and that, Mr Hatch, is one of the things science doesn't attempt to explain. It can be explained some day – it will be explained, but–" He paused. "Darrow hasn't been captured yet?" he said.

"No; no trace of him yet," was the reply. "The police have sent out a general alarm for him all over the country, and today Burdock increased the reward he offered from five thousand to ten thousand dollars."

"One of my objections to dealing with the police is that they are prone to jump at conclusions," remarked The Thinking Machine. "I didn't say, of course, that Darrow was a murderer. He may have killed Miss Burdock, – he probably did, – but it isn't conclusive at all. Still he is the next link in the chain, so his presence is necessary."

Hatch gazed at him in amazement, and a hundred questions rushed to his lips. They were stilled by the sudden appearance in the doorway of a young man. A soft hat was pulled down over his eyes, and he was crouching as if about to spring. One hand, the right, was in his coat pocket, clutching something fiercely. His face was perfectly pallid, and roving, glittering eyes blazed with madness.

"Come in," suggested The Thinking Machine calmly.

"I-I must talk to you, quick!" the young man burst out. "It's a matter of the most vital importance, and—"

"I'm at your service, Mr Darrow," remarked The Thinking Machine pleasantly. "Have a seat."

Darrow! Hatch was startled, made speechless, by the uncanny appearance of this man whom the police of the entire continent were seeking. Darrow was still crouching there in the doorway, staring at them.

"I risked everything to come here," declared the young man – and there was a menace in his tone. "I was on the stoop about to ring the bell when I glanced back and saw Detective Mallory turn the corner. I didn't wait to ring – the door was unfastened and I came on in. Mallory is probably coming here. I must talk to you—and I won't be taken alive. Do you understand what I say?"

"Perfectly," replied The Thinking Machine. "Mr Mallory won't see you. Come in out of the door."

"No tricks!" warned Darrow fiercely.

"No tricks. Sit down."

With furtive glances to right and left along the hall, the young man entered and dropped into a seat in a corner, facing them. There was a long, tense silence, and finally the door bell rang. Darrow half rose and made as if to take his right hand from his pocket.

"That's Mallory," remarked The Thinking Machine, and he started toward the door.

Darrow took one step forward, blocking his way. "Understand, please," he began in a low, even voice. "I am utterly desperate, and I won't be taken! If you attempt to betray me, I—" He stopped.

The Thinking Machine walked round him to the door leading into the hall. Martha, his aged servant, was just passing.

"Mr Mallory is at the door, Martha," said the scientist. "Tell him I am not in; but that I shall be at police headquarters within an hour, and Mr Darrow will come with me."

He stepped back into the laboratory and closed the door, without even a glance at his visitor. They heard Martha open the front door, then they heard Mallory's heavy voice, finally Martha's answer, then the door was closed, and Martha's footsteps passed along the hall. Darrow suddenly rushed to the window and glanced out.

"All right, Mr Darrow," remarked the little scientist, as he sat down. "I know now you are innocent; I know why you have been hiding out, I know why you came here to see me, and I understand too your deep grief; so we can come immediately to the vital things."

The young man turned and glared at the small, impassive figure. "You said I would be at police headquarters with you in an hour," he said accusingly.

"Certainly," agreed the scientist impatiently. "As an innocent man you will go there of your own free will, with me."

The young man dropped into a chair and sat there for a long time with his face in his hands. After awhile Hatch saw a teardrop trickle through the unsteady fingers, and the shoulders moved convulsively. The Thinking Machine sat with head tilted back, squinting upward and fingers at rest, tip to tip.

"This trouble between you and Mr Burdock?" suggested the scientist at last.

"You don't know the malignant hatred he has for me," said Darrow suddenly. "He is not a man of great wealth, but he is a man of great power, great influence, and if I should fall into the hands of the police with the circumstantial case against me that now exists he would bring all that power and influence to bear against me, with the result that I should be railroaded to a felon's grave. I don't know just how he would do it; but he would do it. I'm afraid of him – tha's why I came here to see you when I wouldn't dare go to the police. I won't be taken by the police until I know I can prove my innocence; then I will surrender."

The Thinking Machine nodded.

"The enmity existing between us is of years' standing, and is not of importance here," Darrow went on. "But I know this man's power, – I have felt it all my life, – he has brought me to the edge of starvation half a dozen times, pursued me in every walk of life, until now-now if I should have to commit murder, he would be the victim. I'm telling you this because—"

"All this is of no consequence," interrupted The Thinking Machine shortly. "Who poisoned the rose?"

"I don't know," replied Darrow helplessly.

"You must have some idea," insisted The Thinking Machine.

"I did have an idea," was the reply. "I went this morning to a place to see a-a person whom I intended to accuse openly of the crime, taking the chance of capture myself, much as I dreaded it; but there was no one there. The door was locked; a servant connected with the apartment house told me that the- the person had not been there for a day or so."

The Thinking Machine turned quickly in his chair and glared at Darrow curiously.

"What's her name?" he demanded sharply.

"I don't know that she could have had anything to do with it," warned Darrow. "It seems awful to suggest such a thing, and yet—" He stopped. "I will go there with you to see her if you wish."

"Mr Hatch," directed The Thinking Machine, "step into the next room there and telephone for a cab." He turned again to Darrow. "She threatened you, or Miss Burdock, I imagine?"

"Yes," said Darrow reluctantly.

"And now, please, one last question," said the little scientist. "What relation existed between you and Miss Burdock?"

"She was my wife," Darrow replied in a low voice. "We were secretly married four months ago."

"Um-m," mused the scientist. "I imagined as much."

Detective Mallory impatiently strode back and forth across his private office, his brain turbulent with conjecture. The telephone bell rang; The Thinking Machine was at the other end of the wire.

"Come at once and bring the medical examiner to the Craddock apartments!" commanded the irritable voice of the little scientist.

"Another murder?" demanded the detective, aghast.

"No, a suicide," was the reply. "Goodbye."

Detective Mallory and Medical Examiner Francis found The Thinking Machine, Hutchinson Hatch, and Paul K. Darrow in the sitting room of a small apartment on the fourth floor. Some sinister thing lay outstretched on a couch, covered with a sheet.

"Mr Mallory, this is Mr Darrow," the scientist remarked. "And here," he indicated the couch, "is the woman who murdered Miss Burdock, or rather Mrs Darrow. Her name is Maria di Peculini. Here is a full confession in her own handwriting," he passed an envelope to the detective, "and here are several torn pieces of paper which show how assiduously she practised before show forged Mr Darrow's handwriting in addressing the box in which the red rose was sent to Miss – I should say Mrs Darrow. I may add that Signorina di Peculini killed herself by inhaling hydrocyanic acid – perhaps you know it better as Prussic acid – in a bottle from which came the single drop, allowed to settle in the bloom of the rose, which killed Mrs Darrow."

Detective Mallory remained standing still for a long time to take it all in. At last he opened the confession – only a dozen lines – and read it from end to end. It was a pitiful, disjointed, almost incoherent, revelation of a woman's distorted soul. She too had loved Darrow, and this had changed to hate when he drifted away from her. Then, when by her own hand she had removed the woman he had made his wife, and had sought subtly to place the blame on him by the little forgery, – then had come a revulsion of feeling. She loved again, and overcome by remorse sought relief in death.

"There was no mystery whatever as to the cause of death," The Thinking Machine told Detective Mallory and Hatch a little while later. "Murder by poison was obvious from the fact that both the woman and the dog were dead; and when we knew that there was no mark or scratch on the dog, and the autopsy revealed nothing, we knew by the simplest rule of logic that the poison had been inhaled. The most powerful poison to inhale is hydrocyanic acid, – it kills instantly, – therefore it occurred to me first. It is so powerful that it is never made pure, at least in this country. The strongest you can buy in a drug store, for instance, is about a two per cent solution. One drop of a stronger solution than that, on a rose bloom, would have killed Miss Burdock, and the dog if he sniffed at it, as he must have.

"Therefore, from the very first, we knew the manner of death. When we knew further that hydrocyanic acid is extremely volatile, we see how that single drop on the rose evaporated, was dissipated in the air, as the windows of the room where the young woman was found were open. Still there was a faint odor of it left, – it smells precisely like crushed peach kernels, – and the maid Goodwin was unconsciously affected by it.

"Knowing these things," he continued, "I went to the florist's. Only twelve roses had been bought, paid for, and delivered from there, and the rose that killed Miss Burdock was the thirteenth rose. The roses went from the florist's Mondays, Wednesdays, and Saturdays for four weeks, making twelve roses. They had all been delivered, as the receipt books there showed; but Miss Burdock was killed on Monday; therefore that was the thirteenth rose, and it didn't come direct from the florist's. It was sent by messenger, and the date didn't correspond with any date in the receipt book; therefore it came from another source.

"Incidentally the fact that the roses were sent in that way, – that is one at a time without a card or suggestion of by whom they were sent, – suggested a clandestine arrangement with the girl. In other words, the roses were being sent by some one she knew, in all probability; but no one else must know. It was, I saw, a method of correspondence, I might say a love token of some sort, which would not attract attention at her home as a letter would.

"Thus I established a relationship between Miss Burdock and someone else — unknown. The logic of it all informed me that the reason that unknown didn't communicate with her was because of some objection in her home. Her father! Do you see? I simply asked him about it, and instantly his hatred for a single individual came out, that individual being Mr Darrow. Thus, things pointed toward Mr Darrow, who was away. The letter to the florist was from Washington. The joints were fitting nicely.

"At police headquarters I saw the rose, and by cautious experiments detected a faint odor of peach kernels. Then I saw the handwriting on the box. It seemed to be a man's; yet I knew by the receipt book there that it did not come from the florist's, therefore was not addressed by anyone there. Did Mr Darrow address it? Mr Downey got for me a sample of Mr Darrow's writing (I don't know how he got it), and the two were compared. They seemed to be the same. This fact was connecting with all the others. Clandestine communication – poison – Darrow! Do you see? This development made Darrow's presence necessary, and I told you, Mr Mallory, that he was the man we must find. Yet, from the fact that the handwriting on the box was his I had a first suggestion that he was not guilty of the crime. No intelligent man would address a box like that in his own handwriting.

"The matter rested at this point. Mr Burdock accepted a murder theory and offered rewards, and then Mr Darrow in person came to see me. The moment he stepped inside my door, to tell me an improbable story, I knew he was innocent. Mr Burdock's hatred of him (the cause of the feud between them is not of consequence) told me why he had disappeared; and his mere appearance before me accounted for his not going to the police. So-so that's all. He told me of calling to see Signorina di Peculini, and she was not in. We came here, found the door locked, went in with a pass key, and found the things as I delivered them to you, Mr Mallory." He stopped and sat silently staring for a little while.

"Briefly," he supplemented, "the woman who killed herself knew of the rose being sent regularly, then determined on revenge, bought one, and sent it herself after dropping a single drop of poison in the bloom. The wax paper which surrounded the flower prevented evaporation, and when it was opened,— We know the rest."

Neither Detective Mallory nor Hatch spoke for a long time. But the reporter had one more question to ask; and at last he put it.

"That peach kernel that you sent me to Goodwin with—" he began.

"Oh, yes," interrupted The Thinking Machine. "That was a little psychological experiment, and the result of it disconcerted me a little. It is one of the many things science doesn't fully understand, Mr Hatch—like the little experiment with the frog. For instance, nitrite of amyl is a powerful heart stimulant. It smells precisely like banana oil. A person who has used nitrite of amyl, or to whom it has been administered without their knowledge by inhalation, is momentarily affected the same way when they come suddenly upon the odor of banana oil. Prussic acid has an odor like a peach kernel. I sent you to Goodwin, therefore, to prove definitely whether or not prussic acid had been used, and if she had inhaled it unconsciously. The result gave the proof I wanted."

17

THE SILVER BOX

"Really great criminals are never found out, for the simple reason that the greatest crimes – their crimes – are never discovered," remarked Professor Augustus S. F. X. Van Dusen positively. "There is genius in the perpetration of crime, Mr Grayson, just as there must be in its detection, unless it is the shallow work of a bungler. In this latter case there have been instances where even the police have uncovered the truth. But the expert criminal, the man of genius, – the professional, I may say, – regards as perfect only that crime which does not and cannot be made to appear a crime at all; therefore one that can never involve him, nor anyone else."

The financier, J. Morgan Grayson, regarded this wizened little man of science – The Thinking Machine – thoughtfully, through the smoke of his cigar.

"It is a strange psychological fact that the casual criminal glories in his crime beforehand, and from one to ten minutes afterward," The Thinking Machine continued. "For instance, the man who kills for revenge wants the world to know it is his work; but at the end of ten minutes comes fear, abject terror, and then, paradoxically enough, he will seek to hide his crime and protect himself by some transparent means utterly inadequate, because of what he has said or done in the passion which preceded the act. With fear comes panic, with panic irresponsibility, and then he makes the mistake, – hews a pathway which the trained mind follows from motive to a prison cell.

"These are the men who are found out. But there are men of genius, Mr Grayson, professionally engaged in crime. We never hear of them, because they are never caught, and we never even suspect them, because they make no mistake, – they are men of genius. Imagine the great brains of history turned to crime. Well, there are today brains as great as any of those which make a profession of it; there is murder and theft and robbery under our noses that we never dream of. If I, for instance, should become an active criminal, can you see—" He paused.

Grayson, with a queer expression on his face, puffed steadily at his cigar.

"I could kill you now, here in this room," The Thinking Machine went on calmly, "and no one would ever know, never even suspect. Why not? Because I would make no mistake. In other words, I would immediately take rank with the criminals of genius who are never found out."

It was not a boast as he said it; it was merely a statement of fact. Grayson appeared to be a little startled. Where there had been only impatient interest in his manner, there was now something else – fascination, perhaps.

"How would you kill me, for instance?" he inquired curiously.

"With anyone of a dozen poisons, with virulent germs, or even with a knife or revolver," replied the scientist placidly. "You see, I know how to use poisons; I know how to inoculate with germs; I know how to produce a suicidal appearance perfectly with either a revolver or knife. And I never make mistakes, Mr Grayson. In the sciences we must be exact – not approximately so, but absolutely so. We must know. It isn't like carpentry. A carpenter may make a trivial mistake in a joint, and it will not weaken his house; but if the scientist makes one mistake the whole structure tumbles down. We must know. Knowledge is progress. We gain knowledge through observation and logic — inevitable logic. And logic tells us that while two and two make four, it is not only sometimes but all the time."

Grayson flicked the ashes off his cigar thoughtfully, and little wrinkles appeared about his eyes as he stared into the drawn, inscrutable face of the scientist. The enormous, straw yellow head was cushioned against the chair, the squinting, watery blue eyes turned upward, and the slender white fingers at rest, tip to tip. The financier drew a long breath. "I have been informed that you were a remarkable man," he said at last slowly. "I believe it. Quinton Fraser, the banker who gave me the letter of introduction to you, told me how you once solved a remarkable mystery, in which — "

"Yes, yes," interrupted the scientist shortly; "the Ralston bank burglary — I remember."

"So I came to you to enlist your aid in something which is more inexplicable than that," Grayson went on hesitatingly. "I know that no fee I might offer would influence you; yet it is a case which — "

"State it," interrupted The Thinking Machine again.

"It isn't a crime — that is, a crime that can be reached by law," Grayson hurried on, — "but it has cost me millions, and — "

For one instant The Thinking Machine lowered his squint eyes to those of his visitor, then raised them again. "Millions!" he repeated. "How many?"

"Six, eight, perhaps ten," was the reply. "Briefly, there is a leak in my office. My plans become known to others almost by the time I have perfected them. My plans are large; I have millions at stake; and the greatest secrecy is absolutely essential. For years I have been able to preserve this secrecy; but half a dozen times in the last eight weeks my plans have become known, and I have been caught. Unless you know the Street, you can't imagine what a tremendous disadvantage it is to have some one know your next move to the minutest detail, and knowing it, defeat you at every turn."

"No, I don't know your world of finance, Mr Grayson," remarked The Thinking Machine. "Give me an instance."

"Well, take this last case," suggested the financier earnestly. "Briefly, without technicalities, I had planned to unload the securities of the P., Q. & X. railway, protecting myself through brokers, and force the outstanding stock down to a price where other brokers, acting for me, could buy far below the actual value. In this way I intended to get complete control of the stock. But my plans became known, and when I began to unload everything was snapped up by the opposition, with the result that instead of gaining control of the road I lost heavily. The same thing has happened, with variations, half a dozen times."

"I presume that is strictly honest?" inquired the scientist mildly.

"Honest?" repeated Grayson. "Certainly – of course. It's business."

"I shall not pretend to understand all that," said The Thinking Machine curtly. "It doesn't seem to matter, anyway. You want to know where the leak is. Is that right?"

"Precisely."

"Well, who is in your confidence?"

"No one, except my stenographer."

"Of course, there is an exception. Who is he, please?"

"It's a woman – Miss Evelyn Winthrop. She has been in my employ for six years in the same capacity, – more than five years before this leak appeared – and I trust her absolutely."

"No man knows your business?"

"No," replied the financier grimly. "I learned years ago that no one could keep my secrets as I do, – there are too many temptations, – therefore I never mention my plans to anyone – never – to anyone!"

"Except your stenographer," corrected the scientist.

"I work for days, weeks, sometimes months, perfecting plans, and it's all in my head, not on paper – not a scratch of it," explained Grayson. "Therefore, when I say that she is in my confidence I mean that she knows my plans only half an hour or less before the machinery is put into motion. For instance, I planned this P., Q. & X. deal. My brokers didn't know of it; Miss Winthrop never heard of it until twenty minutes before the Stock Exchange opened for business. Then I dictated to her, as I always do, some short letters of instructions to my agents. That is all she knew of it."

"You outlined the plan in those letters?"

"No; they merely told my brokers what to do."

"But a shrewd person, knowing the contents of all those letters, could have learned what you intended to do?"

"Yes; but no one person knew the contents of all those letters. No one broker knew what was in the other letters – many of them were unknown to each other. Miss Winthrop and I were the only two human beings who knew all that was in them."

The Thinking Machine sat silent for so long that Grayson began to fidget in his chair. "Who was in the room besides you and Miss Winthrop before the letters were sent?" he asked at last.

"No one," responded Grayson emphatically. "For an hour before I dictated those letters, until at least an hour afterward, after my plans had gone to smash, no one entered that room. Only she and I work there."

"But when she finished the letters, she went out?" insisted The Thinking Machine.

"No," declared the financier; "she didn't even leave her desk."

"Or perhaps sent something out – manifolds of the letters?"

"No."

"Or called up a friend on the telephone?" continued The Thinking Machine quietly.

"Nor that," retorted Grayson.

"Or signaled to some one through the window?"

"No," said the financier again. "She finished the letters, then remained quietly at her desk, reading a book. She didn't move for two hours."

The Thinking Machine lowered his eyes and glared straight into those of the financier. "Some one listened at the window?" he went on after a moment.

"No. It is six stories up, fronting the street, and there is no fire escape."

"Or the door?"

"If you knew the arrangement of my offices, you would see how utterly impossible that would be, because—"

"Nothing is impossible, Mr Grayson," snapped the scientist abruptly. "It might be improbable, but not impossible. Don't say that – it annoys me exceedingly." He was silent for a moment. Grayson stared at him blankly. "Did either you or she answer a call on the phone?"

"No one called; we called no one."

"Any apertures—holes or cracks—in your flooring or walls or ceilings?" demanded the scientist.

"Private detectives whom I had employed looked for such an opening, and there was none," replied Grayson.

Again The Thinking Machine was silent for a long time. Grayson lighted a fresh cigar and settled back in his chair patiently. Faint cobwebby lines began to appear on the dome-like brow of the scientist, and slowly the squint eyes were narrowing.

"The letters you wrote were intercepted?" he suggested at last.

"No," exclaimed Grayson flatly. "Those letters were sent direct to the brokers by a dozen different methods, and everyone of them had been delivered by five minutes of ten o'clock, when Change begins business. The last one left me at ten minutes of ten."

"Dear me! Dear me!" The Thinking Machine arose and paced the length of the room thrice.

"You don't give me credit for the extraordinary precautions I have taken, particularly in this last P., Q. & X. deal," Grayson continued. "I left positively nothing undone to insure absolute secrecy. And Miss Winthrop I know is innocent of any connection with the affair. The private detectives suspected her at first, as you do, and she was watched in and out of my office for weeks. When she was not under my eyes, she was under the eyes of men to whom I had promised an extravagant sum of money if they found the leak. She didn't know it then, and doesn't know it now. I am heartily ashamed of it all, because the investigation proved her absolute loyalty to me. On this last day she was directly under my eyes for two hours; and she didn't make one movement that I didn't note, because the thing meant millions to me. That proved beyond all question that it was no fault of hers. What could I do?"

The Thinking Machine didn't say. He paused at a window, and for minute after minute stood motionless there, with eyes narrowed down to mere slits.

"I was on the point of discharging Miss Winthrop," the financier went on; "but her innocence was so thoroughly proved to me by this last affair that it would have been unjust, and so—"

Suddenly the scientist turned upon his visitor. "Do you talk in your sleep?" he demanded.

"No," was the prompt reply. "I had thought of that too. It is beyond all ordinary things, professor. Yet there is a leak that is costing me millions."

"It comes down to this, Mr Grayson," The Thinking Machine informed him crabbedly enough. "If only you and Miss Winthrop knew those plans, and no one else, and they did leak, and were not deduced from other things, then either you or she permitted them to leak, intentionally or unintentionally. That is as pure logic as that two and two make four; there is no need to argue it."

"Well, of course, I didn't," said Grayson.

"Then Miss Winthrop did," declared The Thinking Machine finally, positively; "unless we credit the opposition, as you call it, with telepathic gifts hitherto unheard of. By the way, you have referred to the other side only as the opposition. Do the same men, the same clique, appear against you all the time, or is it only one man?"

"It's a clique," explained the financier, "with millions back of it, headed by Ralph Matthews, a young man to whom I give credit for being the prime factor against me." His lips were set sternly.

"Why?" demanded the scientist.

"Because every time he sees me he grins," was the reply. Grayson seemed suddenly discomfited.

The Thinking Machine went to a desk, addressed an envelop, folded a sheet of paper, placed it inside, then sealed it. At length he turned back to his visitor. "Is Miss Winthrop at your office now?"

"Yes."

"Let us go there, then."

A few minutes later the eminent financier ushered the eminent scientist into his private office on the Street. The only other person there was a young woman, – a woman of twenty-six or seven, perhaps, – who turned, saw Grayson, and resumed reading. The financier motioned to a seat. Instead of sitting, however, The Thinking Machine went straight to Miss Winthrop and extended a sealed envelope to her.

"Mr Ralph Matthews asked me to hand you this," he said.

The young woman glanced up into his face frankly, yet with a certain timidity, took the envelop, and turned it curiously in her hand.

"Mr Ralph Matthews," she repeated, as if the name was a strange one. "I don't think I know him."

The Thinking Machine stood staring at her aggressively, insolently even, as she opened the envelop and drew out the sheet of paper. There was no expression save surprise — bewilderment, rather – to be read on her face.

"Why, it's a blank sheet!" she remarked, puzzled.

The scientist turned away suddenly toward Grayson, who had witnessed the incident with frank astonishment in his eyes. "Your telephone a moment, please," he requested.

"Certainly; here," replied Grayson.

"This will do," remarked the scientist.

He leaned forward over the desk where Miss Winthrop sat, still gazing at him in a sort of bewilderment, picked up the receiver, and held it to his ear. A few moments later he was talking to Hutchinson Hatch, reporter.

"I merely wanted to ask you to meet me at my apartments in an hour," said the scientist. "It is very important."

That was all. He hung up the receiver, paused for a moment to admire an exquisitely wrought silver box – a "vanity" box-on Miss Winthrop's desk, beside the telephone, then took a seat beside Grayson and began to discourse almost pleasantly upon the prevailing meteorological conditions. Grayson merely stared; Miss Winthrop continued her reading.

Professor Augustus S. F. X. Van Dusen, distinguished scientist, and Hutchinson Hatch, newspaper reporter, were poking round among the chimney pots and other obstructions on the roof of a skyscraper. Far below them the slumber enshrouded city was spread out like a panorama, streets dotted brilliantly with arc lights, and roofs hazily visible through the mists of night. Above, the infinite blackness hung like a veil, with star points breaking through here and there.

"Here are the wires," Hatch said at last, and he stooped.

The Thinking Machine knelt on the roof beside him, and for several minutes they remained thus in the darkness, with only the glow of an electric flash to indicate their presence. Finally The Thinking Machine rose.

"That's the wire you want, Mr Hatch," he said. "I'll leave the rest of it to you."

"Are you sure?" asked the reporter.

"I am always sure," was the tart response.

Hatch opened a small hand satchel and removed several queerly wrought tools. These he spread on the roof beside him; then, kneeling again, began his work. For half an hour or so he labored in the gloom, with only the electric flash to aid him, and then he arose.

"It's all right," he said.

The Thinking Machine examined the work that had been done, grunted his satisfaction, and together they went to the skylight, leaving a thin, insulated wire behind them stringing along to mark their path. They passed down through the roof, and into the darkness of the hall of the upper story. Here the light was extinguished. From far below came the faint echo of a man's footsteps as the watchman passed through the silent deserted building.

"Be careful!" warned The Thinking Machine.

Along the hall to a room in the rear they went, and still the wire trailed behind. At the last door they stopped. The Thinking Machine fumbled with some keys, then opened the way. Here an electric light was going. The room was bare of furniture, the only sign of recent occupancy being a telephone instrument on the wall.

Here The Thinking Machine stopped and stared at the spool of wire which he had permitted to wind off as he walked, and his thin face expressed doubt.

"It wouldn't be safe," he said at last, "to leave the wire exposed as we have left it. True, this floor is not occupied; but some one might pass up this way and disturb it. You take the spool, go back to the roof, winding the wire as you go, then swing the spool down to me over the side so I can bring it in the window. That will be best. I will catch it here, and thus there will be nothing to indicate any connection."

Hatch went out quietly and closed the door.

Twice the following day The Thinking Machine spoke to the financier over the telephone. Grayson was in his private office, Miss Winthrop at her desk, when the first call came.

"Be careful in answering my questions," warned The Thinking Machine when Grayson answered. "Do you know how long Miss Winthrop has owned the little silver box which is now on her desk, near the telephone?"

Grayson glanced around involuntarily to where the girl sat idly turning over the leaves of her book. "Yes," he answered; "for seven months. I gave it last Christmas."

"Ah!" exclaimed the scientist. "That simplifies matters. Where did you buy it?"

Grayson mentioned the name of a well known jeweler.

"Goodbye," came the voice of the scientist, and the connection was broken.

Considerably later in the day The Thinking Machine called Grayson to the telephone again.

"What make of typewriter does she use?" came the querulous voice over the wire.

Grayson named it.

"Goodbye."

While Grayson sat with deeply perplexed lines in his face, the diminutive scientist called upon Hutchinson Hatch at his office. The reporter was just starting out.

"Do you use a typewriter?" demanded the Thinking Machine.

"Yes."

"What kind?"

"Oh, four or five kinds – we have half a dozen varieties in the office. I can use any of them."

They passed along through the city room, at that moment practically deserted, until finally the watery, blue eyes settled upon a typewriter with the name emblazoned on the front.

"That's it!" exclaimed The Thinking Machine. "Write something on it," he directed Hatch.

"What shall I write?" inquired the reporter, and he sat down.

"Anything you like," was the terse response. "Just write something."

Hatch drew up a chair and rolled off several lines of the immortal practice sentence, beginning, "Now is the time for all good men—"

The Thinking Machine sat beside him, squinting off across the room in deep abstraction, and listening intently. His head was turned away from the reporter, and his ear was within a few inches of the machine. For half a minute he sat there listening, then shook his head.

"Strike your vowels," he commanded; "first slowly, then rapidly."

Again Hatch obeyed, while the scientist listened. And again he shook his head. Then in turn every make of machine in the office was tested the same way. At the end The Thinking Machine arose and went his way. There was an expression nearly approaching complete bewilderment on his face, as he went out.

For hour after hour that night The Thinking Machine half lay in a huge chair in his laboratory, with eyes turned uncompromisingly upward, and an expression of complete concentration on his face. There was no change either in his position or his gaze as minute succeeded minute; the brow was deeply wrinkled now, and the thin line of the lips was drawn taut. The tiny clock in the reception room struck ten, eleven, twelve, and finally one. At just half-past one The Thinking Machine arose suddenly.

"Positively I am getting stupid!" he grumbled half aloud. "Of course! Of course! Why couldn't I have thought of that in the first place!"

So it came about that Grayson did not go to his office on the following morning at the usual time. Instead, he called again upon The Thinking Machine in eager, expectant response to a note which had reached him at his home just before he started to his office.

"Nothing yet," said The Thinking Machine as the financier entered. "But here is something you must do today. What time does the Stock Exchange close?"

"Three o'clock," was the reply.

"Well, at one o'clock," the scientist went on, "you must issue orders for a gigantic deal of some sort; and you must issue them precisely as you have issued them in the past; there must be no variation. Dictate the letters as you have always done to Miss Winthrop; but don't send them. When they come to you, keep them until you see me."

"You mean that the deal must be purely imaginary?" inquired the financier.

"Precisely," was the reply. "But make your instructions circumstantial; give them enough detail to make them absolutely convincing."

"And hold the letters?"

"Hold the letters," the other repeated. "The leak comes before you receive them. I don't want to know or have an idea of what mythical deal it is to be; but issue your orders at one o'clock."

Grayson asked a dozen questions, answers to which was curtly denied, then went to his office. The Thinking Machine again called Hatch to the telephone.

THE SILVER BOX

"I've got it," he announced briefly. "I want the best telegraph operator you know. Bring him along and meet me in the room on the top floor where the telephone is at precisely fifteen minutes of one o'clock today."

"Telegraph operator?" Hatch repeated.

"That's what I said – telegraph operator!" replied the scientist irritably. "Goodbye."

Hatch smiled whimsically at the other end as he heard the receiver banged on the hook-smiled because he knew the eccentric ways of this singular man, whose mind so accurately illuminated every problem to which it was directed. Then he went out to the telegraph room and borrowed the principal operator. They were in the little room on the top floor at precisely fifteen minutes of one.

The operator glanced about in astonishment. The room was still unfurnished, save for the telephone box on the wall.

"What do I do?" he asked.

"I'll tell you when the time comes," responded the scientist, as he glanced at the watch.

At three minutes of one o'clock he handed a sheet of blank paper to the operator, and gave his final instructions. "Hold the telephone receiver to your ear and write on this what you hear," he directed. "It may be several minutes before you hear anything. When you do, tell me so."

There was ludicrous mystification on the operator's face; but he obeyed orders, grinning cheerfully at Hatch as he tilted his cigar up to keep the smoke out of his eyes. The Thinking Machine stood impatiently looking on, watch in hand. Hatch didn't know what was happening; but he was tremendously interested.

And at last the operator heard something. His face became suddenly alert. He continued to listen for a moment, and then came a smile of recognition as he turned to the scientist.

"It's good old Morse, all right," he announced; "but it's the queerest sort of sounder I ever read."

"You mean the Morse telegraphic code?" demanded The Thinking Machine.

"Sure," said the operator.

"Write your message."

Within less than ten minutes after Miss Winthrop had handed over the typewritten letters of instruction to Grayson for signature, and while he still sat turning them over in his hands, the door opened and The Thinking Machine entered. He tossed a folded sheet of paper on the desk before Grayson, and went straight to Miss Winthrop.

"So you did know Mr Ralph Matthews after all?" he inquired.

The girl arose from her desk, and a flash of some subtle emotion passed over her face. "What do you mean, sir?" she demanded.

"You might as well remove the silver box," The Thinking Machine went on mercilessly. "There is no further need of the connection."

Miss Winthrop glanced down at the telephone extension on her desk, and her hand darted toward it. The silver "vanity" box was underneath supporting the receiver, so that all the weight was removed from the hook, and the line was open. She snatched the box, the receiver dropped on the hook, and there was a faint tinkle of a bell somewhere below. The Thinking Machine turned to Grayson.

"It was Miss Winthrop," he said.

"Miss Winthrop!" exclaimed Grayson, and he arose. "I can't believe it!"

"It doesn't really matter whether you believe it or not," retorted The Thinking Machine. "But if your doubt is very serious, you might ask her."

Grayson turned toward the girl and took a couple of steps forward. There was more than surprise in his face; there was doubt, and perhaps regret.

"I don't know what it's all about," she protested feebly.

"Read the paper I gave you, Mr Grayson," directed The Thinking Machine coldly. "Perhaps that will enlighten her."

The financier opened the sheet, which had remained folded in his hand, and glanced at what was written there. Slowly he read it aloud: "Goldman. – Sell ten thousand shares L. & W. at 97. McCracken Co. – Sell ten thousand shares L. & W., 97." He read on down the list, bewildered. Then gradually, as he realized the import of what he read, there came a hardening of the lines about his mouth.

"I understand, Miss Winthrop," he said at last. "This is the substance of the orders I dictated, and in some way you made them known to persons for whom they were not intended. I don't know how you did it, of course; but I understand that you did do it, so—" He stepped to the door and opened it with grave courtesy. "You may go now. I am sorry."

Miss Winthrop made no plea, – merely bowed and went out. Grayson stood staring after her for a moment, then turned to The Thinking Machine and motioned him to a chair. "What happened?" he asked briskly.

"Miss Winthrop is a tremendously clever woman," replied The Thinking Machine. "She neglected to tell you, however, that besides being a stenographer and typewriter she was a telegraph operator as well. She is so expert in each of her lines that she combined the two, if I may say it that way. In other words, in writing on the typewriter, she was clever enough to be able to give the click of the machine the sounding of the Morse telegraphic code, so that another telegraph operator who heard her machine could translate it into words."

Grayson sat staring at him incredulously. "I still don't understand," he said finally.

"Here," and The Thinking Machine arose and went to Miss Winthrop's desk, – "here is an extension telephone with the receiver on the hook. It just happens that the little silver box which you gave Miss Winthrop is tall enough to support this receiver clear of the hook, and the minute the receiver is off the hook the line is open. When you were at your desk and she was here, you couldn't see this telephone; therefore it was a simple matter for her to lift the receiver, and place the silver box beneath, thus holding the line open permanently. That being true, the sound of the typewriter would go over the open wire to whoever was listening at the other end, wouldn't it? Then, if that typewriter was made to sound the telegraphic code, and an operator held the receiver at the other end, that operator could read a message written at the same moment your letters were being written. That is all. It requires extreme concentration to do the thing – cleverness."

"Oh, I see!" exclaimed Grayson at last.

"When we knew that the leak in your office was not in the usual way," continued The Thinking Machine, "we looked for the unusual. First I was inclined to believe that there was a difference in the sounding quality of the various keys as they were struck, and some one was clever enough to read that. I had Mr Hatch make experiments, however, which instantly proved that was out of the question, – unless this typewriter had been tuned, I may say. The logic of the thing had convinced me meanwhile that the leak must be by way of the telephone line, and Mr Hatch and I tapped it one night. He is an electrician. Then I saw the possibility of holding the line open, as I explained; but for hour after hour the actual method of communication eluded me. At last I found it – the telegraphic code. Then it was all simple.

"When I telephoned to you to find out how long Miss Winthrop had had the silver box, and you said seven months, I knew that it was always at hand; when I asked you where you got it, I went there and saw a duplicate. There I measured the box and tested my belief that it would just support the receiver clear of the hook. When I requested you to dictate those orders today at one o'clock, I had a telegraph operator listening at a telephone on the top floor of this building. There is nothing very mysterious about it, after all – it's merely clever."

"Clever!" repeated Grayson, and his jaws snapped. "It is more than that. Why, it's criminal! She should be prosecuted."

"I shouldn't advise that, Mr Grayson," returned the scientist coldly. "If it is honest – merely business – to juggle stocks as you told me you did, this is no more dishonest. And besides, remember that Miss Winthrop is backed by the people who have made millions out of you, and – well, I wouldn't prosecute. It is betrayal of trust, certainly; but—" He arose as if that was all, and started toward the door. "I would advise you, if you want to stop the leak, to discharge the person in charge of your office exchange here," he said.

"Was she in on the scheme?" demanded Grayson. He rushed out of the private office into the main office. At the door he met a clerk coming in.

"Where is Miss Mitchell?" demanded the financier hotly.

"I was just coming to tell you that she went out with Miss Winthrop just now without giving any explanation," replied the clerk. "The telephone is without an attendant."

"Goodday, Mr Grayson," said The Thinking Machine.

The financier nodded his thanks, then stalked back into his room, banging the door behind him.

In the course of time The Thinking Machine received a check for ten thousand dollars, signed, "J. Morgan Grayson." He glared at it for a little while, then indorsed it in a crabbed hand, "Pay to Trustees Home for Crippled Children," and sent Martha out to mail it.

18

PROBLEM OF THE STOLEN BANK NOTES

There was no mystery whatever about the identity of the man who, alone and unaided, robbed the Thirteenth National Bank of $109,437 in cash and $1.29 in postage stamps. It was "Mort" Dolan, an expert safecracker albeit a young one, and he had made a clean sweep. Nor yet was there any mystery as to his whereabouts. He was safely in a cell at Police Headquarters, having been captured within less than twelve hours after the robbery was discovered.

Dolan had offered no resistance to the officers when he was cornered, and had attempted no denial when questioned by Detective Mallory. He knew he had been caught fairly and squarely and no argument was possible, so he confessed, with a glow of pride at a job well done. It was four or five days after his arrest that the matter came to the attention of The Thinking Machine. Then the problem was—

But perhaps it were better to begin at the beginning.

Despite the fact that he was considerably less than thirty years old, "Mort" Dolan was a man for whom the police had a wholesome respect. He had a record, for he had started early. This robbery of the Thirteenth National was his "big" job and was to have been his last. With the proceeds he had intended to take his wife and quietly disappear beneath a full beard and an alias in some place far removed from former haunts. But the mutability of human events is a matter of proverb. While the robbery as a robbery was a thoroughly artistic piece of work and in full accordance with plans which had been worked out to the minutest details months before, he had made one mistake. This was leaving behind him in the bank the can in which the nitro-glycerine had been bought. Through this carelessness he had been traced.

Dolan and his wife occupied three poor rooms in a poor tenement house. From the moment the police got a description of the person who bought the explosive they were confident for they knew their man. Therefore four clever men were on watch about the poor tenement. Neither Dolan nor his wife was there then, but from the condition of things in the rooms the police believed that they intended to return so took up positions to watch.

Unsuspecting enough, for his one mistake in the robbery had not recurred to him, Dolan came along just about dusk and started up the five steps to the front door of the tenement. It just happened that he glanced back and saw a head drawn suddenly behind a projecting stoop. But the electric light glared strongly there and Dolan recognized Detective Downey, one of many men who revolved around Detective Mallory within a limited orbit. Dolan paused on the stoop a moment and rolled a cigarette while he thought it over. Perhaps instead of entering it would be best to stroll on down the street, turn a corner and make a dash for it. But just at that moment he spied another head in the direction of contemplated flight. That was Detective Blanton.

Deeply thoughtful Dolan smoked half the cigarette and stared blankly in front of him. He knew of a back door opening on an alley. Perhaps the detectives had not thought to guard that! He tossed his cigarette away, entered the house with affected unconcern and closed the door. Running lightly through the long, unclean hall which extended the full length of the building he flung open the back door. He turned back instantly—just outside he had seen and recognized Detective Cunningham.

Then he had an inspiration! The roof! The building was four stories. He ran up the four flights lightly but rapidly and was half way up the short flight which led to the opening in the roof when he stopped. From above he caught the whiff of a bad cigar, then the measured tread of heavy boots. Another detective! With a sickening depression at his heart Dolan came softly down the stairs again, opened the door of his flat with a latch-key and entered.

Then and there he sat down to figure it all out. There seemed no escape for him. Every way out was blocked, and it was only a question of time before they would close in on him. He imagined now they were only waiting for his wife's return. He could fight for his freedom of course – even kill one, perhaps two, of the detectives who were waiting for him. But that would only mean his own death. If he tried to run for it past either of the detectives he would get a shot in the back. And besides, murder was repugnant to Dolan's artistic soul. It didn't do any good. But could he warn Isabel, his wife? He feared she would walk into the trap as he had done, and she had had no connection of any sort with the affair.

Then, from a fear that his wife would return, there swiftly came a fear that she would not. He suddenly remembered that it was necessary for him to see her. The police could not connect her with the robbery in any way; they could only hold her for a time and then would be compelled to free her for her innocence of this particular crime was beyond question. And if he were taken before she returned she would be left penniless; and that was a thing which Dolan dreaded to contemplate. There was a spark of human tenderness in his heart and in prison it would be comforting to know that she was well cared for. If she would only come now he would tell her where the money—!

For ten minutes Dolan considered the question in all possible lights. A letter telling her where the money was? No. It would inevitably fall into the hands of the police. A cipher? She would never get it. How? How? How? Every moment he expected a clamour at the door which would mean that the police had come for him. They knew he was cornered. Whatever he did must be done quickly. Dolan took a long breath and started to roll another cigarette. With the thin white paper held in his left hand and tobacco bag raised in the other he had an inspiration.

For a little more than an hour after that he was left alone. Finally his quick ear caught the shuffle of stealthy feet in the hall, then came an imperative rap on the door. The police had evidently feared to wait longer. Dolan was leaning over a sewing machine when the summons came. Instinctively his hand closed on his revolver, then he tossed it aside and walked to the door.

"Well?" he demanded.

"Let us in, Dolan," came the reply.

"That you, Downey?" Dolan inquired.

"Yes. Now don't make any mistakes, Mort. There are three of us here and Cunningham is in the alley watching your windows. There's no way out."

For one instant – only an instant – Dolan hesitated. It was not that he was repentant; it was not that he feared prison – it was regret at being caught. He had planned it all so differently, and the little woman would be heart-broken. Finally, with a quick backward glance at the sewing machine, he opened the door. Three revolvers were thrust into his face with a unanimity that spoke well for the police opinion of the man. Dolan promptly raised his hands over his head.

"Oh, put down your guns," he expostulated. "I'm not crazy. My gun is over on the couch there."

Detective Downey, by a personal search, corroborated this statement then the revolvers were lowered.

"The chief wants you," he said. "It's about that Thirteenth National Bank robbery."

"All right," said Dolan, calmly and he held out his hands for the steel nippers.

"Now, Mort," said Downey, ingratiatingly, "you can save us a lot of trouble by telling us where the money is."

"Doubtless I could," was the ambiguous response.

Detective Downey looked at him and understood. Cunningham was called in from the alley. He and Downey remained in the apartment and the other two men led Dolan away. In the natural course of events the prisoner appeared before Detective Mallory at Police Headquarters. They were well acquainted, professionally.

Dolan told everything frankly from the inception of the plan to the actual completion of the crime. The detective sat with his feet on his desk listening. At the end he leaned forward toward the prisoner.

"And where is the money?" he asked.

Dolan paused long enough to roll a cigarette.

"That's my business," he responded, pleasantly.

"You might just as well tell us," insisted Detective Mallory. "We will find it, of course, and it will save us trouble."

"I'll just bet you a hat you don't find it," replied Dolan, and there was a glitter of triumph in his eyes. "On the level, between man and man now I will bet you a hat that you never find that money."

"You're on," replied Detective Mallory. He looked keenly at his prisoner and his prisoner stared back without a quiver. "Did your wife get away with it?"

From the question Dolan surmised that she had not been arrested.

"No," he answered.

"Is it in your flat?"

"Downey and Cunningham are searching now," was the rejoinder. "They will report what they find."

There was silence for several minutes as the two men – officer and prisoner – stared each at the other. When a thief takes refuge in a refusal to answer questions he becomes a difficult subject to handle. There was the "third degree" of course, but Dolan was the kind of man who would only laugh at that; the kind of man from whom anything less than physical torture could not bring a statement if he didn't choose to make it. Detective Mallory was perfectly aware of this dogged trait in his character.

"It's this way, chief," explained Dolan at last. "I robbed the bank, I got the money, and it's now where you will never find it. I did it by myself, and am willing to take my medicine. Nobody helped me. My wife – I know your men waited for her before they took me – my wife knows nothing on earth about it. She had no connection with the thing at all and she can prove it. That's all I'm going to say. You might just as well make up your mind to it."

Detective Mallory's eyes snapped.

"You will tell where that money is," he blustered, "or – or I'll see that you get—"

"Twenty years is the absolute limit," interrupted Dolan quietly. "I expect to get twenty years – that's the worst you can do for me."

The detective stared at him hard.

"And besides," Dolan went on, "I won't be lonesome when I get where you're going to send me. I've got lots of friends there – been there before. One of the jailers is the best pinochle player I ever met."

Like most men who find themselves balked at the outset Detective Mallory sought to appease his indignation by heaping invective upon the prisoner, by threats, by promises, by wheedling, by bluster. It was all the same, Dolan remained silent. Finally he was led away and locked up.

A few minutes later Downey and Cunningham appeared. One glance told their chief that they could not enlighten him as to the whereabouts of the stolen money.

"Do you have any idea where it is?" he demanded.

"No, but I have a very definite idea where it isn't," replied Downey grimly. "It isn't in that flat. There's not one square inch of it that we didn't go over – not one object there that we didn't tear to pieces looking. It simply isn't there. He hid it somewhere before we got him."

"Well take all the men you want and keep at it," instructed Detective Mallory. "One of you, by the way, had better bring in Dolan's wife. I am fairly certain that she had nothing to do with it but she might know something and I can bluff a woman." Detective Mallory announced that accomplishment as if it were a thing to be proud of. "There's nothing to do now but get the money. Meanwhile I'll see that Dolan isn't permitted to communicate with anybody."

"There is always the chance," suggested Downey, "that a man as clever as Dolan could in a cipher letter, or by a chance remark, inform her where the money is if we assume she doesn't know, and that should be guarded against."

"It will be guarded against," declared Detective Mallory emphatically. "Dolan will not be permitted to see or talk to anyone for the present – not even an attorney. He may weaken later on."

But day succeeded day and Dolan showed no signs of weakening. His wife, meanwhile, had been apprehended and subjected to the "third degree." When this ordeal was over the net result was that Detective Mallory was convinced that she had had nothing whatever to do with the robbery, and had not the faintest idea where the money was. Half a dozen times Dolan asked permission to see her or to write to her. Each time the request was curtly refused.

Newspaper men, with and without inspiration, had sought the money vainly; and the police were now seeking to trace the movements of "Mort" Dolan from the moment of the robbery until the moment of his appearance on the steps of the house where he lived. In this way they hoped to get an inkling of where the money had been hidden, for the idea of the money being in the flat had been abandoned. Dolan simply wouldn't say anything. Finally, one day, Hutchinson Hatch, reporter, made an exhaustive search of Dolan's flat, for the fourth time, then went over to Police Headquarters to talk it over with Mallory. While there President Ashe and two directors of the victimized bank appeared. They were worried.

"Is there any trace of the money?" asked Mr Ashe.

"Not yet," responded Detective Mallory.

"Well, could we talk to Dolan a few minutes?"

"If we didn't get anything out of him you won't," said the detective. "But it won't do any harm. Come along."

Dolan didn't seem particularly glad to see them. He came to the bars of his cell and peered through. It was only when Mr Ashe was introduced to him as the President of the Thirteenth National that he seemed to take any interest in his visitors. This interest took the form of a grin. Mr Ashe evidently had something of importance on his mind and was seeking the happiest method of expression. Once or twice he spoke aside to his companions, and Dolan watched them curiously. At last he turned to the prisoner.

"You admit that you robbed the bank?" he asked.

"There's no need of denying it," replied Dolan.

"Well," and Mr Ashe hesitated a moment, "the Board of Directors held a meeting this morning, and speaking on their behalf I want to say something. If you will inform us of the whereabouts of the money we will, upon its recovery, exert every effort within our power to have your sentence cut in half. In other words, as I understand it, you have given the police no trouble, you have confessed the crime and this, with the return of the money, would weigh for you when sentence is pronounced. Say the maximum is twenty years, we might be able to get you off with ten if we get the money."

Detective Mallory looked doubtful. He realized, perhaps, the futility of such a promise yet he was silent. The proposition might draw out something on which to proceed.

"Can't see it," said Dolan at last. "It's this way. I'm twenty-seven years old. I'll get twenty years. About two of that'll come off for good behaviour, so I'll really get eighteen years. At the end of that time I'll come out with one hundred and nine thousand dollars odd – rich for life and able to retire at forty-five years. In other words while in prison I'll be working for a good, stiff salary – something really worth while. Very few men are able to retire at forty-five."

Mr Ashe readily realized the truth of this statement. It was the point of view of a man to whom mere prison has few terrors – a man content to remain immured for twenty years for a consideration. He turned and spoke aside to the two directors again.

"But I'll tell you what I will do," said Dolan, after a pause. "If you'll fix it so I get only two years, say, I'll give you half the money."

There was silence. Detective Mallory strolled along the corridor beyond the view of the prisoner and summoned President Ashe to his side by a jerk of his head.

"Agree to that," he said. "Perhaps he'll really give up."

"But it wouldn't be possible to arrange it, would it?" asked Mr Ashe.

"Certainly not," said the detective, "but agree to it. Get your money if you can and then we'll nail him anyhow."

Mr Ashe stared at him a moment vaguely indignant at the treachery of the thing, then greed triumphed. He walked back to the cell.

"We'll agree to that, Mr Dolan," he said briskly. "Fix a two years' sentence for you in return for half the money."

Dolan smiled a little.

"All right, go ahead," he said. "When sentence of two years is pronounced and a first class lawyer arranges it for me so that the matter can never be reopened I'll tell you where you can get your half."

"But of course you must tell us that now," said Mr Ashe.

Dolan smiled cheerfully. It was a taunting, insinuating, accusing sort of smile and it informed the bank president that the duplicity contemplated was discovered. Mr Ashe was silent for a moment, then blushed.

"Nothing doing," said Dolan, and he retired into a recess of his cell as if his interest in the matter were at an end.

"But-but we need the money now," stammered Mr Ashe. "It was a large sum and the theft has crippled us considerably."

"All right," said Dolan carelessly. "The sooner I get two years the sooner you get it."

"How could it be – be fixed?"

"I'll leave that to you."

That was all. The bank president and the two directors went out fuming impotently. Mr Ashe paused in Detective Mallory's office long enough for a final word.

"Of course it was brilliant work on the part of the police to capture Dolan," he said caustically, "but it isn't doing us a particle of good. All I see now is that we lose a hundred and nine thousand dollars."

"It looks very much like it," assented the detective, "unless we find it."

"Well, why don't you find it?"

Detective Mallory had to give it up.

"What did Dolan do with the money?" Hutchinson Hatch was asking of Professor Augustus S. F. X. Van Dusen – The Thinking Machine. The distinguished scientist and logician was sitting with his head pillowed on a cushion and with squint eyes turned upward. "It isn't in the flat. Everything indicates that it was hidden somewhere else."

"And Dolan's wife?" inquired The Thinking Machine in his perpetually irritated voice. "It seems conclusive that she had no idea where it is?"

"She has been put through the 'third degree,' " explained the reporter, "and if she had known she would probably have told."

"Is she living in the flat now?"

"No. She is stopping with her sister. The flat is under lock and key. Mallory has the key. He has shown the utmost care in everything he has done. Dolan has not been permitted to write to or see his wife for fear he would let her know some way where the money is; he has not been permitted to communicate with anybody at all, not even a lawyer. He did see President Ashe and two directors of the bank but naturally he wouldn't give them a message for his wife."

The Thinking Machine was silent. For five, ten, twenty minutes he sat with long, slender fingers pressed tip to tip, squinting unblinkingly at the ceiling. Hatch waited patiently.

"Of course," said the scientist at last, "one hundred and nine thousand dollars, even in large bills would make a considerable bundle and would be extremely difficult to hide in a place that has been gone over so often. We may suppose, therefore, that it isn't in the flat. What have the detectives learned as to Dolan's whereabouts after the robbery and before he was taken?"

"Nothing," replied Hatch, "nothing, absolutely. He seemed to disappear off the earth for a time. That time, I suppose, was when he was disposing of the money. His plans were evidently well laid."

"It would be possible of course, by the simple rules of logic, to sit still here and ultimately locate the money," remarked The Thinking Machine musingly, "but it would take a long time. We might begin, for instance, with the idea that he contemplated flight? When? By rail or steamer? The answers to those questions would, in a way, enlighten us as to the probable location of the money, because, remember, it would have to be placed where it was readily accessible in case of flight. But the process would be a long one. Perhaps it would be best to make Dolan tell us where he hid it."

"It would if he would tell," agreed the reporter, "but he is reticent to a degree that is maddening when the money is mentioned."

"Naturally," remarked the scientist. "That really doesn't matter. I have no doubt he will inform me."

So Hatch and The Thinking Machine called upon Detective Mallory. They found him in deep abstraction. He glanced up at the intrusion with an appearance, almost, of relief. He knew intuitively what it was.

"If you can find out where that money is, Professor" he declared emphatically, "I'll – I'll – well you can't."

The Thinking Machine squinted into the official eyes thoughtfully and the corners of his straight mouth were drawn down disapprovingly.

"I think perhaps there has been a little too much caution here, Mr Mallory," he said. "I have no doubt Dolan will inform me as to where the money is. As I understand it his wife is practically without means?"

"Yes," was the reply. "She is living with her sister."

"And he has asked several times to be permitted to write to or see her?"

"Yes, dozens of times."

"Well, now suppose you do let him see her," suggested The Thinking Machine.

"Lord, that's just what he wants," blurted the detective. "If he ever sees her I know he will, in some way, by something he says, by a gesture, or a look inform her where the money is. As it is now I know she doesn't know where it is."

"Well, if he informs her won't he also inform us?" demanded The Thinking Machine tartly. "If Dolan wants to convey knowledge of the whereabouts of the money to his wife let him talk to her – let him give her the information. I daresay if she is clever enough to interpret a word as a clue to where the money is I am too."

The detective thought that over. He knew this crabbed little scientist with the enormous head of old; and he knew, too, some of the amazing results he had achieved by methods wholly unlike those of the police. But in this case he was frankly in doubt.

"This way," The Thinking Machine continued. "Get the wife here, let her pass Dolan's cell and speak to him so that he will know that it is her, then let her carry on a conversation with him while she is beyond his sight. Have a stenographer, without the knowledge of either, take down just what is said, word for word. Give me a transcript of the conversation, and hold the wife on some pretext until I can study it a little. If he gives her a clue I'll get the money."

There was not the slightest trace of egotism in the irritable tone. It seemed merely a statement of fact. Detective Mallory, looking at the wizened face of the logician, was doubtfully hopeful and at last he consented to the experiment. The wife was sent for and came eagerly, a stenographer was placed in the cell adjoining Dolan, and the wife was led along the corridor. As she paused in front of Dolan's cell he started toward her with an exclamation. Then she was led on a little way out of his sight.

With face pressed close against the bars Dolan glowered out upon Detective Mallory and Hatch. An expression of awful ferocity leapt into his eyes.

"What're you doing with her?" he demanded.

"Mort, Mort," she called.

"Belle, is it you?" he asked in turn.

"They told me you wanted to talk to me," explained the wife. She was panting fiercely as she struggled to shake off the hands which held her beyond his reach.

"What sort of a game is this, Mallory?" demanded the prisoner.

"You've wanted to talk to her," Mallory replied, "now go ahead. You may talk, but you must not see her."

"Oh, that's it, eh?" snarled Dolan. "What did you bring her here for then? Is she under arrest?"

"Mort, Mort," came his wife's voice again. "They won't let me come where I can see you."

There was utter silence for a moment. Hatch was overpowered by a feeling that he was intruding upon a family tragedy, and tiptoed beyond reach of Dolan's roving eyes to where The Thinking Machine was sitting on a stool, twiddling his fingers. After a moment the detective joined them.

"Belle?" called Dolan again. It was almost a whisper.

"Don't say anything, Mort," she panted. "Cunningham and Blanton are holding me — the others are listening."

"I don't want to say anything," said Dolan easily. "I did want to see you. I wanted to know if you are getting along all right. Are you still at the flat?"

"No, at my sister's," was the reply. "I have no money – I can't stay at the flat."

"You know they're going to send me away?"

"Yes," and there was almost a sob in the voice. "I – I know it."

"That I'll get the limit – twenty years?"

"Yes."

"Can you – get along?" asked Dolan solicitously. "Is there anything you can do for yourself?"

"I will do something," was the reply. "Oh, Mort, Mort, why—"

"Oh never mind that," he interrupted impatiently. "It doesn't do any good to regret things. It isn't what I planned for, little girl, but it's here so – so I'll meet it. I'll get the good behaviour allowance – that'll save two years, and then—"

There was a menace in the tone which was not lost upon the listeners.

"Eighteen years," he heard her moan.

For one instant Dolan's lips were pressed tightly together and in that instant he had a regret—regret that he had not killed Blanton and Cunningham rather than submit to capture. He shook off his anger with an effort.

"I don't know if they'll permit me ever to see you," he said, desperately, "as long as I refuse to tell where the money is hidden, and I know they'll never permit me to write to you for fear I'll tell you where it is. So I suppose the goodbye'll be like this. I'm sorry, little girl."

He heard her weeping and hurled himself against the bars in a passion; it passed after a moment. He must not forget that she was penniless, and the money – that vast fortune—!

"There's one thing you must do for me, Belle," he said after a moment, more calmly. "This sort of thing doesn't do any good. Brace up, little girl, and wait – wait for me. Eighteen years is not forever, we're both young, and—but never mind that. I wish you would please go up to the flat and – do you remember my heavy, brown coat?"

"Yes, the old one?" she asked.

"That's it," he answered. "It's cold here in this cell. Will you please go up to the flat when they let you loose and sew up that tear under the right arm and send it to me here? It's probably the last favour I'll ask of you for a long time so will you do it this afternoon?"

"Yes," she answered, tearfully.

"The rip is under the right arm, and be certain to sew it up," said Dolan again. "Perhaps, when I am tried, I shall have a chance to see you and –"

The Thinking Machine arose and stretched himself a little.

"That's all that's necessary, Mr Mallory," he said. "Have her held until I tell you to release her."

Mallory made a motion to Cunningham and Blanton and the woman was led away, screaming. Hatch shuddered a little, and Dolan, not understanding, flung himself against the bars of his cell like a caged animal.

"Clever, aren't you?" he snarled as he caught sight of Detective Mallory. "Thought I'd try to tell her where it was, but I didn't and you never will know where it is – not in a thousand years."

Accompanied by The Thinking Machine and Hatch the detective went back to his private office. All were silent but the detective glanced from time to time into the eyes of the scientist.

"Now, Mr Hatch, we have the whereabouts of the money settled," said Thinking Machine, quietly. "Please go at once to the flat and bring the brown coat Dolan mentioned. I daresay the secret of the hidden money is somewhere in that coat."

"But two of my men have already searched that coat," protested the detective.

"That doesn't make the least difference," snapped the scientist.

The reporter went out without a word. Half an hour later he returned with the brown coat. It was a commonplace looking garment, badly worn and in sad need of repair not only in the rip under the arm but in other places. When he saw it The Thinking Machine nodded his head abruptly as if it were just what he had expected.

"The money can't be in that and I'll bet my head on it," declared Detective Mallory, flatly. "There isn't room for it."

The Thinking Machine gave him a glance in which there was a touch of pity.

"We know," he said, "that the money isn't in this coat. But can't you see that it is perfectly possible that a slip of paper on which Dolan has written down the hiding place of the money can be hidden in it somewhere? Can't you see that he asked for this coat – which is not as good a one as the one he is wearing now – in order to attract his wife's attention to it? Can't you see it is the one definite thing that he mentioned when he knew that in all probability he would not be permitted to see his wife again, at least for a long time?"

Then, seam by seam, the brown coat was ripped to pieces. Each piece in turn was submitted to the sharpest scrutiny. Nothing resulted. Detective Mallory frankly regarded it all as wasted effort and when there remained nothing of the coat save strips of cloth and lining he was inclined to be triumphant. The Thinking Machine was merely thoughtful.

"It went further back than that," the scientist mused, and tiny wrinkles appeared in the dome-like brow. "Ah! Mr Hatch please go back to the flat, look in the sewing machine drawers, or work basket and you will find a spool of brown thread. Bring it to me."

"Spool of brown thread?" repeated the detective in amazement. "Have you been through the place?"

"No."

"How do you know there's a spool of brown thread there, then?"

"I know it because Mr Hatch will bring it back to me," snapped The Thinking Machine. "I know it by the simplest, most rudimentary rules of logic."

Hatch went out again. In half an hour he returned with a spool of brown thread. The Thinking Machine's white fingers seized upon it eagerly, and his watery, squint eyes examined it. A portion of it had been used – the spool was only half gone. But he noted – and as he did his eyes reflected a glitter of triumph – he noted that the paper cap on each end was still in place.

"Now, Mr Mallory," he said, "I'll demonstrate to you that in Dolan the police are dealing with a man far beyond the ordinary bank thief. In his way he is a genius. Look here!"

With a pen-knife he ripped off the paper caps and looked through the hole of the spool. For an instant his face showed blank amazement. Then he put the spool down on the table and squinted at it for a moment in absolute silence.

"It must be here," he said at last. "It must be, else why did he – of course!"

With quick fingers he began to unwind the thread. Yard after yard it rolled off in his hand, and finally in the mass of brown on the spool appeared a white strip. In another instant The Thinking Machine held in his hand a tiny, thin sheet of paper – a cigarette paper. It had been wound around the spool and the thread wound over it so smoothly that it was impossible to see that it had ever been removed.

The detective and Hatch were leaning over his shoulder watching him curiously. The tiny paper unfolded – something was written on it. Slowly The Thinking Machine deciphered it.

"47 Causeway Street, basement, tenth flagstone from northeast corner."

And there the money was found – $109,000. The house was unoccupied and within easy reach of a wharf from which a European bound steamer sailed. Within half an hour of sailing time it would have been an easy matter for Dolan to have recovered it all and that without in the least exciting the suspicion of those who might be watching him; for a saloon next door opened into an alley behind, and a broken window in the basement gave quick access to the treasure.

"Dolan reasoned," The Thinking Machine explained, "that even if he was never permitted to see his wife she would probably use that thread and in time find the directions for recovering the money. Further he argued that the police would never suspect that a spool contained the secret for which they sought so long. His conversation with his wife, today, was merely to draw her attention to something which would require her to use the spool of brown thread. The brown coat was all that he could think of. And that's all I think."

Dolan was a sadly surprised man when news of the recovery of the money was broken to him. But a certain quaint philosophy didn't desert him. He gazed at Detective Mallory incredulously as the story was told and at the end went over and sat down on his cell cot. "Well, chief," he said, "I didn't think it was in you. That makes me owe you a hat."

A fan of Sherlock Holmes?
Then meet Solar Pons

The original fan fiction from the great August Derleth—the Sherlock Holmes of Praed Street.

"the best substitutes for Sherlock Holmes known."
– Vincent Starrett

"an excellent series of adventures in detection in their own right." – *The Chicago Tribune*

For more details and a full list of titles:
visit https://www.hachetteindia.com/home/yellowbacks

Love Golden Age crime fiction? Have you checked out the full yellowback range?

From Locked door mysteries to blind detectives through first women detectives, the yellowback reissues is one of the largest selections of classic crime fictions, in the original format with a modern clean easy read page layout. A sampling below.

For more details and a full list of titles:
visit https://www.hachetteindia.com/home/yellowbacks

H. Rider Haggard MR. MEESON'S WILL	**Melville Davisson Post** MASTER OF MYSTERIES THE COMPLETE UNCLE ABNER COLLECTION 	**Jack London** THE ASSASSINATION BUREAU LTD. 
Baroness Orczy THE SKIN O' MY TOOTH 	**Earl Derr Biggers** SEVEN KEYS TO BALDPATE 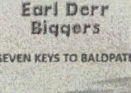	**Horace Walpole** THE CASTLE OF OTRANTO
Sexton Blake THE SEXTON BLAKE COLLECTION VOLUME 1 	**Francis Beeding** THE HOUSE OF DR. EDWARDES 	**A. E. W. Mason** AT THE VILLA ROSE 
Fergus Hume THE MILLIONAIRE MYSTERY 	**Donald Henderson** A VOICE LIKE VELVET 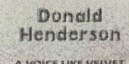	**Richard Hallas** YOU PLAY THE BLACK AND THE RED COMES UP